What She Knew

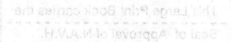

This Large Print Book carries the Seal of Approval of N.A.V.H.

WHAT SHE KNEW

GILLY MACMILLAN

THORNDIKE PRESS
A part of Gale, Cengage Learning

GALE
CENGAGE Learning

Farmington Hills, Mich • San Francisco • New York • Waterville, Maine
Meriden, Conn • Mason, Ohio • Chicago

GALE
CENGAGE Learning

Thorndike Press, a part of Gale, Cengage Learning.

Thorndike Press® Large Print Basic.
The text of this Large Print edition is unabridged.
Other aspects of the book may vary from the original edition.
Set in 16 pt. Plantin.

LIBRARY OF CONGRESS CATALOGING-IN-PUBLICATION DATA

Names: Macmillan, Gilly, author.
Title: What she knew / Gilly Macmillan.
Description: Large print edition. | Waterville, Maine : Thorndike Press, 2016. | © 2016 | Series: Thorndike Press large print basic
Identifiers: LCCN 2015045133| ISBN 9781410487636 (hardback) | ISBN 1410487636 (hardcover)
Subjects: LCSH: Missing children—Fiction. | Mothers and sons—Fiction. | Large type books. | Psychological fiction. | BISAC: FICTION / Suspense. | GSAFD: Suspense fiction.
Classification: LCC PR6113.A269 W47 2016 | DDC 823/.92—dc23
LC record available at http://lccn.loc.gov/2015045133

Published in 2016 by arrangement with William Morrow, an imprint of HarperCollins Publishers

Printed in Mexico
3 4 5 6 7 8 20 19 18 17 16

To my family

Whatever else is unsure in this stinking dunghill of a world a mother's love is not.

— James Joyce

In a real dark night of the soul it is always three o'clock in the morning, day after day.

— F. Scott Fitzgerald

AUTHOR'S NOTE

During the research for this novel I found a number of websites and papers to be very valuable resources. Although I have made some references to these sources within this book, *What She Knew* is entirely a work of fiction and all quotes and references are used fictitiously. Along with the characters and events in this novel, the blog posts, online comments and identities, newspaper articles, email addresses, and many of the websites are entirely fictitious, and any resemblance to actual persons, living or dead, or to actual websites, email addresses, online comments and identities, newspaper articles, and blog posts is entirely coincidental.

Any mistakes in police procedure are mine, with apologies to the two retired detectives who kindly advised me. Bristol is as real as I could make it, although there is no playing field beside the Leigh Woods parking lot, and the descriptions of the interior of Kenneth Steele House are a product of my imagination.

Prologue: November 2013 — One Year After

Rachel

In the eyes of others, we're often not who we imagine ourselves to be.

When we first meet someone, we can put our best foot forward, and give the very best account of ourselves, but still get it horribly wrong.

It's a pitfall of life.

I've thought about this a lot since my son, Ben, went missing, and every time I think about it, it also begs the question: if we're not who we imagine we are, then is anybody else? If there's so much potential for others to judge us wrongly, then how can we be sure that our assessment of them in any way resembles the real person that lies underneath?

You can see where my train of thought's going with this.

Should we trust or rely on somebody just because they're a figure of authority, or a family member? Are any of our friendships and relationships really based on secure foundations?

If I'm in a reflective mood, I think about how different my life might have been if I'd had the wisdom to consider these things before Ben went missing. If my mood is dark, I find fault in myself for not doing so, and my thoughts, repetitive and paralyzing, punish me for days.

A year ago, just after Ben's disappearance, I was involved in a press conference, which was televised. My role was to appeal for help in finding him. The police gave me a script to read. I assumed people watching it would automatically understand who I was, that they would see I was a mother whose child was missing, and who cared about nothing apart from getting him back.

Many of the people who watched, the most vocal of them, thought the opposite. They accused me of terrible things. I didn't understand why until I watched the footage of the conference — far too late to limit the damage — but then the reason was immediately obvious.

It was because I looked like prey.

Not appealing prey, a wide-eyed antelope, say, tottering on spindly legs, but prey that's been well hunted, run ragged, and is near the end. I presented the world with a face contorted by emotion and bloodied from injury, a body that was shaking with grief, and a voice that sounded as if it had been roughly scraped from a desiccated mouth. If I'd imagined beforehand that an honest display of myself, and my emotions, however raw, might garner me some sympathy and galvanize people into helping me look for Ben, I was wrong.

They saw me as a freak show. I frightened people because I was someone to whom the worst was happening, and they turned on me like a pack of dogs.

I've had requests, since it was over, to appear again on television. It was a sensational case, after all. I always decline. Once bitten, twice shy.

It doesn't stop me imagining how the interview might go, though. I envisage a comfortable TV studio, and a kindly looking interviewer, a man who says, "Tell us a little about yourself, Rachel." He leans back in his chair, which is set at a friendly angle to mine, as if we'd met for a chat in the pub. The expression on his face is the sort that someone might make if they were watching a cocktail being made for them, or an ice-cream sundae if that's your preference. We chat and he takes time to draw me out, and lets me tell my side of the story. I sound

OK. I'm in control. I conform to an acceptable view of a mother. My answers are well considered. They don't challenge. At no point do I spin a web of suspicion around myself by blurting out things that sounded fine in my head. I don't flounder, and then sink.

This is a fantasy that can occupy long minutes of my time. The outcome is always the same: the imaginary interview goes really well, brilliantly, in fact, and the best thing about it is that the interviewer doesn't ask me the question that I hate most of all. It's a question that a surprising number of people ask me. This is how they might phrase it: "Before you discovered that Ben had disappeared, did you have any intuition that something bad would happen to him?"

I hate the question because it implies some kind of dereliction of duty on my part. It implies that if I were a more instinctive mother, a better mother, then I would have had a sense that my child was in danger, or should have. How do I respond? I just say "No."

It's a simple enough answer, but people often look at me quizzically, brows furrowed in that particular expression where a desire to mine someone for gossip overwhelms sympathy for their plight. Softly crinkled foreheads and inquisitive eyes ask me, Really? Are you sure? How can that be?

I never justify my answer. "No" is all they need to know.

I limit my answer because my trust in others has been eroded by what happened; of course it has. Within many of my relationships doubt remains like slivers of broken glass, impossible to see and liable to draw blood even after you think you've swept them all away.

There are only a very few people that I know I can trust now, and they anchor me to my existence. They know the whole of my story.

A part of me thinks that I would be willing to talk to others about what happened, but only if I could be sure that they'd listen to me. They'd have to let me get to the end of my tale without interrupting, or judging me, and they'd have to understand that everything I did, I did for Ben. Some of my actions were rash, some dangerous, but they were all for my son, because my feelings for him were the only truth I knew.

If someone could bear to be the wedding guest to my ancient mariner, then in return for the gift of their time and their patience and their understanding, I would supply every detail. I think that's a good bargain.

We all love to be thrilled by the vicarious experience of other people's ghastly lives after all.

Really, I've never understood why we haven't thought of an English word for *Schadenfreude.* Perhaps we're embarrassed to admit that we feel it. Better to maintain the illusion that butter wouldn't melt in our collective mouths.

My generous listener would no doubt be surprised by my story, because much of what happened went unreported. It would be just like having their very own exclusive. When I imagine telling this fictional listener my story, I think that I would start it by answering that hated question properly for the first time, because it's relevant. I would start the story like this:

When Ben went missing I didn't have any intuition. None whatsoever. I had something else on my mind. It was a preoccupation with my ex-husband's new wife.

JIM

Here's the list of everything I used to have under control: work, relationship, family.

Here's the problem I have now: the thoughts in my head.

They remind me hourly, sometimes minute by minute, of loss, and of actions that can't be undone, however much you wish it.

During the week I throw myself into work to try to erase these thoughts.

Weekends are more of a challenge, but I've found ways to fill them too: I exercise, I work some more, and then I repeat.

It's the nights that torment me, because then the thoughts revolve ceaselessly in my head and deny me sleep.

When I was a student I gained a little knowledge of insomnia. I studied surrealist poetry and I read that sleep deprivation could have a psychedelic, hallucinogenic effect on the mind; that it had the potential to unleash reserves of creativity that were profound and could enhance your life and your soul.

My insomnia isn't like that.

My insomnia makes a desperate, restless soul of me. There is no creativity, only hopelessness and frustration.

Each night when I go to bed I dread the inevitability of this because when my head hits the pillow, however tired I am, however much I crave respite from my own mind, every single part of me seems to conspire to keep me awake.

I become hyperaware of all the potential stimuli around me, and each one feels like an affliction.

My shifting movements make the smooth sheet beneath me buckle and form ridges and channels like baked earth that's been torn into by the claws of an animal. If I try to lie still, my hands linked together on my chest, then the pounding of my heart shortens my breath. If I lie without covers, the air in the room makes my skin prickle and crawl, whatever the temperature. Bundled up, I feel only an intense and overheated claustrophobia, which robs the air from my lungs and makes me sweat so that the bed feels like a stagnant pool I'm condemned to bathe in.

As I stew in my bed, I listen to the city outside: the shouting of strangers, cars, a moped, a siren, the rustle of treetops agitated by the wind, sometimes nothing at all. A sound void.

There are nights when this quiet torments me and I rise, usually well beyond midnight, and I dress again, and then I walk the streets under the sodium-orange glow of the streetlights, where the only life is a shadowy turbulence at the periphery of my vision, a fox perhaps, or a broken man in a doorway.

But even walking can't clear my mind completely because as I put one foot in front of the next I dread even more the return to the flat, to the bed, to its emptiness, to my wakefulness.

And, worst of all, I dread the thoughts that will circle once again in my mind.

They take me straight to those dark, vivid places that I've worked so hard to lock away during the day. They find those hidden places and they pick the locks, force the doors, pull away the planks of wood that have been nailed across the windows, and they let light into the dark corners inside. I think of it as harshly lit, like a crime scene. Center stage: Benedict Finch. His pellucid blue eyes meeting mine, and in them an expression so innocent that it feels like an accusation.

Late into the small hours I sometimes get the sleep I crave, but the problem is that it's not a refreshing blackness, a chance for my mind to shut down. Even my sleep allows me no respite, because it's populated by nightmares.

But whether I've been awake or asleep, when I rise in the morning, I'm often fetid and dehydrated, wrung out before the day has even begun. Tears might have dampened my pillow, and more often than not sweat has soaked my sheets, and I face the morning with a sense of dread that my insomnia hasn't just blurred the boundaries between day and night, but has unbalanced me too.

I think, before it happened to me, that I might have underestimated both the restorative power of sleep and the destructive power of a shattered psyche. I didn't realize that exhaustion could bleed you dry so completely. I didn't realize that your mind could fall sick without your even noticing: incrementally, darkly, irrevocably.

I'm too embarrassed to tell anybody else about these things, and the fact that the effects of my insomnia stay with me as day breaks, woven into the fabric of it. The exhaustion it breeds makes my coffee taste metallic and the thought of food intolerable. It makes me crave a cigarette when I wake. It fuels my cycle ride to work with adrenaline, so that I'm nervy, riding dangerously close to the curb, misjudging a junction so that the thud of a car forced into an emergency stop just behind me makes my legs pump painfully fast on the pedals.

In the office, an early meeting: "Are you OK?" my DCI asks. I nod, but I can feel sweat breaking out along my hairline. "I'm fine," I say. I last for ten minutes more, until somebody asks, "What do you think, Jim?"

I should relish the question. It's an opportunity to put myself forward, to prove myself. A year ago, I would have. Now I focus on the chipped plastic shard on the end of my pen. Through the pall of my exhaustion I have to force myself to raise my head and look at the three expectant faces around me. All I can think about is how the insomnia has smeared the clarity of my mind. I feel panic spreading through my body as if infused like a drug, pushing through arteries, veins, and capillaries until it incapacitates me. I leave the room silently and once I'm outside I pound my fist into the wall until my knuckles bleed.

It's not the first time it's happened, but it's the first time they make good on their threat to refer me to a psychologist.

Her name is Dr. Francesca Manelli. They make it clear that if I don't attend all sessions, and contribute positively to the discussions with Dr. Manelli, then I'm out of CID.

We have a preliminary meeting. She wants me to write a report on the Benedict Finch case. I start it by writing down my objections.

Report for Dr. Francesca Manelli on the Events Surrounding the Benedict Finch Case by DI JAMES CLEMO, Avon and Somerset Constabulary

CONFIDENTIAL

I'd like to start this report by formally noting down the objection that I have both to writing it and to attending therapy sessions with Dr. Manelli. While I believe that the Force Occupational Health Service is a valuable asset, I also believe that use of it should be discretionary for officers and other staff. I shall be raising this objection formally through the proper channels.

I recognize that the purpose of the report is to describe the events that occurred during the investigation of the Benedict Finch case from my own point of view. This will provide the basis for discussion between myself and Dr. Manelli, with the aim of ascertaining whether it will be useful for me to have long-term support from her in dealing with some of the issues that arose from my involvement in that case, and some personal issues that affected me at around that time also.

I understand that I should include details of

my personal life where relevant, including where it relates to DC Emma Zhang, as this will allow Dr. Manelli to form a whole view of my decision-making processes and motivations during the period that the case was live. The progress of my report will be reviewed by Dr. Manelli as it's written, and what I produce each week will form the basis for my talking sessions with Dr. Manelli.

Dr. Manelli has advised that the bulk of this report should be a description of my personal recollections of what took place, though it may also include transcripts of our conversations or other material where she feels that is appropriate.

I agree to do this only on the understanding that the contents of this report will remain confidential.

DI James Clemo

■ ■ ■ ■

Before Day 1 Sunday, October 21, 2012

■ ■ ■ ■

In the UK, a child is reported missing every three minutes.
— www.missingkids.co.uk

The first three hours are most critical when trying to locate a missing child.
— www.missingkids.com/keyfacts

Rachel

My ex-husband's name is John. His new wife is called Katrina. She's petite. She has a figure that can make most men drink her in with their eyes. Her deep brown hair always looks shiny and freshly colored, like hair in magazines. She wears it in a bob, and it's always carefully styled around her pixie face, framing a pert mouth and dark eyes.

When I first met her, at a hospital function that John was hosting, months before he left us, I admired those eyes. I thought they were lively and sparky. They flashed around the room, assessing and flirting, teasing and charming. After John had gone, I thought of them as magpie eyes, darting and furtive, foraging for other people's treasure to line her nest.

John walked out of our family home on Boxing Day. For Christmas he'd given me an iPad and Ben a puppy. I felt the gifts were thoughtful and generous until I watched him back his car out of the driveway that day, neatly packed bags stowed on the backseat, while the ham went cold on the dining table and Ben cried because he didn't understand what was happening. When I finally turned and went back into the house to start my new life as a single mother, I realized that they were guilt-gifts: things to fill the void he would leave in our lives.

They certainly occupied us in the short term, but perhaps not as John intended. The day after Boxing Day, Ben appropriated the iPad and I spent hours standing under an umbrella in the garden, shivering, shocked, while the new Cath Kidston Christmas slippers my sister had sent me got rain-soaked and muddy, and the puppy worked relentlessly to pull up a clematis when I should have been encouraging it to pee.

Katrina lured John away from us just ten months before Ben disappeared. I thought of it as a master plan that she executed: The Seduction and Theft of My Husband. I didn't know the detail of how they kindled their affair but to me it felt like a plot from a bad medical drama. He had the real-life role of consultant pediatric surgeon; she was a newly qualified nutritionist.

I imagined them meeting at a patient's bedside, eyes locking, hands grazing, a flirtation that turned into something more serious, until she offered herself to him unconditionally, the way you can before you have a child to consider. At that time, John was obsessed with his work. It consumed him, which makes me think that she must have done most of the running, and that the package she offered him must have amounted to a seductive proposition indeed.

I was bitter about it. My relationship with John had such solid and careful beginnings that I'd assumed it would last forever. It simply never occurred to me that there could be a different kind of ending for us, which was, I now realize, extremely naïve.

What I hadn't realized was that John didn't think like me, that he didn't view any problems we might have had as normal, surmountable. For him things boiled under the surface, until he couldn't cope with being with me anymore, and his solution was just to up and leave.

When I rang my sister right after he'd gone she said, "Didn't you have any idea at all?" and her voice was strained with disbelief. "Are you sure you paid him enough attention?" was her next question, as if the fault was mine and that was to be expected.

I hung up the phone. My friend Laura said, "I thought he was a bit detached lately. I just assumed you guys were working through it."

Laura had been my closest friend since we were at nursing college together. Like me, she hadn't stuck with bedpans and body fluids. She'd quit and switched to journalism instead. We'd been friends for long enough that she'd witnessed the birth and growth of my relationship with John as well as its demise. She was observant and forthright. That word "detached" stayed with me, because if I'm being really honest, I hadn't noticed it. When you have a child to look after, and when you're busy developing a new career as well, you sometimes don't.

The separation and divorce tore me apart, I'll admit to that. When Ben disappeared I was still in mourning for my husband. In ten months you can get used to some of the mechanics of being alone, but it takes longer for the hurt to heal.

I went to Katrina's flat once, after he'd moved in with her. It wasn't difficult to find. I pressed on her door buzzer, and when she answered the door I snapped. I accused her of being a home-wrecker, and I might have said worse things. John wasn't there, but she had friends around, and, as our voices rose, the three of them appeared behind her, mouths open, aghast. They were a perfectly groomed Greek chorus of disapproval. Glasses of white wine in hand, they watched me rage. It wasn't my finest hour, but I never quite got around to apologizing.

You might wonder what I look like, if my husband could be lured away by such a pert little magpie. If you saw the press conference footage, you'll already have an idea, though I wasn't at my best. Obviously.

You'll have seen that my hair looked straggly and unkempt, in spite of my sister's efforts to tame it. It looked like witch's hair. Would you believe me if I said that under normal circumstances it's one of my best features? I have long, wavy dark blond hair that falls beneath my shoulders. It can be nice.

You'll certainly have noticed my eyes. That's the closeup shot they replay most: bloodshot, desperate, pleading eyes, red-rimmed and puffy from the tears I'd shed. You're going to have to take my word for it that normally my eyes look pretty: they're wide and very green and I used to think they flattered my pale, clear skin.

But what I really hope you noticed was the smattering of freckles across my nose.

Did you see those? Ben inherited them from me, and it always pleased me beyond measure to see that physical trace of myself in him.

It would be wrong of me to give you the impression that the only thing I was thinking about was Katrina, when Ben disappeared. On the afternoon when it happened, Ben and I were walking the dog in the woods. It was a Sunday, and we'd driven out of Bristol and across the Clifton Suspension Bridge to reach the countryside beyond.

The bridge traversed the Avon Gorge, a great crevasse in the landscape, carved out by the muddy-banked River Avon, which Ben and I could see flooding its basin far below, brown and swollen at high tide. The gorge was the boundary between city and countryside. The city hugged one side of it, teetering on its edges, and the woods hugged the other, trees running densely hundreds of feet down the steep cliffs until they petered out beside the riverbank.

Once we'd crossed the bridge, it took us only five minutes to be parked and loose in the woodland. It was a beautiful late autumn afternoon, and, as we walked, I was relishing the sounds and smells and sights it offered.

I'm a photographer. It's a career change I made when I had Ben. I walked away from my previous incarnation as a nurse without a single regret. Photography was a joy, an absolute passion of mine, and it meant that I was always looking at the light, thinking about how I could use it in a photograph, and I can remember exactly what it was like as we walked that afternoon.

It was fairly late, so what light remained had a transient quality to it, but there was just enough brightness in the air that the colors of the leaves above and around me appeared complex and beautiful. Some of them fell as we walked. Without a whisper of protest, they let go of the branches that had sustained them for months, and drifted down in front of us to settle on the woodland floor. When we began our walk, it was still a gentle afternoon, allowing the change of seasons to unfold quietly and gradually around us.

Of course Ben and the dog were oblivious to it. While I composed photographs in my mind, both of them, with misty breath and bright, wild eyes, ran and played and hid. Ben wore a red anorak and I saw it flash down the path in front of me, then weave in and out of the trees. Skittle ran by his side.

Ben threw sticks at tree trunks and he knelt close to the leaf-strewn ground to examine mushrooms that he knew not to touch. He tried to walk with his eyes closed and kept up a running commentary on how that felt. "I think I'm in a muddy part, Mum," he said, as he felt his boot get stuck, and I had to rescue it while he stood with a socked foot held precariously in the air. He picked up pinecones and showed me one that was closed up tight. "It's going to rain," he told me. "Look."

My son looked beautiful that afternoon. He was only eight years old. His sandy hair was tousled and his cheeks were pink from exertion and cold. He had blue eyes that were clear and bright as sapphires. He had pale winter skin, perfectly unblemished except for those freckles, and a smile that was my favorite sight in the world. He was about two-thirds my height, just right for me to rest an arm around his shoulders as we walked, or to hold his hand, which he was still happy for me to do from time to time, though not at school.

That afternoon Ben exuded happiness in that uncomplicated way children can. It made me feel happy too. It had been a hard ten months since John left us, and although

I still thought about him and Katrina more than I probably should have, I was also experiencing moments of all-rightness, times when it felt OK that it was just Ben and me. They were rare, if I'm honest, but they were there all the same, and that afternoon in the woods was one of those moments.

By half past four, the cold was beginning to bite and I knew we should start to make our way home. Ben didn't agree.

"Can I have a go on the rope swing? Please?"

"Yes," I said. I reckoned we could still be back at the car before it got dark.

"Can I run ahead?"

I often think back to that moment, and before you judge me for the reply I gave him, I want to ask you a question. What do you do when you have to be both a mother and a father to your child? I was a single parent. My maternal instincts were clear: protect your child, from everything. My maternal voice was saying, No you can't, you're too young, I want to take you to the swing, and I want to watch you every step of the way. But in the absence of Ben's dad I thought it was also my responsibility to make room in my head for another voice, a paternal one. I imagined that this voice would encourage Ben to be independent, to take risks, to discover life himself. I imagined it saying, Of course you can! Do it!

So here's how the conversation actually went:

"Can I run ahead?"

"Oh, Ben, I'm not sure."

"Please, Mum." The vowels were strung out, wheedling.

"Do you know the way?"

"Yes!"

"Are you sure?"

"We do it every time."

He was right, we did.

"OK, but if you don't know where to find the track, just stop and wait for me on the main path."

"OK," and he was off, careering down the path ahead of me, Skittle racing with him.

"Ben!" I shouted. "Are you sure you know the way?"

"Yes!" he shouted, with the assurance of a kid who almost certainly hasn't bothered to listen to what you said, because he has something more exciting to be getting on with. He didn't stop, or look back at me.

And that was the last I saw of him.

As I walked the path behind Ben I listened

to a voicemail on my phone. It was from my sister. She'd left it at lunchtime.

"Hi, it's me. Can you give me a ring about the Christmas photo shoot for the blog? I'm at the Cotswold Food Festival and I've got loads and loads of ideas that I want to chat to you about, so I just want to confirm that you're still coming up next weekend. I know we said you should come and stay at home, but I thought we could do something better at the cottage, dress it up with holly and stuff, so why don't you come there instead. The girls will stay with Simon as they've all got things to do, so it'll be just us. And by the way I'm staying there tonight so try me there if you can't get through on my mobile. Love to Ben. Bye."

My sister had a very successful food blog. It was called "Ketchup and Custard," named after her daughters' favorite foods. She had four girls, each one the image of their father with deep brown eyes and hair that was so dark it was nearly black, and stubborn, willful temperaments. My sister often joked that if she hadn't given birth to them herself she'd have questioned whether they belonged to her at all. And I admit I sometimes wondered if my sister ever truly got the measure of her girls: they seemed such an impenetrable bunch, even to their mother.

Close in age — all of them older than Ben — they formed a little tribe that Ben never quite managed to infiltrate, and in fact he regarded them with some wariness, mostly because they treated him a bit like a toy.

Nicky proved a match for them more often than not, though, scheduling and organizing them down to the last minute, dominating them by keeping them busy. Their lives ran to such a strict routine that I sometimes wondered if these raven-haired girls wouldn't implode once they entered the real world, beyond their mother's control.

On her blog Nicky posted recipes that she claimed would make even the fussiest families eat healthfully and eat together. When she started the blog I thought it was tacky and silly, but to my surprise it had taken off and she was often mentioned when newspapers published Top Ten lists of good food or family blogs.

My sister was a brilliant cook and she combined recipes with good-humored writing about the trials of raising a big family. It wasn't my cup of tea — too contrived and twee by far — but it was impressive and it seemed to strike a chord with lots of women who bought into the domestic heroine ideal.

I called her back, left a message in return. "Yes, we're planning to come up on Saturday morning and leave after lunch on Sunday. Do you want me to bring anything?"

I was making a point by asking that. I knew she wouldn't want anything from me. She prided herself on being a perfect hostess.

Limiting our stay was also deliberate. When I'd thought we were going to visit Nicky at their family home I'd been determined to stay only one night, because although Nicky was the only family I had, and I felt a duty to see her and to give Ben the chance to get to know his cousins, it was never something I looked forward to especially.

Their big house just outside Salisbury was always perfectly presented, traditional, and loud, and it became claustrophobic after one night. I simply found the whole package a bit overwhelming: superefficient Nicky working domestic miracles left, right, and center; her big, jolly husband, glass of wine in hand, pile of anecdotes at the ready; and the daughters, bickering, flicking V signs at my sister's back, wrapping their father around their little fingers. It was a world apart from my quiet life with Ben in our small house in Bristol.

Not that the cottage was my ideal destination either, even without Nicky's family to contend with. Left to both Nicky and me by our aunt Esther, who raised us, it was small and damp and held slightly uncomfortable memories for me. I would have sold it years ago — I could certainly have done with the money — but Nicky remained very attached to it, and she and Simon had long since taken on its maintenance costs entirely, largely out of guilt, I think, that she wouldn't let me release the capital in it. She encouraged me to make more use of it but somehow time spent there left me feeling odd, as if I somehow had never grown up properly, never shed my teenage self.

I slipped my phone back into my pocket. I'd reached the start of the path that led to the rope swing. Ben wasn't there so I assumed he'd gone ahead of me. I made my way along in his wake, squelching through mud and batting away brambles. When I came to the clearing where the rope swing was, I was smiling in anticipation of seeing him, and of enjoying his triumph at having got there himself.

Except that he wasn't there, nor was Skittle. The rope swing was in motion, moving from left to right and back again in a slow rhythm. I pushed forward to give myself a wider view of the clearing. "Ben," I called. No reply. I felt a flash of panic but told myself to stop it. I'd given him this little bit of independence, and it would be a shame to mar the moment by behaving in an overanxious way. Ben was probably hiding behind a tree with Skittle, and I shouldn't wreck his game.

I looked around. The clearing was small, no bigger than half a tennis court. Dense woodland wrapped around most of it, darkening the perimeters, although on one side a large crop of medium-sized saplings grew, spindly and brittle, leafless. They dispersed the light around them, lending it a quality of strangeness. In the middle of the clearing stood a mature beech tree, which overhung a small brook. The rope swing was tethered to one of its branches. I reckoned that Ben was hiding behind its thick trunk.

I walked slowly into the clearing, playing along with him.

"Hmm," I said, throwing my voice in the direction of the tree so that he could hear me. "I wonder where Ben is. I thought he was meeting me here, but I can't see him anywhere, or that dog of his. It's a mystery."

I stopped to listen, to see if he would give himself away, but there was no sound.

"I wonder if Ben has gone home without me," I continued, dipping a booted toe into the brook. The motion of the swing had ceased now and it hung limply. "Maybe," I said, drawing the word out, "Ben has started a new life in the woods without me, and I'll just have to go home and eat honey on toast by myself and watch *Doctor Who* on my own."

Again, no response, and the flutter of fear returned. This kind of talk was usually enough to make him emerge, triumphant at having tricked me for so long. I told myself to be calm, that he was upping the stakes, making me work hard. I said, "Well, I guess that if Ben is going to live on his own in the woods, then I'll just have to give away his things so that another boy can have them."

I sat down on a moss-covered tree stump to wait for his response, trying to play it cool. Then I delivered my trump card: "I just wonder who would like to have Baggy Bear . . ." Baggy Bear was Ben's favorite toy, a teddy that his grandparents had given him when he was a baby.

I looked around, expecting him to emerge, half laughing, half cross, but there was absolute silence, as if the woodland was holding its breath. In the quiet, my eyes followed the lines of the surrounding tree trunks upward until I glimpsed the sky above, and I could feel darkness starting to push in as surely as fire creeps across a piece of paper, curling its edges, turning it to ash.

In that moment, I knew that Ben wasn't there.

I ran to the tree. I circled it, once, twice, again, feeling its bark scrape my fingers as I went around. "Ben!" I called. "Ben! Ben! Ben!" No response. I kept calling, on and on, and when I stopped to listen, straining to hear, there was still nothing. A sickening feeling in my gut pinched harder as each second passed.

Then a noise: a wonderful, glorious crashing sound, the sound of someone rushing through undergrowth. It was coming from the glade of saplings. I ran toward it, picking my way through the young trees as quickly as I could, dodging low, whippy branches, feeling one of them slice into my forehead.

"Ben," I shouted, "I'm here." No response, but the noise got closer. "I'm coming, love," I called. Relief surged through me. As I ran, I scanned the dense growth ahead of me to try to catch a glimpse of him. It was hard to tell exactly where the noise was coming from. Sounds were ricocheting among the trees, confusing me. It shocked me when something burst out of the undergrowth beside me.

It was a dog, and it was big and happy to see me. It bounced at my feet, eager to be petted, its mouth wide and dark red, startlingly so, its big fleshy tongue lolling. A few yards behind it a woman emerged from the trees.

"I'm so sorry, dear," she said. "He won't hurt you, he's very friendly."

"Oh God," I said. I cupped my hands around my mouth. "Ben!" I shouted, and this time I yelled so loudly that it felt as if the cold air was scorching my throat when I drew breath.

"Have you lost your dog? He's not that way or I'd have come across him. Oh! Did you know your forehead is bleeding? Are you all right? Hold on a minute."

She fumbled in her coat pocket and offered me a tissue. She was elderly and wore a waxed hat with a wide brim that was pulled low on her head. Her face was creased with concern and she was short of breath. I ignored the tissue and instead I grasped her, my fingers sinking into her padded jacket until I felt the resistance of her arm beneath. She flinched.

"No," I said. "It's my son. I've lost my son."

As I spoke, I felt a bead of blood trickle down my forehead.

And so it began.

We hunted for Ben, the lady and I. We scoured the area around the rope swing and then returned to the path, striking out along it in opposite directions with a plan to converge at the main parking lot.

I wasn't calm, not a bit. Fear made my insides feel as if they were melting.

As we searched, the woods were transforming. The sky became darker and overcast and in places the overhanging branches were dense enough to form a solid arch, and the path became a dark burrow.

Leaves gusted around me like decomposing confetti as the wind began to build, and great masses of foliage shuddered and bent as it whipped through the canopy above.

I called for Ben over and over again and listened too, straining to decipher the layers of sound the woods produced. A branch cracked. A bird called, a high-pitched sound, like a yelp, and another answered. High overhead was the sound of an airplane.

Loudest of all was me: my breathing, the sound of my boots slapping through the mud. My panic was audible.

Nowhere was the sound of Ben's voice, or of Skittle.

Nowhere did I see a bright red anorak.

By the time I reached the parking lot I felt hysterical. It was packed with cars and families, because there were teams of boys and their supporters leaving the adjacent soccer field. A fantasy role-play enactment group loitered in one corner, bizarrely costumed, packing weaponry and picnic coolers into their cars. They were a regular sight in the woods on Sunday afternoons.

I focused on the boys. Many of them wore red jerseys. I moved among them looking for him, turning shoulders, staring into faces, wondering if he was there, camouflaged by his anorak. I recognized some faces. I called his name, asked them if they'd seen a boy, asked them if they'd seen Ben Finch. A hand on my arm stopped me in my tracks.

"Rachel!"

It was Peter Armstrong, single dad of Ben's best friend, Finn. Finn stood behind him in soccer uniform, mud-streaked, sucking on a piece of orange.

"What's happened?"

Peter listened as I told him.

"We need to phone the police," he said.

"Right now." He made the call himself, while I stood beside him, shaking, and couldn't believe what I was hearing because it meant that this was real now, that it was actually happening to us.

Then Peter organized people. He rallied the families in the parking lot and got some to stay behind with the children, others to form a search party.

"Five minutes," he said to everyone. "Then we leave."

As we waited, raindrops began to speckle the front of Peter's glasses. I trembled and he put his arm around me.

"It'll be OK," he said. "We'll find him."

We were standing like that when the old lady emerged from the woods. She was out of breath and her dog strained at its lead. Her face fell when she saw me.

"Oh my dear," she said. "I'm so sorry. I was sure you would have found him by now." She laid a hand on my arm, for support as much as reassurance.

"Have you called for help?" she asked. "As it's getting dark, I think you must."

It didn't take long, but even so, by the time everyone had mustered, the shadows and shapes of the trees around us had lost their definition and merged into indistinct shades of darkness, making the woods seem impenetrable and hostile. Anybody who had one brought a flashlight. We were a motley crew, a mixture of soccer parents, reenactors still in costume, and a Lycra-clad cyclist. Our pinched faces told not just of the deepening chill, but of the darker and growing fear that Ben wasn't just lost, but that he'd come to harm.

Peter addressed everybody: "Ben's wearing a red anorak, blue trainers that flash, jeans, and he's got brown hair and blue eyes. The dog's a black-and-white cocker spaniel called Skittle. Any questions?"

There were none. We broke into two groups and set off in each direction along the path. Peter led one group; I led the other.

The woods swallowed us up. Before ten minutes had passed the rain worsened and great fists of water broke through the canopy. Within minutes we were wet through, and large spreading puddles appeared on the path. Our progress slowed dramatically, but we carried on calling and listening, the beams of the flashlights swinging wide and low into the woodland around us, eyes straining to see something, anything.

As each second passed and the weather pressed in around us, my fear built into a hot, urgent thing that threatened to explode inside me.

After twenty minutes I felt my phone vibrate. It was a text from Peter.

"Meet parking lot," it said, and that was all.

Hope surged. I began to run, faster and faster, and when I emerged from the path and into the lot I had to stop abruptly. I was in the full glare of a pair of headlights. I shielded my eyes.

"Rachel Jenner?" A figure stepped into the beam, silhouetted.

"Yes?"

"I'm WPC Sarah Banks. I'm a police constable, from Nailsea Police Station. I understand your son is lost. Any sign of him?"

"No."

"Nothing at all?"

I shook my head.

A shout went up from behind us. It was Peter. He had Skittle cradled in his arms. He gently laid the dog down. One of Skittle's delicate hind legs was at a painful, unnatural angle. He whimpered when he saw me, and buried his nose into my hand.

"Ben?" I asked.

Peter shook his head. "The dog hobbled

onto the path right in front of us. We've no idea where he came from."

My memories of that moment are mostly of sound, and sensation. The rain wet on my face, soaking my knees as I knelt on the ground; grim murmurs from the people gathered around; the soft whimpering of my dog; the wild gusting of the wind; and the faint sound of pop music coming from one of the cars that the kids had sheltered in, its windows all steamed up.

Cutting through everything was the crackle of the police radio just behind me, and the voice of WPC Banks calling for assistance.

Peter took the dog away, to the vet. WPC Banks refused to let me go back into the woods. With her sharp young features and neat, white little teeth she looked too immature to be authoritative, but she was adamant.

We sat in my car together. She questioned me closely about what Ben and I had been doing, where I'd last seen him. She took slow, careful notes in bulbous handwriting, which looked like fat caterpillars crawling across the page.

I rang John. When he answered I began to cry and WPC Banks gently took my mobile from me and asked him to confirm that he was Ben's dad. Then she told him that Ben was lost and that he should come right away to the woods.

I rang my sister, Nicky. She didn't answer at first, but she called me back quickly.

"Ben's lost," I said. It was a bad line. I had to raise my voice.

"What?"

"Ben's lost."

"Lost? Where?"

I told her everything. I confessed that I'd let him run ahead of me, that it was my fault. She took a no-nonsense approach.

"Have you called the police? Have you organized people to search? Can I speak to the police?"

"They're bringing dogs, but it's dark, so they say they can't do anything more until morning."

"Can I speak to them?"

"There's no point."

"I'd like to."

"They're doing everything they can."

"Shall I come?"

I appreciated the offer. I knew my sister hated driving in the dark. She was a nervous driver at the best of times, cautious and conservative on the road, as in life. The routes around our childhood cottage, where she was staying for the night, were treacherous even in daylight. In the depths of rural Wiltshire, on the edge of a large forested estate, the cottage was accessible only via a network of narrow, winding lanes edged with deep ditches and tall hedges.

"No, it's OK. John's on his way."

"You must ring me if there's any news, anything."

"I will."

"I'll stay up by my phone."

"OK."

"Is it raining there?"

"Yes. It's so cold. He's only wearing an anorak and a cotton top."

Ben hated to wear sweaters. I'd got him into one that afternoon before we left for the woods, but he'd wriggled out of it once we were in the car.

"I'm hot, Mum," he'd said. "So hot."

The sweater, red, knitted, lay on the backseat of my car, and I leaned back and pulled it onto my lap, held it tight, smelled him in its fabric.

Nicky was still talking, reassuring, as she usually did, even when her own anxiety was building.

"It's OK. It won't take them long to find him. He can't have gone far. Children are very resilient."

"They won't let me search for him. They're making me stay in the parking lot."

"That makes sense. You could injure yourself in the dark."

"It's nearly his bedtime."

She exhaled. I could imagine the creases of worry on her face, and the way she'd be gnawing at her little-finger nail. I knew what Nicky's anxiety looked like. It had been our constant companion as children. "It'll be OK," she said, but we both knew they were only words and that she didn't know that for sure.

When John arrived WPC Banks spoke to him first. They stood in the beam of John's headlights. The rain was relentless still, heavy and driving. Above them a huge beech tree provided some shelter. It had hung on to enough of its leaves that its underside, illuminated by the lights from the car, looked like a golden corona.

John was intently focused on what WPC Banks was saying. He exuded a jumpy, fearful energy. His hair, usually the color of wet sand, was plastered blackly around the contours of his face, which were pallid, as if they'd been sculpted from stone.

"I've spoken to my inspector," WPC Banks was telling him. "He's on his way."

John nodded. He glanced at me, but moved his eyes quickly away. The tendons in his neck were taut.

"That's good news," she said. "It means they're taking it seriously."

Why wouldn't they? I wondered. Why wouldn't they take a missing child seriously? I stepped toward John. I wanted to touch him, just his hand. Actually, I wanted him to hold me. Instead, I got a look of disbelief.

"You let him run ahead?" he said, and his voice was stretched thin with tension. "What were you thinking?"

"I'm sorry," I said. "I'm so sorry."

There was no point in trying to give him an explanation. It was done. I would regret it forever.

WPC Banks said, "I think for now it would be best if all of our focus is on the search for Ben. It won't do him any good if you cast blame."

She was right. John understood that. He was blinking back tears. He looked distraught and incredulous. I watched him cycle through everything I'd been feeling since Ben had gone. He had question after question, each of which WPC Banks answered patiently until he was satisfied that he knew everything there was to know, and that everything possible was being done.

As I stood beside him, and let WPC Banks reassure him, I realized that it had been more than ten months since I'd seen him smile, and I wondered if I ever would again.

Jim

Addendum to DI James Clemo's report for Dr. Francesca Manelli

Transcript recorded by Dr. Francesca Manelli
DI James Clemo and Dr. Francesca Manelli in attendance

Notes to indicate observations on DI Clemo's state of mind or behavior, where his remarks alone do not convey this, are in italics.

This transcript is from the first full psychotherapy session that DI Clemo attended. Previous to this we had only a short preliminary meeting in which I took a history from DI Clemo and we discussed the report that I had asked him to write.

Predictably, given his resistant attitude to therapy, the report that DI Clemo submitted at this stage was lacking in comment on areas of his personal and emotional experience at the time of the Benedict Finch case. The transcripts fill in the gaps somewhat. My priority in this first session was to begin to establish DI Clemo's trust in me.

DI Clemo elected to see me at my private consultation rooms based in Clifton, rather than at the facility provided at police HQ.

Dr. Francesca Manelli (FM): Good to see you again. Thank you for making a start on your report.

***DI James Clemo (JC)** acknowledges this comment with a terse nod. He hasn't yet spoken.*

FM: I've noted your objection to continuing to attend these sessions with me.

JC makes no comment. He is also avoiding eye contact.

FM: So, I'd like to start by asking whether there have been any more incidents?

JC: Incidents?

FM: Panic attacks, of the sort that led to your referral to me.

JC: No.

FM: Can you describe to me what happened on the two occasions that you experienced the panic attacks?

JC: I can't just come in here and talk about stuff like that.

FM: It would be helpful to have more detail, just to get us started. What triggered the feelings of panic, how they grew into a full-blown attack, what you were feeling while it happened.

JC: I'm not talking about my feelings! It's not what I do. I'm sick of the way feelings are all anybody wants to talk about. Watching any sport on TV these days, that's all the commentators ask people. Sue Barker talking to a guy who's played tennis for four hours or collaring someone who's just lost the most important football game of his life. "How are you feeling?" What about "How did you do it? How hard have you worked to get here?"

FM: Do you think that expressing feelings is a weakness?

JC: Yes, I do.

FM: Is that why you don't like talking about the panic attacks? Because they might have been prompted by some very strong feelings that you had?

He doesn't reply.

FM: Everything you say in here will remain confidential.

JC: But you'll make a decision about whether I'm fit to work.

FM: I'll report back to your DCI and make a recommendation, but nobody else will see the contents of your report, or the transcripts of our conversations. Those are for my use only. They'll form the basis of our ongoing conversations. This is going to be a long process, and if you can work toward being open with me, we have a much greater chance of success, and we can hopefully get you back out there doing the work you want to do.

JC: I'm a detective. It's in my blood. It's what I live for.

FM: You need to be aware, also, that the number of psychotherapy sessions that your DCI is prepared to fund is limited.

JC: I know that.

FM: Then talk to me.

He takes his time.

JC: At first it was like being winded, I couldn't get a proper breath in. I kept yawning, and breathing, trying to get air, trying to stop the dizziness, because I thought I was going to pass out. Then my heart was pounding really fast, and I stopped being able to think, I couldn't get my mind to do anything, and then there was panic all over, gripping me, and all I wanted to do was to get out of there, and punch a wall.

FM: Which you did.

JC: I'm not proud of that.

He covers the knuckles on his right hand with his left hand, but not before I've noticed that they're still scabbed and sore.

FM: And you also experienced some bouts of crying in the days after this?

JC: I don't know why.

FM: It's nothing to be ashamed of. It's another symptom of anxiety, just like the panic attacks.

JC: I'm stronger than that.

FM: Strong people experience anxiety.

JC: What I hate most of all is the crying starts anytime, anywhere. I can't stop it. I'm like a baby.

Tears have begun to fall down JC's face.

FM: No. You're not. It's just a symptom. Take some time. We'll come back to this.

He takes a tissue from the box by his chair, wipes his face roughly, tries to compose himself. I make a few notes, to give him some time, and after a minute or two he engages with me.

JC: What are you writing?

FM: I take a few handwritten notes with every patient. It helps me to remember our sessions afterward. Would you like to see what I've written?

JC shakes his head.

FM: I'd like to ask you what kind of support network you might have around you. A partner?

JC: No partner currently.

FM: Family or friends then?

JC: My mum lives in Exeter; I don't see her much. My sister too. My friends in Bristol are mostly colleagues so we don't talk about stuff outside work.

FM: I see from your notes that your father passed away a little before the Benedict Finch case started.

JC: That's correct. About a month before.

FM: And he was a detective too?

JC: He was Deputy Chief Super in Devon and Cornwall.

FM: Was he the reason you joined the force?

JC: A big part of it, yeah.

FM: And you started your career in Devon and Cornwall?

JC: I did.

FM: Was that hard? Did you feel you had a lot to live up to, in your dad?

JC: Of course, because I did.

FM: Did that feel like pressure?

JC: I'm not afraid of pressure.

FM: When you were with Devon and Cornwall was it well known that you were your father's son?

JC: When I started I was known as "Mick

Clemo's boy," but it's the same for anyone who's got a relative in the force.

FM: And when you moved to Bristol, to the Avon and Somerset force, did that change?

JC: It changed completely. Only one or two of the older guys in Bristol knew my dad personally.

FM: So it was a chance for a fresh start?

JC: It was a promotion is what it was.

FM: Has policing been the right career choice for you, do you think?

JC: It's what I always wanted to do. There was never another way for me. Like I said, it's in the blood. It has to be in the blood.

FM: Why "has to be"?

JC: Because you see it all. You see the dirtiest, blackest side of life. You see what people inflict on each other, and it can be brutal.

His gaze is steady now, focused entirely on me. I feel that he's challenging me to contradict what he's said, or diminish it. I remember that I'm not the only person in the room trained to read the behavior of others. I decide to move on.

FM: Your record states that you took an English degree before joining the force.

JC: It's expected to join the force with a degree nowadays. Not like it used to be when you went in straight from school.

FM: Did you enjoy your degree?
JC: I did.
FM: What did you study? Was there anything you especially enjoyed?
JC: Yeats. I enjoyed Yeats.
FM: I know a Yeats poem: "Turning and turning in the widening gyre / The falcon cannot hear the falconer . . ." Do you know it? I think it's by Yeats anyway. I forget the title.
JC can't help himself, he carries on the poem.
JC: ". . . Things fall apart; the center cannot hold; / Mere anarchy is loosed upon the world . . ."
FM: ". . . The blood-dimmed tide is loosed, and everywhere . . ."
JC: ". . . The ceremony of innocence is drowned."
FM: There's more.
JC: I can't remember it exactly.
FM: He's a wonderful poet.
JC: He's a truthful poet.
FM: Do you still read poetry?
JC: No. I don't have time for that sort of thing now.
FM: You work long hours?
JC: You have to if you want to get on.
FM: And do you? Want to get on?
JC: Of course.
FM: Can I ask you once again: is there

anything specific that triggers your panic attacks?

JC covers his face with his hands, rubs his eyes, and massages his temples. I begin to think he isn't going to reply, that I've pushed him too far too fast, but eventually he seems to come to some kind of decision and looks me directly in the eye.

JC: I can't sleep. It makes me confused sometimes. It makes me doubt my judgment.

FM: You suffer from insomnia?

JC: Yes.

FM: How long has this been going on?

He studies me before he answers.

JC: Since the case.

FM: Do you struggle to get to sleep, or do you wake up in the middle of the night?

JC: I can't fall asleep.

FM: How many hours do you think you sleep a night?

JC: I don't know. Sometimes as little as three or four.

FM: That's a very small amount, which could certainly have a profound effect on your state of mind during the day.

JC: It's fine.

He's being stoic suddenly, as if he regrets confiding in me.

FM: I don't think three or four hours' sleep is fine.
JC: Maybe I'm wrong. It's probably more.
FM: You seemed quite certain.
JC: It's nothing I can't cope with.
I don't believe him.
FM: Have you sought any medical help?
JC: I'm not taking pills.
FM: What goes through your mind when you're trying to sleep?
Again, he studies me before responding.
JC: I can't remember.
His answers have become obviously and frustratingly evasive, and I want to delve more into this, but now is not the time, because if this process is to succeed I must first build his trust and that, I suspect, is not going to be an easy task.

■ ■ ■ ■

Day 2
Monday,
October 22, 2012

■ ■ ■ ■

Efforts undertaken by law-enforcement agencies during the initial stages of a missing-child report may often make the difference between a case with a swift conclusion and one evolving into months or even years of stressful, unresolved investigation. While the investigative aspect of a missing-child case is similar, in many ways, to other major cases, few of these other situations have the added emotional stress created by the unexplained absence of a child. When not anticipated and prepared for, this stress may negatively impact the outcome of a missing-child case.

— Preston Findlay and Robert G. Lowery, Jr., eds., "Missing and Abducted Children: A Law-Enforcement Guide to Case Investigation and Program Management," fourth edition, National Center for Missing & Exploited Children, OJJDP Report, 2011

Rachel

John couldn't stand the waiting. He wanted to do something, so he spent most of the night driving around, circling the woods, following the routes back into Bristol, just in case.

Each time he returned, he sat in my car and asked me to go over what had happened.

"I've told you," I said, when he asked for the third time.

"Tell me again."

"How will it help?"

"It might."

"I'm so scared he's hurt."

John winced at my words, but I needed to say more.

"He'll be so frightened."

"I know." His reply was tight, tense.

"He'll be wondering why we haven't found him yet."

"Stop! Just tell me again. From the beginning."

I did. I told him everything I could remember, over and over again, but it was simple really. Ben was there, and then he ran ahead, and then he was gone. No sign, except a rope swing, gently swaying.

"Do you think he'd been on it?" John asked. "How was it swaying?"

"Backward and forward. Gently."

"Could the wind have blown it?"

"It might have."

"Have you told the police?"

"Yes."

"And you heard nothing?"

"No. Just the sounds of the woods."

"And you called out to him?"

"Of course I did."

And so on. In this way, the hours passed slowly, desperately. We punctuated the time by speaking periodically to the police, getting updates that told us nothing. I rang Nicky more than once, passing on the lack of news, hearing the mounting desperation in my voice echoed in her responses.

Inspector Miller arrived before midnight in full waterproof gear, to oversee the search. The men with dogs changed shift twice. Sodden and tired animals handed over to eager, bright-eyed creatures, straining at their leashes. I gave them Ben's sweater to sniff, so they knew his scent. The darkness was our greatest enemy, holding back the possibility of a full-scale search.

At five a.m., Inspector Miller called John and me together to tell us what was happening. They were readying themselves for dawn, he said, which would be at 07:37. He ran through a list of the actions that were planned, using police-speak that I only partially understood. There were to be more dogs, horses, a sergeant and six; Mountain Rescue was coming, and they'd scrambled the Eye in the Sky.

For the next couple of hours I watched numbly from my car as the scene in the parking lot transformed. I felt useless, a voyeur.

The "sergeant and six" turned out to be a grilled van, from which seven men appeared, ready to search on foot. Another van brought a generator, lights, a shelter and maps, and four Mountain Rescue men. Inspector Miller and WPC Banks worked to organize them. They'd both begun to function with the contained, intense kind of energy of somebody who has a bad secret that they're not allowed to tell.

Dawn crept in in fits and starts, the pall

of total darkness reluctant to retreat. Daylight revealed that the parking area had been churned up by the constant comings and goings during the night. The only blessings were that the rain had ebbed to a persistent drizzle and the wind had died down somewhat, though spiteful, icy little gusts still blew through intermittently.

Four mounted officers congregated at the entrance to the path. Their horses were huge and beautiful, with glossy coats and nostrils that snorted visible puffs into the damp, chilly air. Ben would have loved them. One of them startled as the thud-thud of the search helicopter grew louder overhead. It swooped low over the treetops, before disappearing again.

Katrina arrived soon afterward. John emerged from his car to greet her and folded his arms around her in a public display of affection the likes of which had never occurred once in our entire relationship. He buried his face into her hair. I lowered my gaze.

She knocked on my car window, startling me. I wound it down.

"No news yet?" she said.

I shook my head.

"I've brought these for you, in case you need something." She handed me a thermos and a paper bag.

"It's just tea, and some pastries. I didn't know what you like, so I picked for you . . ." Her voice trailed away. She was neatly dressed, and she stood there like a prefect at school, well turned out and eager to please. No makeup. That was the first time I'd seen her without it. I didn't know what to say.

"Thanks," I managed.

"If there's anything I can do."

"OK. Thanks."

"John's asked me to go back home, in case he turns up there."

"OK. Good idea."

It was awkward and strange. There's no protocol for meeting your ex-husband's new wife at the site where your son's gone missing.

"Well, I'd best get back there," she said, and she turned away, returned to John.

After she'd gone, I looked in the bag of pastries. Two croissants. I tried to nibble one, but it tasted like dust. I managed some sips of tea. It wasn't sugared, the way I like it, but the heat was welcome.

It was just after Katrina left that Inspector Miller's radio sprang into life.

They'd found something. It was hard to

hear the detail. The radio crackled and spat, words emerging occasionally from the interference. "What is it?" I mouthed at the inspector as he held up a finger to shush me. He beckoned to WPC Banks to join him and they turned away, conferred. John noticed the action and appeared beside me. I felt electrified by hope and dread. Once again the drone of the helicopter traveled over us, making it even more difficult to hear. The inspector turned to us:

"Can you confirm once again what Ben is wearing, please?"

"Red anorak, white T-shirt with a picture of a guitar on it, blue jeans, ripped at the knee, blue trainers that flash."

He repeated it all into his radio. The voice crackled back at him, asking what size and brand of trainer.

"Geox," I said. "Size thirty."

The inspector turned away again. It took all my self-control not to grab him, to shake out of him what was going on. John was rigid beside me, arms folded tightly across his chest.

It was the awkward twitch of Inspector Miller's mouth that gave it away when he turned back to us. Whatever they'd found, it wasn't making him happy.

"Right." He took a deep breath, drawing

strength from some internal reserve. “The boys have found something that they believe might be significant. It’s not Ben” — he’d seen the question on my lips — “but it might be an item or items of his clothing.”

“Where?” said John.

“By the pond at Paradise Bottom.”

I knew it. It was nearby. I ran. I heard them shout after me, I was aware of the heavy rhythm of someone running behind me, but I didn’t pause; I sprinted into the woods as fast as I could.

Before I even reached the pond I saw them: a group of three men, huddled together, standing in the middle of the path. They watched me as I approached. One man held a bundle in his hands, a clear plastic bag with something in it.

“I’ve come to see,” I said, and the man with the bundle said, “It would be good if you could confirm whether any of these items belong to Ben or not, but please don’t take them out of the bag.”

He held it out toward me, an offering.

John arrived beside me, his breathing loud and ragged.

I took the bag. It had a weight to it. Droplets of water smeared the plastic outside and in. The contents were wet. I saw a flash of red, some denim, bundled-up white cotton fabric. I turned it upside down, and beneath the fabric items were two shoes: blue Geox trainers. They were scuffed, and on one of them the sole was slightly separated from the shoe at the toe, as I knew it would be. I gave the bag a little shake. Triggered by the movement, blue lights flashed along the sole of the shoes.

"The shoes are named," I said. "With his initials, under the tongue."

Through the plastic I managed to pull up the tongue of the shoe. Underneath it were the letters "BF." The ink had bled into the fabric around it.

"Thank you," said the man. He had white hair and a darker gray mustache and eyebrows, and red, pockmarked skin. He took the bag from me, though I didn't want to give it back to him.

"Where's Ben?" I said.

"We're doing our very best to find him," the man replied, and the compassion in his voice robbed me of any shreds of composure that I might have had left.

An ugly fear was growing in me like a tumor; it was an idea that I hadn't wanted to contemplate. John hugged me, tightly. He knew what I was thinking because he was thinking it too.

"No!" I shouted, and it was the sound of

a wild animal, an ululation, an uttering that a mother might make if she saw her offspring being dragged away by a predator.

Jim

The morning after Benedict Finch went missing I woke up early, like I always do. I've got a reliable body clock. I never need to set an alarm, although I do, just in case. You don't want to oversleep. I started the day the way I always do: a cup of good black coffee, made properly in my Bialetti. I drank it standing in my kitchen.

My flat is on the top floor of a tall Georgian building in Clifton. It's the best area in Bristol, and the flat's got amazing views because it's on the side of a steep hill. The front overlooks a big garden, which is nice, but out the back it's better because I can see a proper slice of the city. I've got Brandon Hill opposite, dotted with trees, Cabot Tower on its summit, a couple of Georgian and Victorian terraces below. Just out of sight are modern office buildings and shops, but you can see a bit of Jacob's Wells Road below, leading steeply downhill to the harbor, where you can go for a night out or a weekend walk. I can't see the water from my flat, but I can sense it, and gulls often circle and cry out, diving past my windows.

Until I started going out with Emma I didn't know that this city was built on sea trade that docked there for hundreds of years: sugar, tobacco, paper, slaves. She told me how a lot of human suffering made the wealth that built Bristol, and a lot of men gambled lives and fortunes on that. Emma was an army brat, and the reason she was so well informed was that her dad made her learn a history of every new place they moved her to, and they moved a lot, so she was in the habit of it.

Once she told me about the slavery, I couldn't get it out of my mind, and then I realized how much of the city's noisy, nervy history is in your face, especially where I live. You've got the Wills Memorial Building, pride of the university, towering over the top of Park Street: built on tobacco profits. The Georgian House, perfectly preserved, and a very nice bit of real estate: sugar and slaves. Both of them are less than a quarter of a mile from my flat, and I could name more.

I think about it sometimes because I don't think cities change their character too much; even after hundreds of years it's still there as an undercurrent. Now, when I look out of the window each morning, and watch Bristol wake up beneath me, its messy, complicated past is right there as a little bit of a jittery feeling in my bones.

I'd slept well the night before even though it was obvious that there'd been some serious weather overnight. It was still dark when I finished my coffee, and the flat felt cold and drafty. Outside, rain was pelting down and the tips of the trees were getting pushed and pulled in all sorts of directions. A plastic shopping bag was blown up from the street below and went on a crazy dance over the treetops before it got snagged.

Before I got out the board to iron my shirt, I brought Emma a cup of tea. She was still in bed. She always got up a bit later than me.

She was lying in a mess of bedding and hair. She wasn't a neat sleeper. It was a contrast to the controlled and purposeful way she lived the rest of her life, and one of the rare occasions I was able to glimpse her with her guard down. I felt privileged to be close enough to her to see it.

"Hello," she said when I put the tea down.

"Did you sleep well?" I asked her.

"Mmm. How about you?" She blinked

softly, sleepily. Then she stretched and rubbed her eyes, her movements languid. Emma didn't rush things. She was watchful and clever, and poised, a cocktail of characteristics that I found addictive, especially when mixed with her beauty. Emma turned heads. I was a lucky man.

"Solid eight hours," I said. I got back into bed beside her. It was warm and comfortable and I couldn't resist it. Monday morning could wait a few minutes. Emma nestled into my shoulder.

"I could stay here all day," she said.

"Me too."

She draped an arm across my chest and I watched her tea going cold and saw the face of my clock count nine minutes before I forced myself to leave the gentle rise and fall of her sleepy breathing. As I pulled the cover away, she roused herself and pulled my face to hers and we kissed. "I've got to get up," I said.

"Boring," she replied, but I knew that if I hadn't said it, she would have. Emma was always punctual. She smiled, as if to acknowledge my thought, and then she sat up and reached for her tea, grimacing at the first tepid gulp.

I put the ironing board up in front of the kitchen window and watched the red and white lights of the commuter cars coming into the city as I did my shirt.

"You cycling in?" Emma asked when she appeared in her work clothes, hair smoothed and tamed into a thick ponytail.

"Yep."

"Trying to build up your celery legs?" she said. She loved to tease. This wasn't a side of her she readily showed people either. It made me smile.

"You love my celery legs," I said. "You should just admit it. You driving in then?"

She was wearing a business suit, fitted and shapely, and a pair of low heels. She had bright eyes, and a quick smile that morning. She was ready to take on her day.

"That's correct, Detective Inspector Clemo, an excellent deduction. See you later."

Emma and I traveled separately to work. Police officers are allowed to have relationships with each other, it's not forbidden, but the reality is that it can be frowned upon, because it could complicate things if you end up on a case together. It was my suggestion that we keep our relationship secret for now. We'd only been together for a few months, and I figured what we did in our spare time was our business. Emma agreed. She said she wasn't bothered if it was secret or not. She was easy like that.

First I heard of Benedict Finch was when I was cycling in. I have a portable digital radio that I listen to when I ride. By the time I left the flat the wind and rain had eased up, and, as I dropped down Jacob's Wells Road toward the waterfront, I enjoyed the feel of the acceleration on the steep downhill and skirted around the water that had pooled around the backed-up drains.

I barely had to pedal when I hit the flat beside the harbor, and, as I was cruising past the cathedral, I caught a 07:30 news update on Radio Bristol. It said that an eight-year-old boy called Benedict Finch had gone missing in Leigh Woods. It happened the previous afternoon while he was out on a dog walk with his mum. Police and mountain teams were looking for him. They were worried.

The city center proper was starting to get sticky with early Monday morning traffic, but I made good time, and I hit Feeder Road at 07:40 and cycled alongside the canal. The water level was high, the surface pocked with drizzle. A fisherman sat hunched on the bank beside the road, shrouded in waterproofs.

Overhead, traffic roared across the stained concrete flyover, oppressively low, a grubby landmark that greeted me every day on my arrival at work. Behind it daylight was emerging, a slate-gray sky with low, racing clouds that were purple above and yellow below. It was a poisonous sky: the death throes of last night's weather. I remember thinking that it wasn't a good night for a small boy to be missing. Not a good night at all.

RACHEL

Inspector Miller said that because they'd found the clothing the "game had changed" and they needed to "intensify their operation." He described the woods as "a scene" and said it was a CID case now. What he avoided saying explicitly was what we all knew. Ben wasn't lost; he'd been taken.

A stolen child is every parent's worst nightmare, because the first thing you ask yourself is, "Who would take a child?" The answers are all profoundly disturbing. I slipped into a state of shock. John did too. The faces of the uniformed police around us were grim, and some averted their eyes, a show of respect that was especially unnerving.

WPC Banks guided John and me into her car and drove us to the CID headquarters. At the end of the long lane that led from the parking lot to the main road, photographers and journalists had already gathered, and they thrust their faces and their camera lenses up against the car windows, trying to talk to us, take photographs of us. We recoiled from the noise, and the flashlights. We drew away from the windows and into each other. John clutched my hand.

It was a terrible journey. Coming away from the woods felt like an admission that we wouldn't find Ben; that we were prepared to leave him behind. Within minutes we'd entered the outskirts of the city, and were sucked into its road systems. Busy dual highways carried us past new and old industrial buildings, into dense traffic. In the center the River Avon appeared, parallel to the road, murky water flowing strongly while we lurched to a stop at every light. Plant life clung to its banks, tough and grubby.

My thoughts refused to work coherently and I was gripped by terror, which felt as if it was hollowing me out. My mind couldn't face the present, so it burrowed into the past, looking for distraction, or perhaps solace, looking for anything that wasn't this reality. I felt John's cold fingers clutching mine and I remembered the first time he'd held my hand, as if that would somehow make things right.

It happened the week after we'd met for

the first time at a hospital function. John was an exhausted junior doctor, wearing their standard uniform of oxford shirt and chinos, complete with tired sags in the fabric after a long shift. I was a nursing student, there for the free sandwiches and glass of warm white wine. His dark sandy hair fell over his forehead rakishly, and he had a lovely symmetrical, fine-featured face that was handsome in an old-fashioned way. His eyes were a piercing blue, intense and captivating. Ben was lucky enough to inherit those eyes.

Our first conversation was about music, and on that evening, when I was tired of socializing and a little tired of life, it was a tonic. John spoke in a way that was earnest, but gentle too. He asked me if I knew that Bristol had one of the finest concert halls in the country. It was small, he said, in a beautiful neoclassical nineteenth-century church building, and the acoustics were spectacularly good.

He had a lack of pretension when he spoke that I liked instantly. His inbuilt, unquestioning respect for culture transported me back to conversations overheard at my aunt Esther's cottage, the place I grew up in, and suddenly I felt as if my life had been drifting for too long, and that it was time to stop.

A week later, we sat in St. George's concert hall, waiting for the concert to begin. It's a fine, elegant building, built on the side of lovely, leafy Brandon Hill, just a stone's throw from the shops on Park Street. It's opposite the Georgian House, which Ben has since visited on a school trip, but at the time I hadn't known either place existed.

It was a full house. Tickets had been hard to come by. John was animated, full of information. He pointed out the place where a German firebomb fell through the roof one night in 1942, when the building was still in use as a church, and landed on the altar unexploded.

He talked about himself too. He told me that he used to play the violin, that his mother had been a concert-class performer, and his home had been full of music as a child. He told me that work was going well, and that he'd just decided to specialize in general pediatric surgery. I got a sense that his interest in all things was intense, thoughtful, and absorbing, whether it was music, architecture, or the small bodies and lives of his patients. He had a rare sensitivity.

The concert began. A violinist, dressed in

black, stood center stage and, with utmost care, freed the first few notes from his instrument, and they hung crisply in the air around us. He played with an elegance that captivated and seduced, and I felt John relax beside me. When his hand brushed mine and he didn't move it away, it seemed to give me balance. When he gently held my fingers in his, it felt like a counterpoint to the emotional intensity of the music, and also an encouragement to let myself feel it, become absorbed by it.

This memory — the music, the feelings — flashed through my mind in the car. It was as if I wanted to rewind my life back to that point, and start it over again, to hold on to that perfect moment, so that what came afterward wouldn't turn to crap, wouldn't lead us to now. Which was impossible, of course, because the memory was gone as soon as it arrived. The reality was that instead of comforting me, the cold grip of John's fingers felt desperate and futile, just as mine must have done to him.

The traffic stayed slow as we traveled through the city center: taillights and signposts, concrete shapes and scud clouds under a granite sky. The River Avon disappeared and then reappeared on the other side of the road, brown and choppy still, a shopping cart abandoned on the far bank. I kept my eye on the water, tracking its progress into the city, because I couldn't stand to look at the people outside the car, all the people who were having an ordinary Monday at the start of an ordinary week, the people who knew where their children were.

The police station was a large concrete cuboid building, Brutalist in style. It was three stories high, with tall rectangular windows set into each level at regular intervals, like enlarged arrow slits in a castle wall. In typography from around half a century ago, the sign announcing where we'd arrived sat on a thin concrete rectangle above the doors and stated simply: KENNETH STEELE HOUSE.

The inside of the building was startlingly different. It was state of the art, open plan, busy and slick. We were asked to wait on a set of low-slung sofas by a reception area. Nobody gave us a second glance. I went to the loo. I barely recognized myself in the mirror. I was gaunt, white, a specter. There was mud on my face, and the gash across my forehead was livid and crusty with blood that had strands of my hair caught in it. I looked dirty and unkempt. I tried to clean myself up but it wasn't very effective.

When I got back to reception, John was still on the sofa, elbows on his knees, head hanging. I took my place beside him. A uniformed officer with a pink face and thinning gray hair came out from behind the front desk and approached us across the wide foyer.

"It won't be long," he said. "There's somebody on their way down to fetch you just now."

"Thank you," John said.

Jim

Kenneth Steele House is where I work. It's the CID headquarters for Avon and Somerset Constabulary. It's not a pretty building from the outside, and neither is its location. It's on a strip of commercial and industrial properties behind Temple Meads Station in St. Philip's Marsh. It's a flat inner-city area with an isolated, wasteland feel because there's no housing in the vicinity, and its boundaries are the canal and the River Avon. There's CCTV everywhere and a fair bit of barbed wire.

I was at my desk by 08:05. I noticed the atmosphere straightaway. There was none of the usual Monday morning chatter, only a tension about the place that you get when a big case is in. Mark Bennett — same rank as me but about a hundred years older — popped up from behind the partition that separated his desk from mine before I'd even turned on my PC. "Scotch Bonnet wants to see you," he said. "Soon as."

Bennett had a bald shiny head, a thick fleshy neck, and the eyes of a bull terrier. He looked like a bruiser. Truth was, he was anything but. We'd gone out for a drink once, when I first arrived in Avon and Somerset, and he told me that he'd never gone as far nor as fast as he'd wanted to in CID. Then he told me that he thought his wife didn't love him anymore. I'd gotten out of there as fast as I could. You don't want that mind-set to infect you. "Scotch Bonnet" was Bennett's nickname for our DCI, Corinne Fraser. It was because she was Scottish, and female, and could be fiery. It wasn't especially clever or funny. Nobody else used it.

Fraser was in her office. "Jim," she said. "Close the door. Take a seat."

She was immaculately turned out as usual in a sharp business suit. She was eccentric looking, with frizzy gray hair that didn't suit her short fringe and puffed out over her ears, but she also had an attractive, delicate face, and implacable gray eyes that could look right through you, or pin you to a wall. I sat down opposite her. She didn't waste time:

"As of zero eight hundred hours this morning I've got an eight-year-old boy who has almost certainly been abducted from Leigh Woods. We've got multiple scenes already, the weather's been against us, and we've lost more than twelve hours since he first disappeared. We're going to have the press trying to crawl up our arses before lunchtime. I'm going to need a deputy SIO to take on a lot of responsibility. Are you up to it?"

"Yes, boss."

I felt blood rush into my cheeks. It was what I'd hoped for: a high-profile case, a senior position. I'd been in CID in Avon and Somerset for three years, putting in the hours, proving myself, waiting for this moment. There were DIs above me in the pecking order, older, just as ambitious. Mark Bennett a case in point. They could have gotten the role, but it was my time, my chance. Did I think of turning it down? No. Did I think it was going to be a minefield? Maybe. But the words that were doing cartwheels in my head were these: bring it on. Bring. It. On.

A big part of the thrill was getting to work with Fraser. She was tough and clever, one of the best. It was well known that she'd grown up in a shitty housing project in Glasgow. As soon as she could leave home, she'd moved as far away as possible so that she could train as a police officer and start a new life. Problem was, while she was a young DC she'd ended up married to a DCI from Scotland Yard who reeked so badly of corruption that even the Met had to get rid of him eventually. In his spare time he'd knocked her about. She'd ended up in the hospital once, but her old man was never charged. The police looked after their own in those days, so long as they were white males.

Her good fortune was that her husband had died before going to trial for corruption. He had a heart attack at the pub. He was dead before he hit the floor. She'd responded by moving to Avon and Somerset as a DS and shooting up the ranks with a combination of astute political play and detective work that was respected for its thoroughness. She was the first woman ever to be made a DCI in Avon and Somerset, and must have been one of the first in England. She wasted no words and her authority was natural. It was the right of someone who'd survived her wilderness years and come out tougher and wiser. She didn't tolerate whining and she didn't tolerate bullying.

"First job: interview the parents," Fraser said.

"Yes, boss. Where are they?"

"At the scene."

"Is uniform taking them home?"

"Not yet." She thought about it, tapped her pen on the desk. "We need to be sensitive, that's paramount, Jim, but I'm inclined to bring them in here. Teas and coffees on our terms."

I knew what she meant. When you interview people in their own homes they feel more relaxed, because it's familiar, but they are also in control.

"Use a rape suite," she said. It was a concession to sensitivity. Rape suites are nicer than interview rooms. "And anyway," she added, "we'll need forensics to visit Mum's home at least, assuming that's where the kid spends most of his time, and Dad's home if we think it's worth it. They're both potential scenes."

She picked up the phone. It was my cue to leave. But then she put it down again.

"One more thing," she said. "I was going to ask Annie Rookes to be FLO but she's tied up. Any ideas?"

I don't really know what made me say it so reflexively, but I did, and before I'd had a chance to think. "What about Emma Zhang?"

Fraser looked surprised. "Is she experienced enough? This one's going to be tough whichever way it plays out."

"I think so, boss. She's very bright, and she's done the training." It was too late to back down now, and anyway, I thought Emma deserved the chance, and I thought she'd be good at the job. It would be a real step up for her, and there was so much to learn from working with Fraser.

"Zhang it is then," Fraser said, picking up the phone again.

It was only once I'd left her office that I hoped I'd done the right thing, for Emma, and for the case too. The family liaison officer role is a crucial one. They're there to look after the welfare of the victim's family, but they're detectives first and foremost. They watch, they listen, they offer support, but above all they keep an eye out for evidence and then they report back to the investigation. It's a delicate line to tread. The FLO can make the difference between our success and our failure.

We got an incident room set up, quick sharp. Kenneth Steele House is spot-on because it's been refurbished with CID needs in mind, so we've got the facilities we need to run as slick an operation as possible, as quickly as possible. The room we were allocated was spacious: two runs of tables down each side with monitors on them, room for the Receiver, Statement Reader, and Action Allocator. There was an office set up for DCI Fraser just off the main area, so she could run the show from there, as well as an "intel" room, a CCTV room, an exhibits office, and a store. It was an arrangement that meant we could keep everything close; it was proven to work well.

Straight off, we allocated actions to the officers we already had working, to confirm the whereabouts of all the local sex offenders who were already known to us and to look through records for previous incidents relating to missing children or any peepers, flashers, or attempted abductions in the area. We had four pairs of officers in place and Fraser was adamant that she was going to need ten pairs at least.

At ten a.m. we got a call to say the parents had been brought in. Fraser said, "You should get down there and get straight on with the interviews. Do it by the book, Jim. I want every *i* dotted and every *t* crossed. I'm also going to speak to the Super because I think we've got grounds to get a CRA out already. The criteria are met. You need to ask the parents for a photograph ASAP."

CRA stood for Child Rescue Alert. I knew

the criteria, you learn them by rote: if the missing child is under sixteen, if a police officer of superintendent rank or higher feels that serious harm or death might come to the child, if the child has been kidnapped and there are sufficient details about the child or abductor to make it useful, then you can issue one. The point of it is to inform police, press, and public nationwide that a child is missing. A news flash interrupts TV and radio programs to alert the public, and border agencies and police forces around the country will be primed to be on the lookout. It's as serious as it gets.

I took a last look through the questions I'd been preparing for the parents, made myself take a deep breath. This was it. I was as ready as I was going to be. As detectives, we're trained to know that what you do in the first few hours after a child has disappeared is crucial. Ben Finch had already been missing for more than twelve hours and our investigation was only just launching. I didn't need Fraser to tell me that operationally speaking we were on the back foot already, or that every step we took from now on would be under scrutiny.

"Woodley," I said to a rookie DC whom Fraser had attached to the case. He was a tall, skinny lad with a face only a mother could love. “Get me a tea tray ready. Enough for three. And biscuits. Take it down to the rape suite but don’t take it in. Wait for me outside.”

If a female officer in plainclothes brings a tray of tea into a room, everyone assumes she’s from catering. If a male officer does the same, it makes him seem like a nice guy, puts people at ease. Just a little tip I learned from my dad.

Rachel

They took John and me to different places.

I was interviewed in a low-ceilinged room that was windowless and oppressive. I was met there by a tall young woman, who introduced herself as DC Emma Zhang. She wore a smart, slim-fitting business suit. She had lovely caramel-colored skin, and thick black hair tied neatly into a ponytail, deep, dark eyes that were almond-shaped and beautiful, and a warm smile.

She shook my hand and told me that she would be my family liaison officer and she sat down beside me on an uncomfortable sofa with boxy arms and adjusted her skirt.

"We're going to do everything we can to find Ben," she said. "Please be assured of that. His welfare will be our absolute priority, and my role is to keep you informed about what's happening as the investigation and the search for Ben progress. And you must feel free to come to me with any queries, or anything at all for that matter, because I'm here to make sure you feel looked after too."

I felt reassured by DC Zhang, by her apparent competence and her easy, approachable manner. It gave me a modicum of hope.

There was nothing to look at in the room except for a matching pair of armchairs, a meanly proportioned beech coffee table, and three bland landscape prints on the wall opposite. The carpet was industrial gray. On one of the armchairs a lone purple cushion sagged as if it had been punched. A door was labeled EXAMINATION ROOM.

A man arrived. He was tall, well built, and closely shaven, with thick, dark brown hair, cut in a neat short back and sides, and hazel eyes. He had large hands and he put a tray down on the table clumsily: the stacked cups slid dramatically to one end, the spout of the pot let free a slug of hot liquid. DC Zhang leaned forward to try to save everything but there was no need. The cups wobbled but didn't fall.

The man sat down in the armchair beside me and extended his hand to me. "DI Jim Clemo," he said. "I'm so sorry about Ben." He had a firm handshake.

"Thank you."

Clemo cleared his throat. "Two things we

need from you as soon as possible are the contact details for Ben's GP and his dentist. Do you have those to hand?"

I took my phone from my pocket, gave him what he wanted.

"Does Ben have any medical conditions that we should be aware of?"

"No."

He made notes in a notebook that had a soft acid-yellow cover. It was an incongruously lovely object.

"And do you have a copy of Ben's birth certificate?"

My paperwork was disorganized, but I did keep a file of Ben's important documents.

"Why?"

"It's procedure."

"Am I having to prove he existed or something?"

Clemo gave me a poker face, and I realized I was right. It was my first inkling that I was involved in a process where I didn't know the rules, and where nobody trusted anybody, because what we were dealing with was too serious for that.

Clemo's questions were thorough and he wanted detail. As I talked, I sat with my arms wrapped around myself. He moved a lot, leaning forward at some moments, sitting back and crossing his legs at others. He was always watching me, his eyes constantly searching my face for something. I tried to quell my natural reticence, to talk openly, in the hope that something I told him would help find Ben.

He started by asking me about myself, my own upbringing. How that was relevant I didn't know, but I told him. Because of my unusual circumstances, the tragedy of my parents' death, it's a story I've told a lot, so I was able to stay calm when I said, "My parents were killed in a car crash when I was one and my sister was nine. They had a head-on collision with an articulated lorry."

I watched Clemo go through a reaction that was familiar to me, because I'd witnessed it so often: shock, sorrow, and then sympathy, sometimes barely concealed schadenfreude.

"They were driving home from a party," I added.

I'd always liked that little bit of information. It meant that in my mind my parents were forever frozen as young and sociable, invigorated by life. Probably perfect.

Clemo expressed sympathy but he moved on quickly, asking me who brought me up, where I'd lived, then how I met John, when we got married. He wanted to know about Ben's birth. I gave them a date and a place:

July 10, 2004, St. Michael's Hospital in Bristol.

Beneath the facts my head was swimming with sensations and memories. I remembered a hard and lengthy labor, which started on a perfect scorcher of a day, when the air shimmered. They admitted me to a delivery room at midnight, the heat still lingering in every corner of the city, and as my labor intensified through the long hours that followed, it was punctuated with the shouts of revelers from outside, as if they couldn't think of going home on such a night.

Before morning there'd been the fright of a significant hemorrhage, but later, after the sun had risen high again, I felt the extraordinary joy of being handed my tiny boy, who I watched turn from gray to pink in my arms. I felt the weightlessness of his hair, the perfect softness of his temples, and a sensation of absolute stillness when our eyes met, me holding my breath, him taking one of his first.

I had to detail the years of Ben's childhood for Clemo, and talk about my relationship with my sister, and with John's family. It was painful to speak about John's mother, Ruth, my beloved Ruth, who'd become a surrogate parent to me after my marriage, and who now lived in a nursing home, her brain slowly succumbing to the ravages of dementia.

I also had to talk about the breakup of my marriage, how I never saw it coming, how Ben and I had coped since then. I didn't want to relate these things to strangers, but I had no choice. I steeled myself, tried to trust in the process.

The pace of Clemo's questions slowed as we got nearer to the present day. He asked in detail about Ben's experiences at school. I told him they were happy ones; that Ben loved school, and loved his teacher. She'd been very supportive when John and I had been going through the separation and divorce.

Clemo wanted to know how often Ben had visited his dad lately, or any other friends or family. He wanted to know what our custody arrangements were. He wanted details of all the activities that Ben did in and out of school. I had to describe everything we'd done the previous week and then we were talking about Saturday, and then Sunday morning, and what we'd done in the hours we spent together before we went to the woods.

"Did you have lunch before you went out to the woods?" Clemo asked. There was a sort of apology in his voice.

"Is this in case you find his body?"

"It doesn't mean that I think we're going to find a body. It's a question I have to ask."

"Ben ate a ham sandwich, banana, yogurt, and two Bourbon biscuits in the car on the way to the woods."

"Thank you."

"Do you need to know what I ate?"

"No. That won't be necessary."

Zhang handed me a box of tissues.

We also compiled a list of the people whom I'd seen in the woods: the crowd in the parking lot, including Peter and Finn and the other young soccer players and their families, the group of fantasy reenactors, the cyclist, and the old lady who'd helped me when I first lost Ben. I also remembered a man whom Ben and I had passed early on in our walk. He was carrying a dog lead, though we didn't see his dog. It was frustratingly hard to recall what he was wearing, or even what he looked like, and I became upset with myself.

I promised that if I thought of anything or anybody else I would let the police know. They asked permission to look through my phone records, to search my home, and especially Ben's bedroom. I said yes to it all. I would have agreed to anything if I'd thought it would help.

"Do you have a photograph of Ben? One that we can release to the public and press?"

I gave him the picture that I kept in my wallet. It was a recent school photograph, not even dog-eared yet, as I'd only got it the week before. I looked at my son's face: serious, and sweet, beautiful and vulnerable. His father's eyes and dark sandy hair, his perfect skin, scattered lightly with freckles across the nose. I could hardly bear to hand it over.

Clemo took the photograph from me gently. "Thank you," he said, and then, "Ms. Jenner, I will find Ben. I will do everything in my power to find him."

I looked at him. I searched those eyes for signs of his commitment, for confirmation that he understood what was at stake, wanting him to mean what he said, wanting him to be on my side, wanting to believe that he could find Ben.

"Do you promise?" I said. I reached for his hand, gripped it, startling both of us.

"I promise," he said. He extricated his fingers from mine carefully, as if he didn't want to hurt me. I believed him.

When he'd gone DC Zhang said, "You're in good hands. DI Clemo is a great detective. He's one of our best. He's like a dog with a bone. Once he gets stuck into a case he won't give up."

She was trying to reassure me but I was thinking of only one thing.

"I let him run ahead of me," I said. "This is my fault. If somebody hurts him, it's because of me."

Jim

I was quite pleased with how the interview with Rachel Jenner had gone, but it did shake me up a bit when she took my hand, grabbed it like she was never going to let go. You don't want that. When you're working a case you're always well aware that the victims of crime are real people, but it's important to keep your distance from them to an extent. If you live every emotion with them, you can't do your job. For a moment or two, for me, Rachel Jenner had jeopardized that rule.

I took a close look at the photo she'd given me. It was one of those school pictures that everybody has, taken in front of a dappled background. Ben looked like a sweet kid: blue eyes, very clear and bright. Fine-boned. He had tufty light brown hair and a half-smile. He was looking straight into the camera. Ben Finch was a very appealing-looking child, there was no doubt, and I was pleased because I knew that would help.

I handed the photo over to the team.

"How's the mother?" Fraser asked.

Rachel Jenner had been a ball of nerves, understandably, her eyes darting, flinching at shadows, talking quickly, clearly intelligent, but awash with shock.

"Shocked," I said. "And a bit guarded."

"Guarded?" Fraser looked at me over the top of her glasses.

"Just a feeling," I said.

"OK. Worth watching. Talk to Emma, see what her impressions are. I'm going to go and introduce myself shortly, and we've called the press in at midday to film an appeal. Are you happy to talk to Dad now?"

I nodded.

"On your way then."

I met Emma in the corridor. It was the first chance we'd had to talk.

"Good interview," she said.

"Thanks."

We moved to the side of the corridor to let somebody pass. Emma's hand grazed mine discreetly, lingered there.

"Did you tell Fraser to take me on as FLO?" she asked.

"I might have."

"Thank you." She gave my hand a little

squeeze, then let it go, and stepped away to leave a more respectable distance between us.

"What did you think of the mother?" I asked. "I just said to Fraser I thought she was a bit guarded."

"I agree, but I think it's understandable. I felt as though it was hard for her to talk about her private life, but I didn't think she was being obstructive."

"No, I didn't think that either."

"She's grief-stricken. And she feels guilty too because she let him run ahead of her."

"That's not a crime."

"Of course it's not, but she's going to beat herself up about that forever, isn't she?"

"Unless we find him quickly."

"Even if we find him quickly, I'd say."

"Do you think she's guilty of anything more?"

Emma considered that, but shook her head. "Gut instinct: no. But I wouldn't swear on that one hundred percent."

"You need to keep a very close eye on her. Detailed reports of what you observe, please."

"Of course."

"I've got to go. I'm interviewing Dad now."

"Good luck." She turned to go.

"Emma!"

"What?"

"You will do the best job you can, won't you? This is a big one. We have to be extremely sensitive."

"Of course I will."

She didn't look openly hurt, that wasn't her style, but something in her expression made me regret what I'd said immediately. She was one of the most emotionally intelligent people I knew, perfect for the role, and it was wrong of me to display even the tiniest bit of doubt about her abilities. I was too psyched up myself to be measured in what I said to her; I could have kicked myself.

"Sorry. I'm sorry. That was out of order. I didn't mean it to come out like that. I'm just . . . this is such a big one."

"It's fine, and I'm absolutely on it, don't worry about that."

She cracked a big smile, making it OK, and her fingers made contact with mine again briefly. "Good luck with the dad," she added, and I watched her walk briskly away down the corridor before I went to find Benedict Finch's father.

John Finch was pacing around the small interview room that we'd placed him in. He looked gaunt, and shocked like the mother, but there was also a sense of innate authority. I guessed that in his normal life he was a man more used to being in charge of a room than being a victim.

"DI Jim Clemo," I said. "I'm so sorry about Ben."

"John Finch." His handshake was a quick firm clench with bony fingers.

There was a small table in the room, two chairs on either side of it. DC Woodley and I sat on one side, Finch on the other.

I went through the same process as with Ben's mother, starting him at the beginning with date of birth, childhood, etc. What people don't realize is that one of the first things we have to do is prove that they are who they say they are, and that the crime they've reported really has happened. We'd look pretty stupid if we investigated and it turned out that the people involved didn't actually exist, that they'd spun us a lie from the outset. And God knows the press and public can't wait to make a meal out of any instances of police stupidity.

Finch answered my questions in a muted, economical way.

"I'm afraid we have to spend time on what might feel like irrelevant detail," I said to him.

I felt the need to apologize, to try to make the situation slightly easier for this man who was so obviously sensitive and so obviously trying to hide it.

"But please be assured that it's essential for us to build up a picture not just of Ben but of his family too."

"I know the importance of a personal history," he said. "We rely on it heavily in medicine."

John Finch's backstory was quite straightforward. He was born in 1976 in Birmingham, an only child. Dad was a local boy, a GP, and mum was a violinist. Her parents had escaped Nazi-occupied Vienna while her mother was pregnant with her, and then settled in Birmingham. Finch was close to his parents as well as his grandparents throughout his childhood. He was a scholarship boy at the grammar school. He did well and won a place at Bristol University Medical School. He'd arrived in Bristol to start his degree twenty years ago, in 1992, and never left after that. He'd worked his way up and done well. Proof of that was his current position as consultant at the Children's Hospital. He'd become a general pediatric surgeon. I knew just enough about the world of medicine to know that that must be a coveted position in a competitive world.

Finch's composure first faltered when I wanted to talk in more detail about Ben's mother, and the reason their marriage ended.

"My marriage ended because Rachel and I were no longer suited to each other."

A perceptible stiffening of his body, words a tad sticky as his mouth became drier.

"It's my understanding that this came as a surprise to Rachel."

"Possibly."

"And that there was another party involved?"

"I have remarried, yes."

"Could you give me an idea of why you and Rachel were no longer suited to each other?"

A single bead of sweat had appeared by his hairline.

"These things don't always last, Inspector. There can be a host of small reasons that accumulate to make a marriage unsustainable."

"Including a younger girlfriend?"

"Please don't reduce me to a cliché."

I didn't reply. Instead I waited to see if more information would seep from him, just as the perspiration had. It's surprising how often that works. People have an almost compulsive need to justify themselves. I made a show of looking through notes, and just when I thought he wouldn't spill, he did.

"My marriage wasn't an emotionally fulfilling one. We didn't . . ." He was choosing his words carefully. "We didn't communicate."

"It happens," I said.

"I was lonely."

His eyes flicked away from mine and I saw a frisson of emotion in them when our gazes reconnected, though it was hard to say exactly what. John Finch was definitely a proud man, and unaccustomed to sharing the personal details of his life.

"Is Rachel a good mother to Ben?" I asked him. I wanted to catch him when his guard was down. His reply came immediately, he didn't need to think about it: "She's an excellent mother. She loves Ben very much."

I took the interview back to practicalities. I asked him what he and his wife were doing on Sunday afternoon between 13:00 and 17:30 hours. He said that they were at home together. He was working and she was reading and then she started to prepare their evening meal. He got a call from WPC Banks at 17:30 to inform him that Ben was missing and he'd driven directly to the woods.

"Did you make any calls, or send any emails during that time?" I asked.

He shook his head. "I was catching up on paperwork."

"I've asked Ms. Jenner whether she'd be willing for us to look through her phone records, and she's agreed. Would you be willing for us to do the same?"

"Yes," he said. "Whatever it takes."

"One more thing."

"Yes?"

"Have you had any incidents at work where patients or their families have been unhappy with you? Could somebody be bearing a grudge against you?"

He didn't reply to my question immediately; it took him a moment or two to consider it.

"There are always unhappy outcomes, inevitably, and some families don't take it well. I have been the subject of legal action once or twice, but that's normal in my line of work. The hospital will be able to supply you with details."

"You can't remember them?"

"I remember the names of the children, but not their parents. I try not to get too involved. You learn not to dwell on the failures, Inspector. The death of a child is a terrible thing to bear, even if the responsibility isn't ultimately yours, because you did everything you could."

Even through his fatigue, the look he gave me was sharp, and I felt as though there might be a warning in his words somewhere.

I drove out to the woods after the interview. I wanted to see the scene for myself. I took a pool car. The drive gave me a chance to get out of the city for a bit, and think about the interviews, get my thoughts straight. My impressions were that the parents were both private people, though John Finch was possibly more complicated than Rachel, and certainly more proud. They were both intelligent, and articulate, a classic middle-class profile. It didn't mean that they were whiter than white, though. We had to remember that.

In forensic terms the scenes at the woods were carnage. The combination of shocking weather and multiple people, animals, and vehicles had churned up the paths and especially the parking area. I took a walk to the rope swing where Ben was alleged to have gone missing and regretted forgetting to bring Wellington boots. It was a damp site, with trees crowded around it. It gave me a creepy, sinister feeling like you get in fairy tales, and in some way that was more unsettling than some of the rankest urban crime scenes I've visited.

I talked to the officers working the scene. They were nice guys, cheerfully pessimistic about their chances of finding anything that might be useful to the investigation.

"If I'm honest it's not looking good," one of them said, stepping over the crime scene tape. It was bright yellow and hung limply across the pathway that led to the rope swing. He pulled a plastic glove from his hand so that he could shake mine. "The conditions are atrocious. But if there's anything to be found we'll find it."

I gave him my card. "Will you —"

He interrupted me. "Call you if we find anything? Of course."

We had our first full team briefing with Fraser at 16:00 back at Kenneth Steele House. We gathered around the table, everybody ready to work, tense and serious, trying not to think about where this case could go. A missing kid is the kind of case you do your job for. Nobody wants a kid to be harmed. You could see it on every face there.

"First things first," said DCI Fraser. "Codename for this case is Operation Huckleberry. We're hunting for two people:

Ben Finch, eight years old, and whoever has abducted him. They may or may not be together. The abductor may be a member of his family, or he or she may be an acquaintance or indeed a complete stranger. They may be holed up with Ben or they may be living normally on the surface and returning to Ben occasionally. They may already have harmed or murdered Ben. We need to keep open minds."

She cast her eye around the table. She had everybody's attention.

"Expertise is on our side," she continued. "I'm confident that this team of people represents excellence and I expect it of you. Time is not on our side. It's been twenty-four hours since Ben Finch went missing. Priority is to confirm Mum's story, and speak to all the people she says she saw in the woods that day."

She paused, making sure we were taking it all in.

"I personally feel that the members of the fantasy reenactment group who were in the woods during the afternoon are of particular interest, because I suspect that among them there'll be one or two mummy's boys who are wielding swords on the weekend to make up for being sad, pimply little bastards who can't get a life during the week.

"Which brings me on to another matter. I think we're going to need all the help we can get on this one. The number of actions we've identified already is daunting, and it's certain to get worse before it gets better. I've asked for more bodies, and I've twisted the Super's arm so that he's agreed to fund the services of a forensic psychologist for the short term at least, to help us define our primary suspects. His name is Dr. Christopher Fellowes. He has teaching commitments, and he's based at Cambridge University, so he's not going to be with us in person unless we have a very good reason to bring him over here, but he'll be available to advise remotely."

I knew him. We'd worked with him when I was with Devon and Cornwall. He was good at his job, when he was sober.

"I was going to get Mum and Dad in front of the cameras tonight, but I think we'll wait until first thing tomorrow morning. I've televised a short appeal for information which will do for now, and we'll put that out with Ben's photograph. I've had preliminary reports from most of you, but if there's anything new you want to add, speak now."

One of the DCs put up her hand.

"We're not in school. You can keep your

hand down."

"Sorry. It's just that I've got a possible. We've tracked down all but one of the men on the sex offenders list."

"Who's missing?"

"Name of David Callow. Thirty-one years old. Did time for abusing his stepsisters and posting photographs of himself doing it. His parole officer hasn't heard from him for a fortnight."

"Make him a priority. I want to know who he last saw, and when. Talk to his family, his neighbors, his friends, if he has any. Find out what he's been doing. Anything else?"

Nobody spoke.

"Right. There's a lot to get on with, so let's get on with it. Any leads, any worries, anything gets on top of you, speak to me. I want to know everything, as it happens. No exceptions."

WEB PAGE — BREAKING NEWS POLICE — www.aspol.uk/whatsnew

October 22, 2012, 13:03
AVON AND SOMERSET CONSTABULARY has activated CHILD RESCUE ALERT to assist in tracing eight-year-old Benedict Finch in Bristol.

A dedicated telephone number has been established for anyone who has seen Benedict or has information about his whereabouts.

This number is 0300 300 3331.

Calls to this number will be answered by dedicated members of staff who will take details of any information provided to assist with the inquiry.

By launching Child Rescue Alert, which is supported by all UK Police Forces, it is hoped that the public and media can assist Avon and Somerset Constabulary in safely tracing Benedict.

Police are seeking information specifically from anyone who has seen Benedict or anyone matching his description in the last twenty-four hours.

Benedict is described as being of Caucasian appearance, of slim build, and just over four feet tall. He has brown hair and blue eyes and freckles across the bridge of his nose. It is not known what he is wearing.

A recent photograph of Benedict has been widely circulated. It can be seen on the Avon and Somerset Constabulary website.

He was last seen on the main path around Leigh Woods, just outside Bristol, at around 16:30 on Sunday, October 21, when he and his mother were walking their dog. His mother raised the alarm at 17:00 after extensive searching in the woods did not locate him.

Intensive searches led by trained search officers, and including police dogs and mounted police, are taking place in and around Leigh Woods and the surrounding area, and members of the public have been assisting.

Benedict is described as bright and clever, a fluent communicator, and English is his first language. He is known to his family as Ben.

Spread the word: Facebook; Twitter

Rachel

My sister, Nicky, was waiting for me in the foyer at Kenneth Steele House. She was panda-eyed with strain. I fell into her arms. Her clothing smelled of damp cottage and wood smoke and washing powder.

She looks a lot like me. You could tell we're sisters if you saw us together. She's got the same green eyes and more or less the same face, and a similar figure, though she's heavier. She's not quite as tall as me either, and her hair is cut short and always carefully highlighted, so instead of being curly it settles in brushed golden waves around her face, which makes her look more sensible than me.

Nicky told me she'd driven straight from Aunt Esther's cottage. She held me tightly.

The hug felt awkward. We probably hadn't been in each other's arms since I was a child. I wasn't used to the padded curves of her body, the cotton wool softness of the skin on her cheek. It made me acutely aware of my own frame, its angularity, as if I were constructed from a more brittle material than her.

"Let's get you home," she said, and she brushed a strand of my hair back behind my ear.

Arriving home was my first taste of how it feels to live life in a goldfish bowl.

Journalists had gathered outside my little two-up, two-down cottage. Ben and I lived on a pretty narrow street of small Victorian terraces in Bishopston, an area that has yellow Neighborhood Watch stickers in many house windows and loves recycling and having street parties in the summer. Our neighbors were a mix of elderly people, young families, and some students. Ours was a quiet street. The biggest drama we'd collectively experienced since I'd lived there was waking up to find that drunk students had put traffic cones on top of the car roofs during the night.

The journalists were impossible to avoid. There was a group of them, big enough to spill off the pavement. They called my name, thrust microphones toward us, photographed us as we entered the house, pushed and shoved and tripped up as they ran around one another trying to get in front of us. Their voices were cajoling, and urgent, and to me they had the menace of a mob.

When we got inside, black dots danced at the edges of my vision, the aftereffects of the bright white of their flashbulbs, and I could still hear them calling from behind the door. My heart rate didn't slow until I moved into the kitchen at the back of the house, where it was silent, and I was able to sit, and breathe, and focus on the placid ticking of my kitchen clock.

Zhang stayed with us for a short while. The scenes of crime officers had visited the house while I was being interviewed. She wanted to check that they'd left everything in order upstairs, in Ben's room.

She pulled the curtains in the sitting room tightly shut, so that the journalists couldn't see in. She advised us not to answer the door without checking who was there, and not to speak directly to the press.

"It's good that they're here, though," she said. "It's all good publicity because it means that as many people as possible will be aware of Ben and will be looking out for him."

She made sure we had her card with her number on it and then she left us alone. Part of me didn't really want her to leave.

She was more approachable than Clemo by miles. I felt nervous of him, of the authority he exuded, of his matter-of-factness, and of the power he suddenly held in our lives. But Zhang was different, more of a kindly guide who might be able to help me navigate this horrendous new reality, and I felt grateful for her.

Everything on the kitchen table was as Ben and I had left it: a snapshot of our last few minutes in the house together.

There was a hat that Ben had refused to wear, a packet of Bourbon biscuits that he'd raided just before we left, a much-loved Tintin book, and a Lego car that I'd helped him build.

His school report, received in the post the day before, lay on the table too. It had been a pleasure to read, full of effusive praise from his teacher about how hard Ben tried, how pleased she was that he was finding the courage to speak up more in class, and how he was gaining confidence in his schoolwork.

And it wasn't just the kitchen. There was nowhere in this house that wasn't imprinted with traces of my son, of course there wasn't. It was his home.

Even outside, down the short, uneven

garden path, I knew that there would be signs of him too: in my garden office my computer would be sleeping, its light blinking unhurriedly. If I went out there and brought it to life I knew the Internet history would show a game that Ben had been playing online on Sunday morning. It was called Furry Football and the aim was to play games and earn points to buy different animals, which would form a football team. Ben loved it. I had a daily battle to limit his time on it.

I looked at everything, took it all in, but felt only blankness. All of it was meaningless without Ben. Without him, my home had no soul.

Nicky got busy, typically.

She'd always been like this. She was never still. If there was nothing to do, she would organize an outing, or make an elaborate meal. Activity was her way of relaxing.

When I was younger I could happily spend an afternoon in Esther's cottage doing nothing more than sitting on the window seat in my little bedroom. I would trace outlines in the condensation on the glass, gaze at the frosty trees outside and the shapes they carved against the open sky behind them, and watch the birds on my aunt's feeders fighting for seed. The sharp yellow flash of a goldfinch's wing was a sight I longed for in the monochrome of a snowy rural winter.

Eventually, driven by the cold, I might make my way downstairs to seek the heat of the fire. Nicky would be there with Aunt Esther. Their cheeks would be flushed from the warmth of the oven and the exertions of whatever activity they'd been engaged in. I would admire the freshly baked cake they'd made or smell the stew that was simmering.

Aunt Esther would take my hands and say, "Rachel, you're so cold. Have a cup of tea, darling," and she would rub them, and I would feel rough gardening calluses on her palms. Nicky would say, "Where are your fingerless gloves, Rachel? The ones I gave you for Christmas?" Then I would slip away from them, their cozy domesticity, and slink into a chair by the fire, pull a blanket over myself, and lose myself in a book, or the dancing of the flames.

In those early days after Ben disappeared, when I was practically catatonic with shock, it was natural for Nicky to become the functioning part of me, just as she always had. She returned the increasingly frantic messages that my best friend, Laura, had been leaving on my phone throughout the day, and asked her to come over. She spoke to Peter Armstrong, who told her that the dog's leg had been broken, but he was comfortable at the vet's after having it set. She put her laptop on the kitchen table and spent hours online.

On that first day, she found a missing kids website, based in the United States. On its advice, she made a list of questions for the police. She threw facts out into the room as she learned them. They were ghastly, notes from a world that I didn't want to be a part of. They made me feel queasy, but she was unstoppable.

She told me that the website advised that bloodhounds are essential for a proper search. That they can follow the scent of a child even if their abductor has picked them up and carried them away. She asked me what dogs the police had used in the woods. I said they'd been German shepherds. She continued to read quietly, scratching notes out on a pad, keeping it shielded from me, her mouth set in a grim line.

After a time she said, "Did you see John after your interview?"

"No, they took him somewhere else."

"You should ring him. It would be good to know what they asked him."

"He blames me."

"This is not your fault."

I knew it was.

"What did they ask you? Can you talk about it?"

"They asked me everything, they wanted so much detail: family history, everything to do with Ben since he was born; anything you could think of basically."

I didn't mention that they wanted to know what Ben had had for lunch on Sunday.

"Did they ask about our family?"

"They wanted to know everything."

"What did you tell them?" Her eyes lifted from the screen and they were red-rimmed.

"I told them what happened. What else would I tell them?"

"Yes, of course." She turned back to the screen. "It says here that the family should try to agree on a tactic for how to approach relationships with the police, that it's really effective to do that."

"I can't phone John now." I couldn't face it. I'd committed the worst sin a mother can: I hadn't looked after my child. "I'm going upstairs."

In Ben's bedroom I could see very little sign that the scenes of crime officers had been there. One of Ben's favorite toys lay nestled on his bed, in the tumble of bedding that Ben liked to sleep in. It was Baggy Bear, a doe-eyed teddy with chewed ears, floppy arms, soft fur, and a blue knitted scarf that Ben liked me to tie in a certain way. I held Baggy Bear to my chest. I thought, I can't leave this house now, in case he comes back here. Everywhere, the silence, the absence of Ben, seemed to swell. It felt hostile, like the furtive spread of a cancer.

I lay down on Ben's bed, and curled up. There was something making me uncomfortable and I shifted position, felt for it. It was his old crib blanket. He called it "nunny" and he'd had it since he was a baby. It was very soft and he would wrap it around his fingers and stroke his face with it to get himself off to sleep. He'd never admit it to anybody but me, but he couldn't sleep without it. I tried to push away the thought that he'd already had to spend a night without it, that that might have been the least of his worries.

I balled it up, hugged it to myself, along with Baggy Bear. I could smell Ben on the nunny, on the bedding, and on his teddy bear. It was the perfect smell that he'd always had. It was the smell of baby hair that has no weight to it, and of the skin on his temples, which was still velvety smooth. It was the smell of trust, freely given, and a perfect, innocent curiosity. It was the smell of our dog walks and the games we'd played together and the things I'd told him and the meals we'd shared. It was the smell of our history together. I inhaled that smell as if it could revive me somehow, give me some answers, or some hope, and, like that, I just waited. I didn't know what else to do.

When Laura arrived Nicky let her in and I heard their voices downstairs, hushed and serious. In real life — the life we were living before Ben was taken — they didn't get on very well. I was the only thing that these two women had in common, and their paths had crossed only once or twice before. Without me they would never have spent time together, probably not without a large measure of irritation anyway.

As a foil to Nicky's conservatism, and her serious, thoughtful approach to life, Laura was skittish, playful, inconsistent, rebellious, and sometimes downright wild. She was a bird-like person, tiny-framed, with short urchin hair, wide brown eyes, and a big laugh. When I'd first met her, when we were both nursing students, right from the start she'd made me laugh, taught me how to play. She was the first person I'd met who did that for me. It thrilled me.

She wasn't like that one hundred percent of the time, of course. She had her moments of darkness too, but she kept them private. I only glimpsed them when alcohol had loosened her tongue. "I was a mistake," she said once. I'd known her for a good few years by then. We were no longer students, although we were still in our habit of going for a big night out at least once a week. Her words were heavy with booze.

"My parents didn't want to have me. It's ironic, isn't it, that two people who were among the brightest minds in the country, or so they liked to say, it's ironic that they should have made such a basic error. Don't you think?"

Her tone of voice was attempting to be jokey but the corners of her mouth kept dragging down and her eyes were dull and tired.

"Didn't they want to have children?"

"No. It wasn't the plan. It was never the plan. They were very open about that. If I'm honest, I'm surprised they ever had sex. They were old when they had me too." She laughed. "They must have stumbled across a manual that told them what to do, and had ten minutes to spare before *Newsnight.*"

I didn't have parents, of course, so who was I to pass judgment on how she mocked hers, but there was something unsettling about her tone, and though I'd laughed obligingly at the time, it had made me feel sad.

"Do you want kids?" I'd asked her, for I had a secret that night. It was the reason I was sober.

"Oh, I don't know about that" — I thought I saw a look of sadness flash across her face — "but never say never."

She closed her eyes, giving in to the lateness of the hour, and the soporific effects of the wine. I sat beside her, not ready for sleep yet, and slipped my hand underneath my top. I rested it on my belly and thought of the baby growing there. It was Ben. My mistake. Already loved.

The tread of Laura's feet on the stairs of my house made them creak cautiously, and she paused at the top and said, "Rachel?"

"In here."

At the doorway to Ben's room, she said, "Do you want the light on?"

"No."

She lay down beside me, put her arms around me in a hug that was far more familiar than Nicky's.

"I didn't keep him safe," I said. "It's my fault."

"Sshh," she said. "Don't. It doesn't matter. All that matters is getting him back."

Even in the gloaming I could see that her eyes were liquid. A tear escaped and ran down her cheek, pooling by her nose, a trail of black eyeliner in its wake.

We lay there until the darkness outside was becoming a solid mass, leavened only by the glow of the streetlights and the geometric oddments of light that fell from people's houses.

We'd been told by Zhang to watch the news at six p.m.

At a quarter to six, I realized that I should have been at Ben's school parents' evening, to discuss his report.

Laura said, "Don't worry about that. Don't even think about it. You can go later in the week, once he's back."

The first item on the news was a report on flooding in Bangladesh: thousands of people had died.

Ben was the second item.

DCI Fraser, whom I'd met briefly, stood on the steps at Kenneth Steele House and appealed to the public to "help them with their inquiries."

"We're extremely concerned about this young boy," she said, "and we would urge anybody who has any information about him, or his whereabouts, to get in touch with us."

She was immaculate in police uniform. Wildly curly gray hair and a pair of wire-rimmed glasses that sat at the bottom of her nose, under sharp eyes, gave her the look of a blue-stocking academic.

"We are also requesting that the public do not organize searches of their own," she said. "Though we thank the members of the community who are offering their help."

A helpline number and the photograph of Ben that I'd given the police flashed up, filling the screen.

It's the strangest thing in the world to find that the story you are watching on TV is your own, to realize that you have entrusted a stranger with finding your child, and to then have to accept that you are as disconnected as anybody else watching, that you are essentially impotent. When Ben's face had gone from the screen, Laura turned the TV off. I wanted to howl with sorrow, or to rage, but I did neither, because my hands shook and my stomach was turning, threatening to disgorge the tea I'd been sipping, the tiny morsels of toast I'd forced myself to swallow at the behest of my sister.

The call about the press conference came later that evening. The police wanted me to appear in front of the cameras the next morning, to read out a statement appealing for help in finding Ben. They would send a car for me.

"I can't leave the house," I said. "What if he comes home?"

Laura said, "I'll stay here. You've got to go. I'll stay here."

"Should I stay?" said Nicky. "I could stay."

Both of them looked at me, wanting me to decide.

"Nicky should come with me," I said.

Laura was my best friend, but Nicky was Ben's aunt, our only family.

"She's right," Laura said. "You should be there." She looked at me. "And it can only be good if you appear on TV. People will care more about Ben. They really will. I'll come over in the morning before you leave, and I won't leave the house, not even for a minute. Not until you're back. I promise."

Laura told my sister that she should choose an outfit for me to wear, that I should be as presentable as possible. She said it was important, even if it felt trivial to think about it at a time like this. She looked closely at the gash on my forehead, and I winced when she touched the edge of it.

"I don't think you can put makeup on it, if that's what you're thinking," Nicky said.

"It's too raw."

Laura peered at it. I could see her eyes following its trajectory across my forehead. "Let's see how it looks in the morning," she said.

"Could we cover it with a dressing?" Nicky asked.

"No. A dressing will look ugly on TV, and it'll obscure her face. Worst case, we leave it as it is. It's not that noticeable."

We all knew that wasn't true.

In the kitchen, after Laura had gone, with a promise to return first thing in the morning, Nicky said, "Do you trust her? I'm not sure she should be here on her own."

"What do you mean?"

"She's one of them." She gestured toward the front door, the pack of journalists lingering outside, whose voices we'd heard rising and swelling throughout the evening, breaking into laughter now and then.

"She's not that kind of journalist," I said. "She writes for gossip magazines, about makeup. It's fluff, bullshit. It's not news."

"They're all the same breed."

"She's my friend. My best friend."

"Fine. If you trust her, then that's fine, isn't it?"

"I do trust her. I can't believe you'd say

such a thing."

"Sorry."

The kettle was noisily reaching boiling point. Nicky leaned against the counter and lapsed into a thousand-yard stare, but I knew her and I knew that behind it her mind was turning. For the first time, it occurred to me to ask about her family.

"How are the girls?"

Her attention snapped back to me, a funny look. Guilt, perhaps, swiftly disguised, because she had four daughters safe at home while I was missing my only child.

"Will you tell them?" I asked.

"I think it'll be impossible to avoid. With it on the TV, and in all the papers."

"Do they need you to be with them? Don't you need to go home?"

"No," she said firmly. "My place is with you right now. They'll be fine." She closed the matter by turning her back on me to make tea with concise, measured movements.

After we went to bed, I couldn't sleep. All night I kept vigil in Ben's room. I left the curtains open, and lay in his bed, letting my eyes run over the contours of his belongings. Books, toys, and other stuff, collected and arranged by Ben on his shelves, had the stillness of museum exhibits. I sat up, wrapped his duvet around me, and stared into the shadows in the corners of his room, and then moved my gaze outside.

I watched a fox leap the fence into my neighbor's garden and then slink around, nose to the ground, before finding something it could eat and devouring it, gulping it down in a way that was fast and primitive and ugly. When it was done, it ran its tongue over its chops, savoring, before disappearing into the night.

I felt the various textures of my fear: shivery, visceral, tight, pounding, in turn or all at once. I only fell asleep once, in the small hours, and woke to a sensation of being choked, gasping for air, pushing bedding away from me as if it were hostile, or venomous, and then finding my sister standing in the room with fear on her face, saying, "Rachel, are you OK? Rachel!"

After that we sat together until it was morning, as if it were just the two of us left in the world.

JIM

Addendum to DI James Clemo's report for Dr. Francesca Manelli

Transcript recorded by Dr. Francesca Manelli
DI James Clemo and Dr. Francesca Manelli in attendance

Notes to indicate observations on DI Clemo's state of mind or behavior, where his remarks alone do not convey this, are in italics.

FM: What I'd like to start with today is a discussion of your relationship with DC Zhang.
JC: There's not much to say.
FM: You were seeing each other when the Benedict Finch case started?
JC: Yes.

FM: How long had your relationship been going on?

JC: About four months.

FM: And were things going well?

JC: They were, yes. I thought they were.

FM: But you kept the relationship secret from work?

JC: I didn't want gossip.

FM: Were you embarrassed about the relationship?

JC: No! God no. Anyone would have been proud to go out with Emma.

FM: Why's that?

JC: She's very clever, and very gorgeous. Funny, too, when you got to know her.

FM: She sounds lovely.

JC: She was even better than that though; I'm not describing her very well. She was different from other women I'd been out with.

FM: How was she different?

JC: She was just . . . she wasn't dull like them. It's like she'd lived a different kind of life, and she wasn't afraid to know stuff, and she was always wanting to learn new things, to be a better version of herself. When she was a kid she was an athletics star, and she got top grades, and she'd kept that sense of purpose about her. She talked about life as if it was a given that it was interesting or exciting, not about mortgages or package holidays or where she was going out on Friday night. I don't want to make her sound manic, obsessed with achievement or anything, because she wasn't like that, because she was calm with it all. It's just that she was always striving, you know, to make life better than it was.

FM: So she had high expectations?

JC: Yes, but in a good way. It was refreshing. She was refreshing. That's the word I'm looking for. She had a different outlook and it was infectious, if I'm honest. I felt like it brought me out of myself, if that makes sense.

FM: It sounds as if your relationship with Emma gave you a sort of zest for life that perhaps you hadn't ever experienced before?

JC: It did feel like that, yes. I felt excited about us. I felt a sort of pull to be with her.

FM: Did you meet at work?

JC: We did.

FM: Did you see a lot of each other outside of work?

JC: As much as we could. By the time the case went live, she'd kind of moved in with me.

FM: So things were getting quite serious for you?

JC: She kept her own flat, but she stayed over most nights. We didn't really discuss it, it just sort of happened.

FM: Did you introduce Emma to your family?

JC: Yes, she met them twice, both times when my parents came up to Bristol and we went out for a meal.

FM: How did that go?

JC: It was very nice. They really liked her. She even charmed my dad.

FM: Did you meet Emma's parents?

JC: No.

FM: Any reason for that?

JC: Not really. I suppose I figured I'd meet them at some point, when she was ready. I knew she wasn't close to them. She never went to visit them and they never came to see her, or not that I knew of anyway.

FM: Did you wonder why that was?

JC: She said they'd had a falling-out.

FM: Did she say why?

JC: She didn't really explain. I got the impression her dad was quite strict, classic army type, not an easy man, but I'm not really sure, to be honest. That was one thing about her — she was very private about her family.

FM: Weren't you curious?

JC: A bit. But she didn't make a big deal about it, and we had a lot else going on so I didn't really think about it.

FM: So you recommended Emma for the FLO role?

JC: I did, yes.

FM: Was that a risk?

JC: I didn't think so, no. I thought she'd do a fantastic job. Emma was one of the best new DCs to come through in years, everybody said so.

FM: Was it professional of you to recommend her, given that you were having a relationship?

JC: It wasn't unprofessional.

FM: Are you sure about that?

JC: Yes, I'm sure. Look, I broke a personal rule getting involved with Emma. I never wanted to have a relationship with somebody at work, but when it happened, it felt . . . it felt totally right. So I went with it, but when this opportunity came up I thought she was absolutely the right person for that role. Genuinely. Why would I put my neck on the line otherwise?

FM: OK. I understand that. It's clear from your report that this case was a very big moment in your career. "Bring it on," are the words you used, I think.

JC: That's how I felt.

FM: You were excited.

JC: The challenge of it, the possibility . . .

FM: To shine?

JC: I suppose so. I wasn't going to put it quite like that. It was my first chance to be involved in a very high-profile investigation.

FM: You wanted to prove yourself?

JC: It was a chance.

FM: And your first big task was to prepare for the press conference?

JC: After the initial interviews, yes.

FM: I watched the footage of the conference.

JC: I think everybody did. Once seen, never forgotten.

FM: Indeed. You were there too. I saw you.

JC: I was chairing it.

FM: Why not Fraser?

JC: She believes in giving people a chance. She gave me the responsibility for running it and for drafting the statement that we wanted Rachel Jenner to read. I worked with the forensic psychologist on that. It was a big responsibility.

FM: So your aim was to appeal to Ben's abductor, to use the mother to obtain their sympathy with the hope that that might persuade them to get in contact with you?

JC: With us, or with somebody around

them, somebody they trusted. It was important that they saw Ben as a real person, not just an acquisition, or a means to their own end. It would give him the context of a loving family. It was equally important not to alienate the abductor. We wanted to make them aware that it wasn't too late for them to give him back, if he was still alive, that it was never too late to do that, even if they were scared of what the consequences might be. We wanted to present a friendly face. At that stage it obviously wasn't clear whether it was an abduction or a murder.

FM: So you scripted something for Rachel to read out that would cover all bases?

JC: Yes. That was the idea anyway.

FM: How did you know you could rely on her to get the tone right?

JC: I didn't know.

FM: Did you consider getting his father to do it?

JC: We considered it, but there was something about him that we weren't sure would look good on camera. He was a surgeon, he was used to being authoritative. We were concerned that he might appear arrogant. What you want is a mother, a mother's warmth.

FM: And you were confident in advance that

she could deliver that?

JC: We didn't have time to delve into her psyche. She was his mother. We assumed that she would, because at that stage we had no reason not to.

■ ■ ■ ■

DAY 3
TUESDAY,
OCTOBER 23, 2012

■ ■ ■ ■

Be aware of your public status. Although this might not be the kind of fame you want, you may attain some sort of "celebrity" standing because of your continuous involvement with the media . . . Therefore, for your child's sake, conduct yourself as if all eyes were upon you . . . Don't do things that might cast you in a negative light . . .

— "When Your Child Is Missing: A Family Survival Guide,"

Missing Kids USA Parental Guide,
US Department of Justice, OJJDP Report

WEB PAGE — www.twentyfour7news.co.uk/bristol — 6:18 AM BST Oct 23, 2012

Fears are building for the safety of Benedict Finch, eight years old, who went missing in Leigh Woods near Bristol on Sunday afternoon.
by Danny Deal

Detective Chief Inspector Corinne Fraser last night said that police are "deeply concerned' for the safety of the missing boy. "You've seen the weather we've been having," she said. "Cold, rain, you don't want a small child to be out in that.

"It is possible that Benedict has been the subject of a criminal act," she added, but stressed that all lines of inquiry remain open. "At present, nobody is detained, nobody is a suspect."

Members of the public are being urged to phone in with any information that might relate to Benedict. "We would urge people to come forward if they think they might have any information that could help us find this little boy."

DCI Fraser revealed that they had already received 130 calls to a hotline dedicated to the boy's disappearance.

"I would like to give our sincere thanks to the public for their support in the search for Ben," she said, and urged people to report to Abbots Leigh village hall, where a volunteer center has been set up to co-ordinate search efforts.

Anyone with information can call the missing hotline number 0300 300 3331.

5 people are discussing this article

Donald McKeogh
We should keep this little boy in our hearts. Newspapers have offered a £25,000 reward. Good on them. Hope he's home safe soon.

Jane Evans-Brown
Where's his dad in all this?

Jamie Frick
Something strange about this. How does a kid get lost in the woods? Why wasn't mum looking out for him?

Catherine Alexander
Seems odd. Perhaps the police are not telling everything.

Susan Franks
The police are only releasing what they need to. Let them get on with their jobs and pray for this little boy and his poor family . . . hope he is found safe and well . . .

RACHEL

In the car on the way to Kenneth Steele House, gobbets of sound blurted out of the police radio on the dashboard, and the stop-and-start motions of the commuter traffic made the ride uncomfortable and slow. Nicky had put on makeup and a perfume that was sickly. I wound down the window a little to dilute the smell, but the air I let in was dirty and damply cold.

Nicky and Laura had persuaded me to wear a skirt, boots, and shirt, so that I would appear presentable. They hadn't been able to do anything about my forehead. The gash was too angry and raw. I didn't care what I looked like.

None of us had spoken much, just a few murmurs of advice from Laura about how to face a camera from her college media training, which I hadn't been able to concentrate on, but had nodded at just the same.

In the kitchen, just before we went out, they'd left me alone momentarily, and I saw the notepad Nicky had been using the night before. It lay facedown on the table. I flipped it over, knowing I shouldn't, unable to stop myself.

"Notes," Nicky had underlined, and then she'd jotted down some statistics: "532 missing kids UK 2011/12."

I read on: "82% abductions are family kidnappings. Of non-family abductions, 38% kids taken by friend or long-term acquaintance; 5% by neighbor; 6% by persons of authority; 4% caretaker or babysitter; 37% by strangers; 8% slight acquaintances."

There was more: "Crime is most often a result of interactions between motivated offenders, available targets, and lack of vigilant guardianship to prevent crime."

I couldn't stop reading. I was transfixed by it, carried along by the dry academic tone, and the horror of the content. The next paragraph began: "First law enforcement response is CRITICAL."

She'd underlined that, two lines drawn so hard that they'd gouged the page. What I started to read next was worse: "When abducted child is killed, killer —"

Before I got further Nicky came back into

the room and snatched the notepad from me.

"Don't look at that!" she said. "Not now." She ripped off the pages of notes and put them in her handbag. "You mustn't look. We're not there yet. I'm sorry. I shouldn't have left it out."

"How the hell are you finding this stuff?" I asked. "What is it? Where's it from? Show me!" I held my hand out for the notes, but she wasn't having any of it.

"Don't concern yourself with that. Honestly, Rachel, don't think about it. Let's go. It's time to go. Let me look at you one more time."

She held me gently by the shoulders, looked me over, a frown fleetingly crossing her brow when she looked at my forehead, and all the while I searched her eyes for clues to what she'd read, to how and where she'd found the information so quickly, and to the side of her personality that allowed her the detachment to look at the darkest side of this in a way that I simply couldn't contemplate.

At the police station they showed me into the same room as the previous day. Somebody had arranged four Jammie Dodgers on a plate for us. The centers of the biscuits were crimson and resinous, like excretions from a wound. The room smelled of stewed tea.

I sat there with Nicky, Zhang, and Clemo going over a statement that he wanted me to read out, an appeal to Ben's abductor. I looked over the words with a sense of detachment and surrealism. They didn't resemble my speech in any way. I felt deeply uneasy.

Clemo was like a coiled spring.

"Are you going to be OK with this?" he said.

"I think so."

"It's important that you're calm, and clear, as much as possible. It's absolutely paramount that we don't alienate the abductor."

I took shallow breaths, focused on the page in front of me. The words swam across it.

"Are you sure you can do it?" he asked again. His voice sounded pressured, desperate for a "Yes."

"Do you want me to do it?" Nicky asked. I looked at her, her face straining with the need to help.

What could I say? I was his mother.

"No. I want to do it. I have to do it."

"Good girl." It was enough for Clemo. He

was up out of his chair, checking his watch.

"Will you be ready to go in fifteen?" he said.

I nodded.

"I'll see you in there. I'll be sitting right by you. Emma, bring them down in ten minutes. Cabot Room."

In Zhang's wake Nicky and I traveled carpeted corridors until we reached a set of double doors labeled CABOT ROOM. Inside, I was invited to take my place behind a narrow table that was set up at one end of the room. The lineup was Zhang, me, Clemo, DCI Fraser, and John, who acknowledged me with a nod, his jaw set in an effort to control his emotions.

Nicky found a place at the side of the room. She had to stand because every chair was taken. The room was packed with journalists. TV cameras were set up at the back, photographers beside them. There were more lenses trained on me than I could count.

Those who were sitting had laptops, or tablets, or recording devices, which they were busy checking. Behind us the wall was emblazoned with a large Avon and Somerset police logo, and on each side of that two identical posters had been put up, showing

Ben's photo and a phone number and email address for information.

On the table in front of us was a bank of microphones, wires snaking from the back of them. I poured myself an inch of water from a carafe and sipped it. My mouth was dry, my heart thumping. The noise in the room was oppressive. Motor drives and voices meshed together to make a messy ball of sound from which my name sometimes erupted.

Clemo called the room to order on a signal from DCI Fraser. I clutched my script, forced my eyes to run over the words. I hadn't really come to terms with what they wanted me to say. The carefully modulated phrases that they'd written for me made me recoil.

Clemo started things off and he was concise and authoritative. He spoke briefly and then introduced me, telling the room that I was going to read out a statement. I put my script on the table and smoothed it out, cleared my throat.

"Please," I said, but my voice died away. I started again: "Please can I appeal to anyone who knows anything about Ben's disappearance to contact the police as DI Clemo has requested. Ben is only eight years old, he's very young, and the best place for him to be is at home where he can be with his family and friends because we all love him very much and it is making us very anxious not knowing whether he is safe and well."

I felt tears running down my face. I heard my voice get twisted up by my grief. I felt Zhang's hand on my back, saw Clemo shift uneasily in his seat beside me. I took a deep shuddering breath and went on.

"If you are the person who is with Ben, then please make contact. You don't need to ring the police directly, you can talk to a solicitor, or someone you trust, and they will help you get him home safely. This is an unusual situation for all of us . . ."

I dried up again. I'd reached the bit of the speech I hated. Clemo's words ran around in my head: "Remember, we want to humanize the situation," he'd said, "that's why we're offering the abductor a chance for forgiveness, so that they aren't afraid to get in contact."

I tried to gather myself. Clemo whispered something in my ear, but I couldn't hear what he said, because it was then that I heard John sob. He was hunched over the table, his head in his hands, his face red and distorted. He began to cry noisily, his shoulders heaving, his grief physical and terrible.

I gave up trying to read. I couldn't do it anymore. I couldn't say the words on the script, and, most powerfully of all, I couldn't fight the idea that had crept into my head with a certainty and clarity that almost took my breath away.

I carefully folded up the script, placed it in front of me.

You see, the thought that I had was this: that Ben and his abductor were watching. They were watching John break down and watching me speak words that weren't mine: submissive, tame words.

I was sure of it, and I couldn't stand it any longer.

I stood up, and all the camera lenses in the room rose too, trained on my face. I moved my gaze along them and, in my mind, through each one I met the eye of Ben's abductor.

"Give him back," I said. "Give. Him. Back. Or I will hunt you down myself. I will find you, if it takes me my whole life. I will find you and I will make you pay."

Then, as Clemo was saying "Ms. Jenner!" and standing beside me, not knowing how to stop me, I spoke to my son. I looked deep down those lenses, willing Ben to hear my words, and I said: "I love you, Ben. If you are watching, I love you and I'm going to find you. Love, I'm coming to get you. I promise."

I smiled at him. I was entranced by the fact that I might have just managed the first communication with my son since he disappeared, imagining him hearing my words in a strange place somewhere and feeling less alone, less confused, perhaps even feeling hope.

The reporters began to call to me, but I felt triumphant. If Ben was watching, then I had just made contact with him. He hadn't witnessed his parents simply looking broken, his mother speaking in words that weren't hers. Instead, I'd told him that I was going to find him. Now I felt euphoric, as if I'd done something that was really and truly right and honest, something pure, even, amid the horror of it all, and in my naïveté I felt sure that that rightness and honesty should have some power to lead us to Ben.

I glanced at DI Clemo, wanting a show of support from him, but he looked as though he'd just been slapped, hard, across his hollowed-out cheeks. The cameras were still all trained on me, and the journalists were scribbling in their pads or typing, with fingers flying. The flashguns fired like strobe lights. The noise levels were rising.

DI Clemo, on his feet beside me, begged for calm. He put his hand on my arm and guided me firmly back down into my seat. Patches of sweat had appeared under his armpits, staining his shirt.

"I'm sorry that Ms. Jenner hasn't been able to finish reading the statement," he said. "As you can understand, this is a very distressing time for her. I'll read the rest of it myself, if you'll bear with me."

Frustration crackled in his voice. DCI Fraser stood up and whispered something to him. DI Clemo looked down at the script before continuing, and when he spoke again he sounded calmer, though still tense and tightly controlled. Sitting beside him, I felt powerful, pleased that I'd said my piece. The wound on my forehead began to itch and I scratched it while I listened to him finish reading the script:

"This is a message for whoever might be holding Ben. I would like to reiterate that this is an unusual situation for all of us, and you might not know what to do next. Our suggestion is that you speak to someone, tell someone you trust, it might be a friend or a family member, or, as we've said, a solicitor, and ask them to help you get Ben back home safely. Ben's safety is a priority for all of us. He needs his family. Thank you."

Noise erupted.

"We'll do a couple of questions," Clemo shouted, "but one at a time. Hands up."

He picked a man near the back. "Can you explain why no description of what Benedict was wearing when he was abducted has been issued?"

"No, I'm afraid I can't give you any information about that at this time."

Clemo pointed to a woman who sat in the front row.

"I'd like to ask Ms. Jenner a question," she said.

"I'm afraid that's not going to happen."

"It's OK," I said, foolish me. I leaned forward so that I could hear her.

Her voice rang out, direct and clear. "Why are you smiling, how did you injure your head, and how did it happen that Ben was separated from you in the woods?"

And that was what it took, to make me realize what I'd done and how stupid I'd been. My euphoria disappeared. It was a fizzled-out firework, a limp balloon.

I'd smiled because I'd felt triumphant. I'd felt triumphant because I'd taken the initiative, reached out to my son, spoken to the abductor as they should be spoken to, without mercy.

Now I saw how stupid I had been. If my euphoria and my misguided sense of conviction had been a long stretch of golden beach that I'd basked on momentarily, then reality was the turning tide that was going to swamp it, an unstoppable mass of cold, black water lapping around rocks, shifting pebbles and rising until it engulfed me.

I pushed myself back into my chair until the edges of it dug into my shoulder bones.

"Don't answer that," Clemo snapped at me, and then Fraser was on her feet and she had to shout to be heard: "This press conference is over. We'll update you again this afternoon."

The journalist had one more thing to say: "Rachel! Did you know you've got blood on your hands?"

Her voice drifted up above the other sounds and activity in the room, as if it were a wayward feather, caught on a breeze. It captured everyone's attention. All eyes were on me.

I looked at my hands and there was blood on one of them, greasy red smears like ink, revealing the contours of my fingerprints on my thumb and first two fingers. With my clean hand I touched the gash on my forehead. It felt damp. I'd made it bleed when I scratched it.

"Get me out of here," I said to Zhang. I said it under my breath, but I forgot that the microphones were on and my voice rang out, loud and urgent.

They got me out quickly. Even so, the noise in the room swelled again in a swift crescendo, and by the time I'd traveled the few paces to the door they were all shouting, a chorus of "Rachel, Rachel, just one more thing, Rachel," and they'd got to their feet and were straining toward me.

Zhang propelled me out through the doors. They swung shut behind us and we stood for a moment in the corridor. I could hear Fraser shouting to try to restore order. I sank to the floor.

"Not here," said Zhang. She gripped my arm by my elbow, pulled me up.

"I feel sick," I said.

The urge to vomit was overpowering; faintness was making my head lurch and spin.

"This way," she said.

She swept me down the corridor and more or less shoved me through the doors of a ladies' toilet. I burst into a cubicle and hunched over the bowl, throwing up the liquids I'd had that morning and then nothing but bile.

The retching was painful, convulsive, and it took long minutes to subside.

"Are you OK?" It was Nicky. She crouched behind me, and I felt her hand on my back, rubbing between my shoulders. I couldn't reply. The smell of my vomit was sharp and unpleasant. It made me feel ashamed. I leaned against the cubicle partition.

Nicky extracted a clean tissue from her bag, which she passed to me. She said, "Oh Rachel."

"I've been so stupid."

I dabbed the tissue at the edges of my mouth. She handed me another and I spat on it and tried to rub the blood from my fingers.

"You should have stuck to the script."

She reached over me and flushed the toilet.

"What do we do now?" she asked Zhang, who was watching us.

"We wait, somewhere more comfortable. When you're ready."

"Wait for what?" I asked.

"Honestly," Zhang replied, "at this point, I have no idea."

Jim

Fraser was furious after the press conference. I went to her office. She didn't invite me to sit. Her eyebrows were so far up her face they disappeared into her hairline. Disbelief and disappointment fought to dominate her expression.

"Am I right in thinking that Avon and Somerset Constabulary pays you a salary, Jim? And that's not a rhetorical question."

"Yes, boss, they do."

"Then I need to see some evidence that you're earning it! Not pissing it away! What the hell happened in there?"

"I'm sorry, boss. Rachel Jenner went totally off message. I didn't see it coming. I tried to . . ."

"Did you prepare her properly?"

"I thought I did. We went through the script and she seemed happy with it."

"Seemed? Or was?"

"I asked her if she was happy with it, and

she said yes. I thought she'd cope fine. I didn't have a crystal ball, boss."

"You're not going to have any fucking balls if you carry on like this. I'll chop them off personally and use them as Christmas decorations for the girls' lavvy. Rachel Jenner challenged the abductor. It's the most dangerous thing she could have done. Even the desk sergeant could have told you that. The fucking street cleaner I drove past on my way in this morning could have told you that! I am not prepared to have a dead child on my hands because you're gambling on the mother's state of mind. If you send somebody into a press conference you need to know they're prepared, not send them in on a wing and a prayer."

She was pushing the end of her pen toward me in little stabbing motions.

"I'm sorry, boss."

"This case has the potential to turn into a big hairy beast if we don't find the bastard who's got Ben Finch quickly, and I don't like beasties, Jim. Start using your head."

"I will."

It was a proper dressing down. It was the worst start to the case I could have imagined. I braced myself for more, but she was finished.

"Sit down for God's sake," she said, and

then, "Are we looking at a guilty mother?"

"It's possible. An outburst like that could be masking some kind of intense emotion. It could be guilt."

"Or grief? Or fear?"

"It could be any of those things."

Fraser's pen was tapping again, this time on the desk. "We need to watch her carefully. Make sure Emma knows. Guilty of something or not, Mother's a loose cannon. How did Dad react?"

"He was angry."

I'd had to restrain John Finch outside the press conference. He'd shouted in the corridor, blaming me, blaming Rachel, sobbing again, afraid that Rachel's threats could have done Ben more harm than good. He was right to fear that. It's what we were all thinking.

"Do we think he's genuine?"

"I think he is. His wife's confirmed his alibi. They were both at home together on Sunday afternoon."

"It's a soft alibi."

Fraser was right. We all knew how often spouses or parents offered alibis to keep their families out of trouble, motivated by love, or by fear, or both.

"OK, let's crack on. Damage limitation with the press, I'll see to that, and for you the priority is interviews. I want information. Somebody saw something. Tell Emma to get Mother home."

"Should I interview Rachel Jenner again?"

"No. Just warn her off speaking to the press. There's going to be a reaction to this, I don't think I need to spell that out. When you've done that, I want you to get over to Benedict's school. We need to show that we're being supportive to the school, and the community. You can interview his teacher while you're there, see if she's noticed anything different about Ben lately."

"Yes, boss."

The assignment felt like a punishment for letting the press conference get out of hand, and it probably was. A DC should be doing it, and both of us knew that.

"I'll get down there straightaway."

She softened slightly. "I would ask a DC to do it but the Chief's keen that someone with rank is seen to be there."

If that was supposed to feel like a comfort, then it was a very small one.

Rachel

What happened next was that the attitude of the police toward me tightened, or perhaps I should say sharpened. It was clear as day to me, even though on the surface they still showed appropriate concern.

I first realized it when DI Clemo came to see me after the conference and could barely contain his irritation.

Zhang had brought me yet another cup of tea that I couldn't drink, and sat my sister and me in a boxy interview room until my nausea had subsided to a manageable level and I felt ready to travel home.

When Clemo appeared his eyes were burning. He remained standing, his bulk dominating the space.

"Rachel," he said, "you do understand that things didn't run entirely to plan at the press conference?"

He was handling me. I tried to say something, to justify what had happened, but he held up a hand, even though he'd asked me a question.

"Let me finish if you will," he said. "Our primary concern now is that there may be some kind of backlash against you. We suggest that you keep a very low profile around the press, as low as possible."

"What do you mean by that?"

"Don't talk to them. It's very simple."

"It's for your own protection," said Zhang, "and Ben's."

"What do you mean by backlash?" Nicky wanted to know.

"Precisely that. This is a high-profile case. The press conference was, unfortunately, sensational, and for all the wrong reasons. The public want to find Ben as much as we do, but unlike us they might not be looking for evidence before making accusations. Do I make myself clear?"

"I understand," said Nicky. "They're going to say that Rachel did it."

"They're already saying it."

"So what do we do?"

"Go home, shut the doors, pull the curtains, don't speak to any journalists. DC Zhang will drive you back."

"What about Ben?" I said.

"We're going to continue to do everything we can to find him and we'll keep you posted on our progress." It was a phrase that was as bland and meaningless as a corporate slogan. If I'd ever had a connection with him, I felt as if it was lost now.

"I'm so sorry," I said.

At home, Nicky and Laura and I watched in silence as the footage from the conference played on national TV.

I'd been filmed in close-up. I looked as if I'd crawled out of a primitive encampment after a long siege. The injury on my head was prominent; it drew the eye like a disfigurement, and livid red spots on my pale cheeks made me look feverish, and deranged. My eyes sagged with grief and exhaustion, and roved around the room, restless and jumpy. Every flaw and muscle twitch and emotion was visible on my face, and the moment when I addressed Ben's abductor was the worst. There wasn't a trace of dignity or vulnerability, or love for my son. I simply projected a raw, ugly rage that looked heinous, and unnatural.

And yes, the blood on my hands was visible.

When I finally disintegrated, and was hustled from the room where the conference was being held, I looked like somebody fleeing a crime.

I don't know why I'm describing all this to you, because unless you've been living in Timbuktu you've probably seen it. In fact even if you had been living there you'd have been able to look it up online.

The footage went viral. Of course it did. I understand these things now.

My sister and Laura reacted in ways that summed up what was to be the response of the whole country, Nicky representing the minority view.

Laura: "Everybody's going to blame you. They're going to say you did it. You look guilty."

Nicky: "No, they won't, they can see how much you love him, how brave you are."

Peter Armstrong came around later on. I hadn't spoken to him since he'd taken Skittle away from the woods to get treatment, but he'd phoned regularly and Nicky had kept him updated. He was coming over to bring the dog home. He was sanguine about the reaction to the press conference.

"It'll blow over," he said.

He was a slender man with a stomach that had been concave since his divorce. He had dark hair that circled a significant bald patch, and stubble. He wore jeans, a loose sweater, and trendy trainers that looked too young for him. He worked as a web designer, mostly from home, and I'd always thought he needed to get out more.

"And anyway, it's only ever a minority of people who overreact to these things. As soon as they find Ben, everybody will forget. Don't dwell on it. Keep faith, Rachel. Your friends will still be there for you."

We were kneeling around the dog basket, petting Skittle. The dog's hind leg was in a pristine cast, which dragged behind him when he tried to walk. Now he was lying down, his tail managing a drowsy thump or two, but no more. He was wondering where Ben was. I was wondering what he'd seen.

"The police spoke to the vet," Peter said. "They asked if Skittle's injury could tell them anything about how he got hurt."

"And?" said Nicky.

I could tell she liked Peter. He was the opposite of her husband in looks. Simon Forbes was twice the size of Peter. He had the unruly dark hair that their girls had inherited, albeit a tad salt-and-peppery around the edges by now, and dressed in corduroys, well-worn brogues, and pressed shirts in country checks under old-fashioned blazers. However, aside from this difference, the two men did share a gentle, sensible quality that appealed to my sister.

"The vet said that the leg looked as if it was broken with one clean blow, but that could have happened in different ways. It could have been a fall, or it could have been somebody striking him. No way to tell which."

For a second or two there was silence in the room, an emptiness, which nobody wanted to fill with words, because we were all thinking about what that might mean for Ben, and how bad that could be.

"How's Finn?" I asked Peter.

"Finn's upset. He can't wait to have his buddy back." He struggled to keep himself composed. "But he's OK. He's OK, I think." He didn't look sure. "School is working hard to handle things."

I hadn't thought of that yet, of how Ben's disappearance would affect the other children.

"What are they doing?" Nicky put some tea down in front of Peter.

"Thank you," he said. "Well, they're not ignoring it; the head has spoken to the children about it, I know that much."

"What's he like?" Nicky wanted to know.

"He's new."

"People say he's a drip," I said. I hadn't met him myself, but that was the consensus in the playground, swiftly delivered by parental posses after the man had been in the job for less than two months.

"Well, I wouldn't go quite that far," said Peter.

Peter was a smoother-over of problems, an appeaser. "I think to be fair he's been lying low, getting to know the role, and the staff."

This was a polite way of saying that nobody had seen him since he started because he hid in his office most of the time, and that he hadn't yet begun to tackle any of the school's most obvious and urgent issues.

"He's very experienced, so we're hoping he'll be good for the school in the long run." Peter was also an optimist.

"Miss May?" I asked. She was Ben's teacher, Finn's too.

"I think she's been good." Peter sounded surprised. He wasn't a fan of Miss May. I thought it was because she intimidated him, and maybe because he fancied her just a bit. He'd never admit to it, but I'd seen Peter blush when they talked in the playground. She was young and pretty and had a high attendance among fathers at parents' evening.

I liked her on the whole, which was good, because this was the second year in a row that she'd been teaching Ben. There were certainly worse teachers Ben could have gotten: disheveled and angry Mr. Talbot, for example, who never marked any work and shouted. Or sociopathic Mrs. Astor, who hated children pretending to be animals and was frequently off sick with stress.

Ben had been shy of Miss May at first, but she'd swiftly won him and the other pupils over by demonstrating that she could do a backflip in front of the class, and then cemented their relationship by helping him after John and I separated.

Ben had melted down after John moved out. He'd become tearful and emotional and sometimes angry. It was so out of character, that, very reluctantly, and against all my instincts to be private, I'd had to go into school and tell Miss May what had happened, and ask her to help us pick up the pieces. She'd done that in spades, offering Ben copious amounts of support, and I had to credit her for helping us rebuild our lives since Christmas.

"From what I can gather from Finn, she's been talking to the children about it, but not letting them dwell on it," Peter said. "She seems to be keeping them busy. She was in the playground yesterday after school, talking to parents, as was the head, which people were pleased about. Most of the staff were, actually. It's beyond the call of duty I'd say."

Peter was prone to using military metaphors in his speech. It was one of the things that had put me off accepting his offer of a date when he'd tentatively asked me out after my split from John became public knowledge. It was at odds with his creative-type persona, as if he'd somehow manufactured that personality type for himself, and not arrived there naturally.

"I'm not sure about that," said Nicky. "I'd say it's exactly what they should be doing."

"What are they telling the children?" I asked. "About Ben?"

"They're telling them that he went missing in the woods, that's the phrase they're using, 'went missing,' and that everybody is looking for him." Peter took a noisy sip of tea. "Finn's been having nightmares since Sunday, because of being there in the woods with us I think."

The thought of Finn's concern and the memory of his anxious face in the parking lot made me feel Ben's absence more vividly than ever. I thought of Baggy Bear upstairs, on Ben's bed, and his nunny. I thought of Ben without either of his favorite objects, without me, without comfort, somewhere out there, going through something that none of us could imagine.

I crumpled.

"Oh I'm sorry," said Peter. "I'm so sorry. I've put my foot in it. That's the last thing I meant to do." He looked at his watch. "I should go."

Nicky showed him out, said all the things that I couldn't, like "thank you" and "we'll let you know if we hear anything," and "thank you again."

I found Laura in the front room. She was on the sofa, hunched over her tablet.

"I think this has the potential to go wrong for you," she said.

"What do you mean?"

"It's all over the Net. Facebook, Twitter, comments on news websites, everywhere."

"What is?"

"I was right. They're saying you've done something to Ben."

Jim

Ben Finch's primary school reminded me of my own: small neighborhood school, hodgepodge of portable classrooms clustered around a Victorian building on a cramped site.

Fraser told me to take DC Woodley to the school with me, which was annoying in one way because he had a tendency to behave as though he had L-plates stuck on his back, even though he'd been in CID for more than a year. On the other hand, if anyone was going to witness my humiliation at being demoted, however temporarily, to the role of school liaison officer, I suppose he was a good choice because he was too weedy to gloat. "No gumption," my dad would have said about him, and probably worse.

The school secretary fussed around us, boiling the kettle, and looking disappointed when we didn't want tea or coffee. She wanted to talk. It's not uncommon. When something traumatic has happened, everyone connected to it has his or her own version of the story to tell. It's why the press finds it so damn easy to fill columns; almost everybody wants to get their few minutes of fame.

The secretary told us she'd known something was wrong when Rachel Jenner hadn't returned her calls on Monday morning, because it was so unlike her. The school automatically called parents, she said, when a child didn't turn up and there'd been no word from them. She clutched a mug that read: "Don't talk to me until this is empty!" Fixed to the side of her computer monitor there was a photograph of Ayers Rock under a pink and orange sunset, and a Bible quote, which claimed that faith moved mountains. Both of them irritated me.

"How often is Ben Finch absent from school?" I asked her.

"Hardly ever! He's a lovely boy, ever so polite, ever so good. I couldn't tell you what his schoolwork is like, mind you, you'd have to ask Miss May or the head about that, but I can tell you he's a lovely boy. He brings the register in to me in the mornings and he always has a smile. I say to him, 'Benedict Finch, you'll go far with those super manners.' "

She got teary, removing her glasses to wipe her eyes.

"Sorry," she said, and followed that with a little outtake of air, a puff of distress that dispersed into the room. "You will find him, won't you, Inspector?"

"We'll do our best," I said.

The headmaster's office was cramped. We sat around his desk on rigid molded plastic chairs that didn't fit my body shape in any way.

"I'm sorry, Detective Inspector," he said, "I was in the middle of a special assembly when you arrived and I didn't want to alarm the children by running off. They're rattled enough already. Damien Allen, by the way."

He had a sleepy quality about him, heavily lidded eyes, a jowly face under hair that was in need of a cut, and a ponderous voice that would have had me dozing off before the end of any assembly. I shook his extended hand and found his grip loose.

"I'm new to this job," he added. "It's not ideal."

I took that to mean the situation, not the job.

Ben's teacher shook hands more earnestly; she had a bit of a pincer grip and she was one of those people who shake for longer than you've anticipated. It's an anxiety thing. They don't want to let go of you in case you disappear just when they need you.

Like the head, she was holding herself together quite well, but there were signs of distress in the way she clasped her hands tightly together and she looked on the verge of tears. She was a good-looking woman too: nicely dressed, neat figure as if she went to the gym a lot, soft fair hair down to her shoulders, nice eyes.

They told us that for the past forty-eight hours they'd had their hands full, dealing with children who were understandably frightened and confused about what had happened to Ben, and they'd also been inundated with phone calls and emails from parents who wanted information and reassurance, and were questioning the school's security procedures.

"It's a level of panic," the head said tiredly, "which suggests that there's a precedent for the disappearance of one child to lead to a rash of kidnappings."

I did what I was supposed to do. I promised we'd keep them updated and that we'd send an officer to attend a meeting for parents. We spoke about counseling for the children, but I explained the police view was that it was a bit too soon, that it was something to discuss down the line, depending on the outcome of the case.

"We'll need a list of staff at school," I told the head. "In order of those who have the most direct contact with Ben."

"We thought you might," he said, "so we've started to draw one up, and we'll send that over to you as soon as it's complete."

"We'll need that as soon as possible."

"I appreciate that, Inspector, and I'll prioritize it, of course. However, there are a large number of people involved with the school and we want to make sure we include anybody who Ben might have crossed paths with."

"It's not just teaching staff," said Miss May. "There are the teaching assistants, support staff, catering assistants . . ."

"Domestic staff, site maintenance, parents who help out with clubs . . . ," the head went on.

"Fine," I said. "Comprehensive is good, but why don't you send me over what you've got so far, so we can make a start and then you can forward any other names as you think of them."

"Of course," said the head. "Of course. I'll ask Anthea to do that."

He waved a chubby hand at the glass panel set into his office door. Behind it, the secretary hastily turned away and sat down at her desk, pushing her glasses self-consciously up her nose and trying to look busy. I wondered how many of his conversations she eavesdropped on.

I felt a headache coming on. Dealing with the school was going to be a minefield. We were going to have to work all the hours God gave just to get through background checks on everyone who might have had contact with Ben.

"In advance of the list, is there anyone working at school who's given you cause for concern lately, in terms of their behavior or in any other way?" I asked him.

He shook his head. The frown on his forehead seemed to deepen by the minute.

"Obviously I've been racking my brain since this happened," he said. "But I should say that I am stressing to parents that it didn't happen in or near school property. I think that's worth bearing in mind, Inspector, when you're looking for suspects."

"As is the fact that this place is the single biggest opportunity for Ben Finch to come into contact with a wide range of adults."

"All of whom are CRB checked."

"There's no need to be defensive, Mr. Allen. You know as well as I do that the CRB check is only a reliable check of previous convictions, not of possible impulses or intentions."

"I'm simply keen that the school doesn't become a particular focus of the investigation."

That wasn't worth responding to; it was the kind of bureaucratic comment that made me want to slap a pair of handcuffs on him. I swallowed my annoyance, because I wanted to press him some more on Ben's possible contacts.

"Is there any adult at school who you feel that Ben might have formed an attachment to?"

"Miss May?" asked the head. "You'll know best."

"Well, there's me," she said. The palm of her hand was on her chest, rising and falling with her breathing. "I've been his teacher for just over a year now, I had him last year too; and I work with a teaching assistant called Lucas Grantham, who comes in part-time. He's new this year. The children like him; Ben likes him. We're the ones with the most contact with him."

"We'll definitely need to speak to Mr. Grantham," I said.

"He's here today if you'd like to meet him."

"That would be useful. Anybody else?"

She shook her head.

"Nobody springs to mind, but there are lots of other people Ben comes into contact with on a daily basis."

"And, can I ask, have you noticed anything unusual about Ben's behavior lately?"

"No. If anything I'd say he's been having a good year. Last year was much harder for him, after his parents split up."

"In what way?"

"He didn't know how to react to the separation. We talked about it sometimes at school. He's not the only one in my class going through it, of course, but it's a sad and confusing situation for any child, and I think parents sometimes don't understand how hard the children take it."

"It often falls to the school to deal with the emotional fallout in these situations," said the head.

"Do you think Ben was more affected than you might expect?"

"I couldn't say," said the head. "I'd be lying if I said I knew him well because I've only been here a few weeks, as I said."

I wasn't directing the question at him, but I let it go. The man had an ego. Miss May answered.

"No," she said. "He was affected quite badly, but he's a very sensitive boy so that's what you might expect if you knew him."

The head cleared his throat. "There's one thing on file we thought we should mention. Last spring, when Ben was in Year Four, he had a fall as he arrived in the playground with his mother. It was before school. He came off his scooter and landed badly on his arm. Do you want to tell it from there, Miss May, as you were there?"

"I wasn't actually there when he fell. One of the other teachers saw it happen," she said. "Apparently Ms. Jenner helped Ben up and put him back on his feet and brushed him off. He was crying a bit, because his arm hurt, but she was talking to him and he did calm down."

She paused and looked anxiously at the head.

"And?" I said.

He took over. "And the file says that Ms. Jenner left Benedict at school even though he was complaining of pain in his arm. It turned out that it was fractured."

"So this was when he was in your class?" I asked Miss May.

She nodded. "I've got to say I took one look at him when I was doing registration and I could see there was something very wrong. He was white as a sheet. As soon as he said what had happened I called an ambulance immediately."

"Was he in obvious distress at that point, or when his mother left him?"

"Not obvious distress; he was being very brave."

"Were there signs that the arm was fractured?"

"It was a buckle fracture so there were no snapped bones, or swelling, and he could move his hand. His mother did check all that, but she didn't notice how much pain he was in."

"Did Ms. Jenner return when you realized he needed treatment?"

"Yes, of course, and she went with him to the hospital."

"So it's possible she didn't realize how badly he was hurt?"

"No. She didn't realize." Something in her expression wasn't happy.

"Do you think she should have realized?"

"I do. I really do. And I suppose what's always on my mind is: why did Ben feel he had to be so stoical in front of her? He was only seven years old. And why didn't his mother get him properly checked up right away? Why didn't she see what I saw?"

"We had a similar incident in my old school," said the head. "It's not uncommon for minor fractures to go unnoticed."

"I do know that," said Miss May. "It's just that she always looked so depressed at the time, as if she couldn't cope. This was after the separation. I wondered if it was all getting a bit much for her. Ben always seemed so worried about upsetting her."

"Were there any other signs?" I asked.

Miss May took a deep breath. "No," she said. "Hand on heart, no there weren't."

"Says here she forgot to collect him one day." The head held up a piece of paper from Ben's file.

"Oh! Yes, she did. I'd forgotten that," Miss May said. "Yes, that's true. It was the last day of the spring term, last year, and the children were supposed to be collected at midday instead of at the usual time, so it was understandable."

"Was she commonly forgetful?"

"No, no, it happened just the once, but Ben was very upset. He was inconsolable, actually. It was the last thing he needed at the time. He'd only just moved out of their family home into the new house with just his mum. He was feeling very insecure about the new arrangements, and it was a time when it was important for him to feel wanted, to know that he was their priority."

"So, just to confirm, it wasn't typical of Ben's mother to forget him?"

"No. It wasn't typical, but when it happened I suppose I did think it might be a symptom of how difficult things might be at home."

"So this was last year, and have things improved since then?" I asked. "Any more incidents?"

"No. Nothing else. He's been better generally this year. I think he's settled in the new house with his mum now and things are hopefully a teensy bit calmer." Her inflection at the end of this sentence made it sound like a question.

I looked at the head. "What's your view?"

"Well, I defer to Miss May on this, because, as I said, I don't know Ben very well yet, and I haven't met his mother at all so I can't comment on her. From what I'm hearing, I suspect it's been a hard time for Ben and his mum, but also fantastic continuity for him that he's had Miss May for two years running."

She smiled at him.

"Well, thank you both," I said, "and if you think of anything else we should know then please get in contact." I got up, grateful to be out of the chair.

"We shall," the head said. He looked even more weary as he stood, and, in spite of his attitude earlier, I felt sorry for both of them, having to go back out of this room and deal with the confusion and fear of a school full of traumatized children. He smoothed his tie against his shirt and treated me to the same loose handshake as before.

"Could we have a quick word with Ben's teaching assistant before we leave?" I asked. "Mr. . . . ?"

"Lucas Grantham," said the head. "Miss May, could you show the officers where to find him?"

She walked with us down the corridor. On either side, the walls were plastered with work that the children had done.

"Lucas is in the classroom," she said. "Right here."

Before I could ask her to fetch him discreetly, she pushed open the door. A class of kids was working at low tables, in groups of four, sitting in those miniature chairs that you forget you ever fitted into. A young man was overseeing them from the front of the room. He looked early twenties at a guess. He had thick tufty ginger hair, and his face was pretty much one big freckle with a bit of white skin peeking through here and there. He was perched on the desk.

The children's eyes turned to us and they started to get to their feet. Chairs scraped and papers fell off tables as they stood.

"This is Mr. Clemo and Mr. Woodley," said Miss May. She whispered to me, "I'm not going to tell them you're policemen." Then she addressed them again: "What do we say, children?"

"Good afternoon, Mr. Clemo, good afternoon, Mr. Woodley," they chanted.

"Well done, class," said Miss May, and she favored them with a big smile. "Sit down and carry on."

They sat down with a collective bump, duty done. The young man came to the door. "This is Lucas," said Miss May. "Or Mr. Grantham, as the children call him. He's our teaching assistant for Oak Class."

"Nice to meet you," he said. No handshake; instead he held his hands in front of him, fingers interlocked, and in motion, as if he were working his way along a set of prayer beads. "It's just awful, I can't believe it." He had freckles on the back of his hands too.

"We'll need to have a word with you at some point very soon," I said.

"Right! Of course, whenever," he said. Close up, he looked tired and slack-jawed. He had a weak chin and he hadn't shaved for a couple of days.

"Have you noticed anything different from usual about Benedict Finch's behavior lately?" I asked him. I kept my voice down so the kids didn't hear me.

"No," he said. "Nothing at all."

Behind him a space at one of the tables caught my eye, an empty chair where presumably Ben Finch should have been sitting, surrounded by his schoolmates, having an ordinary day.

"Nothing? Are you sure?" I said. He was starting to irritate me.

"No," he said. He shook his head slowly, his lips tucked in between his teeth. I felt my phone buzz in my pocket.

"We have to get going," I said. "Though we'll need to interview you as soon as possible. Somebody will be in touch to arrange that."

The children were starting to fidget and talk. Miss May hushed them gently.

"Whenever you like," said Lucas Grantham. "Of course. If it'll help."

In the car, Woodley said, "It's a bloody nightmare how many people could have had contact with him."

"I know, and we're going to need background and alibis on every single one of them. Plus we need to check out the incident with the broken arm with the hospital."

"Do you think there's anything in it?"

"No, because it seems completely clear that Rachel Jenner didn't inflict the injury on him. It was an accident. But we'll check it out anyway and I think we should take the possibility that she was depressed seriously. We'll pass that on to Fraser and Zhang straightaway."

"What did you think of the teaching assistant?"

"Of interest," I said. "Definitely."

"Yeah, I thought he was a bit shifty."

Woodley sat in silence for a few moments, then he said, "Strange, isn't it? Being back at school?"

The car was poised at the school entrance, indicator light ticking.

"Why do you say that?"

"You forget how small you were once. Don't you think?"

"I suppose so. When did you leave primary school then? Last week? Short memory you've got. Is that why they kicked you out? Couldn't remember your times tables?"

It was a sport in the office, ribbing Woodley because he looked young, or because he had a nose you could ski off.

"Ha ha, boss," he said, but he shut up then and I was glad because I was actually thinking about how vivid my memories of being primary-school age were, and it was making me scared for Benedict Finch, because of all the bad things that can be done to a child that age, so very easily.

Rachel

Laura and Nicky wouldn't let me go online. They said I shouldn't read the stuff people were saying, that it would upset me. They were united in this. I was still in denial, still sure that people wouldn't actually, really accuse me. Even then, in those first hours after the press conference, I was naïve enough to retain a delicate mesh of middle-class confidence around me. I'm a good citizen, I thought. People will know that. I used to be married to a doctor.

I should have had more sense though, because outside the house the journalists were gathering in greater numbers than before, drawn there since the press conference.

Inside, we'd had to take the phone off the hook, and seal the letter flap with masking tape. I stayed in the back of the house, as far away from them as possible.

Nicky went out for supplies and bustled

back into the house within minutes, holding bags from the local corner shop. "I couldn't get any farther," she said. "They followed me. And they've dropped rubbish everywhere."

She found a black bin liner under my sink and took it back out to the front of the house, where, in tones strident enough for me to hear, she ordered the journalists to clear up what they'd dropped in the street and in my postage-stamp-sized front garden.

Back inside, still bristling, she started to unpack a selection of canned food. "They're lovely in the shop," she said, "aren't they? They locked the door so I could shop without the journalists and then they gave me this to give to you."

It was an envelope. On the front was handwritten "To Benedict and His Mother."

"They said they can order in anything you want," Nicky went on, shoving the cans into cupboards. "Or if we can't get to the supermarket they said they can get stuff for us that we can pick up, which might be nice because we can't live off this." She held up a loaf of sliced white bread.

I opened the envelope. Inside was a small card. An elegant pair of hands was drawn on the front, with tapered fingers and palms together, in prayer. Beaded bracelets hung around the wrists.

"What religion are they?" Nicky asked, looking over my shoulder.

"Hindu," I said. "I think."

Inside the card was a handwritten message, in careful, formal lettering. "We have shed tears for you and we wish you and Benedict every strength and we pray that he will be home soon. Ravi and Aasha and family."

"I barely even know them," I said. I thought of my frequent visits to the shop, the small talk with the owners, a lovely couple, but strangers really, and I felt deeply moved by the card.

"You've had other messages," Nicky said. "I just wasn't sure you were up to them."

"Show me."

Nicky had commandeered my mobile phone, in order to field calls and messages from friends, and other families that we knew well and not so well.

They were mostly texts from people I knew, an outpouring of reaction to the story appearing on the news. The texts ranged from the predictable:

> Devastated to hear about Ben please let us know if there's anything we can do. Clarke Family xxx

Can't imagine what you're going through. We're thinking of you and Ben. Sacha x

To the insultingly practical:

Don't worry about returning Jack's coat with what's happening we understand completely. Thinking of you. Love Juliet xx

"What's that supposed to mean?" I said. "What the hell's that supposed to mean?"

Nicky read it. "It's nothing. It doesn't matter. They're trying to be nice."

"As if I care about a stupid coat."

"They don't expect you to. Don't think the worst. It's supposed to be a nice message."

There were emails too, but I tired of reading them. The messages made me feel either sad or angry or resentful and I was feeling all of those things enough already. Needling at me, too, were the messages that weren't there, from friends who I would have expected to support us. "Have there been voicemails?" I asked Nicky. "Don't you think people should leave a proper message?"

"There've been one or two," she said. "I wrote them down. People probably don't want to tie up the phone line."

I looked over the messages she'd carefully recorded. There were still at least two friends conspicuous by their absence from these lists. Were they being kind by not contacting me? Was that a thoughtful response? Or had they backed off now that I was tainted by misfortune, now that I was the person to whom the worst had happened, the one at the sharp end of the statistical wedge, where nobody else wants to be.

I sat there, the card in my hands, while Nicky trawled the web again, searching deeper and deeper for advice and information, for anything that might help us, as if it were a sort of addiction.

I had an impulse to phone John. I wanted to tell him I was sorry about the press conference, and that I was sorry I had let Ben run ahead in the woods. I increasingly felt a desperate need for him to absolve me of the things I'd done wrong. It felt like the only way I could lessen my pain. But he didn't answer his mobile, and Katrina answered their landline.

"He's not here," she said. "He's out driving the streets, looking for Ben. He hasn't been home since the press conference."

"You've seen it?"

"Yes."

I didn't want her to say anything about it. "I've got to go," I said quickly.

Laura went home. She had cats to feed. I marveled at how the mundane activities that life demanded still needed to be done, even while the worst was happening.

I even felt resentful toward my body, toward its demands for sleep, for food, for drink, for bodily functions. I thought that life should stop until Ben was found. Clocks should no longer tick, oxygen should no longer be exchanged for carbon dioxide in our lungs, and our hearts should not pump. Only when he was back should normal service resume.

Anything else was an insult to him, to what he might be suffering.

Nicky continued to work, propelled by some kind of manic internal engine, as if an Internet search might yield a vital clue, or trigger a revelation. Once she'd finished looking online, she began to design a flyer, and to come up with plans for distributing it.

I tired of being in her orbit, and I went upstairs, my fingers running along the dado rail. Just above it, visible against the white paint, were Ben's finger marks. He always ran, never walked, whether he was going up or down the stairs. Ignoring my shouts to slow down, he would have one hand on the banister and one hand on the wall to steady himself, and I would hear rapid footfalls. Usually I only noticed the marks made by his grubby fingers when they exasperated me, but now they seemed unbearably precious. I traced over them with my own fingers as I went up.

The house had been in a total state when we moved in. John, who'd viewed it because he was paying for some of it, advised me not to buy it. Horrible dark colors and tacky plastic cupboards had put off many people, but I could see that underneath the tatty decor and the tack there were some pretty, original features and I'd been excited by their potential. I'd tackled Ben's bedroom first. Ben and I had spent a brilliant day putting the first coat of paint over the horrible dark maroon color left by the previous owners.

"Go on," I'd said to Ben, "just slap the paint on."

"What, anywhere?" he'd asked, hardly believing his luck, a wide smile dimpling his cheeks.

"Anywhere," I'd said, and to prove my point I'd dipped my brush in the tub of pristine white undercoat and written "BEN" in huge capital letters on the wall. He'd loved the forbidden thrill of painting all over the walls, and he'd quickly got into it. We'd drawn pictures, written silly words, and had much fun until the room was covered in a patchy layer of undercoat.

It had felt good for both of us: we were taking possession of the house. The plan had backfired a bit because we never quite managed to smooth the wall out afterward, and even now that there were two coats of pale blue covering the undercoat it was possible to make out raised areas where some of our pictures and words had been. Neither of us minded that though. In fact we liked it.

Remembering, I eased my body down into the dent in his mattress that had taken on my shape now, obliterating his, and I touched the wall, feeling for those raised areas of paint.

I tried to make myself focus, to think through what had happened in the woods, to recover every detail. I was desperate to discover, somewhere in my mind, something significant, but I remembered nothing new.

Then I thought about John, driving the streets, desperately searching for Ben, and I thought about Katrina, and I regretted every moment that I'd let Ben be with them over the past year, and not with me.

She hadn't even wanted him in their home at first. That had been clear from what Ben had told me. "She doesn't let me slide on the floor in the hall," he'd complained, and I'd been furious, imagining him tiptoeing through their perfect house, unable to relax in case he did something wrong. I recalled Ben's reluctance to spend weekends with them after the breakup, especially in the beginning, when things still felt raw, and unstable. I came bitterly to my usual conclusion that Katrina didn't deserve Ben, and I didn't deserve to have to go through her to get to John.

My thoughts circulated fruitlessly like this until finally sleep conked me out, knocked me into my unconscious, where I dreamed of being surrounded by looming trees and by foliage with sharp edges, and by shadows and dark tunnels where you could get lost forever.

In the small hours I woke up and reached for my phone. I opened the Internet browser and Googled "News Benedict Finch." When the results came up I only needed one or two clicks before a feeling of dread coursed icily through me.

Jim

Addendum to DI James Clemo's report for Dr. Francesca Manelli

Transcript recorded by Dr. Francesca Manelli
DI James Clemo and Dr. Francesca Manelli in attendance

Notes to indicate observations on DI Clemo's state of mind or behavior, where his remarks alone do not convey this, are in italics.

FM: So not a good day on the case for you, your second day?

JC: No. It's not what I would have wanted, but you pick yourself up, keep on going, try to put things right. By the end of the day we had lots to think about.

FM: I wonder if you feel that the press conference knocked your confidence?

JC: Because of what the mother did?

FM: Yes.

JC: No. It didn't. I'd make that call again. Nobody could have predicted that she was going to do what she did. If I'm honest, I didn't think it was fair for me to take the rap for it.

FM: Did you say that to DCI Fraser?

JC: No. I'm proud, I'm not suicidal. She was just venting anyway. That's what she's like so I didn't take it too seriously.

FM: How was the case progressing overall?

JC: We had stuff going on. We all sat down together at about fourteen hundred hours that night. Fraser was still bitching and moaning about the press conference to start off with, but she settled down because we had a few obvious leads so there was a feeling that we might be getting somewhere.

FM: What were the leads?

JC: We were still looking into the fantasy role-play folks. The majority had alibis, but one of them in particular was being difficult, refusing to answer questions, and that got Fraser's goat. He didn't have an alibi and she liked him for the abduction.

FM: How was he being difficult?

JC: He claimed that the only authority he would recognize was the Order of Knights who ruled his fantasy world, which basically meant that he refused to talk to us. Wouldn't answer any questions. On a point of principle.

FM: Is that allowed?

JC: He can claim what he likes and we couldn't make him talk to us. Fraser decided to interview him herself. She wanted Woodley and me to go with her the next day, pay him a visit at home and see if we couldn't shake something out of him.

FM: And the pedophile? The one you were trying to trace?

JC: He was a definite concern. We still didn't have a location for him, but the DC who was on the case reckoned his mum knew where he was and it was eating her up not telling us. She was going to pay her another visit. We had the psychologist working on possible profiles for abductors and other than that we were drawing up lists of people to interview, checking alibis, and responding to all the calls that had come in after our appeals.

FM: Did you have a large response?

JC: Huge, almost overwhelming. Fraser had pulled together as big a team as she could but it was still going to be hard to follow up everything quickly. As a priority, we needed IDs on the cyclist Rachel Jenner mentioned seeing in the woods and the lone male walker, so we were focusing on those.

FM: What was the atmosphere like among the team?

JC: Totally adrenalized. Everyone wanted to get on with it, find the kid.

FM: Had there been a public reaction to the press conference?

JC: That was an issue. Even that first night there was already a massive online backlash against Rachel Jenner. People were saying, or insinuating, everything under the sun, online news sites included. We were dreading the headlines the next morning.

FM: What kind of things were they saying?

JC: The headings were "Mother's Angry Outburst," that kind of thing. Not too bad yet but it was the comments that people were making that were worrying us. On Facebook hundreds of people were discussing the case and they weren't holding back. They thought she was guilty.

FM: And what did you think?

JC: Couldn't rule it out. She certainly had the opportunity to do something to Ben, and we hadn't verified her story yet.

FM: What was your gut instinct?

JC: That she was volatile.

FM: Meaning?

JC: She could have done it.

FM: You weren't convinced of her innocence after her display of grief at the press conference?

JC: Grief isn't proof of innocence. If she'd done something to Ben she could still have been feeling distress.

FM: True.

JC: I felt she could have murdered him, or killed him by mistake, and hidden the body and made up the story about the woods. It's a pretty unlikely scenario but by no means impossible. We asked the forensic psychologist to look at the footage from the conference and give us his thoughts about Rachel Jenner.

FM: So apart from the negative press, were you happy with the response to the press conference? Did any good come of it?

JC: We did get some positive response. Like I said, we had a lot to manage but once we'd weeded out the nutters, we were hoping something would come of it, maybe a sighting, maybe people to add to the list we had to interview.

He's got me interested. If truth be told, this case fascinated me at the time, as it did many people. I must have let this show, the fact that

I'm finding what he's telling me compelling, because he leans forward, asks me the question that's really on his mind.

JC: How many sessions do you think it will take until you can sign me off?

I have to put my professional face firmly back in place.

FM: That's impossible for me to say. All I can say is that you're making good progress so far.

He sits back again, but he's agitated. His right knee jiggles up and down.

FM: I'm interested in the work that the forensic psychologist was doing. Can you tell me more about that?

JC: He'd not submitted anything in writing at this point, but Fraser and I had both talked to him.

FM: And what were his thoughts?

JC: They were a mixed bag.

FM: Can you describe them to me?

JC: It's not nice stuff.

FM: I'm interested. It's not a million miles away from what I do.

JC: The main distinction that profilers make in child abduction cases is between family and nonfamily abduction.

FM: Is either one more likely?

JC: Statistically, a family abduction, because it's usually the result of divorce or custody arrangements that have gone bad. You often read about kids who are kidnapped and taken abroad by a parent. Rarely, a family abduction involves a member of close family: an uncle, or a stepfather maybe, who harbors an unhealthy sexual interest in a child, but in those cases the victim is usually a girl.

FM: Presumably those cases are easier to solve.

JC: Absolutely. The nonfamily perpetrator is much more challenging for us. If a child is snatched right out of the family's lives, without trace, the pool of potential suspects can become vast. Obviously we look at everyone they know, but once you've ruled them out, it could be anyone. And time is always against you.

FM: It must leave the parents in a living hell.

JC: You wouldn't wish it on anyone.

FM: No, you wouldn't. There's a term we use for it: "ambiguous grief." It can be a life sentence. It's a kind of unresolved grief. You might feel it if you have a child or another family member who is mentally impaired. You might mourn the person you think they could have been if things had turned out differently. That person is physically present but psychologically absent. Conversely, and this is what happens in cases of abduction, or more commonly in divorce, the child or the person is psychologically present but physically absent. And in the case of abduction the parents have the added uncertainty over whether the child is alive or dead.

JC: It's what we wanted to avoid. We wanted to get that kid back safe and well. We were waiting to get written profiles from the psychologist, but he'd told Fraser he was veering toward a nonfamily abduction, because of the circumstances of the abduction.

FM: Why?

JC: Based on Ben's age and gender it was likely to be a lone male abductor with a sexual motive, probably acting opportunistically.

FM: And how did he come to this conclusion?

JC: Past cases, the circumstances of Ben's life and his disappearance. He advised us to look out for someone odd when we were interviewing and looking through statements.

FM: Odd? You surely didn't need a profiler to tell you to look out for somebody odd?

JC: I don't mean overtly odd. There are signs to look for. Often they are craving control, in sexual relationships perhaps, or just in their lives.

FM: Which presumably might have been a fit for your fantasy role-play suspect?

JC: That's right.

Describing his work has given him an energy I haven't seen before. I change the subject, hoping he'll carry this momentum into talking about his personal life.

FM: And Emma?

JC: What about her?

FM: What were her thoughts?

JC: To be honest, we hadn't really had a chance to talk properly. She was getting on with the job though. Fraser was pleased with her.

FM: I'm very surprised you hadn't talked. I understood that you were living together.

JC: It was hard once the case started. You don't keep sociable hours. When you get home you're so tired you just want to sleep. It was easier for us both to sleep at our own places some nights. And Emma could be hard to read sometimes, you know?

FM: What do you mean?

JC: I don't know. You know how people sometimes get very quiet, go into themselves a bit when they're focused on the job?

FM: Yes.

JC: She's like that. So when she wanted to keep herself to herself I respected that. And, to be honest, we didn't really have time for our relationship once the case started because it consumed us both. It's the nature of it.

FM: Do you think Emma was prepared for that?

JC: Absolutely.

FM: You put a lot of responsibility on her, recommending her for the post.

JC: I've already told you, I had faith in her.

FM: Did you talk about that?

JC: I wasn't going to patronize her. That would have been out of order. And she didn't need me to.

His foot begins to tap a swift staccato on the floor, signaling that he knows it's only minutes until the end of our session.

FM: Just one last thing before you go.

He raises an eyebrow inquiringly.

FM: Did you feel that you were able to keep your distance from the case? Personally?

JC: What do you mean?

FM: The age of Benedict Finch, the visit to his school. Occasionally when I read your report I get the feeling that he might have got under your skin a bit.

JC: I was professional.

FM: I'm not suggesting for a moment that

you weren't.

He stares at me.

JC: It's not wrong to care.

FM: Was this the first case you worked on where a child was involved, or in danger?

JC: Yes.

FM: Was that hard?

JC: It was hard in that we had to find him. It was our responsibility to him. He'd done nothing wrong. He was just a kid. But that didn't make any difference to anything I did.

FM: Do you think your response to the case could have been affected by the relatively recent death of your father?

JC: What?

FM: Sometimes when we lose a parent it makes us reflect on our childhoods. It's not an uncommon response to parental bereavement. That might have made you more vulnerable to identifying with Benedict Finch, and what could be happening to him?

He doesn't reply. He looks incredulous.

FM: DI Clemo?

JC: No. It didn't. You've got the wrong end of the stick. I was doing my job. Isn't this session supposed to be over by now?

Although there's a clock in plain view on my

desk, he glances at his watch. It's obvious that he's not going to engage with this today.

▪ ▪ ▪ ▪

Day 4
Wednesday,
October 24, 2012

▪ ▪ ▪ ▪

Crimes against children, particularly cases involving abduction and homicide, continue to be problematic as both a social phenomenon and judicial responsibility. Such cases routinely receive intense community, media, and law enforcement attention, and can rapidly overwhelm local investigative resources.

— M. C. Boudreaux, W. D. Lord, and R. L. Dutra, "Child Abduction:

Aged-Based Analyses of Offender, Victim, and Offense Characteristics in 550 Cases of Alleged Child Disappearance,"
Journal of Forensic Sciences 44(3), 1999

Stay united in your fight to find your child. Don't allow the stress of the investigation to drive a wedge into your family life. When emotions run wild, be careful that you do not lash out at or cast blame on others . . . Remember that everyone deals with crises and grief differently, so don't judge others because they do not respond to the disappearance in the same way you do.

— "When Your Child Is Missing:
A Family Survival Guide,"
Missing Kids USA Parental Guide,
US Department of Justice, OJJDP Report

Email

To: Corinne Fraser <fraserc@aspol.uk>
Cc: James Clemo <clemoj@aspol.uk>;
Giles Martyn
<martyng@aspol.uk>
From: Janie Green <greenj@aspol.uk>
October 24, 2012 at 06:58

OPERATION HUCKLEBERRY — PRESS REVIEW 10/24/12

Morning, Corinne

Roundup of this morning's press coverage relating to Operation Huckleberry below. This is just the nationals and locals. Due to the vast quantity of material, we've yet to go through everything that's online, so I'll forward that later. As usual, "highlights" below with link to scanned copies.

I'm copying this in to DS Martyn at his

request. The material is concerning him and he'd like us all to get together later this morning to discuss tactics. He and I can do 10 or 11?

Janie Green
Press Officer, Avon and Somerset Constabulary

THE SUN
"ANGRY"
Blood: On her hands
Rage: In her eyes
Gashed: Across her forehead

THE DAILY MIRROR
"BLOOD ON HER HANDS"
Loner photographer mum says on her website she "likes to work alone"
Neighbor says she "never saw Benedict"

THE DAILY MAIL
"DO WE NEED TO LOOK ANY FURTHER?"
Could the answer to Benedict Finch's disappearance lie close to home? . . .

RACHEL

I slept only fitfully after looking online. The phrases I'd read repeated in my head over and over again. When I woke up for what felt like the hundredth time, the Stormtrooper clock beside the bed read 4:47 a.m. Ben's bedding was twisted around me and I felt exhausted and cold. Nicky was sleeping in my room, with the door open. I didn't want to wake her. I crept downstairs quietly and didn't turn any lights on.

On the kitchen table I found her laptop. I opened it and the glow from the screen lit up my fingers, poised over the keyboard. It asked me for a password. I watched the cursor blinking as I tried to think what it might be. I knew it wouldn't be the name of any of her daughters. She'd lectured me once on password security and the foolishness of using your children's or pet's names. I tried "Rosedown," which was the name of the cottage we grew up in. "Incorrect password" was the computer's response. I tried "rhubarbcustard" — a reference to Nicky's blog. It didn't work. I had one more shot at it, and no clue what to try. On a whim, because it was my password in spite of her advice, and because my exhausted brain couldn't come up with anything else, I tried "Benedict."

It worked. I leaned back in my chair in surprise, but then I felt a rush of affection toward Nicky: my bossy sister, a proud-enough aunty to use Ben's name as her password.

Now that I was in, I searched "Benedict Finch Missing." News items from all different sources appeared on the screen. The story had exploded. Images of me from the press conference appeared alongside Ben's photo: my bleeding head, my white pallor, my body language, and my angry eyes. Many of the news headlines were blatantly aggressive toward me.

But I still couldn't help myself.

Like a moth to a flame I clicked on the Facebook site.

There were hundreds of posts. The top one was from somebody called Cathy Franklin.

Cathy Franklin The mother has done something to him thats obvious
2 hours ago • Like

Stuart Weston Police wouldn't have let her tlk at press conf if they suspected her
2 hours ago • Like

Cathy Franklin Stuart that's not true has been seen before that people crying in press confs have been convicted.
1 hour ago • Like

Rich Jameson Some people hang themselves like that perhaps they're trying to catch her out. U wouldn't believe how many people have done this go to www.whereisbenedictfinch.wordpress.com u wd be amazed.
42 minutes ago • Like • 6

Write a comment . . .

I clicked on the link. My heart was pounding, my mouth bone dry.

The page appeared instantly:

WEB PAGE — www.whereisbenedictfinch.wordpress.com

WHERE IS BENEDICT FINCH? For the curious . . .

FACTS

Posted at 03:14 by LazyDonkey, on Wednesday, October 24, 2012

Benedict Finch went missing at 15:30 on Sunday, October 21.
The last person to see him was his mother.
She let him out of her sight.
And she never saw him again.
Yesterday she appeared at a press conference to appeal for help finding Ben.
This blog wants to draw your attention to some things that have happened in the past.

CASE HISTORIES

Ian Huntley

This man appeared on television shortly after the disappearance of Holly Wells and Jessica Chapman. He was later convicted of their murders. He was the last person to see them alive.

Shannon Matthews

Shannon's mother appeared on television on numerous occasions after the disappearance of her daughter. She was later convicted of her kidnapping.

Tracie Andrews
This woman appeared at a televised press conference to appeal for help finding her fiancé's killer. She blamed a road rage incident. She was later convicted of murdering him herself.

What do these things tell us?
They tell us that nothing is what it seems.

54 people are discussing this post with 94 comments

Cathy_07926
I'm very troubled by what I'm reading here. Why don't we all stop persecuting the mother. Have any of you ever heard of "innocent until proven guilty"?

Jen loves cookies
Cathy, I agree with you. As a human being who lives and breathes I want to hold out my hand to Rachel and Ben and the father so they know there are people out there praying for them and their little boy. I was awake all night thinking of them. What that family must be going through.

SelinaY
OMG you only have to look at that mother to know she's done something. She is guilty until innocent for me, get real everybody, how else will we stop evil scum hurting our kids.

Mountain biker
Why did the mother let her kid run off like that? Asking for trouble. And what about the father?

JuliaPeachy
That dad is a doctor. Saved my baby girl's life. Heart goes out to him at this time.

JohnDoe
A kid running alone in the woods? Seriously? Did she want something to happen to him? That's out of a nightmare.

Joker_864
Trees can walk. Ivy wraps around your feet. Branches carry you up and away. Little finches are prey for bigger birds.

RichNix
I wouldn't want her for my mum. Scared me.

Cloud99
She shouldn't be allowed a kid. It's disgusting what she did. U don't realize how stupid people are till you read this stuff. A child is a gift. I wouldn't let my kids run off, doesn't she know the risks.

HouseProud
I feel sorry for Benedict Finch with that mum I hope his dad can take him after this.

Forever twenty-one
As a mum of four I would want people to stop speculating and start praying for that little boy.

Rational_Dawn_to_Dusk
Speculation is a drug. It fuels our society.

Happyinmydressinggown
People need to stop being sat in front of their screens and get out there and help look for this little boy. Police should give us more information. Whatever the mother has done we must pray for god to protect this poor little boy wherever he is.

The kitchen light came on suddenly. Nicky was standing in the doorway. She looked crumpled and sleepy in her nightie.

"What are you doing?"

I gestured to the laptop. "Who would write something like this? Do you know what they're saying?"

She took a quick look, and pushed down the lid of the laptop.

"Don't look at it! You mustn't. There's no point. It's sick people using Ben to get their moment. It's grotesque. It's a feeding frenzy. Promise me you won't look again. Promise me!"

"It's not just people. It's the newspapers too."

"Promise me you won't look!"

I promised, but my hands shook for a long time afterward.

Jim

I spoke to Emma before I left for work, a quick call because I'd missed her the night before.

She answered her phone quickly — "Hey how are you?" — but I could hear the drag of fatigue in her voice and she yawned generously.

"Good. You? Did you sleep well?"

"What do you reckon?"

"I reckon you were awake half the night like me."

"I was."

"Are you OK?"

"I've survived on less."

"Everyone on the investigation's going to be feeling it."

"I know."

She still sounded flat, and I didn't like it, because it wasn't like her to let things get to her. I wanted to buoy her up.

"But it's what we do it for, isn't it? A case

like this."

"Yes, you're right. If we get a result, that is."

She stifled another yawn, apologized for it, and then she snapped back into something resembling her usual efficient tone, as if she'd suddenly realized how dispirited she sounded.

"I was worried about you yesterday," she said.

"What do you mean?"

"The press conference, Rachel Jenner out of control, and the whole country watching? Don't be obtuse."

I didn't really want to answer that.

"I'm fine."

"Are you sure?"

"If I say I'm sure, then I'm sure."

"OK. Good. Sorry, I'm not fully awake yet, I don't think. I overslept. I didn't mean to upset you. Can I give you a quick call back in a few minutes, when I've finished getting ready?"

"I'm on my way in already, I'm literally about to step out the door, so I'll see you at the briefing."

"OK — I'll see you then. I'll be more with it by then, I promise."

We said our good-byes, and they were affectionate enough, but I ended the call feeling a bit cheated, because the conversation hadn't lifted my spirits the way I'd thought it would.

At work our priority for the morning was to go and talk to the member of the fantasy role-play group who'd already given some difficulties to the pair of DCs who went to interview him. First thing in the morning checks had thrown up some previous on him, indecent exposure no less, meaning that he'd just shot straight to the top spot on our interview list.

DCI Fraser stuck to her guns by insisting that she'd like to talk to him herself. "We'll see this young chappie in his home, I think, Jim," she said. "But let's not book an appointment, eh? We'll surprise him."

It was a long time since I'd been accompanied to an interview by a senior officer, and I tried to fight off the thought that she wanted to keep an eye on me after the balls-up at the press conference. More likely, I hoped, she was living up to her reputation as somebody who liked to stay in touch with the roots of her investigations. She asked Woodley to come along too.

We took an unmarked pool car. I drove and Fraser studied the stereo, glasses halfway down her nose. Woodley sat in the back, but took the middle seat and leaned forward each time Fraser said anything.

Fraser asked, "Did you see the email from Press Office this morning?"

"I did. Pretty brutal."

"Indeed. I'm meeting DS Martyn about it at eleven and he's not going to be a happy bunny."

DS Martyn was the officer ultimately overseeing this case, and Fraser's senior officer. He was never a happy bunny. I waited for her to say more, but she turned on the radio.

"What do you like to listen to, Jim?" she asked.

"Five Live usually, boss," I said. "Or Radio Bristol."

"Those are very pedestrian choices," she said. "How about a little culture? Have you ever heard of culture, DC Woodley?"

"I played the recorder at school," he said.

I glanced in my rearview mirror; he had a deadpan expression, hard to know if he was teasing. Fraser looked amused. She put on a classical music station, turned up the volume.

"I would have had you down for a Radio Four listener, boss," I said.

"No, no. There's far too much danger of hearing one of our pals from Scotland Yard crucifying himself and the entire force on Radio Four. I like to avoid that if I possibly can."

She leaned her head back on the headrest and when I glanced at her as we stopped at traffic lights, she had her eyes closed.

We turned up at the address at 09:00. Our man lived in a basement flat, in a shabby street in Cotham. From the looks of it, the street was mostly student flats, which had been carved out of a terrace of tall flat-fronted Victorian buildings. The Bath stone facades had probably been attractive once, but were now dirty and cracked in places. Not a single building looked well looked after. Wheelie bins littered the pavements or were crammed into the tiny areas that fronted the street. Most of them were disgorging overstuffed black bin liners. In front of our man's property, a bin for food waste had tipped over and deposited its rank contents on the threshold.

"Not a proud household then," said Fraser, stepping carefully around the muck in a pair of little heels.

We had to repeatedly press the buzzer to get an answer. Our man eventually buzzed us in through the communal door and we waited in the hallway for him to appear. Fraser flicked through the post that had been dumped on a hall table. Food delivery flyers littered the floor, and these, together with Fraser's shoes and lipstick, were the only sources of color in the drab space. The light was on a timer and clicked off just as he inched open the door to the basement.

"Edward Fount?" asked Fraser.

He nodded. Fraser introduced us. We produced our badges and he squinted at each one in turn. He was a slight man, with very pale skin and hair so black that it must have come out of a bottle. It fell in greasy tendrils around his face and made him look feminine.

He lived alone apparently. There were only three rooms: his bedroom, a corridor that was pretending to be a kitchen, and a room that must have been a bathroom if the smell coming from it was anything to go by.

"They don't like him," Fraser had told Woodley and me before we left. "The organizers of the fantasy meetings — the ones we've spoken to — are wary of this boy. He's a new member, and they don't know him well. And, on top of that, nobody saw him leave the woods on Sunday. Some of them say that he doesn't play by the rules, which is a cardinal sin in role-play apparently. Some of them complained that he's dirty too."

He was dirty. His body odor was powerful even before we stepped into his squalid bedroom, which had only one small window through which you could see a small section of the backyard: all concrete and the winter carcasses of rampant self-seeded buddleia plants.

The bed was a single, with bedding on it that had probably never visited a launderette. A desk, roughly constructed from bits of MDF, was the centerpiece of the room. It had a PC on it, and a dusty iPod dock, which cradled his phone. Music was playing: Celtic sounding, the lyrics in German. It wasn't mainstream. The walls were covered with posters and artworks depicting dark and bloody fantasy worlds.

Edward Fount sat down on the side of his bed and was unafraid to study us intently from behind his fringe. Fraser took the computer chair, adjusting it for wobble before she settled on it, crossing her legs. I saw Fount's eyes run down her calves and linger on her shoes, which were a dark maroon patent leather. Woodley and I stood against the wall. There weren't more than a few feet between us all.

"Does that window open?" said Fraser.

Fount shook his head. "It's painted shut. Doesn't matter, it's always cold down here anyway."

"You need ventilation," she said, "or you'll get sick."

"I take vitamins," he said. A feeble gesture indicated a tube of vitamin C tablets on his desk, beside a warped black plastic tray with the remains of a microwaved meal in it.

"Well, that's good," said Fraser. "It's important to take care of yourself."

Fount nodded.

"Especially, I'd say," she continued, "when you are out doing battle every weekend. Would I be right?"

"Not every weekend," he said. "Once a month. And it's not always a battle. It's a narrative, a storyline we enact."

" 'Narrative' is a very grown-up word, Mr. Fount, and so is 'enact.' I'm impressed. So tell me, what character do you play in these 'narratives'? I understand you all develop roles for yourselves, would that be right?"

"I'm an Assassin," he said. He knew she was toying with him now, there was nothing stupid behind those furtive eyes, but still he couldn't disguise the pride in his words.

"Uh-huh. And would Assassin be an important role in the game?"

"Very. It's very, very important. The Assassins lie in the shadows, they watch, they wait, they know secrets."

"Do they now?"

He nodded, his chin up, trying to assert confidence.

"And would an Assassin have a lot of power?" Her voice lingered mockingly on the sibilants.

"Yes."

"Would an Assassin be a match for a big man like, say, DI Clemo here?"

"Assassins have their methods. They're afraid of nobody and everybody fears them."

"That's very clever. Good for you. By the way, are you not curious to know why we're here?"

"Is it because of the boy who went missing?"

"You've shown a remarkable lack of interest. Why is that?"

"It's nothing to do with me. I didn't see anything."

"What happened to Benedict Finch wouldn't be one of your secrets then?"

"I never tell my secrets."

"And why's that?"

"Because they're secret." He laughed, a quick, high-pitched sound, a fish gulping air.

"Or is it perhaps because you're ashamed of them? You have a previous conviction for exposing yourself, don't you? I can understand why you'd like to keep something like that under your hat, or should I say under your Assassin's cape? Probably wise."

"I never did it."

"That's not what two little girls who were trying to play a nice game of tennis said. How old do you think they were? I'll tell you. They were eleven years old, and their nice game was interrupted by you sticking your wee tadger through the netting around the court, was it not?"

"It's not how it was. I promise."

Fraser leaned forward, fixing her gaze on Fount. "Did you see Benedict Finch in the woods on Sunday afternoon?"

Fount shuffled his backside across the bed until he was sitting with his back against the wall. He had a sharp Adam's apple and angry ingrown hairs along his jawline. He said nothing, but there was defiance in his expression.

"So did you?" asked Fraser. "See Benedict Finch in the woods on Sunday afternoon?" She hadn't looked away from him.

Fount crossed his arms. "I only answer to the authorities of my kingdom," he said.

Fraser snorted. "You've got three authorities in the room with you now; how much more authority do you want?"

"I only answer to the authorities of my

kingdom."

"How about: how did you get home from the woods on Sunday? Nobody saw you after three o'clock."

"You don't understand. I inhabit the Kingdom of Isthcar. I recognize the Isthcarian authorities only. Assassins answer only to the Knights of Isthcar, the Holders of the Hammer of Hisuth."

"What? What nonsense is that? You'll answer to us. Let me tell you something, you'd better grow up, young man, and you'd better do it quickly. We're investigating the disappearance of a child here. There are two facts we can't ignore: you were there, and you've got previous."

She stared at him until his eyes dropped. He picked at a frayed hole on the knee of his jeans.

"Can you tell us anything about what you saw?" I asked, inserting my words carefully into the stalemate that was brewing, although I felt like wringing his scrawny neck. "It would be very helpful."

Fount closed down his face. He wasn't going to talk.

"If I find out later that you know something that could help in the investigation, and you're not telling us, then you'll pay for that," said Fraser. She got to her feet. "Have no doubt about that. Right, we're finished here for now, but we're certainly not finished with you."

"You can see yourselves out," said Fount to Fraser's back. There was a hint of a smirk on his face. We paused at the bottom of the stairs when we realized Woodley wasn't behind us. He'd waited in the doorway of the room.

"Isthcar," he said to Fount. "Isn't that an ancient tribe? From Nordic mythology?"

"The finest tribe," said Fount. "The most noble."

"It sounds fascinating. Is the game very complex?" Woodley sounded impressed.

"To play properly, there's a lot you have to understand."

"Awesome," said Woodley. He said it simply, his voice light. "See you again maybe." He nodded at Fount, a man-to-man gesture.

"Bye," Fount said to him.

"What a prick," said Fraser. "It's meeting pricks like that that makes me actually look forward to getting back to my desk."

I knew that wasn't true. However high she'd climbed, at heart she was a street cop through and through.

We were in the car. Woodley and I had

pulled on our seat belts, we were ready to leave; Fraser was taking a few moments to rage. "I bet he wishes he was still sucking at his mammy's breast. What do you reckon?"

"I think we need to be careful. He's almost too much of a cliché, he looks so good for it on paper. Young, single male, all of that. But I think we need to be careful not to make assumptions about him."

She ignored me. "You know as well as I do that if there's a cliché there's usually a good reason for it. Christ! That little prick's given me a headache with his skanky flat and his self-obsessed, smug little bucket-and-spade ideology. He needs to get out of the sandpit and get into the real world. Knights of Isthcar, what's that about when it's at home?"

She sighed. She looked tired. She was putting in the hours this week, just like everyone else.

"I suppose it makes a change from asking for a lawyer. I feel like I've got something in my eye, have I got something in my eye?" Fraser pulled down the mirror and pulled down an eyelid.

"I don't think he did it," I said.

She flicked the mirror back up brusquely. "What makes you say that?"

"I agree that he looks good for it on paper,

but he couldn't take his eyes off your legs in there, and your . . ." I felt shy suddenly.

"My what, DI Clemo?"

"Your shoes, your red shoes."

"Oh right. Well, for a moment there I thought you were going to say something else."

Woodley snorted from the backseat and then tried to turn it into a cough.

"So what's your point, Jim?"

"My point is that somebody interested in children is not usually interested in women, especially not in a fetishistic way. He couldn't take his eyes off the red shoes. I was watching him."

"I still want him brought into the station. We can't possibly rule him out because he looked at my shoes. You know that as well as I do. Woodley, I saw what you did at the end there. Very smart. When we bring him in, I want you to interview him and get to the bottom of his dirty little mind whichever way it bends."

"Yes, ma'am." I could hear the sound of a grin in Woodley's voice.

"I'm not your 'ma'am,' " she said. " 'Boss' will do. Right, come on, Jim, what are we waiting for?"

Rachel

Halfway through the morning Nicky announced, "I've spoken to John. He wants us to go around to his house so we can agree together on a design for a 'Missing' flyer, and print some there. He's got a laser printer."

I'd never been to John and Katrina's new house. Not past the front door anyway. I'd spent plenty of time standing on the gravel outside when I'd dropped Ben off for the weekend.

"Will Katrina be there?"

"I expect so, yes, but at this point I think you need to think of her as another pair of hands. She wants to help and we need all the help we can get."

I thought of the blog and the comments I'd read this morning.

"Any port in a storm?" I said.

"Exactly!" she said, and she smiled just a little.

It pleased Nicky when I said that because it's what our aunt Esther used to say. "You'd been through a storm," she would say if we ever discussed the circumstances that had led us to live with her. "A terrible storm, and I was your port."

"A safe haven," Nicky would say and Esther would agree.

Esther had taken us in after our parents' death. She was our mother's much older sister. She brought us to her house immediately after the accident that killed our parents and we never left after that. She sheltered us from gossip, which sometimes hung around us like a cloud of biting midges. She gave us the chance to have a childhood, or her version of one.

It wasn't a usual upbringing, because Esther was a spinster, who'd always lived alone. She taught English literature A level to the children of the local wealthy at a small private school and could quote a huge amount of poetry by heart. She also played bridge and had a passion for growing roses. She wore knee-length skirts and flat shoes, with simple cardigans, and had bobbed flyaway white hair that she clipped back with bobby pins. She kept gold-topped milk in the fridge, which the birds had invariably pecked at before she brought it in in the morning, so each lid had neat puncture marks in it when it arrived on the breakfast table.

I don't think Esther was a naturally maternal figure. She was unaccustomed to young children apart from a regular annual visit she'd made to our family before our parents died, so when Nicky and I arrived suddenly in her life she treated us as miniature adults, and shared her passions with us. She surrounded us with art and music and books, she pointed out the possibility of beauty in life. Nicky drank this up as if it were nectar, and fell into Esther's arms gratefully.

I was different. When I was growing up I always felt like the baby that I'd been when we arrived there, a bit of an addendum to their lives, too little to understand things, always in bed when the proper conversations took place. It was ironic, as I'd never known our mother or father, that I was the one who found it most difficult to accept Esther in her role in loco parentis, while Nicky, nine years old when we arrived, wouldn't leave her side.

As a teenager I'd meanly thought that Esther was fusty, tweedy, and better suited to another era, more like other people's grandparents than their parents. I'd rejected her gentle offerings of culture and knowledge because they hadn't immediately bolstered me, or given me an obvious direction or purpose. That came later in life, when I took up photography, when I sat beside John in St. George's concert hall and fell in love with him and with classical music, and then I regretted that I'd never thanked her for what she did for us before she died.

It was because things hadn't always been easy when we were growing up that it pleased Nicky whenever I said a kind word about Esther. It pleased her immensely.

I agreed to go to John's house. Laura came around to house-sit because I still couldn't stand to leave it empty. Just in case. Nicky and I had to fight through the journalists to get to her car. They jostled us, shouted questions at us. We ignored them, but the questions hurt. They were aggressive, and accusatory. Some of the photographers ran alongside the car as we pulled away, lenses at the windows, snapping away at our white, scared faces.

John and Katrina's house was only ten minutes' drive away, on a quiet suburban street where everybody had driveways and two cars parked in them on the weekend. The house was semidetached, art deco in style, painted white, and had long, linear windows along the front of it, which would normally give a view into both their sitting room and office. When we arrived the curtains were drawn in both rooms, and there were journalists lounging on their low front wall like teenagers at a bus stop. They leaped to their feet at the sight of us.

John opened the door and ushered us in quickly. He looked disheveled, and he was unshaven.

"In the kitchen," he said.

"John," I said, before we stepped out of the hallway. "I'm so sorry about the press conference, so, so sorry. I didn't mean to . . ."

"It's OK," he said. "At least you didn't just cry like a baby."

It hadn't occurred to me that John might be berating himself for his own behavior. I'd thought mine so much worse.

"Don't be ashamed," I said, but he was already on his way into the kitchen.

Before I joined him I couldn't help noticing the parquet floor in the hallway, and remembered what Ben had said about it: "There's a shiny floor, but I'm not allowed to skid on it."

Katrina stood in the kitchen beside a small

round table. Like John, she appeared haggard and undone somehow. She was dressed in jeans, a T-shirt, a cardigan over it. She looked very young. She glanced at John as if expecting him to play host and when he didn't she asked, "Can I get anything for you? Would you like a cup of coffee? Or water? Or tea?"

It was awkward being in their house, I can't deny it, but together we made a flyer, and in some ways it was a relief to have something constructive to concentrate on.

Ben's photo was prominent in our design, as was the phone number to contact. The word "MISSING" ran along the top of the page. The plan was to print out one hundred copies there and then and Katrina said she would get more done at a local print shop. She and Nicky discussed how and where we should distribute them.

When we were done, Nicky said, "John, Katrina, do you mind if I ask, can either of you think of anybody who might have done this? Anybody at all?"

John's reply was curt. "I've told the police everything I can think of."

"Are you sure you can't think of anything odd at all, people behaving strangely around him, anything like that?"

Katrina said, "We've gone round and

round in circles talking about this, haven't we, John?"

He had his elbows on the table, his hands flat on its surface. It was almost a position of surrender. He nodded at her. "We have," he said. "And I can't think of anything." His eyes were so bloodshot they looked painful.

"It's the teaching assistant I wonder about," said Katrina.

"He only started this term," I said. "I don't know anything about him."

"Exactly," said Katrina. "That's what bugs me. We don't know who he is. He's an unknown quantity."

"Have you spoken to him?" I asked John.

"No. You?"

"Not once, he's never out in the playground."

John shrugged. "The police will be talking to everybody," he said. "They've assured me of that. I don't see what we can do."

"Anybody else you've thought of?" Nicky asked.

John had had enough. "Don't you think I haven't spent every second of every day going through this in my mind? I can't think of anything else that would help. God knows I wish I could!"

He slammed the flat of his hand down on

the table and it juddered.

"Of course," Nicky said. "I'm sorry."

In the silence that followed, Katrina stood up and began tidying up mugs. My eyes roved around, taking in John's new home. Their kitchen was white and shiny, the granite surfaces immaculate. The only sign of disorder in the room was a large pin board, covered with stuff. I stood up and went to look at it, lured over there by one image in particular. It was a drawing, made by Ben.

The drawing was of three adults and a child. Each person was named underneath: Mummy, John, Katrina, and Ben. We all stood equidistant from each other. Ben stood between John and me. "My family," he'd written above it, and on each of our faces was a smile.

And in that moment I realized that Ben had managed to do what I hadn't done, couldn't do: he'd moved on. I began to cry.

I felt an arm around my shoulders. It was Katrina, and what she said next made me think for the first time that she had a heart, and feelings of her own.

"Would you like to see his room?" she asked me.

"Yes."

She took me upstairs. On the landing, the

first door we came to had three colorful wooden letters on it that spelled out "BEN." She opened it and I stepped inside. "Take as long as you like," she said. She went back downstairs.

The room had been beautifully decorated. It was light, and fresh, with pale walls and striped bed linen. The bed was made up with care. The duvet had been smoothed and tucked in and somebody had carefully arranged three or four soft toys against the pillows, which were plumped up and welcoming.

The walls were hung with two framed pictures of Tintin book covers, Ben's favorite ones, and a Minecraft poster. There was a child's desk in the corner, and on it a stack of scrap paper, a container full of coloring pens and pencils, and a lamp, bright red, in the shape of an elephant. A half-finished drawing lay waiting to be completed beside the iPad that John had given me the day before he left us, but which had ended up belonging to Ben. It had felt impossible for me to deny him that, in the absence of his father, and he often left it at John and Katrina's house so that he didn't have to negotiate with them over computer use, because there was only one in the house.

A large rug covered the floor and there

was an electric railway set assembled on it, a train with carriages attached, ready to depart. A light shade, patterned like the moon, hung in the center of the room, and from it, carefully suspended on a thread, one above the other, hung three homemade paper airplanes.

I sat on the bed for a long time, until John appeared in the doorway.

"This room is lovely." I wanted him to know that.

"Katrina planned everything with Ben and she painted it herself."

There was no reproach in his voice, which he might have been entitled to, just a dreadful sadness.

I could see that an extraordinary amount of care and attention had gone into the creation of the room. It was painful to me to hear that Katrina had done the work, but not nearly as painful as the fact that Ben had never once described it to me.

"It's beautiful," I said, and I saw suddenly how I'd taken everything Ben told me about his life at his dad's and twisted it into a sordid, unhappy shape.

No skidding on the floor had meant that Ben wasn't allowed to play, and that wasn't the end of it. Every time Ben had come here I'd festered at home, and questioned him afterward, mining him for information that I could use to paint their marriage, and especially Katrina, in a negative light. I'd never allowed for the fact that Ben might have been happy here, that John and Katrina might have made an effort to make things nice for him, that she had, in fact, welcomed him with open arms.

Everything my son had told me, I'd taken and made into something unpleasant or sad, until he'd simply stopped telling me things. He was a sensitive child. He knew what upset me.

"I'm so sorry," I said to John, and he said, "I am too.'

I heard in his voice the self-blame that was my companion too.

"I keep thinking about how scared he must be, without us," I said.

"He misses you even when he's here, so God knows how he's feeling."

"Do you think he knows we're looking for him?"

"I'm sure he does."

They were words of reassurance, but John's eyes told a different story. I read in them a quality and depth of despair that matched my own, and that frightened me even more.

■ ■ ■ ■

When we got home, Nicky and I decided to park the car a few streets away and see if we could approach the house via the alleyway that ran along the back, avoiding the press pack. It was a narrow passage, not wide enough for a car, and occupied mostly by rubbish bins and foxes. It separated the ends of our gardens from the allotments behind. From it, you could directly access my garden studio, where I did my photography. Once in the studio, it was only a few meters across the garden into the house. Our garden wasn't big. There was just enough room for a small soccer net and a Swingball set.

Our gamble paid off because the journalists hadn't bothered to camp out there. As we squelched along, avoiding puddles, we saw it at the same time. On the fence panel facing my studio door somebody had been busy with a can of spray paint. In scorching orange letters, neon bright against the dull gray slats of wood, dripping in places because it was so fresh, two words had been sprayed: "BAD MOTHER."

When I sank onto the sodden, stony ground in front of the panel of defaced fencing, grit digging into my hands and my knees, Nicky knelt down beside me and coaxed me up. She took me indoors and phoned Zhang.

"Who would do such a thing?" I asked Nicky, but she just shook her head, and lifted her hands in a gesture of, Who knows?

It boiled over: the fear, and the anger, the frustration, and the terrible impotence I felt too. I was being persecuted. It was personal, and that was terrifying. And it wasn't just in cyberspace; it had come to visit me at home.

Some of my anger was directed at myself, because of Katrina, because I'd got it so wrong about her and John, because I'd been so bitter and so stupid that I'd forced Ben to lie to me. At eight years old, he'd felt he had to protect me from the fact that they had a nice life together, that they cared for him.

But my anger was mostly directed at whoever painted those words, because they made me feel very, very afraid.

In my kitchen, in front of Nicky, I threw a plate across the room and it shattered into pieces against the wall. Another followed it, and then a mug, some cutlery. I threw everything as hard as I could, and then I looked for more things to throw.

"Don't!" shouted Nicky. "Don't do this.

Please!"

She manhandled me. She took hold of me, gripping my upper arms. She sat me down on one of the kitchen chairs and she knelt on the floor in front of me.

"Where is he?" I asked her. "What's happening to him?"

"Don't," said Nicky again, her voice quieter this time, and her face close to mine. "Please don't."

I stopped resisting her, and I sobbed until my throat was sore and my eyes were swollen almost shut.

Jim

Fraser and I had a pre-meet before the whole team got together for the evening briefing. She was looking at her computer screen as I took a seat.

"Woodley's bringing in our friend Edward Fount of fantasy world fame in the morning," she said. "And Christopher Fellowes, the forensic chappie, has sent me a profile that we can use when we're considering the nonfamily abduction option. You'll not be surprised to hear that it's an almost perfect description of Mr. Fount."

"I still think he's not our man."

She took off her reading glasses to study me. "I know that, I take your point, but I can't dismiss him on a hunch. This isn't an episode of *Columbo.*"

In spite of everything, that made me smile. *Columbo* had been a favorite childhood show.

Fraser went on. "Can we run through who

else we're looking at? Rachel Jenner?"

"Chris emailed me his thoughts on her."

"He's been a busy boy today, which is good, because he's expensive enough. He should have copied me in on that. Can I see it?"

I got the email up on my laptop, winced a little in anticipation of her reading the first paragraph.

Email
From: Christopher Fellowes
<cjfellowes@gmail.com>
To: James Clemo
<clemoj@aspol.co.uk>
October 24, 2012 at 15:13

Re: Rachel Jenner
Jim
Thanks for your mail — good to hear from you. I've had a chance to watch the footage from the press conference. Would it be terribly wrong of me to say WHAT A COLOSSAL BALLS-UP? I hope it's not your neck that's on the line for that one, but somebody's ought to be. We'd worked up a good script for her. What a waste.

You wanted me to pull together some

thoughts about Rachel Jenner as a potential suspect. Seeing as we don't yet know whether this is an abduction, or a murder, I think the way forward for now is to keep in mind that these are very different crimes which throw up differing motives and therefore profiles. I've detailed these for you:

Family abduction

In my view this is only a small possibility in this case, because in the vast majority of family abductions a mother taking a child would keep the child with her, and both would travel somewhere where they felt the father would not be able to reach them or harm them. However, it is worth looking into whether other family members might have helped her to conceal the child, in order to keep him away from his father. Family abduction by a parent almost always takes place after a divorce where custody arrangements are disputed.

NB I am not excluding the possibility that another family member (i.e., somebody who is not a parent) could have taken Benedict, for motives of his or her own that don't relate to the ones I've outlined above. That would be a separate scenario entirely.

Filicide

Much more complicated, this. Generally there are a few different motives, not all of which are relevant to this case. The two most likely to be relevant to Benedict Finch's disappearance, in my view, are as follows:

Accidental filicide/battering — usually an impulsive act characterized by a loss of temper; often occurs in context of psychosocial stress and lack of support. Did she lose her temper with him in the woods? Or perhaps before they left home and hid his body somewhere en route?

Mentally ill filicide — complex, this one. Filicide often seems like a rational act to these women; older children more likely to be victims. A large percentage of these women are already known to social services or mental health services and have preexisting diagnoses that could include melancholia, manic depression, schizophrenia, or assorted character disorders. Munchausen syndrome's also worth considering here, in which case the family would certainly already be known to medical services, though probably unlikely if Dad is a medic.

Worth mentioning also two other categories:

Mercy killing — a murder committed out of love, usually to spare a child suffering, which could be caused by disease or perhaps the potential loss of a mother if the mother herself is contemplating suicide. It's not unusual for a parent or parents to take their own life simultaneously in this scenario.

Spouse revenge filicide — the killing of a child in "revenge" for something, often infidelity. The aim is to "get back" at the spouse.

Please bear in mind that these are first thoughts only but they should give you something to go on. I'd be on the lookout for custody disputes; previously existing psychological or psychiatric issues; previous involvement with social services; mother's predisposition to suicide; revenge impulses pertaining to her husband (did he cheat on her?); and check out her support network. No doubt you've done many of those things already.

I would need to come and meet Rachel Jenner if you want to progress these any further in terms of getting a detailed psychological picture of her. On the basis of what I saw in the press conference, she certainly possesses the capacity for uncontrolled outbursts of anger and a potential impulse for revenge (i.e., her threats to Ben's abductor).

Of course none of this rules out the possibility that the perpetrator of this crime (whether it be abduction or murder) is a nonfamily member — which DI Fraser and I have spoken about. I'm currently formally writing up my thoughts on that and will send directly to DI Fraser and cc you in on.

Please give me a call if you'd like to discuss.

Best, Chris
Dr. Christopher J. Fellowes

Senior Lecturer in Psychology
University of Cambridge
Fellow of Jesus College

"Forward it to me please, Jim," she said once she'd read it. "There's some good stuff in there. I'll edit and pass on to the rest of the team. We should also take note of his point about the wider family."

"The sister interests me, but that's all the wider family there seems to be. There's also a friend, Laura Saville, who Emma's met at the house."

"Has she been interviewed?"

"Not yet, but she's a priority. And on top of that the school has sent over a very long list of people that Ben could have had contact with."

"Anybody stand out?"

"I met with the head teacher and Ben's class teacher. They were very obviously stressed out, but trying to be helpful. The head's a little defensive, I'd say, it's obviously a nightmare for him, especially because he's only been in the job since the beginning of this school year. They raised one or two concerns about Rachel Jenner that you already know about."

"You mean the broken limb that the child had?"

"Yes, but I can't see any evidence of wrongdoing there. I do think she's been depressed though, that's pretty clear, and it might be the most significant thing from our point of view."

"Teacher?"

"Late twenties, I'd say, eager to assist, perhaps not the sharpest tool in the box, but seems perfectly nice. They're behaving like people struggling to cope in a difficult situation."

"Understandably."

"The only one who rang a few alarm bells was the teaching assistant."

"He's got an alibi, doesn't he?"

"He does, the head does, and the teacher does, and they all check out."

"So what rings bells for you?"

"He was just a bit shifty. Woodley thought so too."

"Who interviewed him formally?"

"I can't remember off the top of my head."

"Did they raise concerns, do you know?"

"No."

"Do you want to interview him yourself?"

"No. It's only a feeling, and I don't want to spook the school unless we've got a very good reason to. The headmaster sent over the full list of people Ben might have had contact with yesterday evening, and I think we should wait and see what that might throw up. There are at least twenty people on it, so it'll take time to check them out and interview them, but let's leave the teaching assistant alone until we see what comes of that."

"Agreed. We don't want another witch hunt on our hands. It's bad enough already. By the way, have you seen the blog?"

"Blog?"

But she was looking at her watch. "We should go. People need briefing. I'll talk about it in the meeting."

We walked into a packed briefing room and took our seats. Prominent at the head of the table was DS Martyn.

"Don't mind if I join you, do you, DCI Fraser?" he asked. He had an unusually low voice.

His presence at the meeting was a sign of how high profile the case was. He wore full uniform. His hair was curly but thinning so it looked like spun sugar. He had slab cheeks and a drinker's nose. He reminded me of some of my dad's friends. He was on his way to a function at the Marriott hotel, he told us, so he couldn't stay long.

His presence was a downer; it gave the meeting a formal edge, took away the conspiratorial atmosphere that Fraser usually managed to foster. She kicked things off. First bit of news was that there'd continued to be a high rate of calls to the tip line, so she was pleased about that.

Fraser talked people through progress and shared our thoughts with the room, told them about the stuff Chris Fellowes had sent over. She divvied out the workload and allocated actions. Priority was given to trawling through the list that the school had provided.

"Speak to as many people as you can," she said. "We need to form as clear a picture as possible of the networks around this child."

Fraser asked for updates and a sharp-faced DC called Kelly Dixon started us off. She told us that she'd located the pedophile. He'd been at a comic convention in Glasgow on Sunday afternoon, manning a stall. He hadn't been anywhere near Benedict Finch. He had, however, crossed paths with an incalculable number of under-sixteens during the course of the afternoon, a clear breach of the terms of his release, and as a result he was cooling his heels back in the cells.

"Jesus," said Fraser. "That's a result of sorts anyway."

The next item was the blog. If things had been bad for Rachel Jenner up to now, then it turned out that they were about to get worse.

"It won't have escaped anybody's attention," said Fraser, "that our victim's mother behaved in an unconventional manner at the press conference yesterday."

"Understatement," boomed DS Martyn.

Fraser tried to contain her irritation. "That behavior seems to have triggered somebody to write a very vindictive blog, which aggressively targets Rachel Jenner, implying that she is responsible for Ben's abduction, or worse. Woodley, would you like to explain?"

Woodley cleared his throat. His mouth was dry when he spoke. Nerves. "Normally we wouldn't expect a blog like this to attract very much attention," he said, "but the author has placed several links to it on Facebook, which has inevitably led to it being shared and mentioned on Twitter and retweeted over and over again. It's had thousands of hits."

He looked at Fraser, who said, "In English, please, for the older generation."

"It's gone viral," he said.

"Still none the wiser," she said. I saw Emma smile discreetly. We all knew Fraser was more IT-savvy than she let on, but there were others in the room who might need this spelled out.

"Everybody's looking at it. Thousands of people already, with the potential for it to spread to tens of thousands."

Fraser continued. "Right. Which means it's a possible problem for us because it could stoke people up, and the last thing we want is trial by Internet. We must remember: in spite of her performance in front of the press we have no evidence to suspect that Rachel Jenner's done anything at this stage, although if she's charged in the future, this is a potential contempt of court issue."

"Can we find out who the author is?" asked DS Martyn.

"Not easily," said Woodley. "It's somebody calling themselves LazyDonkey, but we've got no way of knowing who they are."

"We're monitoring closely for now, hoping things will calm down," said Fraser. "I'll get legal eyes on it if it's still a problem in twenty-four hours. Right! Anyone got anything to add?" She looked around the room.

"Excuse me, boss," Emma said. Her phone was vibrating. "It's Rachel Jenner's home number."

"Speak of the devil," said DS Martyn. His

fingers were working at a red lump on his neck.

"Can I take it?" Emma asked Fraser.

Fraser gave her the nod.

Rachel

Nicky phoned the police and then she and Laura scrubbed the fence. They wouldn't let me help them in case there were photographers, and I was in no state to anyway.

While I sat on the sofa, cocooned in a blanket to try to stop my body shaking, they worked together in the cold to erase the evidence that somebody out there wanted everybody to think that I'd hurt my son.

It was pointless though, a Sisyphean task, because while they scrubbed, fingers frozen and arms aching, we all knew that other people were at work elsewhere, spreading the message far more effectively, and without getting their hands dirty.

It has a very destructive effect, being publicly vilified, or being aggressively targeted by others, however much you rationalize it and tell yourself that only the worst kinds of people do that sort of thing.

I felt hemmed in by hatred, and I felt

physically afraid. If somebody was brazen and motivated enough to graffiti that close to my property, what would stop them going further? Would they break in? Would they hurt me?

Fear for Ben had inhabited every cell in my body since Sunday, and governed my every thought and every action, but now it was to be joined by something else: fear for myself.

Jim

While Emma stepped out to take the call from Rachel Jenner, the rest of the team murmured quietly. The biscuit tin had been emptied. Energy drinks were scattered around the table and people were rubbing gritty eyes. Bennett tried to cover up a monstrously large yawn with his case papers. We were all battling our ebbing energy levels and trying not to be disheartened by lack of progress.

Fraser summarized: “There’s two trains of thought here, a twin-track approach: family or nonfamily. Bear that in mind, please, everybody, as we go forward. The MOs are significantly different for each.”

She was interrupted by Emma returning. “That was the sister,” Emma said. “They’re frightened. There’s been some abusive graffiti on the wall behind the house.”

Fraser swallowed an expletive. “That is not what we need,” she said once she’d got her vocabulary under control. "How's the mother?"

"She's very upset apparently," said Emma. "As you would be. And frightened."

Fraser sighed. "We should respond to that. The only problem is that if we station somebody at the house, we'll need one out front and one out back."

DS Martyn shook his head. "We can't commit budget to that at this stage. Once you've got protection there, how do you take it away? What if this lad isn't found? We'd need the threat to escalate to justify it."

Fraser made a note. "I'll ask uniform if they can drive by throughout the night, and check out the back alleyway too, when they're there. It'll help if we're seen to take some action at least. The family need to know we're supporting them."

"Have they asked for protection?" Martyn again.

"No," said Fraser. "But I think it pays to preempt these things. If we take it seriously now we might head off a situation where they panic."

Martyn nodded, approving. Fraser's solution was neat and free. I wondered if he actually kept the department budget spreadsheets constantly running across the front of his eyeballs.

"Did they say what the graffiti said?" Fraser asked.

"It says 'Bad Mother,' " said Emma.

"Christ," said Fraser.

"I'm not surprised," said Emma.

Fraser's head snapped up. "And what exactly do you mean by that?"

Emma flushed deeply. "Sorry, I only meant that I'm not surprised because there's been such a backlash against her. That's all, boss. I didn't mean to insinuate anything."

"OK then," said Fraser. "I'm glad to hear it."

She shot an assessing look at Emma before moving on, and I saw Bennett's fat lips form into a sneaky smirk, which I could have throttled him for.

"Which brings me to the next thing, because I think it would be wise to inform the family of this in person too."

The next thing was a big disappointment to everybody. Forensics had reported that they'd found nothing of interest on the items of Ben's clothing that were discovered in the woods. Fraser felt it would be a good idea to send somebody to break the news to the family in person. With a glance at her watch, she sent Emma back out to Rachel Jenner's house.

"Better go now before it gets too late. It won't do their nerves any good if we go banging on their door in the middle of the night. You can take a look at the graffiti too, while you're there. Jim can update you on anything else we cover tonight."

I nodded, kept my eyes on my own notepad.

"And, Emma," Fraser added.

"Yes, boss."

"Keep up the good work. Your role is to observe, but also to support the family, so remember to be careful what you say."

"Got it, boss. I'm really sorry. I didn't mean to —"

"I understand," Fraser cut her off. "Go on, get out of here now."

As she left I noticed that Emma's cheeks were still flushed.

There wasn't much else. We discussed re-interviewing the parents but decided to hold on that for a day. In spite of everything, Fraser was still working up a head of steam about Edward Fount. She wanted further background checks on him, and she ordered actions galore: our team of DCs was tasked with talking to anyone they could dig up who was associated with him.

When all was done, Martyn reared up out

of his seat and gave us a short speech about teamwork and dedication and how important this case was and how the eyes of the nation were on us, and then put on his cap and left to attend the event for the great and the good at the Marriott.

One by one the team left the room, packing up papers wearily, some just moving a few yards to their desks, planning to burn the midnight oil. We were at that stage in a case where it's taken over: it's exhausting, it's addictive, and you can't get enough of it. Your nerves are frayed and you're running on adrenaline and caffeine. It's hard to do anything normal because the case is always in your thoughts. It's like a drug.

Fraser and I were the last to leave. She looked tired, and thoughtful.

"You OK, boss?" I said.

"I'm OK," she said. "Go home, Jim. Get some sleep."

RACHEL

Zhang arrived after Nicky and Laura had come back in, knuckles red and swollen from scrubbing.

She was there to break it to us gently that the forensic tests on Ben's clothing hadn't turned up anything. It meant that they couldn't get any specific leads from the clothing, she said, but they were still pursuing lots of "interesting avenues."

"What are those?" asked Laura.

"I can't tell you any more than that, I'm afraid," Zhang said. She took my hand. "But know that we're doing everything we possibly can. Don't lose heart."

She turned her attention to Laura. "I heard today that you're a journalist."

"I am." Laura wasn't afraid to look directly at her, but she twisted a bracelet on her wrist, a black silk band with a small jade rose on it. "Why do you mention it?"

"I wondered if that puts you in a difficult

position professionally. Being at the heart of things here."

"I write gossip," said Laura. "Who turned out to the launch of a new lipstick at Harvey Nichols, that kind of thing. It's a different world."

"Oh," said Zhang. She paused before asking, "Do you get lots of freebies?"

The tension in the room dissolved just a bit and Laura softened. "It's a perk — definitely. Though I sometimes wonder what I'm going to do with six bottles of black nail polish."

"Donate it to my daughters," said Nicky. "They seem to enjoy anything that's in incredibly bad taste."

After that, the silence was a bit awkward. Zhang started to excuse herself, she wanted to check the alley, but Nicky insisted that she have a cup of tea. Nicky was keen to share the plans she was hatching.

"I think we need a vigil," she said, "if he's not found by next week. It's what they do in America. It keeps public awareness up."

Desperate not to leave any stone unturned, Nicky had been in email contact with somebody who worked for the Missing Kids website in the States, taking advice on what we could do.

Zhang took a sip of her tea. Her mug was

one that Ben had decorated in one of those pottery places when he was very little. Covered in splotches of blue, in different hues, it was apparently supposed to be a sea scene. He'd been very proud of it when he made it, although now that he was a bit older he was embarrassed by it. "It's babyish," he'd said the last time I'd used it.

"I'm not putting it away, Ben," I'd replied. "I love it."

"You can obviously do what you want, but I'd be very careful about a vigil," said Zhang. "The press can be a law unto themselves. You don't know how they'll react, and we mustn't compromise the investigation."

"What would be very useful then," said Nicky, "is if we could arrange a proper meeting with the police, with yourselves, to discuss some of these things together, agree on a proper course of action. We don't want to do anything that would affect the investigation, but there must be something we could do to help."

"I'll ask," said Zhang. "I promise I'll ask. But be warned, everybody's already working all hours on the investigation, so manage your expectations, and for now it's best to keep channeling your questions through me."

Before she left, she went out the back to see where the graffiti had been. She stood in the glare of my neighbor's security light and looked at the newly scrubbed fence, where the words had gone but an orange wash remained. It struck me what a neat person she was. Alongside her warmth, she had a reserve about her and a sort of economy of both speech and dress that both impressed me and slightly intimidated me.

"I'm going to check out the rest of the alley before I go," she said. "We'll speak tomorrow."

In both directions the alley stretched out into darkness. We could hear scuffling behind the fence as something took cover. Farther away, the wind was making somebody's back gate creak and bang.

"Go back inside," she said to me. "Stay safe."

Jim

I did go home, but the flat felt hollow and cold, and I was unsettled. I called Emma.

"Where are you?" I said when she answered.

"I'm in the alleyway behind Rachel Jenner's house."

"And?"

"Well, they've washed most of the paint off, but you can see where the words were written in massive letters."

"How is the family?"

"Rachel's not good, she's really fearful. Looks ill actually. Nicky's holding the fort — she's tough that one, proactive, I like her — and they've got Rachel's friend Laura with them."

"Are you going back in with them?"

"I don't think I need to. They're coping for now. I'm cold, Jim, I need to get going."

"Are you coming round?"

"I've got to go and see John Finch, tell

him about the forensics."

"Afterward?"

"I'm so tired. I might just go to mine."

"Please, Em. I missed you last night."

She didn't answer right away. The line went bad as the wind whistled into her handset and it was hard to hear her when she said, "Are you sure it's a good idea, now that I'm working for you?"

"With me, not for me, and it doesn't have to make a difference, of course it doesn't. Please, come round tonight."

"I'll come round after I've seen John Finch, but I'm warning you I won't be good for much."

"Are you OK?"

"I hope I'm the right person for this job."

"Of course you are. Of course! Don't start getting wound up because of what you said at the meeting. Fraser knows you didn't mean it."

"The way she looked at me . . ."

"Honestly, don't worry about it. Don't. She'll have forgotten about it by now. I promise you. You are the right person for this job. You're tired tonight, that's why it all feels bad. Just remember why you're doing it: it's for the boy. Emma? Are you there?"

"Yeah. I heard you. It's for the boy."

"Are you coming round?"

"I'll see you in about an hour. Don't wait up."

After we spoke I turned on all the lights in the flat and put the heating up. Then I went to the shop around the corner and got supplies for breakfast, and a Mars bar, because Emma liked chocolate. I made a coffee and waited for her to arrive. I couldn't wait to see her, but I wanted her to be her normal self. I wanted her to tease me, take me out of myself, and make me forget work for a while. I wanted to hold her.

RACHEL

When I got back inside, Nicky held the phone out to me. "It's John."

"The nursing home rang," he said. "My mother's distressed because you didn't bring Ben to visit her today."

"Oh God."

I'd forgotten about Ruth. Ben and I made a regular weekly visit to see her in her nursing home. Spending time with her grandson was one of the only things she looked forward to.

"Does she know?" I asked.

"No." His voice was quiet. "I've asked them to keep her away from the media."

I knew it would be easy to keep Ruth away from the TV — she didn't have a television in her room, and she was fiercely dismissive of the communal areas of the nursing home, keeping to her own room mostly. She loved to listen to Radio 3, though, and I wondered how they were managing that. She'd be desolate without it.

John was one step ahead of me. He said, "They've told her that her radio's broken, and Katrina dropped off some CDs for her, and a player. It should keep her going for a while."

"You'll have to go and see her," I said.

"I can't see her." This said so quietly that I could hardly hear him.

"Well, one of us has to go. We don't have to tell her."

I wanted it to be him who went. I didn't want to have to look into Ruth's eyes and lie to her about Ben, but to tell her would break her heart.

"No. Don't ask me to," he said. "I can't."

"John!"

"I'm sorry," he said, and he hung up. I stood there with the phone in my hand, incredulous.

"How does he think I can deal with this any better than him?" I said.

"I'm not sure he's coping," said Nicky.

"Nobody's coping," I said.

"He's really on the edge."

"We're all on the edge."

"Don't argue." Laura tried to be peacekeeper.

"I just don't see why everybody has to be so worried about John."

"We ought to be thinking of him," said Nicky. "It's not just you who's affected by this."

"Oh and it's so hard for you with your perfect husband and perfect daughters safe in their perfect home?"

Nicky gasped. "That's just not fair."

She got up and left the room. I'd gone too far.

"She didn't deserve that," said Laura.

"I know."

"She's trying to help."

I knew I should apologize to Nicky, but I couldn't bring myself to. She came back down soon afterward, eyes red, but face composed.

"Rachel, I know this feels unbearable, but we're all on your side, and there are even people out there who are on your side too. The stuff online, it's not all bad. People are out there searching for Ben. People we don't know."

"They're organizing themselves online," said Laura. "Using social media."

"And the police are going to meet with us," said Nicky. "Don't forget what Zhang said earlier. We'll be working with them to find Ben. It'll give us the best chance."

She held my hand and squeezed it gently, but all I could think of was those people out there who hid behind online nicknames, or anonymous blogs, or found safety in numbers on the payroll of newspapers. I thought about how they'd started hunting me from the moment I went off message at the press conference, and I felt preyed upon. Just like my son.

Jim

On the night of Wednesday, October 24, after working all hours, basically until I was ready to drop, I dreamed of Emma and I dreamed of Benedict Finch too. I remember this because in the moment before waking properly, when the dream was most intense, I clutched her, pulled her to me, and expected her to understand why. She'd been in the dream with me, after all.

Instead I scared her. She yelped and sat up, confused by being woken abruptly.

"What?" she said. "What is it?"

I realized my mistake then. Her voice, her actual real voice, chased the shadows of the dream away.

"Sorry," I said.

She relaxed, fell back onto the pillows, and looked at me with sleepy eyes. She said, "You look exhausted," and then, "What time is it?"

I'd forgotten for a moment that dreams

are private.

The dream starts at Portishead lido, where I'm meeting Emma for a coffee in the café. I sit down opposite her. We're the only customers. Across the room, among a host of empty tables, there's one that has a RESERVED sign on it. Outside, the water in the Bristol Channel looks gray and squally under clouds that are darkening, filthy, and low. I feel as if we're in the last place on earth. I crave a cigarette.

"I like it here," says Emma.

"Really?" I say. "I feel as if I'm in an Edward Hopper painting."

She laughs. "*Nighthawks?* I know what you mean."

"Something like that," I say. I don't know what the painting is called, just that it shows a stark bar, only four people in it, muted colors, and a big dose of bleakness as its theme.

"You don't like it?" says Emma.

"No, it's fine. It's nice."

Emma starts talking fast. She's brimming with ideas that spill out of her and bounce off in different directions, as if you'd tipped out a basket of tennis balls and suddenly they're bouncing everywhere at once, their individual trajectories too fast and too random to track.

Her dark eyes flash and dart, and her skin is a soft, dusky brown. Her lips are full. In repose, her face is symmetrical, perfectly proportioned. When she's animated she looks intelligent, intense, and engaging. When she smiles it's surprisingly mischievous.

As she talks, Emma disentangles the string of her tea bag from the handle of her cup and dances the bag up and down. It releases dark curlicues of flavor that creep through the hot water and mesmerize me. I'm enjoying the moment, loving her company, but my cozy trance is broken abruptly by a silence that's weighted with suspense, like a breath held, because Emma's stopped talking, and she's fixated on the table that's on the other side of the café, the one that's reserved.

"Jim," she whispers. "He's right under our noses. Look."

I turn and I see him too. Benedict Finch is sitting a few feet away from us, and I realize that the table was reserved for him. He's wearing his school uniform, just like in the photo we put out of him. He's a really beautiful child.

I get up, but my motion is retarded, and I can't move toward him as quickly as I want to. The air around me is viscous and intolerably heavy. Where my bones should be I feel only weakness, a confusing absence of strength.

While I make only a few paces of progress, Benedict Finch stands up and peels off his school sweatshirt and top, and then his trousers, shoes, and socks. He's wearing swimming trunks. He smiles at me and says, "I'm going to take a dip," and still I can't move any faster. I haven't even covered half the ground between us.

Benedict Finch strolls toward the doors that separate the café from the pool outside, and disappears through the glass, ghostlike. I reach the doors just after him but I'm trapped behind them. I hear Emma say, "Jim, we've got to get him. I don't think he can swim."

Outside Benedict Finch is standing on top of a very high diving board. I don't know how he got there because I can see that it's been cordoned off, and the ladders removed. I bang on the doors, I shake the handles, and I shout until I'm hoarse, but Benedict Finch, bold as brass, jumps, and it's then that I realize the worst thing of all, which is that there's no water in the pool. None at all.

And I can't look. I pull Emma into my arms.

Of course then I wasn't dreaming any longer. I was awake, and I'd woken Emma up and I had to say sorry and I told her it was three o'clock in the morning and she should go back to sleep.

She didn't though. After a while, she said, "Jim? Are you awake?"

"Yes."

"I'm bothered by Rachel Jenner. There's something about her."

"What do you mean?"

"She's unstable."

"I know."

"Even her sister seems to treat her like she's made of china or something."

"What's your point?"

"I don't trust her."

"Do you think she's harmed Ben?"

"I don't know. It's just a feeling right now. But I think she could have."

"Trust your instincts. Talk to Fraser about it, and keep your eyes peeled when you're with the family. If Rachel Jenner's done something she might well let it slip."

"I am already. I will."

I reached over and ran my hand up and down her arm, then let it rest on her skin, which was always perfectly soft. I felt myself getting drowsy, but after a while Emma got up. "Where are you going?" I asked, and she said, "I can't sleep. I'm going to read for a bit next door. I'm fine. Go back to sleep."

After she left, I was asleep again in moments, my hand resting on the warm spot on the bed where she'd been.

■ ■ ■ ■

Day 5
Thursday,
October 25, 2012

■ ■ ■ ■

You and law enforcement are partners in pursuit of a common goal — finding your lost or abducted child — and as partners, you need to establish a relationship that is based on mutual respect, trust, and honesty.

— "When Your Child Is Missing:
A Family Survival Guide,"
Missing Kids USA Parental Guide,
US Department of Justice, OJJDP Report

WEB PAGE — www.whereisbenedict finch.wordpress.com

WHERE IS BENEDICT FINCH? For the curious . . .

FOOD FOR THOUGHT
Posted at 04:47 by LazyDonkey, on Thursday, October 25, 2012

On Monday, October 22, police discovered a bag of clothing in
Leigh Woods near Bristol.
They belonged to Benedict Finch.
According to his mother, they were the clothes he was wearing when he disappeared.

That's why police haven't issued a description of what he's wearing.

Because they don't know.

Because they've got to take the mother's word for it.

Would you?

Rachel

I slept the night in Ben's bed again, inhaling the perfect smell of him, worrying that it was fading away. I couldn't think of sleeping anywhere else.

When I woke up my body ached, crying out for proper sustenance, which it hadn't had for days. I could feel my hip bones protruding where they hadn't before, my stomach concave.

My eyes drank in what they could in the dim light before dawn.

I could see Ben's posters, his *Doctor Who* figurines, the silhouette of his piled-up boxes of Legos.

I could just make out the dark stain on his carpet where he'd left a felt-tip pen with its cap off and I remembered how cross I'd been with him when he did it.

It had been our first week in the house, one of the first weeks in years when I'd had to wonder how I was going to pay for everything, now that I wasn't cushioned by John's salary. I'd shouted at Ben, and he'd cried. Had he thought, I'd raged at him, how many hours somebody would have to work to pay for a carpet like that? Had he? Did he realize what life was like for most people? I'd been so angry.

The memory was a sharp pain. It made me sit up and pull a cushion to myself, hunch over it, and cry with great gulping sobs. It made me detest my previous self-absorption and shallowness. It made me wonder whether I'd been everything I could be to Ben, especially in the past year. Whether I'd let him down terribly, filtering his needs through my own, letting my anger and depression seep between us, where it shouldn't have been.

I couldn't forgive myself.

It was a noise from outside that got me out of Ben's bed to stand at the window. It was the creak of a fence, the thump of a landing. In my back garden was a man; he was standing in the shadows, beside my studio, half concealed by shrubbery, but only half. He wore a dark coat and a beanie hat. A camera obscured his face, its long lens trained on the back windows of my house. Kitchen first, then a slow tilt up toward me.

He was scavenging, like the fox. I stepped back, snapped Ben's bedroom curtains shut. From behind the curtain I pounded on the window.

"Get out!" I shouted. "Go away!"

My sister ran into the room. She moved me aside and peered through the curtains to see the shadow of him disappearing over the fence into my neighbor's garden. The stairs rumbled as she rushed down and outside to confront him, but he'd gone.

Out front the rest of the press pack feigned ignorance. As I watched, standing back from the window in my own bedroom, shaking from cold, Nicky went out into the street in her rosebud-print nightie, hair greasy and wild, nipples on show, goose bumps on her flesh, and told them what she thought of them.

"You are vandalizing our family!" she shouted and her words echoed up and down the quiet street, interrupted only by the mechanical dawn chorus of the camera motor drives.

JIM

Sometimes on a case you get a bit of information that feels electric, like static under the skin, especially when it's very unexpected.

I was awake before six a.m., feeling bruised from my dream at first, because it had lingered with me into the morning and gotten mixed up with the tiredness I felt, and the disappointment that we weren't making as much progress as we'd have liked.

But that didn't last long, because I checked my phone and saw an email that had just arrived very late the night before from one of the blokes we had digging up background on people.

It was a new bit of information, and it changed what we knew about somebody close to Benedict, and to be sure that I acted on it properly, I knew I had to damp down my feeling of excitement and follow procedure. I had to make sure I did things right.

So in order to do that, I had four conversations before I paid a visit to Rachel Jenner's house that morning.

6:15 a.m.: FRASER

I paced around my bedroom, waiting for her to answer. She picked up quickly.

"Jim," she said. "I'm hoping there's a good reason for this. You do know I bite the heads off orphans before I've had my first coffee?"

"Nicola Forbes," I said.

"What of her?"

"She hasn't been entirely honest with us. Understatement."

I gave her a synopsis.

"OK, you've got me interested. I'll see you in my office in an hour."

"If you don't mind, boss, I'll go and talk to John Finch first."

"Do you think you should talk to Rachel Jenner first?"

"My feeling is that she doesn't know about this."

"OK. Keep me posted."

6:45 a.m.: EMMA

I was up and dressed by now, one espresso down, and the Bialetti foaming on the stove again already, because although I was more fired up than I had been for days, I'll admit I was feeling my lack of sleep just a touch, and I needed to drive that feeling back, so I could stay on the ball completely.

Emma was on the sofa and groggy as hell, her forehead all scrunched up as she tried to fight her way back to consciousness from a deep sleep. I knelt down beside her, whispered that I'd made her a cup of coffee, and held it near her face so she could smell it. When she'd managed to open her eyes, I filled her in on what I'd learned. That woke her up properly, like a shot of adrenaline straight into the arm.

7 a.m.: Ex-DI TALBOT

Ex-DI Talbot was the man who'd sent me the information. Officially, he was retired, but now and then he came in to work on cases as a civilian when extra bodies were needed. We always wanted him on a case because he was a proper bloodhound. He'd been digging into background on the individuals closest to Ben, and he'd stumbled on this information about Nicola Forbes. I wanted every detail from him. I wanted to hear it from him directly; to be sure I hadn't misinterpreted his email.

■ ■ ■ ■

8:30 a.m.: JOHN FINCH

The last was John Finch. When he opened the door to his house he was in checked pajama bottoms and a crumpled T-shirt, a pair of reading glasses pushed up onto his head. His knees buckled and I realized I should have called ahead.

"I'm sorry, sir," I said. "There's no news on Benedict's whereabouts just yet, but if you wouldn't mind, I would like to have a word with you about Nicola Forbes."

He regained his composure impressively well. The man had nerves of steel. By the time his wife had reached the bottom of the stairs in the hallway behind him, wrapping a white dressing gown around herself, he had pulled the door open farther and invited me in graciously.

Rachel

Nicky opened the door. It was midmorning, and DI Clemo was standing on the doorstep with Zhang.

"Is there news?" Nicky asked. It was all any of us ever seemed to say to each other. It was starting to sound pathetic to me, as if we would be punished just a little bit more each time we asked it, as if there were a vengeful God somewhere up there, counting each display of misplaced optimism.

There wasn't any news. Clemo said that they were here to "have a chat," though something in his tone of voice suggested otherwise. It made me feel wary, but Nicky seemed oblivious to it.

"I could have used a little bit of notice," she said, "to get properly prepared for you, but I'm delighted you've made time to talk. We're so very grateful. We've got so much to ask."

She pulled some papers together, and

tapped at her laptop, looking for a document.

"Here it is," she said. "I've got a list here. It's roughly broken into two categories: questions we have about the investigation and suggested actions to help in the search for Ben. Do you have a preference for which we should start with? And how would you like your tea? Or would you prefer coffee?"

I was watching Clemo and Zhang. He was waiting for Nicky to finish. Zhang looked at her notebook, which she'd laid neatly on the table in front of her, then glanced sideways at Clemo. Whatever they were here to say, he was going to be the one to say it, and I was becoming certain that it wasn't to discuss Nicky's wish list.

"Coffee, please," he said. Zhang wanted some too.

As Nicky filled a French press with boiling water and set it down in front of us, Clemo watched her in a way that made frost settle on my skin.

"From our point of view," she said, "this is so valuable. I've been doing some research, as you can see" — she smiled at them — "and everywhere it says that there's a much higher chance of success in finding the child if there's a close relationship between law enforcement and the family.

So — thank you. So much. Help yourselves to milk and sugar." She set down a sugar bowl and a small china jug. Steam rose from its contents. She'd warmed the milk.

DI Clemo opened his notebook and had a quick look inside it. He closed it again. Nicky finally heard the silence.

"I'm so sorry," she said. "I'm gabbling, aren't I? Sorry." She pulled out a chair, sat down, and looked attentively at Clemo and Zhang.

Clemo cleared his throat before he spoke. "Do either of you know of a couple called Andrew and Naomi Bowness?"

I shook my head. "No."

"Nicky?" he asked my sister.

Her face had emptied of color, instantly. It was extraordinary.

"Oh God, no," she said, and the tendons on her neck appeared stretched and odd as she looked first at me and then back at Clemo, searching our faces for something. She stood up abruptly but didn't seem to know what to do then.

"This will be easier if you can sit down and talk it through with us," said Clemo.

"No," said Nicky. "Don't do this." Her hands were clasped together, the edges of her fingers white from the pressure of her grasp.

"Please sit," Clemo insisted.

She didn't sit; she crumpled back into her chair, as if he'd sunk his fist into her stomach.

"What about their son, Charlie Bowness?" asked Clemo, in a tone that seemed carefully controlled to sound light. He adjusted his chair, moving it just a little closer to Nicky. She wouldn't look at him.

"Nicky?" he asked. "You know who they are, don't you?"

"You know I do," she whispered.

"And you?" he asked me. "Do you know?"

"I've never heard of them," I said.

I was transfixed at the sight of my sister so vulnerable and defenseless. I was aware that I should probably move, and go to her, but there was a ghastly momentum in the room now, and it felt unstoppable.

"She doesn't know," said my sister. "She hasn't got a clue and that's the way it should be." Hatred had crept into her voice, and it was directed at Clemo.

He persisted. "And what about Alice and Katy Bowness? Do you know who they are?"

Nicky began to shake her head violently.

"Alice and Katy Bowness," he repeated. "Do you know who they are?" He spoke slowly, giving each word space and a weight, as if it were a rock being dropped into water.

She looked right at him, and it seemed to cost her an enormous effort to do that. Defiance and defeat waged war in her expression. She spoke her next words quietly. "I know who they are."

"Have you heard of them?" he asked me.

"No!" I said. "Who the hell are they? Have they got Ben?"

"Are you sure you haven't heard of them?"

"No! She hasn't! She's telling the truth," said my sister.

Clemo remained impassive. He contemplated me, and then my sister, in turn. I felt my chest tighten.

"Will you tell her, or will I?" he said to Nicky.

"You bastard."

Zhang started to speak, but Clemo held a hand up to silence her.

"Careful," he said to Nicky.

"You're frightening me," I said. "I don't understand."

Nicky turned toward me. I was sitting at right angles to her, at the head of the table. She wanted to take my hand and I let her.

"Who are these people?" I said.

"Andrew and Naomi Bowness . . . ," said Nicky. It was hard for her to go on. A sob escaped her. "I'm sorry, Rachel," she said. Her gaze flicked back to Clemo and he nodded at her, willing her to continue. She placed one trembling hand upon the other, so that my hand was buried beneath both of hers. I saw in her eyes that some kind of battle was lost.

"Rachel," she said, "Andrew and Naomi Bowness are our parents. Our mum and dad."

"What do you mean? No, they're not. That's not what our parents are called." I tried to pull my hand away but Nicky was gripping it now.

"It is. Those are the real names of our parents," my sister said. Her eyes were begging me to understand but I didn't, not really, not yet.

"And Charlie Bowness?" I said.

"He . . ." She was welling up again, but she got herself under control. "He was our brother."

"Brother?" I'd never had a brother. "And the others? I suppose they're our sisters are they?"

"Tell her everything," said Clemo.

He'd broken Nicky, drained the fight out of her. In her expression I saw terrible suffering, terrible vulnerability, and, most frightening of all, what looked like a plea for forgiveness.

"Alice and Katy Bowness are us. Those

were our names before they were changed. We were, we are, Alice and Katy Bowness."

Clemo briskly pulled something from between the pages of his notebook. It was a newspaper clipping.

If he hadn't showed it to me there and then I'm not sure that I'd have believed any of them. I'd always been told that my parents died in a car accident. You could tell the story in an instant and I'd been doing that for years: our parents died in a head-on collision with a lorry. It had been nobody's fault, just a tragic accident. The steering on the lorry was proved to be faulty. My parents were cremated and their ashes scattered. There was no headstone. End of story.

Except that apparently it wasn't.

I wasn't who I thought I was, nor was Nicky.

Clemo handed me a photocopy of a newspaper article from March 30, 1982, thirty years ago. There was a photograph of a couple that I recognized as my parents. My aunt Esther had had one photograph of them on her mantelpiece and this grainy image showed the same two people. The difference was that in this image they were with three children.

I recognized my sister. She stood beside

our mother. I could see a baby, a chubby little thing of about one year old in a smocked dress, and I supposed that she could be me. I didn't recognize the boy who sat in the middle of the picture. Around four years old, he was so like Ben it took my breath away. He had the same messy hair and balanced features, the same posture and the same grin, the one that could light up your day, and the same smattering of freckles across his nose. He was nestled between my parents. It was a lovely image, a perfect family.

The headline beside it told another story:

BATTEN DISEASE FAMILY IN
FATAL DEATH LEAP

I scanned the article, snippets of it jumping out at me: "Local couple Andrew and Naomi Bowness leaped to their deaths . . . driven to the act by lack of support for their terminally ill son . . . no grandparents surviving . . . friends and neighbors expressed surprise . . . had coped so well . . . feel sorry for their two surviving daughters . . . wanted to end his suffering."

I looked at Nicky, who was watching me, stricken.

"They killed themselves?"

"And Charlie."

The way she said his name, the tenderness in those two words, the loss, told me that it was Charlie who she mourned above all.

"But what about us?"

Nicky looked away.

"Why did they leave us?"

"Don't you think I've been asking myself that all my life?"

"And why didn't you tell me?"

She didn't answer.

I looked at the article again, and stared at the photograph.

Clemo cleared his throat. "There was a report from the coroner. Would you like to know what it said?"

"I've read it," said Nicky.

"I want to know," I said.

He took another sheet of paper from his notebook, ran his eyes down it.

"It says that your brother, Charlie, was diagnosed with Batten disease at the age of five and that his condition began to deteriorate rapidly after that. His diagnosis came about a year after you were born, Rachel, at around the time that this picture was taken, but he was already experiencing some of the symptoms."

"He looks OK in the photo," I said. He

did. He was lovely: sunny-looking, vibrant, snug in his family's embrace.

"He's not," said Nicky. "He was beginning to lose his sight. Look at the photo. You'll see that he's not looking at the camera properly. He's looking above it. It's because he only had peripheral vision when that was taken. He had to look out of the bottom of his eye to see anything."

She was right. The little boy was staring at a point that was above the camera.

"He was totally blind soon after that," Nicky said. "And then he stopped being able to walk and stopped being able to talk, and he had to be fed with a tube because he couldn't swallow and he had epileptic fits. The disease took him away from us piece by piece."

"You loved him."

"I worshipped him."

Her words seemed to hang for a moment between us, and when she spoke again it was hushed.

"He didn't deserve it. I would've helped them. I would've helped them to look after him until the end, but they couldn't stand his suffering. Mum blamed herself."

"Why?"

"It's an inherited condition."

"But we don't have it." I was struggling to

understand.

"Not every child gets it. It's a matter of luck."

"So they jumped off a cliff with him? That's so extreme."

Nicky simply nodded. She'd turned her head away now, and I could only see her profile, as she looked fixedly toward the dim winter light that filtered through the kitchen window, washing her features with gray.

"But why would you do that if you had two other children?" I asked.

Clemo replied, "The coroner's report does shed a bit of light on that. Apparently, because the condition was inheritable, they had had you tested. They were waiting for the results when they took their lives."

"But I'm fine," I said. "Why didn't they wait for the results?"

"Your mother had convinced herself, and your father, that you would not be fine. By then she was, as far as we can gather, extremely depressed and unstable. She told her sister, your aunt Esther, that she would not be able to cope any longer if you were also diagnosed with Batten disease, and your father had never coped well. The report mentions that she spoke of feeling very isolated. There was a stigma to mental and physical disability in those days and your mother was not very strong emotionally. The coroner concluded that the strain of caring for Charlie had affected your parents profoundly. They felt that they had no option."

"It makes no sense."

"Things don't always make sense," said Clemo, "especially when people are under duress. We see things you wouldn't believe."

I resented the way he was trying to reassure me, as if he hadn't just turned my world upside down, and I didn't want his words to distract me, because there was something else I needed to ask.

"Why did our names get changed?"

Nicky said, "Aunt Esther thought it would be better. She didn't want it to be hanging over us, or herself either. She thought people would judge us, that they'd say it was a shameful thing. Luckily, for us anyway, the Falklands War started four days later, so that article was all the press attention our little family story got. The papers were full of battleships and submarines after that. Better to be safe than sorry, though, Esther said, and social services approved the idea of having new names. I chose them, you know! I renamed us!"

She forced a sarcastic enthusiasm into her voice but there was nothing in her expression to suggest that this fact actually gave her any pleasure.

I picked up the article and studied the photograph. I'd never seen an image of myself as a baby before. I was chubby-faced with a curl in my hair that I never knew I'd had. I was balanced on my father's knee, with fat little arms protruding from my dress. My hands were blurry, as though I might have been clapping. My sister stood beside my mother in the photograph. She wore shorts and a T-shirt and her hand rested casually on my mother's shoulder. Her feet were bare and she had the skinny coltish legs of a prepubescent child. She was smiling widely. When I studied the faces of my parents I felt a new emotion: a stab of betrayal. They'd been willing to leave me. Whether I was healthy or ill, they'd relinquished care of me at just one year old. They weren't taken from me by chance. They'd abandoned me and they'd abandoned Nicky too, in the most final way possible.

I swallowed and just that small physical reflex felt like an effort. I felt as if the blood had drained from me, just as it had from my sister minutes earlier, and with it any strength that I might have had left, any fight. I was a husk, robbed of all the things that had made me who I am, all the things that had made me vital.

"Am I Alice or Katy?" I asked.

"Katy." It was a whisper, and Nicky's face contorted tearfully around it, mirroring mine.

In the photo, my parents' expressions were impossible to read. They were both smiling for the camera and I tried in vain to imagine what was actually going through their minds. I looked at my brother. He sat in the center, cocooned by their bodies: a terminally ill little boy who was never going to get to live a proper life. I wondered whether they'd had the diagnosis before this photograph was taken, or were they just worried about his eyesight at this stage, thinking that was bad enough and having no idea what horrors lay just around the corner for their little boy. A boy who looked just like Ben.

I said to Clemo, "Why are you telling me this now?"

He addressed Nicky. "We spoke to your sister's ex-husband this morning."

She looked at him warily and raised her chin slightly, with a touch of defiance. She let go of my hand. The light in the room fluctuated, growing darker and more riddled with shadows as the clouds lowered outside.

"I know what you're going to say, and it's

bullshit," she said.

"What makes you say that?"

"I know what you're trying to do, but you're wrong."

"What am I trying to do?"

"I don't have to listen to this."

"I think we both know that you do."

She crossed her arms, stared down at the table.

I sat in a state of pure, simple shock. I knew well enough by now that you could lose your child in just a few minutes, but I was shocked into silence by the new knowledge that in a similar space of time you could also gain and lose a brother who was the image of that child, and parents who were more imperfect than any version of them that I'd ever imagined.

Clemo spoke to Nicky: "John Finch told us that when Ben was born, he was concerned that you might have what could be described as an unhealthy interest in Ben. Would you like to comment on that?"

"You revolting man," said my sister. "You haven't got a clue who's got Ben so you've decided to pick on me. Easier to get to someone close to home, is it? Stops you having to do so much work?"

Clemo's gaze never left her face. "Would you care to comment?" he asked her. "I'd be very interested to hear what your response might be."

"I'm sure you would," she replied.

"I expect your sister would as well," he said.

Nicky looked at me. "I've tried so hard, and for so long, to protect you. I just wanted you to have a life where you didn't feel rejected. I wanted it to be straightforward for you. But you were so . . ." She searched for a word, frustrated.

"What?"

"Difficult, and ungrateful."

"For what? Ungrateful for what?"

"And irresponsible! You never understood anything. You just took it all for granted. You did what you wanted to do, when you wanted to do it. You had no burden. You had no loss to bear."

"I had the loss of my parents to bear." I said this quietly, because I understood that she'd had more to cope with, but she was angry now, and so was I.

"You were clueless! Totally clueless!"

"How could I have been any other way, if you didn't tell me anything? That's not my fault."

She didn't respond to that; she had more to get off her chest. "You never thanked me."

"For what?"
"For protecting you."
"How could I have known?"
"They never thanked me either."
Suddenly she lost her momentum, as if that statement summed up the hopelessness of it all.
Clemo leaned in toward her. "Who never thanked you?"
"Mum and Dad."
"What did they never thank you for?" he asked.
"For loving Charlie, for watching him when they'd had enough, for making him smile when they were too tired, when they couldn't cope any longer."
Her eyes were glassy with loss. His were intent.
"Nicky. Were you jealous when Rachel had Ben?"
She snapped an answer at him as if he were running through a questionnaire.
"Yes, I was jealous, yes."
"But you had the girls," I said.
"I wouldn't expect you to understand," she said.
"Why were you jealous?" said Clemo.
"Because he looked like Charlie, right from the start. All I could see when I looked at him was Charlie."

"Did you feel that Rachel might not be able to care for Ben properly?" said Clemo.

"I was worried," she said simply, and she turned to face me. "You were so feckless, you know, so young?"

My sister spoke as if she'd rehearsed these words for years. Her speech gathered pace, as if she were confessing something.

"You messed about for years, you never bothered with schoolwork although they said you could have done brilliantly if you'd tried. You never cared about anything, and then all of a sudden you got John. God knows how, because you were pissing your life away, partying all the time, and suddenly everything was so perfect and what had you done to deserve it? Nothing."

"We fell in love," I said, but she took no notice. She couldn't seem to stop herself now.

"I knew you'd have a boy the minute you told me you were pregnant. And when he was born and I went to see him and I held him, I saw Charlie in him. It was as if he was Charlie, reborn. He was so precious, and I wasn't sure you'd be able to look after him."

"So you called John Finch," said Clemo.

"Just to check that she was coping, that she was doing the right thing."

"Mr. Finch says that you were rather insistent with your phone calls."

"Well, he wouldn't give me any information!"

I interrupted them. "John never said anything to me."

They ignored me, their eyes were locked, Nicky's gaze furious, his eyes hard like ice; their terrible dialogue unpicking yet more of the stitches that had held my life together. I was relegated to the role of spectator.

"Nicky," he said, "did you want to have Ben for yourself? So you could look after him properly?"

"That's the thing," she said, "I didn't. I didn't want her to have him, but I didn't want him either. He would just have reminded me every day of what I'd lost, and that's why you're wrong.'

"Wrong about what?"

"For pity's sake!" She laughed. It was a shrill, upsetting sound. "Stop playing games with me! What would I do with him? Where do you think I would keep him?"

"I think you might like to have him. I think you've always wanted him."

The baldness of this, the slow, calm way he said it, made my sister pause and collect herself before she spoke again, as if she realized she couldn't combat his accusations with emotion alone.

"Well, you're not sure, are you? If you'd got any actual evidence you'd have arrested me, so this is a pathetic attempt to get me to confess to something I haven't done."

Now she leaned across the table toward him.

"You made me tell my sister about our family. That was low. You're not getting anything else. I've told you that I've got nothing to do with Ben's disappearance and that's all you need to know. The rest is private. Why don't you get out there and start looking for him before it's too late?"

She got up and went into the garden, slamming the kitchen door behind her. Zhang went after her.

I was left sitting at the table with Clemo.

He cleared his throat. "I'm sorry to land this on you like this. I hope you understand that we have to follow everything up."

I just stared at him, wondering why anybody would ever do a job like his and believing for the first time that he would do anything it took to find Ben.

JIM

Addendum to DI James Clemo's report for Dr. Francesca Manelli

Transcript recorded by Dr. Francesca Manelli
DI James Clemo and Dr. Francesca Manelli in attendance

Notes to indicate observations on DI Clemo's state of mind or behavior, where his remarks alone do not convey this, are in italics.

FM: So if you're happy to, I'd like to talk about your interview with Ben's mother and his aunt.

JC: Fire away.

His manner is hard for me to decipher today. He seems more willing than usual to talk but he has a professional mask on too, he's controlling his emotions.

FM: What an extraordinary revelation. I find it amazing that Nicky Forbes could have kept that information from her sister for all those years.

JC: It wasn't just her; it was their aunt as well.

FM: How did Rachel Jenner react?

JC: Total shock, obviously. I don't know what happened just after we left, but I can't imagine it was pretty.

FM: Am I right in thinking that this was a real moment of triumph for you in the case?

JC: Fraser was pleased. Yes. Especially because they'd ruled out Edward Fount, the role-play guy, that same morning.

FM: So you were right about him?

JC: Yep. When Woodley went to pull Fount in — this was while I was with Nicky Forbes — he found him waiting with a woman, another role-play member, and she gave Fount an alibi. They'd gone back to Fount's flat together after the afternoon in the woods — shagging basically, if you'll excuse my language — and in spite of the fact that she was nearly twice his age.

FM: And neither of them had mentioned this before because?

JC: Oldest reason in the book: she was married, to the "Grand Wizard" apparently.

FM: Oh my.

JC: Yeah. A bit messy. I won't repeat what Fraser said when she found out.

He almost smiles.

FM: So you were able to move on from that line of investigation.

JC: Absolutely. Fraser was happy with how things had gone, but she had concerns about how we should handle Nicky Forbes going forward, so she felt that the best course of action would be to reinterview her the following day. Give her and Rachel Jenner time to cool off.

FM: Did Nicky Forbes have an alibi for the Sunday afternoon?

JC: She'd told us that she was at a food fair. A big event, lots of stalls, very busy. It was research for the blog she writes. We sent out DCs to interview all the people she might have had contact with, but they were scattered far and wide, as you might imagine, so we knew we'd need a little time to put together a picture of her movements.

FM: Did you speak to her husband?

JC: Again Fraser felt we should wait on that just a short while. Her strategy was to look into the alibi first, and give the family space while we worked out whether Nicky

Forbes could actually be good for it or not.

FM: Did you agree?

JC: Absolutely. You've got to fit the pieces into the jigsaw in the right order. Gathering evidence is the single most important objective when you have a suspect. That, and not being sued by your victim's family. You can't just apply continual pressure without evidence.

FM: Or you could alienate the family?

JC: Exactly, and they could talk to the press, and so on. You can imagine it and it wouldn't look good for us. The press had jumped all over the case by then and they'd have been only too ready to have a go at us as well. And, on a practical level, we were nowhere near understanding how the mechanics of an abduction could have worked if Nicky Forbes had carried it out. She had a family in Salisbury so her setup didn't look like the perfect profile for a child abduction.

FM: Unless she didn't want her sister to have Ben, and she'd killed him.

JC: That was one of my hypotheses, and abductors don't always kill on purpose, sometimes things go wrong and it happens then, but we had to build a proper case before we could act further. I asked

Chris Fellowes, the forensic psychologist, to send me his thoughts on Nicky Forbes.

FM: But the profile that your forensic psychologist made for you, the one that fitted Fount so perfectly, hadn't been much use.

JC: I disagree — we were still considering the nonfamily abduction as a strong possibility, and that profile could have fitted any number of suspects for that scenario. The thing about the profiles is that you shouldn't just attach them to one suspect. They're a resource that you have to use as part of your armory as a detective. Profiles never solve cases on their own, but they can make you think in different ways sometimes, or look at people in a new light. And it's always good to have another pair of eyes on the case, especially when everyone closely involved is getting tired. You can be in danger of losing perspective.

FM: What was Emma's view on Nicky Forbes?

JC: To be honest, I didn't see much of Emma that afternoon. I was too busy holed up with Fraser making a plan.

FM: Did you see her that night?

JC: She said she was knackered. She wanted to go back to her place to get a proper night's rest and I didn't blame her for that. I was feeling that way myself. I could have slept on my desk.

FM: But I get the sense you were fired up too.

JC: I was, yes. We all were. Without a doubt. It felt like things were starting to happen.

Rachel

The immediate aftermath was the first in a series of new body blows.

Nicky swept everything up from the table, all her hard work, gathered it hastily, and tried to push it into her bag. Her movements were rough and clumsy.

"Don't," I said. "Please don't."

I felt as though she was falling apart right in front of my eyes. I wondered if that's what it had been like when she first went to Esther's, to live in the cottage, right after it happened, when I was a baby, when her grief must have been unbearable.

And I realized that in the future I would wonder about everything.

From now on it would be impossible to unpack every detail of my history, every assumption that had led to me building a sense of my own identity, and of Ben's identity. My past had been crumpled up and thrown into the fire, and I would have to sort through the ashes, with only Nicky as my guide. Nicky, who had lied to me for a very long time; Nicky, who said that she'd lied to protect me; Nicky, whom I needed.

"I should leave," she said. "You're better off without me. You know, I would never, ever hurt Ben. Can I just say that? I would never hurt Ben."

Her distress pushed her voice to an acute pitch, and I went to comfort her.

"I know you wouldn't."

She let her bag slide down her shoulder and onto the table, and the papers spilled back out of it. Her head fell onto my shoulder and her body shook.

Are you surprised at my reaction to her? At my willingness to accept what I'd heard and offer her comfort?

It wasn't the end of it. Of course it wasn't. If I think back to that day I can remember the stages I went through. I suppose it was like the stages of grief, although this was different. This was the processing of what felt like a betrayal, this was the seeping away of trust.

After the door had clicked shut behind an adrenaline-pumped Clemo and a Zhang who couldn't meet my eye for the first time, that first interaction Nicky and I had was of course a reflex, an urge to keep Nicky by me, to deny that anything had changed. She'd been my rock, always, and I couldn't contemplate any other existence. It wasn't in my DNA. Or I'd thought it wasn't.

After that exchange we separated. Nicky unpacking her bag robotically, calling on those massive reserves of strength to anchor her to my table, to keep her going as she delved deeper and deeper into whatever the web had to offer her.

I went to my safe place, to Ben's room, and I immersed myself in him, as was my habit. It was the only place I felt secure. His bedroom had become my womb.

This was my second stage.

I sank onto the beanbag on the floor of his room and I felt as if I had been cast adrift in a small wooden boat, shrouded by a watery gray mist. And suspended within each of the millions of fine droplets that made up the mist was the news, the bombshell that I'd just heard. And in this stage it simply surrounded me, existing, but not yet understood. And within it I felt baseless, disorientated, and lost.

The third state was the inevitable churning of my mind, the processing of what I'd learned, and of its implications, the moment the droplets of mist began to settle on my skin and permeate it. It was when the knowledge became part of me and it was irreversible. I had to face up to it.

It led swiftly to the fourth state.

That was the erosion of my trust, where the droplets on my skin turned to acid and began to burn, producing a feeling that was intense and painful, a pins and needles of the mind and the body, and it was so creepy and unsettling that I couldn't remain still any longer.

I got out of Ben's bed and looked out of the window, and I saw Nicky below in my garden with the dog, petting him, encouraging him to pee. They stood on the soggy, shaggy lawn by the abandoned relic of Ben's soccer goal, the net broken from the frame in places, the grass in front of it worn from where he'd played. I backed away from the window, not so that the press wouldn't see me, but so that my sister wouldn't.

And as dusk fell again, wrapping itself around the edges of the day, I ran back through events, until I thought about how I had started the day: the photographer in my garden, Nicky's anger with him, her outburst on the street, her loyalty.

And then I thought about the previous day, and how it had started with an Internet search, and with a laptop that belonged to

Nicky, that needed a password, and how that password was the name of my son.

And each intake of breath felt sharp in my lungs and my mind roved further and I thought of Nicky's discontent with her daughters, and what Clemo said about her wanting a son. And then I thought of her words: "It was as if he was Charlie, reborn."

I began to cry hot, silent tears, and they had sharp edges just like my breath did, and they ran down my cheeks and soaked into Ben's nunny, which I held tightly to my face.

When I heard Nicky's footsteps on the stairs I got into Ben's bed, covered myself up, turned away from the door, and tried to breathe slowly so she would think I was asleep.

When she put her head around the door of the room and asked if I wanted any food I didn't answer her.

When she reappeared some minutes later with a tray of supper I still couldn't look at her, couldn't speak to her.

"I just wanted to protect you," she said.

She shut the door quietly behind her, respecting my privacy, and all I could feel was a throbbing. It was the pulse of the time since Ben had been missing. And it felt as if it had begun to beat faster.

Jim

Email
From: Christopher Fellowes
<cjfellowes@gmail.com>
To: James Clemo
<clemoj@aspol.uk&gp;
October 25, 2012 at 21:37

Re: Nicola Forbes
Jim
Good to speak. Fascinating development!

I'll send you a full report tomorrow but, as agreed, here is a précis:

Psychological markers for predisposition to sociopathic behavior in Nicola Forbes might include any of the following: tendency to control; affective instability (which could include jealousy and identity diffusion); unnatural interest in Ben

— you've already mentioned this as a possible, if father is to be believed. Other generalized signs might include obsessive-compulsive spectrum behavior (OCSD) and/or delusional beliefs (though these can be well hidden).

She's certainly been quick to be on the scene, which could indicate that she enjoys the attention that the case is bringing the family (just speculation, but maybe an unresolved desire from her earlier experience, which was handled so discreetly by the aunt?).

There's more — I'll follow up asap with a full report. It'll be with you end of tomorrow, latest.

Best, Chris
Dr. Christopher J. Fellowes
Senior Lecturer in Psychology
University of Cambridge
Fellow of Jesus College

Email
From: Corinne Fraser
<fraserc@aspol.uk>
To: Alan Hayward
<alan.hayward@haywardmorganlaw.co.uk>

Cc: James Clemo <clemoj@aspol.uk>; Giles Martyn <martyng@aspol.uk>; Bryan Doughty <doughtyb@aspol.uk>
October 25, 2012 at 23:06

Blog Warfare

Alan

We're in need of your services, as the weird and wonderful worldwide web is once again involving itself in our police work. Could you cast your keen legal eye over this blog please: www.whereisbenedictfinch.wordpress.com

You'll see that it relates to the Benedict Finch case (Operation Huckleberry).

I've got two primary concerns.

First, there could be contempt of court issues, should we ever get to trial.

Second, there's stuff appearing on there that's making me nervous because it shouldn't be in the public domain. We're concerned that somebody within the investigation (either family or within our organization) could be authoring the blog or leaking information to it.

What I want to know is, can we find out who the author of the blog is, the self-styled "LazyDonkey," and what do we need to do to get it shut down? Is that even possible?

I'm copying this to DS Martyn and Inspector Bryan Doughty from Internal Affairs.

Quick response appreciated, obviously.

Cheers, Corinne

■ ■ ■ ■

DAY 6
FRIDAY,
OCTOBER 26, 2012

■ ■ ■ ■

Cases involving child victims are not only burdensome from an investigative standpoint, but are also emotionally exhausting. Law enforcement agencies are commonly tasked with the simultaneous pursuit of multiple, time-sensitive avenues of investigation, often with inadequate resources (i.e., financial, logistical, manpower).

— M. C. Boudreaux, W. D. Lord, and R. L. Dutra, "Child Abduction:

Aged-Based Analyses of Offender, Victim, and Offense Characteristics in 550 Cases of Alleged Child Disappearance,"
Journal of Forensic Sciences, 44(3), 1999

WEB PAGE — www.whereisbenedictfinch.wordpress.com

WHERE IS BENEDICT FINCH? For the curious . . .

NOTHING TO WATCH?
Posted at 05:03 by LazyDonkey, on Friday, October 26, 2012

This blog wants to recommend a television program to you:

Go to: http://www.itv.com/jeremykyle

You could try:

Episode 198:
I can't trust you with our son! You spend all your time texting instead of watching him.

Or you might enjoy this:

Episode 237:
Admit you're a bad mom and you can't look after your children.

Just a thought. Up to you.

Oh, and one more thing:

Did you know Benedict Finch fractured his arm last year, and his mother didn't get it treated? He must have been in a lot of pain. Guess she wasn't bothered. Or perhaps she was just busy doing something else.

Rachel

First thing in the morning, facing each other across my kitchen table in our dressing gowns, our eye contact patchy, the air between us oscillating with tension, Nicky told me that she was going to leave.

"I think we probably both need some time," she said. It was a quiet statement, and a very controlled one, but it was also damp with the undercurrent of what we'd been through the day before.

"Just for a day or two, then I'll come back. Will you be OK do you think?"

I had to clear my throat before replying in order to moderate my own tone and maintain the perfect neutrality of our exchange. The alternative was shouting, or weeping, or accusation, hastily spat out. After spending the night imagining darkly, now the sheer reality and familiarity of my sister's presence and her own attempt at composure kept me in check.

"OK," I said. "That's fine."

"It's the girls," she said, turning away, slotting bread into the toaster.

"Of course you should go." And I did feel a twinge of guilt then, because Nicky's girls needed her too.

Steam billowed up from the kettle and settled in a moist coating on the front of one of my kitchen cabinets. Skittle dragged his cast laboriously across the floor and flopped heavily onto my feet. Nicky burned her toast and I watched her back as she took it to the sink and used a knife to scrape the black crumbs from it with sharp motions. They fell in a layer of coarse powder.

"Cook some more," I said.

"I wanted to leave some for you."

"It's OK, I'll have —" I started to say.

"You need to eat, Rachel!" It was an outburst, her composure splintering abruptly, and she dropped her toast and the knife into the sink and leaned heavily on her palms on the edge of it, so that her shoulders became sharp points on either side of her bowed head. She looked up at the window and the darkness outside meant that her reflection was razor sharp in the glass and our eyes met in that way. She was the first to lower her gaze.

"Sorry," she said. "I'm sorry. Can I show

you something?"

It was an email that had come from America during the night. Via the Missing Kids website, Nicky had contacted another family whose child had been abducted and they'd replied to her, a message of support.

"Read it," said Nicky. "They understand."

She handed me her laptop. Two pages were up: one her blog, the other her email. I couldn't help noticing that she'd updated her blog:

> Dear Custard & Ketchup friends and followers,
>
> This is a heartfelt request for you to please bear with me just for now. I'm sorry to say I need to take a short break from blogging for family reasons. I was hoping to keep you busy with some new Tasty Halloween Treats, but that hasn't been possible. If you're looking for Halloween ideas my post from last year is available still and you'll find lots of fun stuff to make and decorate there. Next to come: Christmas Cheer! Watch this space, I'll be back as soon as I can . . .
>
> Nicky x

She saw me reading it. "Simon posted that. He updates it for me sometimes," she said, and then, "I'm wondering whether we should do a web page for Ben. I could link to it from the blog."

I didn't know what to say. I looked at my sister's blog quite frequently, usually with some awe, especially at its mythologizing and professionalizing of family life. It was like a glossy food magazine, an enviable social diary. It was not my world.

I clicked on the email instead.

Email
From: Ivy Cooper
<ivycooper@brettslegacy.com>
To: Nicola Forbes
<nicky_forbes@yahoo.com>
October 25, 2012 at 23:13

Re: Ben
Dear Nicky
BRETT'S LEGACY "DO SOME GOOD"

This is a time of tremendous pain for you and your family. We are praying for Ben, and for your family.

Our son Brett was taken from us seven years ago, and since then we've been through things that we never thought we would have to experience. Before he was taken from us, one of Brett's favorite things to say was, "Mom, let's do some good," and we decided to make this a choice for our future, so that we could offer some help to other families who find themselves in the same situation.

We made this decision five years ago, soon after Brett's body was discovered, and . . .

I stopped reading. I looked at my sister. "What happened to Brett?" I said.

"Have you read it all? Read to the end, you must. They actually understand what it's like and it's such a relief, honestly, I can't tell you what a relief that is. I've been struggling so much to find anyone out there who knows what —"

"What happened to him?" I had to know. I didn't like the email. I didn't want to be part of this club: a family of devastated families. I wasn't ready for that. Ben was going to come back to me. I wasn't going to be like them.

"It's not relevant."

"It's relevant to me."

"Brett died," Nicky said. "Unfortunately."

"How did he die?"

"Rachel."

"How did he die?"

"He was murdered, by his abductor. But that's not the point, and they would never have found out what happened to him if the family hadn't worked really hard to get the police to pursue the case."

"Ben's coming back."

"I hope he is, God knows I do, you know I do" — she was twisting a tea towel tight between her hands — "but we have to accept the possibility that he might not be back soon, that some harm might have come to him. It's been six days."

I couldn't hear it. Not from Nicky. Not from anybody. Not now. Not ever.

"I'm going to see Ruth," I said.

"I'm sorry," she said. "This wasn't how I wanted this morning to go."

Jim

When you work a case like this one, you long for a lead. When you get one, you're all over it, and that's how I felt about Nicola Forbes. I'd been ready to chase her to the end of the line.

What you don't expect is for something else just as strong to turn up, because then it's a bit like being in a shooting range, trying to decide what to aim at, what's a decoy and what's real. Friend or enemy? Where should your sights land?

You can't always tell straightaway, but sometimes you are presented with a clear and immediate threat, and it's obvious that you must respond to that.

That's what happened on day six of the case. The letter arrived, and it changed the game completely.

It came in the morning post. Postmark BS7, addressed to Fraser directly, at Kenneth Steele House. Fraser's secretary opened it. Her scream could be heard out in the corridor at the far end of the incident room, and she bolted out of her office.

Fraser pulled us in immediately. The letter was in an evidence bag by then, and the secretary was already having her fingers inked next door so we could eliminate her prints. She was shaking and tearful, an extreme reaction for somebody who regularly got to file crime scene photographs.

'Jim," Fraser said once we'd closed the door behind us. "Get John Finch in."

Emma was there too. She didn't look as though she'd slept. Under her makeup her skin was dull and strained. To anybody else she probably looked more or less her usual self — a tired version of herself, of course — but I could see a few extra small signs of disarray. Her hair wasn't tied up as neatly as usual, and her shirt didn't look fresh. You can do that if you want to know every inch of somebody better than you know yourself. I wanted to put my arm around her, ask her if she was coping, but I couldn't of course. Not there, not then.

Emma's phone rang just as Fraser finished filling us in. She glanced at it. "It's Rachel Jenner, boss," she said. "Should I tell her?"

"Nuh uh," said Fraser. "Not a word, not yet."

Rachel

Zhang agreed to come and give me a lift to the nursing home. She drove carefully and we didn't talk.

Sitting beside her in the silence, I felt, for the first time since Ben had gone, a sort of awakening, an impulse from within, which told me to lift my head up from the sand, to stop burrowing into my memories of Ben, and instead to look around me, to be more alert.

I needed to consider people, to assess them, as a detective might, as Clemo might, and I needed to do it now. I'd placed my trust in my husband and my sister in the past, and both of them had proved themselves unreliable.

I needed to consider my assumptions about life too.

I'd also placed my trust in the veneer of a civilized society, the lie that is sold to us daily, which is that life is fundamentally good and that violence only happens to those who warrant it; it tarnishes only the trophy that's already stained. That's the same logic as the age-old accusation that a raped woman somehow deserves it, and based on that, without questioning it, I'd trusted that if Ben ran ahead of me in the woods, then he would come to no harm, because I believed myself to be fundamentally good.

And, worse, the betrayal had been a double one because Ben had also put his trust in me, in the way that children must, and so I'd failed him as well as myself: abjectly and possibly finally.

I looked at Zhang's hand on the wheel, her knuckles white as she gripped it firmly at ten to two, and I realized that beyond my first impressions I hadn't before thought about who she really was, or what she might be like.

"Do you have a family?" I asked her, as the car idled at a junction.

"I have a mum and dad," she replied.

"I mean children of your own?" Though as I said it, I realized she was probably too young.

"No." She shook her head. "I won't have children for a while, if ever."

"Oh. You know that already?"

"I do."

"Can I ask why?"

"Because I'm not ready to be responsible for somebody else's life yet."

She said it so simply that it gave me a frisson of shock because I realized that she already knew what I was only just working out — that we should look very carefully indeed before we leap, or believe, or trust — and that this younger woman had recognized that before I did only made me feel more foolish.

I didn't know how to respond so I fixated on what was around me. Outside, the sky was the kind of gray that looks perpetual and heavy, and the clothing of the people in the street was flattened against them by a strong wind. I retreated back into silence and the slow unfurling of the thoughts in my head, where I was starting to doubt everything I ever thought I'd known.

There was one consolation at that moment when everything weighed unbearably heavily and when suspicion was beginning to edge into every corner of my mind. It was that I was on my way to visit Ruth. I desperately wanted to see her because she was one of my favorite people in the world. Ever since Ben was a baby, she'd been a reassuring presence in my life, offering me gentle, unconditional support, and our friendship had grown alongside him.

Life hadn't been easy for Ruth. To those who didn't know her she would appear dignified, proud, and fragile, always chic in a uniform of dark clothes with a scarf neatly tied at her neck, a silky flash of color. As a young woman, she'd had the talent to be a concert violinist, but she'd also felt things so deeply that they could wound her.

Her violin playing had captivated John's father. "I fell in love with her the first time I saw her play," Nicholas Finch would proudly tell everyone, in his Brummy accent. In fact, most people who'd heard her play were entranced. She'd trained and performed on the instrument for years, but ultimately found public performance an intolerable pressure, and as a result, when she was in her twenties, shortly after marrying John's father, she'd sunk deeply into the first of many bouts of depression that she suffered throughout her life.

I first met Ruth in early 2003, a good year for her. She and Nicholas were enjoying his retirement. After a long career as a GP, which had kept him working all hours, finally having him around had helped Ruth remain stable. They were planning to buy a small apartment in the Alps, and they'd taken a successful trip the previous year to Vienna, to see the buildings and neighborhoods that Ruth's parents grew up in. Lotte and Walter Stern had been musicians too, both successful and well-respected performers before the war, but they'd become refugees, driven from Vienna after Kristallnacht, when Lotte Stern was heavily pregnant with her daughter.

In the summer of 2003, John and I made our first visit together to his parents' home in Birmingham. I found Ruth and Nicholas charming and welcoming. Their contrasting personalities intrigued me. Nicholas was a big, warmhearted man with a kindly, relaxed manner, which had won him many friends among his patients during his years as a GP. His bonhomie was the opposite of Ruth's nervous disposition, but she welcomed me cautiously.

Ruth's mother and father both died in 2004, and she took it hard. As a tribute to them, she preserved many of their traditions long after their deaths. Lotte Stern had kept a special white tablecloth just for making the delicate strudel pastry that she took much pride in. Ruth kept the tablecloth, and more than once made what we called "Lotte's strudel" with Ben, asking him to stir the filling while she showed him the methods she used to stretch and roll the wafer-thin pastry.

In fact, it was the tiny Benedict Finch, only six pounds, thirteen ounces when he was born in July 2004, who brought Ruth back to us after her parents' death. She adored him instantly. She opened her arms to him and never wanted to let him go, and to all of our surprise, she included me in that embrace. Right after Ben's birth, she came to stay and she helped me through the difficult first weeks and months, and then she never stopped helping. She became a companion to me, a friend, and a wonderful grandmother to Ben.

John told me a story about Ruth once. It was a rare confidence about his childhood that he told me just after I'd met her. I think he wanted to explain her to me. It was a story that showed her darkness and her light.

When John was about nine years old, he'd gone to see Ruth after school. It was during one of her periods of depression, and he was ushered quietly into her darkened bedroom to show her a prize that he'd won that day.

Ruth examined his certificate, and then propped it up on her bedside table. She patted the bed beside her. It was a rare invitation and John sat down carefully, desperate not to break the moment, daring to do nothing more than glance around the room, which the drawn curtains had given a chiaroscuro quality, so it felt to him as if he and his mother were drawn characters in a children's book.

"Where I am weak," she said to him that afternoon, "you can be strong. Like your father."

She held his hand tenderly, examining with the tips of her fingers each of his. He remembered that sensation. Then she spoke to him of music. John explained to me that when Ruth was drained of life, she seemed always to have music left in her, and it was this that was her gift to him, even when she lacked the energy to get him up, make his packed lunch, or take him to school in the morning.

After sitting with his mother until she was too tired to talk anymore, John left her room with his little heart beating, relieved to escape her intensity yet longing for more of it.

When we arrived at the nursing home, Zhang said she'd wait in the car.

Ruth was in her room. It was a generous

size, one of the nicer rooms upstairs, with large windows overlooking a garden and some mature trees below. It was a thousand times nicer than some of the gray and murky spaces we'd looked at before placing Ruth here.

Those homes were like holding pens, where residents waited for death with little more status than corpses. Loneliness, confusion, pain, and the smell of urine and boiled food seemed to be their only companions as the light faded on their lives. Those places had made me shudder, and sometimes weep.

Carpe diem was the lesson to be learned. It's what I had been trying to teach Ben when I let him run ahead in the woods. Seize the day — be brave — be independent — be thoughtful — don't be scared to make mistakes — keep learning — all of those things, all the time. And somebody had taken him. More fool me.

Ruth's chair was turned to face the window. Her hand rested on its arm, her arthritic knuckles gnarled and inflamed, her fingers resting at unnatural angles. Macular degeneration was starting to steal her vision, and she had to keep her head at a sideways angle to see me properly. Somebody had done her makeup; there was rouge on her waxy skin, a smudge of the bright lipstick she'd always favored.

Classical music was playing softly and I was relieved to see that it was a CD as John had requested, and there was no sign of her radio so there was no chance of her hearing about Ben on the news.

"Rachel," she said. "Darling." She reached for my hands with her own and cupped them stiffly, a favorite gesture of hers.

"Where's Ben?" she said. "I missed you on Wednesday. People think I know nothing anymore, but I do know when it's Wednesday."

She was putting a brave face on it, attempting to maintain her dignity, but I knew from her carers that her agitation had been more extreme than she was letting on. She was also more lucid than I'd expected, and I didn't know whether to be grateful for that or not.

"He wanted to try chess club," I said. "I was planning to bring him over here after it finished, but he was feeling poorly when I collected him. I'm sorry. I should have phoned."

"You should have," she said. Manners mattered to Ruth. "I thought it was half-term, that I'd forgotten, I'm a little forgetful nowadays you know," she told me, as if this were news, as if I hadn't been minutely tracking the destructive progress of her dementia since her original diagnosis, "but Sister told me she was sure it was next week."

I'd forgotten that half-term was about to start, of course I had.

"What was wrong?" Ruth asked.

"He had a sore throat, a bit of a temperature, I think it was a virus."

"Should he be back at school? Is he wrapped up warm?"

"Yes," I said, and the lie felt as though it might wind its way around my throat, and tighten.

"Is he working hard?" she said. Her eyes were milky, and the impotence of her condition wandered around their depths. "At the hospital?"

She was confusing Ben and John. It happened often, and I went with it.

"Not too hard. He's doing well."

"He must practice, when he's better, because when he is big enough and good enough he must have the Testore."

The Testore was Ruth's violin: a beautiful instrument, made in eighteenth-century Milan, her most valued and valuable possession.

"He's not showing any signs of growing

out of his half-size yet," I said.

"No, but he will. They do, you know." A half-smile played on her lips, a memory, and then died away again.

"What's he playing?"

"Oskar Rieding. Concerto in B minor."

"The whole thing?"

"Just the third movement for now."

"He must be careful with his bow control. In this passage in particular."

Ruth began to hum the Rieding concerto, her hand beating time. She had an extraordinary memory for music. Each note she'd ever played, or taught, seemed to have found a place to lodge in her head, all its resonance still alive to her. She'd started Ben on the violin when he was six, insisted on paying for his lessons. He was showing promise, some of the musicality that had traveled from Vienna, through her family, and that thrilled Ruth.

She stopped abruptly. "Have you got that?" she asked, as if I was her pupil myself.

"Yes. I'll remind him."

She pulled herself forward. Her dress shifted over her skeletal knees, catching on the surgical stockings that she wore on her calves. I noticed a small stain on her pretty yellow scarf. On a table, just within her reach, a shiny golden sweet sat in the middle of a crocheted doily. Her hands scrabbled uselessly to grasp it, but I knew better than to offer to help because that would have upset her. Finally, her fingers got a purchase on it.

"For Ben," she said. "I saved it."

On the rare occasions that Ruth took part in the communal activities in the home, she was ruthless about acquiring the sweets that were sometimes offered as prizes. She hoarded them for Ben.

"Thank you," I said.

She went through the same rigmarole to reach something else, a book. She passed it to me. "Look at this. I got it from the library. Does it remind you of anything?" A smile passed across her lips, a rare sight nowadays, usually bestowed only on Ben.

I took the book, ran my hand over its shiny cover, and felt the dog-eared edges. It was a monograph, and its subject was the artist Odilon Redon.

"The museum," I said. "When we took Ben to see the dinosaurs and ended up looking at the paintings."

"Yes!" she said. "I've marked the page. Can you see?"

I opened the book where she'd inserted a bookmark. It was a garish yellow strip of leather with a design of the Clifton Suspension Bridge embossed in it in gold. Ruth didn't have many ugly possessions, but this was one of them and she kept it because Ben had bought it for her on a school trip.

"We looked at the William Scott painting first, do you remember?" said Ruth.

I did. It was a huge canvas, wall-sized, with an ink-black background and four large formless abstract shapes floating within it, in white, darker black, and a complex shade of blue that brought to mind a sunlit Cornish coastline. "What is it?" Ben had asked me, his hand nestled in mine. "It's whatever you want it to be," I'd said. "I like it," he replied. "It's random." "Random" was a new word that Ben had learned at school, and he used it whenever he could.

In the next gallery Ben had been drawn to a small canvas by Odilon Redon, and a copy of this was revealed when I opened the book. In the museum, Ben had stood in front of it, just inches from it, while Ruth and I stood behind him.

"What is this one?" he asked us. In the center of the painting was a white figure, mounted on a rearing white horse and holding aloft a long stick with a green flag at the top of it, which looked to be fluttering in a hot breeze. Behind the figure were two boats, barely emerging from the thickly painted background, with its suggestions of land, sea, clouds, and sky in dusty shades of brown and blue.

"It's a bit messy," said Ben.

"The artist has done that on purpose," Ruth told him. "He wants to suggest a dream to you, a world where stories take place and where you can use your imagination."

"What is the story?"

"Like your mummy said about the other painting, the story is anything you want it to be. It's everything or nothing."

"I would like to have a green flag," said Ben.

"Then you could be an adventurer too, like the person in this painting. Would you like a white horse?"

Ben nodded.

"And what about a boat?" Ruth asked him.

"No thank you," he said, and I knew he would say that, because Ben had a fear of the sea.

"Do you know what I see in this painting?" Ruth asked him.

He looked up at her.

"I see a brave person riding a magnificent horse and I wonder where that person is going and where they've been," she told him. "And I also see music."

"Where is the music?" he asked.

"It's in there. It's in the paint, and the sea and the sky and in the story of the person and their horse and the ships," said Ruth. "All those things give me the idea of music, and then I can hear it in my head."

"And for me too," he said. He smiled at her, his face lit up. "It's lots of fast notes, like an adventure."

"And slow ones too," said Ruth. "Do you see here — that thick bit of paint, where you can see how the painter smeared it on with his brush? That's a slow note for me."

Ben considered that. "Can you hear it, Mummy?"

"Definitely," I told him, and in that moment just the sound of his voice, the innocence ringing in it, the eagerness to listen, was music enough. On that day, my son was seven years old, and I suspected already that he might not be the kind of child who could win a running race, or triumph on a rugby pitch, so to see him respond in this way to the paintings was a joy. It gave me so much hope for his future, that sensitivity he had, the way that he might be able to respond so positively to beauty and to ideas. I felt it would enable him to create reserves that he could draw on when he needed to, and I knew I could guide him through that, or at least set him off on his way.

What I hadn't realized on that day, as Ruth and I took him downstairs to find tea and cake, was that he might need to draw on his reserves so soon. Before he would be ready. Or that he might never get a chance to build them up before they were shattered forever.

"Do you want to borrow the book?" Ruth asked. I was lost on the page, in the image, and her voice pulled me back to now. "Ben might like to see it."

What to answer? How to disguise my emotions? I managed only to say, "He would. Thank you."

"Bring him to see me next week. Promise you will."

I was struggling to hold myself together. I went to stand at the window, keeping my face turned away from her, looking out at the beds of pruned roses in the garden below, at the sweeping, gracious branches of a mature cedar tree. But Ruth was no fool, dementia notwithstanding.

"What is it, dear?" she said.

"I'm fine."

"I don't like to see you like this, my darling. Come, sit with me, talk to me."

I wanted to, I so wanted to. But the thing

is that if I'd told her, it would have destroyed her. So I didn't.

"I've got to go now," I said. "I'll see you next week."

I put my face to hers, said good-bye, kissed her. She clasped my head to hers and for a moment the sides of our faces rested together. Her skin felt as smooth as gossamer, her cheek bony and delicate, barely there.

"Bye-bye, darling," she said. "Be strong. Remember: you are a mother. You must be strong."

Jim

I got one of the DCs to pick up John Finch and bring him in. He was with us within the hour. He looked thinner than he had at the beginning of the week. I put the letter down in front of him.

"Don't take it out of the bag."

He picked the bag up. Fingernails bitten to the quick. Shaking hands. He read out loud:

John Finch will now understand
how it feels to lose a child.
It serves him right.
He has been arrogant, and
now he will be humbled.
"By medicine life may be prolonged,
yet death will seize the doctor too."

I watched him closely. He looked as if I'd swung a cudgel at his head, and made contact.

"Who sent this? What is this?"

"It arrived this morning. We don't know who sent it. We're hoping you can help us find out."

The shaking in his hands spread to his wrists.

"Is this my fault? Have I done this?"

"Let's not talk about fault. That's not going to get us anywhere at this point. Do you have any idea who might have sent it? We think it implies that the sender has had contact with you in a professional capacity. I know I've asked you before, but I really need you to think about this again now. Do you know of anybody who might have a grudge against you? A former patient?"

John Finch looked like the most beaten person in the world. He looked like a man watching all his worst nightmares come true. His voice was tight with the effort it was costing him to control it. If I'm honest, I found the interview unexpectedly hard, and I think that's because I recognized myself in him. I knew that if I was him, I would be broken too, and somehow, although it shouldn't have, that got under my skin. I don't know if it was my fatigue, or the way he tried so hard to hold on to his dignity, or perhaps both, but there it was, a small feeling of solidarity with him that I shouldn't have allowed myself.

"My patients are children, Detective. They don't tend to bear grudges. In fact their view of the world is often beautifully simple, beautifully fair."

He ran the fingertips of one hand around his eye socket.

"But they have families, and, sometimes — rarely — you lose a child during surgery, and the families can't accept it. They blame you. Even when there's nothing you could have done. Even when the surgery was your only option because without it the child would have died."

"Can you think of any families who might have cared more than others?"

"Cared enough to take my son in revenge? An eye for an eye?"

"Yes."

He shook his head. "Like I said before, there were one or two who tried to sue the hospital, but even that isn't very unusual. It's a risk we take in our profession." He passed a hand across his forehead, squeezed his temples. "I can't imagine them doing anything this extreme, I really can't, but I suppose there is one family that sticks in my mind as being more persistent than the others. I can give you the name of the child; the father's details will be on the records at the hospital."

I pushed a piece of paper and a pen across the desk toward him. "Write down the name for me," I said. "The one that springs to mind. And write down the person to contact at the hospital."

He wrote. He passed the paper to me. "Does Rachel know?" he said.

Rachel

This time, I made no attempt at conversation as Zhang drove me home.

I stared out of the window and thought about Ruth and Ben, and how much they loved each other's company. I was transfixed by the sight of schoolchildren walking home with parents, or in messy groups without adults, shouting, laughing, jostling each other, dropping bits of rubbish, which the wind picked up and blew around them. It was the start of half-term this afternoon, as Ruth had said, and they were in a celebratory mood.

"Can we go to Ben's school?"

"We can. Why?" Zhang said.

"I want to get his stuff. It's half-term."

She hesitated only momentarily. "Of course," she said. She pulled into the forecourt of a gas station to turn around and we got stuck behind another car. It was impossible not to see the headlines, murky as they were behind the thick plastic of the forecourt newsstand. The front pages of two newspapers showed a photograph of me at the press conference, beside one of my sister in her nightie, berating the journalists outside my house. This is what I read before Zhang pulled away:

FINCH FURIES
INTIMIDATING: Benedict's auntie lets rip
SISTERS: who aren't afraid to look SAVAGE
FEARS GROWING: 5 days missing and counting

And on another paper, underneath a photograph of my boy:

MYSTERY OF BEN'S CLOTHING
New Timeline of Ben's Disappearance Inside

Zhang still said nothing. I wasn't sure if she'd seen them or not. I pulled up the hood of my coat and sank down into my seat. I was afraid of somebody recognizing me and I was afraid of what they might say if they did.

Ben's school was almost deserted as we arrived. We had to maneuver around some orange traffic cones that had been placed as a loose barricade across the entrance to the teachers' parking lot. Only a few cars remained there; most of the spaces were empty. Zhang parked in a spot where we had a view of the playground, a small tarmacked space with soccer posts painted on one wall and colorful murals on the others. It was a modest little school, with the old Victorian schoolhouse at its heart, and various unprepossessing modern additions tacked on to it over the years.

Right up until the moment when we parked, I thought it was a good idea to visit the school, but as Zhang undid her seat belt and pulled the keys from the ignition, I found myself paralyzed by the fact of actually being there.

It was the sight of the playground. It reminded me that this was Ben's world, his other world, and that the last time I was here was to pick him up the previous Friday afternoon.

As Zhang turned to me, wondering why I wasn't moving, images flooded my brain.

The playground on Friday: it had been heaving as usual, crowds of parents waiting for children who were being disgorged from the building in various states.

Some looked as if they'd been catapulted

out with the sole purpose of expending excess energy, chasing each other around between huddles of mothers; others looked beaten down by the week, bags weighing heavily on their shoulders. Some were sporting stickers proudly on their sweatshirts; one or two burst into tears at the sight of their parent after a long day of pent-up frustration.

I saw all this in vivid little bursts: baby carriages, mothers laden like packhorses, snacks being distributed, tales of injustice or triumph. Children sent back into the building to get forgotten things. A teacher with a cup of tea in hand; the headmaster wearing a novelty tie on a rare outing from his office, a few parents flocking around him. Cutout figures strung like bunting in the windows of the classroom behind them.

"Are you having second thoughts?" asked Zhang.

"No," I said. "I want to do this."

I made myself focus, take a deep breath. In front of me the playground was empty, except for a green plastic hoop, which had been discarded in the middle of the tarmac, and the remnants of colorful chalk marks on the ground, only partially washed away by the rain. I got out of the car.

"Be warned that the school's hired security," Zhang said as we crossed the playground to the entrance, "because of the press. They caught a journalist snooping in the school office."

As we walked, my legs felt as though they weren't working properly, and there was faintness in my head and my chest. Everything seemed to take on a cartoonlike quality. I visualized the press as an invasive plant, its roots and tendrils growing implacably into every area of my life and Ben's, looking for action or information to feed off. I felt distinctly unwell, and I wondered if I should go back to the car and let Zhang go in without me, but we'd arrived at the door by then and to articulate how I felt was impossible.

We were admitted to the building by a burly man whom I'd never seen before. He had a shaved head, an earpiece, and a strikingly large beer belly. He checked Zhang's ID and then let us in.

I led the way to Ben's classroom. All I wanted was to get Ben's PE uniform from his peg, and anything else he might have left behind. That's what I would normally have done at half-term. I would have washed his uniform, and checked he had everything he needed for the next few weeks in the run-up to Christmas. Not to do that would have felt wrong.

It wasn't to be that simple though. As we neared the door to Ben's classroom, I saw a big display of artwork, and in the middle of that display was a picture that I recognized, because Ben had made it. My knees buckled.

After that I have only snatches of memory and sensation: confusion, when I came around, because I was on the floor of the corridor and Zhang was propping me up; eyes refocusing again on the display of artwork, seeing painted leaves and branches in all the shades of brown and orange and green and black that wrapped themselves around Ben and swallowed him up when we were in the woods; seeing Ben's picture among the others and feeling sure that I could see the imprint of his fingers in the smears of paint; feeling an impulse to stand, and put my fingers where his had been, and then an inability to do that.

When they'd got me upright and they were sure I wasn't going to faint again, they moved me into the classroom and sat me in the teacher's chair.

Miss May was there, and also the teaching assistant. I heard Zhang's voice, saying, "She wants his things, that's all, that's why we're here."

I watched Miss May go over to a row of pegs that ran along one wall of the classroom, and take down the only PE bag that remained there, and behind it there was a label. It was a photograph of a dog, black and white like Skittle, and the name "Ben F."

Then Miss May said, "Lucas, can you please get . . ." and I watched the teaching assistant go into the corridor and carefully take down Ben's painting from the autumn display and put it into a plastic folder. Noticing his receding chin and very red hair. Noticing the sweat under his arms.

Then Miss May was offering to help me to the car, but I found my voice and said no, because I didn't want the fuss of it, and Zhang said we could manage just fine.

Outside in the corridor, with her arm linked firmly around mine, we walked past the new headmaster. He said, "I'm so sorry," but the way he looked at me made me feel like an exhibit so I didn't reply. I just wanted to be at home.

Miss May ran down the corridor behind us, her shoes tapping fast, and just as we reached the door she caught up with us. She had an armful of Ben's books, which she passed to me, and she said, "I thought you might like these, since you didn't make it to parents' evening this week. I thought you might like to look through them."

So I took them and as Zhang helped me into the car I held them to myself as carefully as if they were an actual baby.

Jim

Addendum to DI James Clemo's report for Dr. Francesca Manelli

Transcript recorded by Dr. Francesca Manelli
DI James Clemo and Dr. Francesca Manelli in attendance

Notes to indicate observations on DI Clemo's state of mind or behavior, where his remarks alone do not convey this, are in italics.

FM: So the letter?
JC: We threw everything into it. Obviously.
FM: Was that your call?
JC: It was Fraser's, actually it was both of ours, and it was the right one.
FM: Was the investigation team excited?
JC: You're always excited when you've got a lead, but you have to be cautious too. You

don't want mistakes. But it was a development and that was good because by then it had been five days and that was getting to people. They were tired; the media were going insane around us. We had the blog to worry about.

FM: What was happening with that?

JC: Behind the scenes Fraser was putting everything she could into finding out who might be behind it. Among others we were looking at Laura Saville and Nicola Forbes as possibles for the leak. We knew that both of them were involved in online journalism in some way already, and they were obviously close to the heart of things. She had to be discreet internally though, partly because we didn't want to put the wind up anybody if they were up to something, and also because everybody working the investigation was feeling the pressure, and that kind of thing is very bad for morale, putting it mildly.

FM: Including you? Were you feeling the pressure?

JC: Of course. There was a kid's life at stake.

FM: And did you have any strategies to cope with that?

He speaks to me as though I am an imbecile.

JC: A little boy, eight years old, was still missing after five days. We didn't have time for "coping strategies."

FM: OK. I understand that it must have been a stressful period for everyone involved in the investigation. My question is —

He interrupts me; his temper has risen.

JC: Don't patronize me.

FM: I'm not intending to. That's a very defensive reading of what I said. I'm simply acknowledging the fact that you felt under pressure and looking at ways that we might explore what that meant for you, and for the investigation.

JC: You have no idea what it's like to be in the middle of something like that.

FM: So would it be fair to say that by this point in the case you'd moved on from the attitude that you felt when you took on the case? The "bring it on" attitude?

JC: It would, yes, because have you ever thought about what five days of being removed from your family and living in fear could do to a child? That's one hundred twenty hours and counting. That was on my mind every single second. Why do you think I threw a hand grenade into the middle of that family? Because that's what it was, making Nicky Forbes confess that stuff to her sister; don't think I don't understand that. But I did that for Benedict. Because we had to find him, and if there was collateral damage, then so be it. The letter was no different.

I end our session here, because I fear I'll push him away entirely if I press him further today. I do wonder whether, if this man doesn't successfully go through this process and get back to work in CID, I might fear for his long-term stability.

Rachel

When I got home, Zhang asked me if I wanted her to come in with me but I declined, saying that my sister would be there, even though I didn't know if that was true. I still felt detached and strange, as if all my senses were dulled and the only thing that mattered were the thoughts that were at a rolling boil inside my head.

Nicky was there. She was sitting in the kitchen and her packed bag was by the front door, her coat draped over it.

"I waited because I didn't want to leave without saying good-bye," she said.

She didn't notice my disorientation. She did ask me what I was cradling in my arms.

"Ben's books," I said.

I put them carefully down on the table and then we just stood facing each other and she reached forward to hug me. It was an awkward hug, just as it had been the first morning at the police station, although this time it was worse because her body offered none of the softness that it had before. We were both too wary of each other, and we made do with the minimum of contact, because for the first time in our lives neither of us knew where we stood with the other. And then, as if she knew that was inadequate, Nicky stood in front of me and put her hands on either side of my arms, and rubbed them up and down.

"Will you be OK?" she asked.

I nodded.

"I can come back whenever you want, just call me, if it's too much being on your own."

"I can ask Laura to come over," I said, and my voice sounded strange, as if I were speaking with a thick tongue.

She hesitated just slightly before saying, "OK, good."

Then we stood there again and her hands fell away from my arms and she looked at me in a way that made me want to start screaming with the uncertainty and the awfulness of it all, so with the last reserves of my strength I said, "Just go, Nicky."

"Now I'm not sure I should," she said. "Looking at you now. You're not OK, are you?"

And I shouted. I shouted, "JUST GO!" because I felt as if I would implode if anybody said anything else to me, and it shocked her so much that she took a step back, and from her reaction I could tell that my expression must be ugly.

She stared at me, and then started to say something, but I couldn't stand to hear it, so I shouted "NOW!" and it was more of a scream than a word, and then I ran up the stairs so fast that they pounded and I didn't hear the sound of the door clicking shut behind her, but I did hear the press badgering her to tell them who had been shouting and why, and if she replied to them she did it very quietly or not at all, because within minutes all I could hear were the sounds of my empty house.

Laura came to mop me up. I didn't ask her to, she just arrived. As I went to answer the door I heard her chatting with one of the journalists on the doorstep. When I let her in she said, "How funny. I trained with one of those guys out there." She said it lightly, as if they'd run into each other at a party. I wondered which one of them it was. There were a few regulars. Most likely, I thought, to be the youngest of the bunch, the one who could outrun the others and was the last to stop beating on the windows of the car when I was driven away. I didn't ask her.

She'd brought takeaway food and a bottle of wine with her. Before she arrived I thought I'd tell her everything that had happened. But I didn't. I couldn't find the words; they felt trapped inside me, made prisoner by my numbed senses and my decaying ability to trust. Within my head I was jittering, like a withdrawing addict, obsessing over my sister, and what she'd told me, replaying my loss of consciousness at the school.

Laura let me jitter. She calmly laid out our food on the kitchen table and poured us glasses of wine. "I know you probably don't feel like this," she said, "but I'm going to do it anyway and I won't be offended if you don't want it."

The food and drink she'd brought looked like ancient relics of a life that I'd once enjoyed, but I went through the motions of appearing grateful. I picked at one or two of the dishes, managed just a sip of the wine, which had lost all of the comforting qualities it had before Ben disappeared and tasted like acid in my mouth.

"Do you want to talk about him?" Laura asked, breaking our silence. "Would it help?"

Laura never ate much; she had the appetite of a sparrow. She toyed with her food for a few moments, while I failed to answer her question, and then she said, "Do you remember when you had him? At the very beginning? We couldn't believe how tiny he was, do you remember that?"

I found my voice. "You wouldn't hold him at first."

Laura hadn't been able to take her eyes off him when she came to see me in the hospital. I lay exhausted in the bed, my body bruised and sore, hormone-drenched and soft, and watched her while she'd stood beside his Perspex crib, all trim and well dressed and tanned and pretty in a little summer dress and big sunglasses pushed up on her head — like a postcard from my life before motherhood. I told her she could pick him up, but she'd shaken her head at first.

She smiled at the reminder. "I'd never held a baby before. I didn't want to break him, or to drop him."

"But I made you."

"And he puked on me."

"He puked everywhere for the first few months. It was constant washing."

"But it was love at first sight, wasn't it? For you?"

"Yes."

"I envied you that. It was so intense, so private."

Her fingers sat on the stem of her wineglass and she turned it slowly, delicate wrists flexing. Then she refilled it. More than half the bottle was gone, and I hadn't had more than a sip.

For the first time I noticed that lines were beginning to form on her elfin face. It was just an impression, they seemed to be there one moment, and gone the next, but they were a reminder that she was aging, that we were all aging. I stretched my hand across the table toward her and our fingers linked briefly.

"I can't believe this is happening to you," she said. "It's like a bolt of lightning came out of nowhere and struck you, and Ben. I can't imagine what you must be going through."

"All my feelings hurt."

Her eyes brimmed with unshed tears, and she said, "Can I tell you something? I want to say it so you know that other people know how you feel. Just a little bit of what you feel anyway."

"Tell me," I said, and instinctively I felt a reawakening of the feelings of dread that our reminiscences about Ben had briefly put to sleep.

"I had an abortion."

"When?" This was startling news, shocking too. I thought Laura and I had had the kind of friendship where you lay yourself bare, where the only secrets you keep are to do with your plans for each other's Christmas or birthday presents.

"Before you had Ben."

"I don't know what to say. Why didn't you tell me before?"

"You were pregnant."

And there it was: a wedge in our friendship that I'd never known about.

"Who was the father?"

"Do you remember Tom from Bath?"

I did. He was a married man, whom she'd met through work.

"Did he know?"

"He paid for it. God, Rach, I'm sorry. It's stupid of me even to mention it now. I don't even know why I'm telling you. It's nothing compared to what you're going through."

And here's the thing: I couldn't deal with it. If Laura wanted us to feel solidarity at that moment, then she'd just said completely the wrong thing. It was simply too much to cope with: the intentional loss of a child.

A week previously I would have been there

for her, supported her, but at that moment it was viciously, unbearably painful to hear, and my brain, addled with her news, with everything, did a flip.

The exquisite and painful pleasure of our reminiscences about Ben disappeared in an instant. The earlier warmth of her friendship, and her company, suddenly felt frosty and brittle. Goose bumps ran across my skin like squalls agitating glassy water.

"No," I said. "No, no, no. I can't hear this now. Why are you telling me this?"

And then another thought, a corrosive one, as the distrust that my sister had sown as a seed now bloomed freely in my mind. I voiced it with a tone that was raw enough to surprise even myself, the tone of somebody who has reached the end of her tether. "Are you feeding stories about me to the other journalists? To your friends out there? Is that why you wanted to talk about Ben?"

I got to my feet, and my wineglass tipped over in my hurry to stand, the wine everywhere, pooling on the table, on me, dripping onto the floor, and Laura stood too and shock had peeled away any softness in her expression so that her cheeks looked cold and smooth as marble.

"Jesus, Rachel! I know you must be feeling desperate, but . . ."

I pushed her. She came around the table toward me, wanting to hug me, and I pushed her away. I grabbed her coat and her bag and I shoved them at her and I hounded her all the way to the front door, ignoring her pleading words, and her tears, until she was out and gone, like Nicky, and the press, her so-called friends, took photographs of her on the doorstep while I sat back down at the kitchen table, on the chair that was damp with wine, and I sobbed.

Jim

We worked closely with John Finch all day. The feeling of recognizing myself in him didn't abate; if anything it got stronger as we talked. It troubled me.

He waited at Kenneth Steele House with me while my officers began checking out families whom he'd identified for us. We sent a pair of DCs down to the hospital, hoping there weren't going to be too many confidentiality issues and bureaucratic hoops to jump through before they would release information to us.

"Do you ever tire of it?" Finch said to me in a long moment of silence when my thoughts had flown to Emma, to when I might see her next. "Do you ever tire of the daily contact with people when their lives are shattered?"

We sat in a windowless interview room around a gray-topped table. A strip light above us threw out a glare that made my temples ache. I didn't answer him. If I had, I would have lost my separateness, my professional distance. I had to remember that John Finch was not my friend, but it was hard not to answer, because there were parallels between what he did and what I do. For a moment or two I was overwhelmed with a desire to say yes, to talk to him, to compare notes and admit that there were times when it was very, very difficult to stand back. In another universe, I thought, we might have been able to do that, and it would have been nice, but not here, not now.

"Do you know what this room reminds me of?" he asked.

I shook my head.

"We call it the bad news room at the hospital. It's where we take families when we have to tell them the worst. It's exactly like this, except that there are brochures."

I kept my reply neutral. "We're hoping to bring you good news, Mr. Finch."

"Do you know how they know?" he said. "The smart ones, the clever families? They see the china teapot and the china cups with saucers, and the door closing behind them, and the unusual number of staff all together in one room, and they ask themselves why all this fuss, just for us? It doesn't take them long to work it out. They read the situation before we've even started talking. They start to grieve before the milk goes into the cups."

"Well, you're safe on that count," I said.

In front of us was a tray of four polystyrene cups with gray coffee remains swimming in the base of them. Torn and half-emptied sachets of sugar littered the table like doll-sized body bags.

He understood why I'd given such a shallow response. "I'm sorry," he said. "Of course you don't want to have this conversation because to do so would be unprofessional. That was stupid of me. I'd do the same in your situation." He barked out a noise that was supposed to be a laugh, but instead was a noise that crept sullenly around the edges of the room, mocking his attempt at forced jollity.

I wondered then if all the pain and difficulty of his profession, the hopelessness and the encounters with death, had become toxic for John Finch, too toxic to bear any longer.

I let my guard down then, just for a moment, because I was curious.

"Do you get emotional when you lose a patient?" I asked him. I wanted to know how much failure hurt him; I wanted to know if he was like me.

"Very occasionally there's one that gets to

you, no matter how hard you try. It's very rare. You learn early on, when you're training, that you have to keep your distance emotionally, because if you don't, you can't do your job."

"What makes that one stand out?"

"Sometimes you don't even know. Once I operated on a boy who reminded me a little of Ben, and I met his mother, she wasn't unlike Rachel. They reminded me of us, of our family. It wasn't that long ago, Ben was about seven at the time. The boy's operation was quite a simple one, but there was bleeding, and he died. His heart failed. There was nothing we could do. It was an unexpected death and when I went to tell his mother, I . . . I'm afraid I broke down."

Distress swam deep in his eyes, but John Finch had obviously learned to be stoic too. He didn't lose control; he said, "It was unprofessional of me."

"It's understandable."

"Do you think so, Detective? Has it ever happened to you?"

I looked at my watch. It was late. I was in danger of confiding. I had to get things back on track. "I think we could do with something to eat," I said. "Chances are, it's going to be a long night."

■ ■ ■ ■

We took John Finch home at ten that night. By midnight, we'd narrowed things down based on the information he'd given us, and we had a standout suspect for the letter. By the early hours of the morning we'd disturbed countless colleagues and we were as certain as you can be. We'd checked and double-checked the details, gone into background, and triple-checked that we had the correct address for our suspect.

Fraser, on what must have been her fiftieth cup of coffee, tasked me with leading a dawn raid. We wanted the element of surprise, and that's the best time to get it. I chose my men, and we went through our preparations carefully.

We were due to go in at five a.m.

■ ■ ■ ■

Day 7
Saturday, October 27, 2012

■ ■ ■ ■

An abduction may occur for many reasons, including a desire to possess a child, sexual gratification, financial gain, retribution, and the desire to kill. Research findings indicate that when a child is killed, the motivation may be either emotion-based, where the abductor seeks revenge on the family; sexual-based, where the offender seeks sexual gratification from the victim; or profit-based, which involves most often ransom for money (Boudreaux et al., 2000 & 2001). Moreover, child homicide usually follows an abduction and is not the reason for the abduction.

— Marlene L. Dalley and Jenna Ruscoe,
"The Abduction of Children by Strangers
in Canada: Nature and Scope,"
National Missing Children Services,
National Police Services, Royal Canadian
Mounted Police, December 2003

WEB PAGE — www.twentyfour7news.co.uk/bristol — 7:22 AM BST Oct 27, 2012

Where is Benedict Finch?
The blogosphere rises — people power or vigilante justice?
by Danny Deal

Officers working on the Benedict Finch case have been frustrated by the emergence of a blog, which has stirred up the media frenzy.

Apparently written by somebody close to the case, the blog has been blamed for leaking details of the case and stirring up suspicion against the family of Benedict Finch.

DCI Corinne Fraser said last night, "We don't know who is writing this blog, but it is a vindictive piece of work. At this time we are very concerned for the well-being of the family of Benedict Finch, as well as for the lad himself, and we would ask people to remain calm, and respect this family's situation, and not pay heed to this blog, which is the work of an uninformed and unreliable individual. Our efforts at this time are all concentrated on finding this lad."

She also added that police are still "pursuing multiple lines of inquiry" and are "hopeful of a significant development soon." She declined to comment on what that might be.

James Leon QC stated that "anybody, either a media organization or an individual, can be prosecuted under contempt of court laws if their comments published online are found to be prejudicial at trial."

3 people are discussing this article

Donna Faulkes
People should be able to say what they like.

Shaun Campbell
If the police cant find him then at least somebodys saying what everybodys thinking.

Amelie Jones
Its stupid to write this and not say what it is that people cant say.

Rachel

In the early hours of the morning I woke to find myself drenched in sweat again, consumed by that scooped-out feeling of loss that was brutal and all-consuming and was no longer tempered by having people close to me.

I began to consider the thought that Ben might not come home.

I began to consider the reality that I might have to exist in, should that happen.

It would be intolerable.

My obsessive, jumpy thoughts drove me downstairs, and out of the back door into the night. The wind was still sharp and it sent me running across the garden to my studio, and in that short distance made its way coldly between the folds of my nightwear so that by the time I let myself in, I was shivering so violently that I felt like a shaken bag of bones.

I didn't dare turn on the lights, in case of

being seen through the glass doors, top-lit in all my falling-apart glory. My neighbors, like my friends, felt like adversaries now, potential spies. Instead I just turned on my computer, and sat in its frigid blue glow. Then, compulsively, slowly, knowing I shouldn't, feeling unable to stop, I began to look online.

I found myself castigated further. In the absence of news about the case, editorial pieces had emerged, primarily in the broadsheets. And if I'd ever hoped before reading them that they might provide a more balanced view of our family's situation, then I was wrong, delusional. They were as brutally judgmental as the tabloids.

Almost without exception they discussed the case, and my performance at the press conference, in the context of my single motherhood, and they used it as a stick to beat me with, or a label with which to stigmatize me.

Those editorial pieces asked a lot of questions about me, and about Ben's case. You can imagine that, can't you? Perhaps you read them. They questioned my morals and they cast doubt on my fitness to raise a child. They condemned me roundly for my slack parenting in letting Ben run ahead in the woods. They blamed me, made a social pariah of me. Single mother, failed mother, person of dubious social status, target.

Here's what they didn't ask: they showed no curiosity whatsoever about whether I'd considered the decision to let Ben run ahead, or any of the factors I might have taken into account; they didn't examine the sense of loss I had to overcome when John left me, or my efforts at rebuilding, or my longing to be a good mother in his absence; they didn't ask how much I loved Ben.

Nowhere did any journalist mention the hardship of single parenthood, the evenings spent alone, the pressures of making difficult decisions without support, the painful absence of a partner who might have been there if life had turned out differently.

These were people, I thought, with a growing sense of desperation, who would have put me in a workhouse a hundred years ago, and a few centuries before that strapped me into a scold's bridle, or built a tall bonfire just for me to sit atop, and lit it with flaming torches, which underscored with flickering light their hard-bitten features, their lack of mercy or compassion.

And nowhere, in any of the hundreds of words written, did any of them lay a scrap of blame at John's door. In contrast, he was the object of sympathy, protected by his gender and his profession: pediatric general surgeon, his new wife a deserved salve for his pain, not a cause of the breakdown of our marriage. One of them even featured a photograph of John and Katrina looking like a perfect unit, irreproachable in their togetherness.

I was their target because I was socially unacceptable, and so they did everything they legally could: they publicly lanced me with words which were written, examined, and edited, each process carefully honing them in a calculated effort to push people's buttons once they were published, to froth up public opinion around them so that my situation could titillate others, could thrill and bolster the minds of the smug and judgmental. Schadenfreude. Conservatism. Better the worst happens to somebody else, because, quite frankly, they must have done something to deserve it.

And they felt entitled to do that, these so-called "thinkers," as they sat comfortably behind their desks with their reference books and their own unexamined moral compass, because I was nothing to them. Ben and I were simply the commodity that would sell their papers, nothing more. And these were the very papers that I used to read, that I used to carry down the road from the shop and bring into my home.

It was cowardly, yellow journalism, and I knew that. The problem was, knowing it wasn't enough to stop every single word from chipping away any final scraps of self-respect or dignity that I might have had left. I was only human, after all.

And I suppose I'm interested now to know whether it troubles you to read these things, to know that the rug you're standing on so securely can be whipped out from under your feet rapidly and completely? Or do you feel safer than that? Do you assume that your foundations are more secure than mine, and that my situation is too extreme to ever befall you? Have you noted the moments when I made mistakes that you might have avoided? Do you imagine that you would have behaved with a more perfect maternal dignity in my situation, that you would be unimpeachable? Perhaps you wouldn't have been stupid enough to lose your husband in the first place.

Be careful what you assume, is what I'd say to that. Be very careful. I should know. I was married to a doctor once.

I'm also interested to know how uncomfortable you feel now. Whether you're regretting our agreement. Remember the roles we allocated each other? Me: Ancient

Mariner and Narrator. You: Wedding Guest and Patient Listener. Do you wish you could shuffle away yet? Refill your glass perhaps? Now that my grip is loosening whose side are you on? Mine, or theirs? How long will you stay with the underdog, given that she's so beaten now, so unattractive? Displaying here and there signs of mental instability.

If I were to make a final bid to keep your attention I suppose I would say that if it troubles you to hear these things from me, to witness my descent, then perhaps you can take heart from the fact that it pains me very, very deeply to confess them.

When, finally, the darkness outside my studio began to dissolve that morning, I pulled my chair away from the computer, tore my horrified eyes from the screen. With ice-cold fingers I pulled my dressing gown around me and I watched the grainy night contours of my garden morph slowly into a strangely lit morning where the rising sun tinted the pendulous clouds so that they were not entirely black, but colored instead with bruised fleshy tones, burnished in places. It was the kind of light that nobody would mistake for hope.

Back in the kitchen, it felt as though I was

meeting my possessions after an absence. I boiled the kettle, and realized that I hadn't done that myself for days, because Nicky had done everything. Almost out of curiosity I opened the fridge, having no idea what was in it, and found cooked meals, in labeled containers, prepared by Nicky before she left, and half a pint of fresh milk.

At the kitchen table, warming slowly as the heating in the house cranked up around me with its familiar clicks and clonks, I began to look at Ben's schoolbooks.

There were five of them. There wasn't a great deal of work in each one as it was so early in the school year, but I started to work through them: math, literacy, spellings, a history project, and a news book.

The first page of the news book made me smile.

Ben had drawn a picture of a huge bed, which filled the entire page. In it was a small stick figure. Underneath it he had written: "I spent the hole weekend in bed." There was a comment beside it in red ink: "Are you sure that's all you did, Ben? I expect you did something else. The drawing of the bed is nice."

It even made me smile, because it was nonsense, and I thought simply: this is the world I want to be in, the imaginative, funny world that's my son.

I knew then, with perfect clarity, that if Ben didn't survive this, then neither could I.

Jim

Five of us turned up: me and four men in full gear. Black clothing, bulletproof jackets, caps that hide your eyes, and shoes with soles that were thick enough to do damage. All my men were armed. All of us wore earpieces, to keep in radio contact. I was leading.

It was 05:00 hours. It was dark. Early morning hush was settled over the neighborhood like a blanket.

We parked quietly around the corner, killing the car engine quickly, and when we got out we didn't talk, communicating with gestures only. Three of us stayed at the end of the driveway, in the shadows and out of sight, and we waited there silently while I sent two around the side of the property.

We didn't want anybody slipping out of the back.

Streetlights revealed that the bungalow was in bad condition, in contrast to the neighboring properties, which were immaculate, their front gardens displaying neatly trimmed lawns, and tended borders containing closely clipped shrubs like shiny suburban trophies.

The flower beds in our bungalow's garden were overgrown, and the lawn was muddy and unkempt, but the metal gate at the side of the house had shiny black paint on it and its latch didn't squeak when my two DCs opened it and sidled through it.

My guess was that its decline was recent.

There was a single garage to the side of the bungalow; its door was shut but in good shape, and the driveway had been expensively relaid at some point recently. There was no crunchy gravel to give us away. There was also no vehicle in the driveway, no curtains drawn at the front, and no lights on in the house, and I hoped to God the place wasn't empty.

On my signal, two of the men approached the front door and stood on either side of it, tucked in, so that they weren't visible through the frosted glass in the door, not until they were ready to be.

There was a security light above them, but it didn't come on. They had a battering ram with them, a black metal cylinder, so that they could break down the door if necessary.

They didn't look at me. They were focused on the door, waiting to hear my voice in their earpieces. "Go," I whispered into my radio. I knew the command would transmit loud and clear, and they didn't hesitate. They rang the bell, hammered on the door, shouted through the letter flap: "Police, let us in. Police!"

The noise ripped through the predawn stillness.

By the time a light came on in the hallway of the bungalow the other properties around us were lit up like Christmas trees and we were about to bash the door in.

A woman opened it, just an inch or two at first, suspicious eyes peering through. She looked as though she'd been asleep. She wore tracksuit bottoms, plastic clogs, and a nurse's tabard. My men pushed past her. I followed.

"Where is he?" I said.

She pointed toward the end of the hall opposite. One of my men was already down there; the others had gone into the front rooms. I ran down the hall, but even before I'd traveled those few paces I knew it had gone wrong when my man said, "In here, boss," and his voice sagged. He stood in the doorway just ahead of me and his body language had relaxed, adrenaline gone. There was no threat.

As I pushed past him, he said, "He's not going anywhere."

In the middle of the room was a hospital bed. In the bed lay a man, his eyes wide balls of fear. He was underneath a white sheet that he'd pulled up to his neck with fingers that scrunched the material tight. A hospital band was visible on his wrist. The only clue to his relative youth was his brown hair. His face hung from his bones and his skin was gray apart from high red spots on his cheekbones, from fever, or morphine. He was hooked up to a pump. An oxygen mask was attached to his face, the elastic digging into his cheeks, and a bag of dark orange urine hung from the side of the bed.

Beside the bed was an armchair, and a table, with books on it, along with a laptop computer, a remote control for the TV that sat on the chest of drawers in a corner, and a cardboard tray for collecting vomit. Beside the door was a wheelchair.

The nurse was beside me now. "He's dying," she said. She had tribal scars on her face, two rough, raised lines on each cheek, and eyes that told me that she'd seen death before.

I turned to my man. "Search the garage,"

I said, but I already knew that there'd be no sign of Ben Finch.

Rachel

Zhang phoned me midmorning. She'd just parked on my street, she said, and, no, they hadn't found Ben but could I let her in? She wanted to speak to me.

I listened at the front door for her footsteps, reluctant to open it until I knew she was there. A peek from my bedroom window had told me that overnight the numbers of journalists had dwindled to just two or three, but I didn't want to give them a photo opportunity.

When I heard her footsteps, and I heard the journalists call out to her, I began to undo the latch, but the expected ring on the bell didn't come. Instead I heard her curse. I opened the door a crack.

My doorstep was awash with milk. It covered the front door and dripped down onto the doormat at my feet. It pooled onto the short front path and it was littered with broken plastic. A pair of two-pint bottles, my twice-weekly delivery from the milkman: full fat for Ben and his growing bones, semi-skimmed for me. Smashed to pieces.

I pictured hands throwing them, feet kicking them, the impact, the explosion of white liquid, the dirty, messy aftermath, and I knew I was meant to understand it as a rebuke, that it labeled me as a woman with a filthy doorstep: such an old-fashioned taint that marks you out as the worst, sluttish kind of woman. I read it as snide vigilante justice, the domestic equivalent of a white feather through the door.

You can see how my mind was rampaging, now that I was cornered, and alone.

"Rachel, go back in," Zhang snapped. "I'll deal with this. You go in."

I did as I was told. She borrowed a mop and a plastic bag to gather the debris, and when she came in after cleaning up I said, "Do you think somebody did it on purpose?"

"I can't say that for sure. It might have been an accident."

"You know it wasn't."

"I don't know anything."

"Did they see who did it?" I gestured toward the journalists.

"They say they didn't. They say it was like that when they arrived this morning."

"They're liars."

"Rachel, it's nothing. It could have been an accident. Don't let it get under your skin."

But it was too late for that.

We went down to my studio, taking the dog. I couldn't bear to be near the front door, with its smeary residue of vandalized milk that shamed and frightened me.

In the studio I put the heater on this time, embarrassed in front of Zhang to indulge in the predawn masochism that had compelled me to sit in the cold while I looked online.

Zhang told me about the letter then, and about the dawn raid that had turned up a dying hoaxer.

"He was a broken person," she said. "His child died during surgery, when Mr. Finch was operating."

"Was it John's fault?"

"No. It was a very risky operation. The father had been informed of that, and the child would have died without it. John wasn't at fault. Nobody was."

"Was it a boy or a girl, the child?"

"I don't know. Apparently the death drove the father mad. He'd been bringing the child up alone anyway because the mother had died. Also to cancer. He wrote a series of letters to the hospital threatening legal action, but he had no case against them, so it was hopeless. And now he has terminal cancer himself. The whole family, wiped out by that disease."

"How did he know about Ben?"

"He saw it on the telly, recognized John, and he thought it was a chance to get back at him. That's all it was, a spiteful act. I'm sorry. We're not back at square one though. We've got other avenues to pursue."

Her words were reassuring in themselves, but I could see that it cost her an effort to arrange her features into an expression of optimism.

As she stood up to leave, my photographs caught her eye.

On the wall above my desk was a collage of pictures I'd taken over the years, and almost without exception they were portraits of Ben. They were my best work.

They were mostly in black and white, and mostly taken on old-fashioned film and developed and printed by me, in a darkroom I'd rigged up in the garage of our family home. John had been happy to hand the garage space over to me. He wasn't a DIY man.

My camera of choice had been a Leica M20, given to me by Ruth and Nicholas. I processed the films myself, and spent hours poring over the negatives, deciding which ones to print.

The printing process was a joy: the murky red light in which images of Ben emerged from the chemical soup, a kind of alchemy, painting with light, bringing something from nothing. It was a wobbly, unreliable, unpredictable process, yet it yielded images of such beauty and power, and I never tired of it.

The photographs I took weren't the brightly lit studio prints that are ubiquitous now, where families are pictured against glaring white backgrounds, mouths agape, dental work on show, in poses they've never before adopted. Artifice, all of it.

I preferred to work with light and form, with what was there already. I started with the idea that I would be lucky to capture just a scrap of the beauty of my child.

Once, when Ben was about five years old, I came downstairs very early one summer morning to find a dawn light so softly crystalline that it seemed to have an ethereal presence of its own.

I roused Ben gently and before he was fully awake I asked him to sit at the breakfast table. It had been a hot night and he wore just pajama shorts. He sat and gazed at the camera with a frankness that was perfect. In the finished photograph, it's as if you can see into his soul. His hair is messy, his skin has the texture of velvet, and the contours of his slender arms are perfect. There are no harsh lines in the picture. Blacks fade into grays and into whites, and shadows draw the features of his face and torso. They describe sleepiness and innocence and promise and truth. Only deep in Ben's eyes is there a glint of something that is of its moment. It's a flash of light, a white pearl, and although nobody else could tell, I know that the pearl is the reflection of the window, and of me, taking the photograph.

It's the best photograph I've ever taken, and probably the best I ever will take.

Zhang stared at that photograph for a very long time. She held her coffee and stood in front of it and in time steam stopped curling above her hands. Then she looked at the others too, the various manifestations of Ben, of Ben as he was to me.

He was a toddler examining something on a summer lawn, with a lightly furrowed brow just visible under a sun hat; he was a close-up of two chubby baby feet and a study of hands with tiny, fragile fingernails and knuckles that had newborn wrinkles but not yet any solidity; he was his profile, the softness of the skin on his temples, the crisp curls of his eyelashes just visible behind; he was a distant silhouette jumping a rock pool on a spectacular cliff-edged winter beach.

There were so many and Zhang studied each one. Occasionally her radio made a sharp noise, a crackle or static or a voice. She ignored it.

"These are just beautiful," she said.

I was lost in the pictures myself when she said it, and her sincerity was unexpected, and felt unfiltered.

"You're the first person outside the family to see them," I said.

"Truly? I'm honored. I really am."

Her voice caught. She had to take a moment to compose herself.

"I tried to learn photography when I was younger," she said. "My dad bought me a camera, an old-fashioned one. It was a film camera. I was fifteen years old. He set me a project. He told me to go out and take photographs. He drove me to a place called Old Airport Road, in Singapore, where I grew up, because he was in the army, you see. Anyway, on Old Airport Road there's an old-fashioned food court, so you know what I mean, lots of stalls selling street food of every different kind, a photographer's dream really. My dad told me to take photographs of the food. I had to ask permission from the stallholders and my dad sat and watched while I spent ages preparing my shots and looking at the different angles and shapes, and after two hours I'd taken my twenty-four photographs. We dropped the film off to be developed and I couldn't wait to go and collect it the next day, I was so excited. I had one of those ideas you have when you're young, you know: I'm going to take one roll of film and be a famous photographer. I was that excited. But when I went back the next day and the girl in the shop gave me my packet of photographs, I pulled them out, and every single one of them was black."

It was the most I'd ever heard her talk. "What happened?" I asked.

"Well, I looked at my dad, I had the same question on my lips, and he said, 'That will teach you not to leave the lens cap on.' I was so angry with him for not telling me."

"Did he know? While you were taking the photos?"

"He did. That's what he's like though. He believes you should learn things yourself, do things the hard way." She smiled wanly. "It worked. I never did it again."

"That's what I was trying to do for Ben," I said. She kept her eyes on the photographs. "In the woods, when I let him run ahead. Because I thought that being independent would let him feel life, be enchanted by it, not fear it, or feel that he has to follow a set of rules to get through it. Because it's tough."

She said nothing. She turned away for a moment and the silence was awkward. When she turned back her eyes were red and she put a hand on my arm, and said, "I'm so sorry, Rachel. I really am."

Once Zhang had gone I went back into the house, driven by the need to be near the landline in case of news. The silence was hard to bear, and I tried to console and calm myself by looking at Ben's books again. I revisited the page where he'd drawn himself spending the whole day in bed, before I turned over to see what he'd written next.

The following page was startlingly colorful by comparison. Greenery filled every corner: trees and plants in strong confident lines, and a dog that was obviously meant to be Skittle. Short straight lines slanted across the page, over the other images, as if somebody had spilled blue sprinkles across it.

"On Sunday Mummy and Skittle and me walked in the woods," he'd written. "It was raining all the time."

I turned another page. The next week's drawing was very similar. Ben had written: "We walked in the woods agen on Sunday. I found a very big stick and brung it home."

There was a comment in red ink: "Your walks sound lovely, Ben. Excellent drawing."

Another page. A different drawing: a picture of a bowling ball, a crowd of children. "I went to Jack's bolling party and Sam B won," he'd written.

Red ink: "Brilliant!"

Another page: trees and foliage again, a swing hanging from a branch, a child beside it, wearing red. Ben was a good artist for his age; the images were clear.

"In the woods I went on a big swing and mummy went on her phone."

Red ink: "That sounds like so much fun for you!!"

A thud of understanding in my chest that was so violent it felt as though it was knocking the breath out of my lungs. It turned my lips and mouth dry and made me look again at the book, as if my eyes were attached to it by strings, and rifle the pages backward and forward until I was sure.

"It's somebody at school," I said, although there was nobody there to hear me. In response there was just a single thud from Skittle's tail, an acknowledgment that I'd spoken out loud.

With shaking hands I picked up my phone and I dialed Zhang over and over again, but every time I just got a message telling me to leave her a voicemail.

Jim

A phone call from Emma woke me up. Fraser had sent me home to catch up on a couple of hours' kip since I'd worked through the whole of the night preparing for the raid. The buzzing of my mobile dragged me up out of a deep sleep, where the disappointment that we'd wasted so much time and budget and were no nearer to finding Ben Finch was feeding me vivid, uncomfortable dreams.

Emma said she wanted to talk, said she would come over, wouldn't say what it was about.

I was out of the shower and dressed by the time she arrived, about to call Fraser to check I hadn't missed anything that morning. "I'll come down," I said to the intercom. "Do you mind if we talk on the drive in?"

I pounded down the stairs of my building and I took her in a hug when I found her on the pavement outside, but she was somehow awkward and I got only a bit of a dry-lipped peck on the cheek in return. She had a pool car with her, a green Ford Focus that hadn't been properly cleaned out since a couple of sweaty DCs camped in it for a surveillance job. She handed me the keys. She was old-fashioned like that sometimes. My dad would have loved it.

We set off into the city, and within minutes we'd got locked in a traffic system around Broadmead, where Saturday shoppers and roadwork had brought everything to a standstill.

It was one of those moments where it seems surreal that ordinary lives go on around you, that other people can actually afford to tolerate delays, when all you can focus on is the gigantic ticking clock that's your head, counting time on somebody else's life.

We were diverted onto Nelson Street, the city's so-called open-air street art gallery, where graffiti murals covered every dank, depressing concrete facade available: psychedelic art meets calligraphy meets art deco meets the recesses of the minds of a dozen artists from around the world. A dreamscape all of its own.

I waited for Emma to start talking, but the whole time she sat motionless beside me, coat buttoned, collar pulled up, scarf wrapped high on her neck, just staring out front.

"Em?" I said when the silence started to get to me. "What do you want to talk about?"

Still she said nothing. If anything, her silence seemed to have settled deeper on her, like it meant to bury her. I pulled over into a loading bay.

"What's going on?" I said. "What's wrong?"

The ignition was still running and the wipers squealed as they made a pass across the windshield.

There was so much happening in her eyes that I felt my insides wrench.

"Emma?" I said. Whatever the thing was, I was desperate to sort it out, to make it right. I put my hand on hers, but she kept her fingers curled away from mine, pressing her palm flat onto her leg.

"I don't know how to say it." Her voice was small, as if she'd swallowed half of it.

"For Chrissakes try."

She made me wait for an answer until I was fit to burst.

"I've done something bad and I don't know what to do."

"What have you done?" And even then I

was thinking, it can't be so bad, Emma's so hard on herself that whatever she's done will be easy to put right. I thought that even as I watched her shut her eyes, and press her lips together until her face folded around them and she didn't look like the girl I knew. Not one bit.

Her next two words were her confession, her downfall, and the first sparks of a wildfire that was to burn through everything we'd had together with startling speed.

"The blog."

I was slow; I didn't understand at first. She had to spell it out for me, blow on the sparks until I could see that they were dangerous, and that they would spread uncontrollably.

"I've given information to the 'Where is Benedict Finch?' blog."

"You're the leak?"

She nodded.

I gave myself a nasty bruise on the side of my hand where I slammed it on the dashboard. Pain shot up my arm. It made Emma jump and then she seemed to contract into herself a little more.

"Why?" One puny word, to express all the incredulity and anger that I felt.

"I feel so stupid."

"Tell me why!"

"Don't shout," she said. "Please."

I watched her as she tried to compose herself. She carefully tucked her hair behind her ears in a gesture that I knew and loved. She took a deep breath, exhaling audibly, and just when I was about to shout at her again she said, "I wanted to punish Rachel Jenner for letting Ben out of her sight in the woods."

I didn't expect that.

"What? Why? For fuck's sake, why would you do that? Why's that even your business?"

"It got to me, I'm sorry. I started looking at the blog, for research, and I got sucked into it. First I just put a comment, because people were saying some stupid things, but then I found myself agreeing with some of them, and I've got strong feelings about it, because it's a massive issue for me. And I know none of it's an excuse but I was getting tired, it was hard to cope with the family and I was scared I wasn't up to the job. I know I shouldn't have. It was weak. I just couldn't help thinking about how if she'd been a bit more responsible, then it wouldn't have happened. Oh God, Jim. I'm so sorry. My head gets so fucked up sometimes. It's complicated. It's personal. Something happened that I've never told you."

"What happened?"

She didn't answer. Instead she shook her head, and covered her face with her hands.

"Emma! What happened?"

Her hands fell away and her voice veered into hysteria.

"Stop shouting! I said stop!"

She wiped at her face brusquely, streaking the sleeve of her coat.

Then she turned to look at me with an expression of vulnerability that I'd never seen on her before and she pleaded. It was awful, that diminishment of her. She said, "Oh God, I've been so stupid. It's so hard for me to explain but please know that I'm trying to be honest with you because I love you. I do. I know we've never said that to each other but I think I actually do."

But I was too angry to hear it. I was facing the charred remains of our relationship, of Emma's career, possibly of mine too. I said, "Do you know how many resources Fraser's had to put into finding out who the leak is?"

"I'm sorry." A bright, high note on a scale.

"You've risked that boy's life!"

"I'm sorry." The scale descending into tones of hopelessness.

"You owe me a proper explanation."

"I know. I'm scared you won't understand." Just a whisper.

"Try me." My tone was cynical now. I'd become my professional self, tucked away the things I wanted to say. It was self-protection. I hated myself for doing it, but what choice did I have, really?

She talked then, a slow stream of words and it was breaking her to say them.

"Because I saw the photographs Rachel took, they were photographs of Ben. She loves him. I saw it for the first time, how much she cares about him, because they're such beautiful pictures and they made me feel so guilty." She clutched at my arm. "I'm telling you because I don't know what to do and I want you to help me make it right. You won't tell anybody, will you? I've stopped already. I won't do it again."

"You can't come back from this. You cannot," I said, but she was pulling her handbag onto her lap, digging through it.

"I've got a personal email address for the author of the blog. We can track them down. I'll get it for you, I'll get it now."

She took her phone out. I could see that she had missed calls, but not who they were from, and she ignored them, as she tried with trembling fingers to access her mailbox.

"It's gone too far. You can't make it right."

"We don't need to tell anybody else," she

said. She looked pale and fearful, her eyes darting nervously from me to the phone and back. "If you help me we can do it. We can get the blog removed."

"You, not we. I didn't do this, it's got nothing to do with me, and actually you do need to tell them. You're kidding yourself if you think you can get away with it. And you're compromising me just by telling me, let alone expecting me to help you!"

"Please. I'll lose my job." Her eyes were locked on to mine now, wide and wild with panic.

"Do I really need to say that you should have thought of that earlier? What you leaked was spiteful, wicked stuff. Jesus! And now you want me to put myself on the line for you. Do you have any idea what you're asking me to do?"

"Jim." It was a plea. "I thought you would help me."

"I thought I knew you."

She tried to reach out and touch my face, but as her fingers grazed my cheek I said, "Don't," and she withdrew her hand quickly, as if I'd scalded her.

I massaged my temples, and I felt an exhausted, debilitating sadness because I knew that this was the end of us, and that I'd made my own bed on this one. It was my own fucking fault. End of.

She took another deep breath. "I did it because of what happened to my sister," she said, and I could hear that there was bravery in her voice, that she was working up courage for what she was about to say, but for me it was too late for that, because she'd betrayed the police force and the investigation, betrayed Benedict Finch, and betrayed me.

"No," I said. "I'm not interested. I don't want to hear it."

She opened her mouth to reply but something she saw in my face made her close it again, and her features drained of hope.

"Jim . . ." was all she managed.

"No."

I didn't want to hear it because Emma wasn't the person I thought she was, and I wouldn't lie for her.

She started working at her phone again, desperately tapping at the screen, and it was too much for me; it was delusional.

I snatched the phone from her, opened the car window, threw it out, and watched it clatter across the pavement and break against the urine-stained wall, pieces of it scattering among dark black puddles, fag butts, and other unidentifiable scraps of filthy rubbish. A passerby paused to give me a look and I told him to fuck off.

"Tell Fraser," I said to Emma. "Or I will."

"Jim."

"You need to go and do the right thing or this could hang us all. Now."

I started up the car and eased back into the traffic. I couldn't look at her. In the rearview mirror I could see a vast mural covering the side of an office building: a mother and child. It was a pure image, made of black lines and a white background, the mother's lips as sensual as Emma's. I thumped the dashboard again, felt the pain again, and then I took the car in the direction of Kenneth Steele House. On the way, we didn't speak at all.

When we parked at Kenneth Steele House, Emma got out of the car without a word and I watched her walk across the parking lot, and climb the steps to the entrance, slowly, straight-backed. I gave it a full twenty minutes before I followed her. Twenty minutes of gazing through the windshield at the sharp-tipped silvered-metal railings that encircled the parking lot and wondering whether she was doing the right thing in there.

When I finally got out of the car, my body was protesting with fatigue, and I checked my face in the side mirror to be sure I wasn't wearing the whole episode for anybody to read. Inside, I said my normal hello to Lesley, who was on reception, and she smiled at me, and I hoped she didn't notice that I felt like I was wading through shit.

Rachel

With Zhang not answering her phone, and somebody in the incident room telling me that Clemo and Fraser were unavailable too, I had to turn to John. Or, as the papers would have it, the unimpeachable Mr. John Finch, Consultant Pediatric General Surgeon, and proud owner of a lovely new wife.

He answered the phone with the same haste with which I jumped on every call I received. To give him credit, he quickly managed the disappointment he obviously felt when I said I didn't have news, took me seriously when I explained about the pictures in the book, and didn't demur when I asked him to drive me, and the book, to the police station.

Heading up the steps of Kenneth Steele House, I realized I could barely even remember our arrival nearly a week before. The receptionist told us that if we'd like to leave the book with her, then she'd ensure that it was taken up to the incident room.

I said that I'd like to speak to somebody in person. I mentioned DC Zhang and DI Clemo.

She asked us to sit, and we perched side by side on the same sofa we'd occupied on Monday morning.

She made some hushed calls, head down, covering her mouth as if we could lip-read. Then she crossed the foyer, heels clipping the floor noisily, and said, "Someone will be down to see you soon. If you wouldn't mind being patient."

She brought us hot tea in plastic cups so thin you could burn your fingers.

John passed the time by looking through Ben's book methodically, page by page, over and over again. I could barely sit down; I was pulsating with impatience, and after what felt like an interminable wait I approached the desk again.

"Somebody's coming, they're rather busy up there this morning," I was told.

"Can we interrupt them? This is very important."

"They know you're here, they're just in a meeting."

"Can I just speak to DC Zhang?"

"Please be patient, Mrs. Finch."

"My name is Jenner."

"Sorry, Ms. Jenner. DC Zhang and DI Clemo have only recently arrived themselves, and I've rung the incident room but they're both tied up just at the moment. If you can try to be patient, one of them will be down before long, I assure you."

"Please."

"I would ask you to sit down again if possible."

I sat, my knees jigging, hands wringing.

John said, "Perhaps it's best if we just leave the book here."

"What if they can't read Ben's writing?"

"Rachel . . ."

"No. I want to hand them over myself, explain them."

After another ten minutes I felt my patience snap. I took the book from John and said, "If they're not coming down here I'm bloody well going to go up there."

"No, don't do that," John said, but he was too slow to stop me. I marched to reception, propelled forward by my certainty, and my outrage that nobody had come to listen to us.

"Where are they?" I said to the receptionist.

"Ms. Jenner, if you can just be a bit more patient —"

"Stop asking me to be patient. How can I

be patient? My son is missing and if they can't be bothered to come down here I'm going to go to them. What's more important than a piece of new evidence that they don't know about? How is it that I can get the immediate attention of any journalist in the country but not of a single officer investigating my son's case? Should I take this to the press? Should I?"

I was waving the book at her, brandishing it in her face.

"Please don't raise your voice, Ms. Jenner."

"I will raise my voice if I fucking well feel like it. I will raise my voice until SOMEBODY COMES DOWN AND LOOKS AT THIS BOOK!" I slammed it down on the desk in front of her. "THEY NEED TO KNOW ABOUT THIS BECAUSE I WANT MY SON BACK. I WANT BEN AND IF YOU DON'T WANT ME HERE, THEN YOU CAN FUCKING WELL ARREST ME."

She was no pushover, the receptionist. She spoke to me in a voice that was steel-reinforced. "If you take a seat, I shall phone the incident room once more. If you continue to make a scene, I shall ask one of my colleagues to escort you from the building."

Up close to the desk, I saw that her

handbag was tucked into a corner behind it. It had a newspaper folded on it, and I realized that even here, in this environment, I was probably being judged through the filter of what was written about me; that the receptionist was seeing, in front of her own eyes, the Rachel Jenner from the press conference.

John was at my side, and he coaxed me away then, back to the sofa, and I stared at the few people coming and going through the foyer in front of us with an empty gaze that made many of them take a second look at me.

Within minutes, a man stood in front of us.

"DI Bennett," he said, sticking a hand out to John first, and then to me. His handshake was painfully strong, and I didn't recognize him. "Is this it then?"

John stood up and handed him the book and DI Bennett's big hand seemed to dwarf it. He had a neck that sat in rolls on his collar, narrow wide-set eyes, and the shiny crown of his head took on the glow of the ceiling lights.

"Right," he said. "Do you want to show me what's worrying you?"

I showed him the pages that haunted me, and he pored over them, brow hunched.

"I see what you mean," he said, and then, "He's a good artist your lad, isn't he?"

"Will you show it to DI Clemo, or DCI Fraser?"

"Of course I will. I'll do that right away."

"Should we stay, in case you have questions?"

"Honestly, the best place for you right now is at home. We know where to find you, and we'll be in touch with any questions or any information we have, I promise you. And if you phone us with any concerns, at any point, we will always send somebody to talk to you at home about it; there's no need for you to come here."

"I tried to phone DC Zhang," I said.

"Ah well, she's a bit busy in a meeting right now."

"We wanted to get it to you quickly."

"We appreciate that, Ms. Jenner, we really do, and we'll deal with it immediately. I'm going to personally hand-deliver this to DCI Fraser as soon as I leave you."

"Thank you," John said.

Bennett tucked the book under his arm. "I suggest you both go home and get some rest now. The more you rest, the better you'll cope. Thank you for bringing it in."

He offered each of us his hand again and then disappeared through a set of double doors that swung dully on their hinges in his wake.

In spite of his politeness, and of the care he took looking at the book, he left me overwhelmed by my own impotence, feeling it in great shuddering waves. John looked at me with fright, as if he was terrified of another scene that he didn't have the resources to handle, and it was the receptionist who came to my rescue. She emerged from behind the desk and came to me, and sat beside me on the sofa, and put her arms around me. She smelled of perfume and hairspray and she had liver-spotted hands.

"I know," she said over and over again. "I know."

And that act of kindness surprised me, and then upset me more, and finally calmed me down, until I was ready for John to take me home.

Jim

In the incident room the blinds on the windows of Fraser's office were drawn but I could glimpse her silhouette and Emma's through the slats. Nobody else might have noticed it, but to me their body language spoke volumes: Emma had come clean.

I thought I'd feel relieved but instead it was the final straw, and I couldn't stand to witness it.

I took myself down to the canteen, tucked myself in a corner to try to write up a report on the morning's raid with a cup of coffee that would have made British Rail ashamed, but I just got wound up, thinking about it all, and it was hard to concentrate with every nosey parker who walked past my table asking me how the case was going.

I went to the men's room, locked myself in a stall, and tried to get control of myself.

I sat in there on the closed lid of the toilet bowl, my head resting against the partition wall, eyes shut, breathing through my mouth and trying to pull myself together. I don't know how long I stayed, but at some point somebody else came in and the shame of it made me get to my feet.

It was Mark Bennett, undoing his fly at the urinals. He was hyped up; his cheeks flushed red with excitement.

"The proverbial's hit the fan," he said, not caring that his piss was going everywhere. "Something's going on. Benedict Finch's parents came into reception and his mum made a massive scene and brought in one of Ben's schoolbooks they want us to look at. They asked for you and Zhang, but we couldn't find you and Zhang was holed up with Fraser 'not to be disturbed.' Where the fuck have you been? Got the runs or something?"

I started to answer but he said, "So I went and got the book myself, calmed the mother down, but that's not the fucking end of it. I took the book straight into Fraser's office, potential new evidence, thought that was worth disturbing them for, only now she's got Internal Affairs in there with her and Zhang. I gave her the book, but got my head bitten off for interrupting. Something massive is going on, definitely."

I washed my hands for show, and he

joined me at the sink and then stayed on my heels like a pesky younger sibling as we went back to the incident room, Bennett full of ignorant speculation that made my jaw clench.

As we entered the incident room, the door of Fraser's office swung open at the other end and Emma walked out, flanked by two men. Fraser was hovering behind, but shut the door before I could read her face. I recognized one of the men: Bryan Doughty, the biggest cheese in Internal Affairs. Bennett and I stood aside as they approached.

"Clemo," he said, as he passed me.

"Sir," I replied. He was a shark of a man, intellectually and physically well equipped to take a bite of you. Perfect for the job. He didn't slow his pace. Emma's gaze was fixed front and forward.

Even though it was Saturday, about fifteen faces watched them walk the length of the incident room, Emma's small frame dwarfed by the men beside her. When they exited and disappeared from sight, I realized I'd been biting the inside of my cheek so hard I'd drawn blood.

"I think she's been a naughty girl," said Bennett. "Tut, tut, tut. And Doughty's not going to be happy about being called in on a weekend either." He was buoyant: the sight of someone else's career ending in a car crash was actually bolstering his self-esteem.

"Do me a favor and keep your fucking opinion to yourself," I said.

"What's the matter with you? Anybody would think you wanted to get into her knickers." Brave words, but as he said them he was wiping my spittle off his face with an injured expression.

I walked away. I don't know what I would have done to him otherwise. I knocked on the door of Fraser's office.

"What's going on?" I said. I tried to keep my face steady, put my hands in my pockets so the shake didn't show.

Her expression was grim, her eyes were bloodshot, and she had that pallor you get after days on a case, when your skin's sagging and you can't remember what it felt like not to have your shoulders in tight knots.

"Take a seat," she said. "We found our leak."

"Emma?"

"Yes, I'm very sorry to say."

"Fuck me," I said. "I didn't have her down as a Judas."

My head felt tight around the lie. I hoped

my voice wasn't giving me away.

Fraser looked at me hard. "My sentiments exactly," she said. "And I expect this to be especially hard for you because I know you two were working closely together." She let her words hang there for a moment, between us, before she went on. "Emma's confessed to leaking confidential information to the blog. Personal motivations. That's all I can say at this time. Apart from the bleeding obvious, which is that she's thrown a promising career down the pan, and the press will have all of our guts for garters if they get hold of it."

"I feel responsible," I said. "I recommended Emma for the role. I'm sorry."

"I'm a big girl. I don't do things just because one of my DIs has a bright idea. You've no need to take this all on yourself."

She looked at me intently and I still couldn't work out what the subtext was, whether she knew about Emma and me or not.

She said, "You don't seem too shocked."

"I'm shocked, boss, trust me. I just . . . don't really know what to say. I feel like we can't let this hold us back."

She gave me a brisk nod in agreement. "We're in the shit. There's no doubt about that. We don't have time to waste on this, and we can ill afford to be a man down. We need to regroup quickly, figure out how to fill the gap Emma's left us, and somebody's going to have to go through all the work she did."

"I can do that."

"But before anything is done, I want you to have a look at this. Bennett's just brought it up. Hand-delivered by Benedict's parents. With some drama."

"Bennett told me," I said.

"They asked specifically to see you or Emma but we couldn't find you. Where the hell were you, by the way?"

On the bog, shaking like a school kid hiding from bullies. I didn't say that. "I went to the canteen to get on with the report on this morning."

"Without your phone? Ah, never mind. Take a look at this."

She handed me a child's exercise book. On the cover, in uneven handwriting: "Benedict Finch. Oak Class. News Book." I flicked through it. Seeing Ben Finch's clumsy handwriting gave me a bit of a start, it was such a vivid trace of him. Page after page seemed to be filled with pictures from the woods. It made him very real, very present, disturbingly so.

He'd written descriptions of their regular

dog walks and drawn pictures of them too, including the swing.

"So what are we thinking?" I said.

"Well, Ben's parents are thinking that this means that anybody at school might have known about the regular walks they took, and the route they took, and they're thinking that there might be something in that."

"But anybody they knew could have known about the walks. People with dogs walk them regularly and mostly to the same places. There's only so many routes you can take in the woods."

"Point taken, but we do have an obligation to look into this, and I think we should. We're not overrun with options at this point, and I am not going to miss anything, Jim. I'll not have that on my conscience."

"So what this actually means is that we can include school staff, or anybody else who might have had access to this book, in the circle of people who might have known about the dog walks. So what do we do? Reinterview school staff?"

Fraser was scribbling a note. "That's exactly what we do."

"Start with the teacher and teaching assistant?"

"Yep. And the headmaster. And don't forget the school secretary too. They always know everything."

"You know they've all got alibis, don't you, boss?"

"Yeah, yeah, I do. Teacher having lunch with parents, school secretary at cinema with a friend, TA shagging his girlfriend, headmaster playing golf. That good enough recall for you? Do you think I've gone senile all of a sudden?"

"No, I just want to be sure we're not wasting our time on this."

"I'm looking for information here. I want to dig deeper with these people. Maybe the books will trigger a memory for somebody. And I need to tell you that we've had a turn-up on the CCTV as well," she added. "Confirmation that Ben was with his mother when they drove across the bridge on the way to the woods. They're still scouring and cross-checking a final half-hour of footage but we should have the results later today."

Other than that, Fraser said we still hadn't tracked down the man Rachel said she and Ben spoke to in the woods. She had a DC looking into that, but he was banging his head against a wall because nobody had come forward. It seemed like Rachel Jenner was the only one who'd seen him. Even the regular dog walkers weren't sure who he might be. In the office they'd started to call him Big Foot.

"Nicky Forbes?" I said, when we were nearly done. My thoughts had kept returning to her, I couldn't deny it.

"Definitely still of interest, but softly, softly."

"Of course."

"First job — get Bennett to look through Emma's work, clear her desk; everything she was doing, I want to know about."

"I can do that, boss."

"I think it's better if somebody else does it, don't you, Jim?"

This time, the subtext was crystal clear. She knew. I managed to nod an affirmative and got myself out of her office as quickly as I could.

Rachel

John drove me home, and came inside with me, guiding me past the three or four journalists who remained doggedly outside my door.

They should have seen me at the police station, I thought. That would have got them going.

For now, they were loitering a few lampposts away from my house and they called out to us in a desultory way, trained like Pavlov's dogs to know that neither John nor I would talk.

They still frightened me, but not as much as their colleagues who were probably piecing together juicy commentary on our lives for their Sunday supplements, making me into a comment on society, doing it just as John and I unlocked the front door of my home and contemplated the absence that was our son.

Inside, John kept shooting surreptitious

glances at me, which made me feel like he was assessing me, gauging my stability.

I let him go up to Ben's room alone, and he was there for a long time. I expected he was doing what I did: touching objects, remembering, smelling bits of clothing, holding things that Ben had held.

When he was down, I asked him a question that had been on my mind since Nicky had gone.

"Why did you tell the police that Nicky was worried about me after Ben was born?"

He was surprised, but he had a quick answer. "Because she was. She phoned me a lot."

"Why didn't you tell me?"

"At the time? I didn't think you needed to know. You were so tired, and trying so hard. I thought she was being neurotic. It would have upset you."

"And afterward?"

"I just forgot. She stopped, and it didn't seem important. Why are you bringing this up now? Did the police mention it?"

"I just wondered," I said, and I realized that he didn't know yet, about Nicky, about our family. And I kept the news folded up like a piece of paper I'd tucked into my pocket, because I didn't know how to say it, and didn't want to admit that there was a part of me capable of distrusting my own sister.

Later on, John said he should go home. I wanted him to stay, but I didn't trust myself to admit it out loud, for fear of how it would make me sound. I was aware of my own instability by then, I could feel it seeping out into my speech and my actions, and I didn't want that look from John again. The one that evaluated me, worked out how to handle me.

He saw I didn't want to be alone, he saw that at least. "Should I phone Laura?" he asked, and I said, "It's OK," but he began to insist and I didn't know what to do apart from to nod mutely because I couldn't tell him about her either. About how I'd shooed her away too.

It took her a while to answer the phone and when she did he immediately frowned and he left the room. I listened, my house was too small for secrecy, and heard him say, "Are you drunk?" in an incredulous tone.

I knew he'd have thumb and finger pressed to his temples, as if trying to hold his thoughts together; I knew he'd look as if his weariness were falling off him in pieces.

His end of the conversation was mostly

listening noises, murmured words of agreement or appeasement. He spoke very little; she must have been speaking a lot.

"Rachel will understand," he said after a while. "I'm sure she will." And then, "I think it's best if she calls you tomorrow."

"She's drunk?" I asked when he reappeared.

"She's been drinking all afternoon as far as I can tell. You don't want her around here."

"What's she saying?"

"She's not making much sense. She says to tell you she's sorry. That the thing is too big for her, whatever that means. That she just wanted to support you. She's not in a fit state to be coherent. What happened?"

"It's my fault," I said, but it was a whisper and he didn't hear. He asked me again.

"I don't know if I trust her," I told him. "I don't know who I trust."

"I've never trusted her."

"What do you mean?"

"I don't know, I've just never liked her. I thought she used you."

"You never told me."

"You never asked."

I was absorbing this when my phone rang.

"Can you answer it?" I said. It was still in his hand.

The phone call was short, it furrowed his brow, but I couldn't decipher it from hearing his responses.

After he'd ended the call with a thank-you, he said, "That was a DC Justin Woodley calling to say that DC Zhang isn't our family liaison officer anymore."

"What? Why not?"

"He just said she's had to step away from the post, didn't give a specific reason, and that they'd appoint somebody new as soon as they could, Monday at the latest, but in the meantime we should speak to him. Have you met him?"

"I don't think so. What could possibly have happened? Did you ask?"

"It's very odd," said John, "because I thought they said she was in the office this morning."

"They did." I curled my legs up onto the sofa, wrapped my arms around myself, and felt the disappointment keenly. I minded very much that DC Zhang was gone because I'd got used to her, started to trust her, and I knew I would miss her. I didn't like the idea of having a man as our liaison officer, however temporary. It wouldn't be the same.

"I really liked her," I said.

"I'm sure DC Woodley or whoever they appoint will be fine." John wasn't as perturbed as I was; he had Katrina to lean on. He looked at his watch.

"Look, I can stay here a bit longer, but I have to go home later tonight. You could come to our house."

"I can't leave here again. I shouldn't have left this morning."

"Are you sure?"

"Yes." And I knew I'd be up all night, fearing for Ben and fearing for myself too, but that I had no choice.

"If that's what you want."

Later John and I warmed up some of the food that Nicky had left in the fridge: wholesome, beautifully cooked food. It should have sustained us, given us strength, but both of us could only pick at it.

It was at the precise moment that we were getting up to clear the table that we heard a powerful crash, high-pitched and violent. It came from the front room and seemed to make the air cave in around us. It was the sound of shattering glass, and it made us motionless for a moment and the dog barked and then whimpered and then all was quiet again except for the noise of footfalls, somebody running away.

John was up on his feet in an instant. He ran outside.

I followed him, but by the time I got to the front door it was swinging wide open and he was gone.

A bitter wind blew into the room, not just through the door but also through a gaping jagged hole where the front window had been. The curtains, drawn to shield us from the press, were dancing, flapping and turning in the wind like dervishes. Pieces of glass littered the floor, sharp edges everywhere, and in the center of the room lay a brick.

There were letters painted on it. It took me a moment to realize that there were two words on its side, the same two that had screamed at me from the back fence: "BAD" and "MOTHER." Small, printed carefully. It couldn't be easy to paint on brick.

"John!" I screamed.

I ran to the door. Glass crunched underfoot. From one end of the street footfalls rang out, the sound echoing. I saw John and, just ahead of him, another figure, both running as fast as they could. They were moving shadows and, in an instant, they'd disappeared around the corner.

The street stretched away from me, dark and wet, the glow from the streetlamps looking three-dimensional in the rain, orbs of orange fluorescence. I stood in a shard of white light that spilled out of my house and fell around me, making the slick wet surface of the pavement gleam blackly. Opposite, a neighbor opened his front door just a crack.

"Help," I said. "Help us."

From the corner the men had disappeared around, I heard a scuffle, a thud, a cry of pain, and then I began to run too.

JIM

Addendum to DI James Clemo's report for Dr. Francesca Manelli

Transcript recorded by Dr. Francesca Manelli
DI James Clemo and Dr. Francesca Manelli in attendance

Notes to indicate observations on DI Clemo's state of mind or behavior, where his remarks alone do not convey this, are in italics.

We're getting to the point in our process where I would like to see some real progress from DI Clemo. He's still very closed emotionally, and our time is running out.

FM: I'm so sorry about Emma.
JC: Don't be.
FM: That must have been an extremely difficult situation for you.

JC: It didn't help.

FM: Do we know why she did it?

JC: I know now, but I didn't then. It was partly because she just couldn't cope with the role. That was my fault, I know it was, I fucked up. But that wasn't the only reason. It was because of something that happened to her . . .

FM: Take your time.

JC: Sorry.

FM: There's no need to be sorry. You don't need to tell me now. I'm curious about whether either of you tried to contact each other that night?

JC: No. We didn't. I made a choice — my loyalty was to the investigation.

FM: That's a very selfless choice.

JC: Is it?

FM: I think so. Others might have protected their own interests more.

JC: I protected my position in the investigation.

FM: But the personal cost to you was extremely high.

He tries to answer this, but he can't seem to find the words. He's done well so far today and I don't want this subject to become taboo, so I change tack.

FM: Tell me what happened that afternoon once you turned your mind back to the investigation.

JC: Well, that's the thing. First thing was, I called Simon Forbes, Nicky Forbes's husband, and asked him to contact me to arrange an interview. But after I did that, we got a break that we didn't expect. That evening the boys got to the end of the CCTV checks and turned up something significant.

FM: Which was?

JC: They traced one of the cars that crossed the bridge about an hour before Ben's abduction. It was registered to Lucas Grantham, Ben's teaching assistant.

FM: I understood that he had an alibi.

JC: He did, but a piece of evidence like that is enough to make you take a much closer look at an alibi.

FM: And Nicola Forbes?

JC: Still a person of interest, but you don't argue with CCTV. And we had the school-book evidence too.

FM: I felt as if you didn't put much store in the schoolbook.

JC: Not on its own. I thought we needed to be careful to understand that it only widened an already considerable pool of people who could have known about the dog walks. But in the context of the

CCTV discovery it was much more significant.

It gives him satisfaction to say that. He is born for this job, I think. But I have another question.

FM: DI Clemo, did you rest at all that night?

JC: I did go home, yes. I knew I couldn't pull another all-nighter.

FM: And did you get some sleep?

This question makes him edgy.

FM: Were you able to sleep?

He doesn't answer.

FM: Were you thinking of Emma?

JC: I might have been.

FM: You suffered a very traumatic loss that day. You lost a relationship with somebody you had extremely strong feelings for.

JC: It was nothing compared to what Benedict Finch might have been going through.

FM: That doesn't mean it wasn't significant. Would you say this time might have been the start of the insomnia that plagues you now?

JC: I don't want to talk about it.

FM: I believe we have to talk about this, or we can't make progress.

JC: It's not relevant.

FM: I believe it is. Think about it. I'd like to discuss it at our next session.

JC: Fine.

He coaxes his lips up into a smile for me, but the look in his eyes is far from happy. I can see that he's just being polite and I have to remind myself that that is, after all, progress. The problem is, it's too slow.

Rachel

It was John who had cried out in pain. I found him on the corner of the street, fallen, his head smashed open against the side of the curb, his face damaged too, his ear pulpy. The amount of blood on his face and beneath him was sickening. It was matted in his hair, sticky and dark on the pavement, and it soaked into my knees and covered my hands as I knelt beside him.

He was unconscious; eyes glassy. I peeled off my sweater and pressed it against his head, trying to stem the blood flow. I screamed over and over again for help.

When the paramedics came they moved quickly and worked with a quiet urgency that frightened me. There was no joking, and no smiling. Uniformed police officers arrived too. They lent me a phone to ring Katrina, and I told her and then handed the phone to one of the paramedics, who instructed her to meet them at A & E at the

Bristol Royal Infirmary.

When they were finally ready to move John, they rolled him carefully onto a stretcher and eased it into the ambulance, one of them seated in the back beside his inert form. It was shocking, that, the absence of him. That, and the amount of blood.

"Will he be all right?" I asked.

"Head injuries are very serious," they told me. "Unpredictable. You did well to call us so quickly." There were no reassurances.

Part of me didn't want to let him go on his own, but the police knew Katrina was meeting him at the hospital and they wanted to take a statement from me. As the ambulance disappeared into the night underneath its pulsing halo of blue light, I walked back down the street. A uniformed officer accompanied me. Two police cars were still parked at drunken angles, blocking off the scene.

In the house, they took my statement. More officers arrived and took photographs, and then they put the brick in a plastic bag and took it away. They helped me clean up the glass while somebody they'd called boarded up my window. They said they'd station somebody outside the house for the rest of the night.

One thing the police all agreed on, and they even had a laugh about it, was that it was ironic that nobody from the press had been there to witness the incident. The three journalists and one photographer who'd had the stamina to stake out the house overnight had wandered down the road to get food.

They'd reappeared, kebabs in hand, shreds of iceberg lettuce falling from them, as the ambulance doors had been slammed shut and John had been driven away.

It was the only thing to be grateful for.

I slept in the front bedroom that night, in my own bed, wanting to know that the police car they'd stationed there for the night was just outside, wanting the security of that. In case I had to shout out. Bang on the window. In case I heard somebody creep into my house, wanting to do me harm.

I took Ben's duvet and pillow from his bed and brought them with me. I stripped away my own bedding, piling it on the floor, and arranged Ben's stuff carefully on my bed, with his nunny, and his Baggy Bear.

I listened all night for the sound of footfalls again, and I lay rigid when voices loomed out of the darkness. They were the usual Saturday night revelers returning home, but their shouts and their drunken laughter sounded hostile to me now. Every noise I heard that night was laced with menace.

JIM

It was Emma who I thought of all the way home. I thought of telling her about the CCTV, that grainy image of Lucas Grantham driving across the bridge in a blue Peugeot 305, his bike on a rack on the back. I thought of driving to her flat and holding her, trying to find a way forward. I felt my exhaustion drug me, dull my senses and my reactions, addle my brain. I felt like part of me was missing.

I went to bed after midnight. I'd treated myself to a packet of cigarettes, a consolation prize for the demise of the best relationship I'd ever had, and I sucked on one after the other, the smoke hitting my lungs like a wallop, making them ache. I drank most of a pot of coffee far too late. I felt like I should keep working, scouring Lucas Grantham's background, but my concentration was shot to pieces and so I got under my covers and tasted the bitter residue of the fags mixed with toothpaste on my tongue and thought about the CCTV and what it meant, and thought about what Emma might be doing.

It wasn't her that got into my head for the rest of that night, though.

When I finally shut my eyes and tried to sleep, my brain had a different plan.

It pulled me back to my past, and it did it swiftly, like an ocean current that's merciless and strong. It took me back to my childhood, where it had a memory to replay for me, a videotape of my past that it had dug out of the back of a drawer where I'd shoved it, long ago, hoping to forget.

When the memory starts I'm on the landing at my parents' house, looking through the banisters. I'm eight years old, exactly the same age as Benedict Finch. I'm at home, and it's well past my bedtime.

Down below, the hallway is dark because it's night and it's hard to see, but when the front door opens I know it's my sister, Becky, because of the way she closes it ever so softly, trying not to make a sound. She's wearing a party dress, which looked pretty when she went out earlier, but now it's a mess and her tights have got a big rip on one leg. Her eyes look horrible, like she's been crying black tears.

She yelps when she realizes my dad's standing in the hall opposite her. He's wearing his day clothes and holding a cigarette that glows red. Becky doesn't move.

"What did you see?" Dad asks her. His face is in shadows.

She shakes her head in a tight way, says, "Nothing."

"Don't muck me about, Rebecca."

A sob comes from her; it makes her body buckle. "I saw the girl," she says. "And I saw you."

"You shouldn't have been there," he says.

"She was hurt, but you didn't care." Becky chokes out her words. "You gave her to that man, I saw you do it, she was begging, she was crying, and you did nothing, you let it happen. They shoved her in the car. I wasn't born yesterday, Dad!"

She tries to lift her head and look at him all proud, like she usually is, but instead her back slides down the wall so she's on the floor. Dad crouches in front of her.

"Keep your voice down," he says to her, "or you'll wake your mum." He takes her chin between his fingers and wrenches her head up so she's looking at him.

I don't know what to do. I want to look away but I can't stop watching. I want to stop them both from arguing. I don't want him to hurt her.

I see a big china dog on a shelf beside me. It belongs to my mum. She loves that dog. She likes the smooth, nubbly texture of its ears. I pick it up. I don't want to smash my mum's china dog and I don't want to hurt anybody, but I'm desperate to distract Dad and Becky, to stop the thing that's happening. I throw it, as hard as I can, but it hits the top of the banister and so it smashes right by me and rains shards of china around my feet as well as down onto my dad and Becky below. I see this as if it's in slow motion.

Becky screams and I do too, and then my mum comes from her room and turns on the landing light. It freezes the three of us: Becky, my dad, and me. Mum's wearing just her nightie, long sleeves, hem brushing the carpet, soft fabric, and she just stands there really quiet for a second, then she says to Becky, "Go to bed, love," and Becky runs up the stairs past us. My dad comes up after her fast, two steps at a time, and before I realize what's happening his hand is on my arm and it feels so strong and my bones feel like brittle sticks, but my mum is calm, and she says, "Mick, give him to me, he's hurt. Look, Mick, he's cut himself on the broken china. Mick . . . Please . . ."

■ ■ ■ ■

I don't remember any further than that. Just as if it were a dream, my mind cut the memory there, at the point when it felt like the stress of it was nipping unbearably hard at the edges of me. And then it replayed, even though I was desperate to sleep, and I felt as if tiredness was collapsing my veins.

And I knew what it was telling me. It was telling me that people aren't always what they seem, and it was telling me to fear for Benedict.

And both of those things made me break out in sweat, even though the night was cold and the duvet was too thin to stop the chill from creeping in around me, and there was no extra body in my bed to keep me warm.

But, worst of all, it compounded both my guilt that we hadn't found him yet and my fear for what could be happening to him at that very moment.

Deep into the small hours of the morning, I felt as if I was coming undone.

■ ■ ■ ■

Day 8
Sunday,
October 28, 2012

■ ■ ■ ■

The Prolonged Investigation: This phase in the investigative process occurs when it becomes apparent the child will not be quickly located, most immediate leads have been exhausted . . . While some observers might view this stage as one of passively waiting for new information to emerge, in reality, it presents an opportunity for law enforcement to restructure a logical, consistent, and tenacious investigative plan eventually leading to the recovery of the child and arrest of the abductor.

— Preston Findlay and Robert G. Lowery Jr. (eds.), "Missing and Abducted Children: A Law-Enforcement Guide to Case Investigation and Program Management," fourth edition, National Center for Missing & Exploited Children, OJJDP Report, 2011

Researchers reported that abductors seldom "stalk" their victim. However, they are usually very skilled at manipulating and luring children. Those lures commonly involve requests for assistance, to find a lost pet, to claim an emergency, calling the victim by name, posing as an authority figure or soliciting the victim by internet computer chats.

— Marlene L. Dalley and Jenna Ruscoe, "The Abduction of Children by Strangers in Canada: Nature and Scope," National Missing Child Services, National Police Services, Royal Canadian Mounted Police, December 2003

Email
To: Corinne Fraser <fraserc@aspol.uk>
Cc: Giles Martyn <martyng@aspol.uk uk>; Bryan Doughty <doughtyb@aspol.uk>; James Clemo <clemoj@aspol.uk>
From: Janie Green <greenj@aspol.uk>
October 28, 2012 at 08:13

OPERATION HUCKLEBERRY — WIBF BLOG UPDATE

Morning, Corinne

Bryan and I have spoken about developments relating to the WIBF blog this morning — much of which he's asked me not to refer to directly in email — so we'll speak about that. However, I can say that activity continues on the WIBF blog, in that last night a post appeared suggesting police incompetency. In spite of that we are confident that what we discovered yesterday has taken the sting out of its tail so that while it remains unpleasant and accusatory, no further privileged information was made public.

As of this morning, the blog owner has been contacted by ourselves by email and has been asked to take down the blog. We reminded the blog owner of contempt of court and other legal issues and made it clear that we would take action against them if necessary. We've not yet received a response, and we are not overly hopeful of their agreement, because the blog has a rapidly growing number of followers. Best-case scenario might be that the knowledge that we are monitoring extremely closely at least keeps the content somewhat under control, while we look into tracing the identity of the owner from the email address (apparently this could be complicated depending on how smart they've been at covering their tracks). However, now that the blog lacks a source of confidential information about the investigation, Bryan, Giles, and I all feel that it shouldn't be a worry to the extent that it was, even if it remains vindictive and aggressive, which, as you'll see below, seems to be the tone of much of the media this weekend. Anyway, I'll keep you posted.

Roundup of this morning's press coverage relating to Operation Huckleberry to follow. The supplements are all over it — double spreads, etc. — usual mixture of sensible and scurrilous, some editorial and thought pieces too, and Rachel Jenner in particular is still a target.

Looking forward, I'm hopeful that with the blog out of the running or at least under control, we might be able to get some more positive material out there to reinforce our efforts and encourage people to come forward.

Janie Green
Press Officer, Avon and Somerset Constabulary

Rachel

When dawn came there was no respite from the grip of my nighttime fears, because it was Sunday.

One week since Ben went missing.

A lifetime of loss in one week.

And still no news.

I looked at myself in the bathroom mirror, as I brushed my teeth with slow, ineffective strokes, and I didn't recognize myself.

The police ordered a taxi to take me to the hospital. They promised that a squad car would remain outside the house. They promised me that they would protect me.

The police asked the taxi to collect me from the back of my house so the driver wouldn't see the press and work out who I was. The driver was an older man, wearing a Sikh turban, with a white beard and white eyebrows. I slunk into the backseat behind him.

"BRI is it?" he asked.
"Yes please."
"Do you mind which route?"
"No."
On the passenger seat beside him was a newspaper, opened out, and I could see a photograph of Ben. He wanted to talk about it.
"You heard about this little boy then?"
"Yes," I made myself say. I was desperate he shouldn't recognize me. I pulled my scarf up around my chin, moved my hair so that it obscured my face.
"Terrible, isn't it?"
"Yes it is." I pressed myself against the window, staring out as the taxi descended into the city. We were driving through deserted residential streets where the only sign of life was a mangy fox panting sickly in the shelter of an evergreen hedge.
"My wife, she says the mother's done it. She can feel it in her bones. That's what people are saying, you know, the mother's done it. But you know, I don't think she did. It's unnatural, to do that. We had an argument about it last night, you know?"
I could sense he was trying to meet my eye in the mirror, gauge my opinion. I looked away. It was impossible to answer him.

We turned onto Cheltenham Road, abruptly in the city center now, pubs and bars all shut up on either side of us. A pair of homeless men sat on a stoop together, shrouded in blankets. They were sharing a cigarette. They had bulging red alcoholic faces and broken teeth.

"The thing is," he said, "this is what I said to my wife . . ."

He wanted to give me his wisdom. Perhaps his wife turned away from him at this point last night, wanting to stick to her own view, perhaps he won her over with it.

"I said to her that if you've been called those things, accused like the mother is, you never get over it. That's the shame of it. If she's guilty, she deserves it; if she's innocent, then people have done her wrong."

We swung around the Bear Pit roundabout, the swift curve of it making my stomach quail, dirty shop windows advertising bridal wear and discount trainers blurring in front of my eyes. Yards ahead, I saw the magistrates' court and the hospital buildings.

"I'll get out here," I said at a red light. "Can you stop?" Desperate to escape him, that kind man, before he saw who I was.

"Are you sure, love?" Eyes in the mirror again, a frown line above them. "Are you

OK? Are you sick? You don't look too well. Sorry, I thought you were visiting somebody, I didn't know you were sick. Shall I take you to A & E?"

I opened the door while we were at the light, pushed some cash at him, got out. He had to drive on because the light turned green and somebody behind him landed a fist on their horn.

My scarf wound tightly up my face, my hair arranged like a pair of curtains that were mostly shut, in the plate glass outside the hospital entrance my reflection told me I looked like somebody with something to hide.

Jim

Nine o'clock Sunday morning, on Fraser's instructions, Bennett and I were knocking at a heavy wooden door set in a stone wall on a wide sidewalk in the posh end of Sea Mills and listening to the sound of birdsong while we waited for a reply.

The woman who opened it had the same flaming red hair as Ben's teaching assistant. She wore an extravagantly colorful kimono over a pair of pajamas and had bare legs and feet. Her toes curled in as the cold hit them. She was polite but perturbed. She was Lucas Grantham's mother.

"He's here but he's still asleep," she said, when we asked if we could have a word with him. "He got in late last night."

"Anybody else at home?" Bennett asked her.

"No. Just us. Nobody else lives here."

The house was unusual, built in the sixties I'd have guessed, single story, wrapped in an L-shape around a large garden. Impenetrable looking from the outside, the interior was flooded with light because almost every wall facing the garden was made of glass.

She asked us to wait in a modest-sized sitting room. There was nothing showy about this home apart from the architecture. The furnishings weren't new and the walls were lined with shelves in cheap brown wood, which carried hundreds of books. Visible across the garden was a room at the end of the house, which looked like an artist's studio.

In a far corner of the garden was a very large mound, covered in grass, and at one end of it was a corrugated metal door that you reached by walking down a few steps.

"Do you know what that is?" Bennett said, in a voice that told me he'd quite like to educate me.

"It's an Anderson shelter," I said. I wasn't going to give him the pleasure of engaging in his usual one-upmanship. I'd wanted to do this interview with Fraser, but she was still firefighting back at HQ after Emma's confession. We'd only been out together for half an hour, but already I was tolerating Bennett at best.

When Lucas Grantham appeared, his pale skin was whiter than I remembered, freckles running over it like a nasty rash. He wore a crumpled T-shirt, which looked like he'd slept in it, and a pair of tracksuit bottoms.

His mother had dressed herself, and Bennett said, "Make us a cup of coffee, would you, love? While we have a chat with Lucas."

I winced as I saw pride flicker in her face before she made a calculation and quelled it in the face of our authority. She left us with her son.

The three of us sat down around a low coffee table, and I pulled a photograph from my file and put it down in front of Grantham. It showed his car, crossing the suspension bridge, at 14:30 on Sunday, October 21, time and date clearly printed on the photograph.

"Fuck," he said. "Oh fuck. I told Sal we shouldn't have done this, I told her."

"Done what, son?" said Bennett.

"Now you're going to think that I've done something to Ben Finch. Truth is, I don't even know him very well! I don't. He's a nice kid, he's good at art, but that's all I know!"

"Reel it back in, son," said Bennett. "Reel it back in. Let's start at the beginning."

Grantham's panic was palpable now, hands rubbing up and down along his thighs, clawing at his knees. Eyes darting from Bennett, to me, to the photograph, to the doorway where his mother might re-appear.

"Who's Sal?" I asked him.

"That's my girlfriend."

"The one who gave you the alibi?"

"Yeah."

"The alibi that said that the two of you were at Sal's flat the afternoon of Sunday, the twenty-first of October?"

"Yeah."

"Is that true?"

"No." His face twists.

"Why did you lie, Mr. Grantham?" Bennett again.

"Because I knew what you'd think."

"What would we think?"

"That it was me that took Ben. Of course you'd think that! I would, anybody would. That's why Sal helped me get an alibi."

"And did you? Did you take Ben Finch?" I took back the questioning.

"No!" He shook his head violently.

"Did you hurt Ben Finch?"

"No."

"Did you see Ben Finch?"

"No! I swear it. I wasn't even in the same bit of the woods as him."

"So what were you doing?"

"I was cycling the trails at Ashton Court."

"With anybody?"

"On my own."

"What time did you get home?"

"About five o'clock. Sal can confirm that."

"Sal who helped you fabricate an alibi?"

"Sorry. I'm sorry."

"Do you know we could charge both of you for this?" I was so angry I could have throttled him.

"Do you mind, Mr. Grantham," Bennett said, standing up, moving to the window, "if we take a look in your Anderson shelter?"

"Why? Why would you do that? I was cycling, that's the truth, it's the truth, I swear it."

His mother was in the doorway now, as he knew she would be, and she had a tray of mugs in her hands. It wobbled.

"Oh my God, Lucas," she said. "What have you done?"

"Mum, I've not done anything. I promise."

"God help us," she said. "You've always been secretive, God knows you have, but please tell me you've nothing to do with this."

It wasn't the display of loyalty you might have expected from a mother. Bennett and I exchanged a glance.

"Do you think you might be willing to

come to the station with us for a bit more of a chat?" I asked Lucas.

He nodded, his pale eyes cast down, his cheeks flaming.

RACHEL

The hospital receptionist sent me to a ward in the old part of the building. I walked down a corridor that was long and square, an exercise in perspective, with a pair of double doors at the end. Rectangular strips of lighting hung from the ceiling at regular intervals, each one emitting a pale bloom of fluorescence, as if it were undernourished.

Old linoleum that was the color of ripe cherries covered the floor, and on each side there were private rooms where patients lay. Some were propped upright, reading or watching TV. Others were just contours under the sheets, still as a landscape, in rooms that seemed more dimly lit, as if they were advertising their role as a potential place of transition, a conduit between illness and health, or between life and death.

I saw Katrina emerge from a room at the far end of the corridor. She stepped out, then turned and closed the door gently behind her. She stood for a second or two, looking back into the room, her hand against the window. She wasn't aware of me.

"Katrina," I said. I hardly dared to look into the room, and when I did I saw that John looked barely alive. He lay on his back, his head was heavily bandaged, an oxygen mask was over his mouth, and what I could see of his face was swollen and disfigured by bruising. He was connected to tubes everywhere. Two nurses were tending to him.

"Hello," Katrina said softly, and I was disarmed by her humility and vulnerability. Her face was taut with exhaustion and shock. She looked very, very young, just as she had at her house a few days earlier.

"They want to do some checks," she said. "I was in the way."

"How is he?"

"He has bleeding and swelling on the brain," she said. "They hope the swelling will reduce. They say he's stable."

"How long will that take?"

"Nobody can say. And nobody can say what damage it'll leave."

I put my hand on the glass, palm pressed against it.

"Did you see what happened?" she asked me.

"Somebody threw a brick through the window and he ran out into the street after them. He was chasing them. I didn't see what happened after that. I found him just around the corner. He was already hurt, he was lying on the ground."

"The doctor said it looks as though he was kicked in the head repeatedly." Her voice cracked. "Who would do a thing like that?"

"I don't know," I said.

We stood side by side like sentries, watching him, and it was long moments before we were interrupted by brisk footsteps. It was a nurse, and the soles of her shoes squeaked on the linoleum.

She gave some leaflets to Katrina. "I grabbed what I could," she said. "The ward's miles away and I got paged as soon as I got there so I hope they're what you need."

"Thank you," said Katrina. She took the leaflets hastily, held them against her stomach. She was trying to hide them from me, but there was no point. I'd already seen enough. "Folic Acid," I'd read as they were handed over, "an essential ingredient for making healthy babies."

"You need rest," said the nurse, "and you need to keep your strength up. Would you consider going home and getting some sleep? We don't expect to see any change in him today."

Katrina nodded, and it satisfied the nurse. "I'll see you later no doubt," she said. She disappeared the way she'd come, still squeaking.

"You're pregnant," I said. My words sounded soft, and distant, as if they'd drifted in from elsewhere, but she heard me.

"I didn't want you to find out like this. I'm sorry."

I turned away from her, and looked at John. The nurses were in conference, standing at the end of the bed, annotating his notes. He was motionless, apart from the almost imperceptible rise and fall of his chest under the sheet.

"Does he know?" I said.

"No."

Now I let my forehead fall gently onto the glass of the window. I wanted the cool, hard surface to counteract a spreading numbness in my head.

"Congratulations." I said it flatly, and I didn't mean it to sound hurtful, though it might have.

"He hasn't coped," she said, indicating John. "This. Ben. Everything. It's destroying him. He thinks this wouldn't have happened if you and he had stayed together."

I had to try very hard. The numbness was everywhere, threatening to make me callous. Something about her touched me though. It could have been her vulnerability, or perhaps the fact that she was carrying a new life.

"John's a good father," I said.

I put my hand out to touch her, but the impulse died before I made contact and my arm dropped.

I turned and walked away, and, as I did so, I noticed that my shoes weren't squeaking on the floor, they were tapping, in a beat that was painfully slow. I counted my steps as I walked.

It was all I could do.

Jim

Addendum to DI James Clemo's report for Dr. Francesca Manelli

Transcript recorded by Dr. Francesca Manelli
DI James Clemo and Dr. Francesca Manelli in attendance

Notes to indicate observations on DI Clemo's state of mind or behavior, where his remarks alone do not convey this, are in italics.

FM: I'm very interested in something you wrote when you described your childhood memory.
JC: Don't put too much store in that.
FM: Do you mind if we discuss it?
JC: If you like.
FM: You said, and I'm just going to refer to it directly here, because the way you

phrased it interested me. You said, "It was telling me that people aren't always what they seem."

JC: Yes.

FM: So does that mean that your father wasn't who people thought he was?

JC: He was everything they thought he was, people respected him, you should have seen the turnout at his funeral, but he had another side too. People do.

FM: Was your father violent?

JC: He was a different generation.

FM: Meaning?

JC: They did things differently then.

FM: Including hurting his children?

JC: It was just a slap here and there. Did nobody give you a slap when you were growing up?

FM: I'd rather not comment on my upbringing.

JC: I bet they did. Everybody did it, before the Internet started policing our lives. My dad was just part of his generation.

FM: What your sister saw, do you think what he was doing was legal?

JC: I don't know.

FM: Did you ever speak to your sister about that incident?

JC: No. We weren't close. She left home soon after that anyway.

FM: What do you think she witnessed?

JC: I've no idea. She was a hysterical teenage girl. She was always kicking off. You're putting too much significance on this. I shouldn't have written it. I only wrote it because it's what you look for when you're working, that person who's not who you think they are. That was a stupid example, I'm not even sure I remember it right anyway. I was a kid.

I'm not sure I believe this, I think he's obfuscating. I wait for him to continue, to fill in the silence.

JC: Look, I admired my dad. He had people's respect because he'd earned it. He was one of the best detectives of his generation. Can we move on?

FM: How did he earn respect?

JC: He had a saying: "You can't put the shit back in the donkey."

FM: Meaning?

JC: Meaning you try not to fuck up, you don't let things get out of your control.

FM: Was it hard to grow up in his shadow?

JC: It made me want to be a detective, and to do well, if that's what you mean.

FM: Was that a good thing?

JC: It was better than being a bum, or pimping, or boozing, or raping old ladies for kicks, or getting so shitfaced that you think it's OK to smash your wife's head against a wall until she loses her teeth as well as her self-respect. What do you mean "Was that a good thing?"

FM: I'm interested that my question is making you feel angry.

JC: Because it's a joke! It's actually insulting.

FM: I think it might mean that being a successful detective was a matter of honor for you?

JC: Yes! Yes, it was, it is, and I don't think there's anything wrong with that.

He's displaying a level of anger that I feel is excessive, though he's trying to disguise it.

FM: Would it be fair to say that at this point in the case you were under almost intolerable personal pressure in addition to the pressure the case was putting on you?

JC: You're totally missing the point.

FM: What was the point then? Tell me.

JC: Benedict Finch was the fucking point. Finding Benedict Finch. Giving him safely back to his mother. That was the only thing that mattered. Why can't you see that?

His fists are clenched, his teeth gritted. I thank him for coming and say that I'll see him next week. I don't wish to be cold with him but he is challenging, and I need him to understand how important it is for him to open up completely during our discussions. Our time together is running out.

RACHEL

My cabdriver on the way home didn't want to talk any more than I did and I was grateful for that. I sat noiseless and motionless in a corner of the backseat, seeing John's still body and his disfigured face, thinking about his new child.

The cabbie dropped me off around the front and a uniformed police officer clambered stiffly out of his squad car to ensure that I got in safely.

Inside the house, a silence deeper than any I'd ever experienced before. A void where everything that I'd ever lived for should have been.

A buzz from my phone was a pull back to reality. A text from Laura:

> Love, I'm so sorry about being pissed yesterday when John called and I'm so so sorry about what I said to you. I'm not supporting you well and I'm being a shit friend,

it's just such a big thing and I'm frightened too, but I'm here now if you need me, I promise, and I hope you're not too angry with me.

I deleted it, appalled by it, by her self-absorption.

There was another text, which I hadn't seen earlier, from Nicky:

How are you doing today? Fine here, and I should be able to head back to you in a day or two, I'll call later today. Thinking of you ALL the time. xxx

How to reply? Faced with a decision about what to tell her, and how to tell her, I bottled. Trust is like that. Once you lose it, you begin to adjust your attitudes toward people, you put up guards, and filter the information you want them to know.

I wasn't prepared to actively hide things from Nicky, or to be completely open with her, as I might have been three days ago. So I didn't reply. She'd said she would call me, and I decided I would tell her everything then.

There was nothing from the police. Not a word. Part of me wanted to phone them, to ask what they'd thought of the schoolbook, but the night's events seemed to have raked out of me any last bits of fight that I might have had left.

They'll phone me if there's news, I thought, but as I thought it, it felt somehow defeatist, as if I was letting hope ebb away.

I went to Skittle, who was in his bed. I sank to the floor beside him and sat there, my hand in his fur. I shut my eyes, and let my head fall back against the wall behind me and I allowed myself to imagine a reunion with Ben. The feel of him in my arms, the expression in his eyes, the scent of his hair, the sound of his voice, the silky perfection of the moment I'd been longing for all week, and as I imagined it I wept quiet hot tears that felt as though they'd never stop.

Jim

We had the TA in an interview room at Kenneth Steele House.

His mother, her face drained of color, had spoken to him quietly and fiercely in the hallway of their home, telling him that she'd call their family solicitor, while he shouted at her that she always thought the worst of him, that he hadn't done anything wrong, that he wasn't being arrested.

"Not yet," Bennett had muttered under his breath. "But it won't be long, sonny boy."

He'd come with us voluntarily, but odds were that we weren't going to let him leave. We knew that, but he didn't yet. He sat slumped in a chair looking like a bad boy. His chin was at a defiant tilt, and his pupils were pinpricks swimming in irises that were the palest blue.

We had enough to arrest him, but we were debating when to do that, because, as soon as we did, the clock would start ticking until the deadline to release him, unless we could come up with evidence or a confession.

Fraser's view was simple: "I think we should caution him now."

"He's come in of his own volition."

"I don't want him talking when he's not under caution and us not being able to use it in court later."

"A solicitor will tell him to keep silent."

"It's a risk that I think we're going to have to take. Otherwise he could walk out of here and do a disappearing act. What's this I hear about an Anderson shelter in the garden?"

"Empty, boss, apart from a lawnmower and some bags of compost."

"What do you reckon?"

"He was near the scene, he's lied to us, he knows Ben well, and we've got the schoolbook."

"Motive?"

"Don't know enough about him yet."

"What's the mother like?"

"Angry with him."

"Get Bennett to caution him, and get her in for an interview while we're waiting for his brief. And is somebody getting hold of his lying girlfriend?"

"Yes, boss."

"Good work, Jim."

■ ■ ■ ■

I had a spring in my step as I went back to the incident room. It might have been adrenaline-fueled, but that was good enough for me. I wanted to be thoroughly prepared for the interview, not one little pebble left unturned. I knew the real work started now because we only had twenty-four hours to charge him.

I sat down at my desk and got on with reading all the background we had on Lucas Grantham. I thought back to when I'd first met him at the school, the way he'd seemed a bit pathetic. I'd had no inkling then that he'd been lying to us, though Woodley had thought he was a bit shifty. I didn't want to think I'd missed something I should have noticed.

But I never got to finish my research, because we had another turn-up. Nicky Forbes's husband arrived. Unexpectedly. Asking for me.

Simon Forbes was as posh as I might have expected. I'd Googled his wine company the day before. It was high end, the website slick and impressive, and he was obviously very well connected. He was a tall bear of a man, with very dark hair that was graying at the temples and red veins on his nose, which probably came from years of wine tasting. He was dressed in corduroy trousers, a checked shirt, and a tweed jacket, the kind of thing that people wore at the country shows my mum used to take us to when we were growing up.

"It's very kind of you to come in," I said. "It wasn't necessary."

I'd found somewhere to take him and we'd just sat down opposite each other.

"What I have to tell you might be best said face-to-face," he said. "It's about my wife, but it's a very delicate situation because I have four daughters to consider."

There was a quality of warmth about him that I hadn't anticipated. He had a kind, patient manner that was appealing, even under the circumstances.

"I believe," he said, "that you might have been under the impression that my wife was living at our family home in Salisbury?"

"Entirely under that impression, because that's what Mrs. Forbes informed us."

"I'm afraid that she hasn't been living at that address for just over a month. She moved out at the end of September."

He spoke quietly and clearly while my

mind frantically tried to process what this meant.

"Do you know where your wife moved to?"

"She's living in the cottage where she grew up. It's in the Pewsey Vale, about a forty-five-minute drive north of Salisbury."

"Did your daughters go with her?"

I wondered if this had been an acrimonious separation, if he was here to cast blame on a wife he loathed, to muddy the waters around her in advance of a custody dispute.

"No. Nicky didn't just leave me; she left all of us."

"Can I ask why?"

"The specific occasion was" — he cleared his throat — "the specific catalyst for her to actually pack her bags and leave was an argument we had."

"What did you argue about?"

"It's a bit complicated, but we had recently talked about having another child."

"A fifth child?"

His reply bounced off my surprise.

"Yes. I'm aware that some people might think that five children is an excessive number, but Nicky wanted to try again, and I'd previously agreed to support her wish, happily I might say, because of something she'd suffered. I felt I should support her.

Do I need to explain about her background?"

"We know about that."

"So you understand she has a longing for a son. To replace Charlie."

Those words felt solid to me, like a remnant jettisoned from an explosion, a twisted shard of metal, turning in midair, glinting.

"I understand," I said. "You said you'd previously agreed to having another child, so had something changed? Did you no longer feel that way?"

He looked like a man who was having to haul up strength from a great depth.

"My wife gives the appearance of coping, always coping, she makes a career of it, but it takes its toll. She's become very controlling of our time. That was the source of the argument. I was trying to ask her to relax, to give us space to breathe in the house. This scheduling of the girls' time down to the last minute affects them, and affects us too. In my view, life had become a bit joyless. We had no time to do things together as a couple, or a family, ever, and I told her that I'd begun to wonder if another baby would be too much, for both of us."

"How did she react?"

"Badly. Very badly. She felt that I'd betrayed her."

"Did she say that?"

"She did. She freaked out, for want of a better expression. I've never seen her so angry, or distraught. And I'm afraid I lost my temper, I was at the end of my tether, and I told her that I thought we might need some space from each other."

"And how did she react?"

"She stormed out of the room, the expression on her face was awful, and I didn't follow her, I let her go. Grace, our second daughter, was waiting in the hall, ready to go to a riding lesson. That's how scheduled our lives were — we barely had time for an argument! Anyway, I didn't want to make any more of a scene in front of Grace so I called out to Nicky that I was driving Grace to her lesson, and I cooled off a bit while I was there, and I regretted some of the things I'd said, and I hoped Nicky had too, that we might discuss things more calmly that evening. But when Grace and I got home, she'd gone."

"Gone?"

"Completely. She'd packed a case, and driven away. She'd told our eldest daughter to look after the two little ones until I got home but didn't tell her why. And, unfortunately, the girls saw Nicky put her suitcase in the car, and they could see that she was very upset, so when I got back they were in a bit of a state, to put it mildly. It was a terrible shock for all of us."

"Have you spoken to her since?"

"We speak a lot, but it's very frustrating. She won't discuss the future with me. She won't plan or meet up to talk. She just says she needs more time. I'm trying to be patient, but I'm angry about the effect it's having on the girls. We all love her, that's the thing, of course we do, but we can't always be what she wants us to be."

If I'd judged Simon Forbes harshly at first, on the basis of his website, his profession, and his appearance, then I'd been a fool. This was a sensitive, intelligent man, with apparently extraordinary reserves of patience, and he'd been hurt.

I drew breath. "Do you think your wife is unstable?" I asked him.

"She's walked away from her children. That's not the behavior of somebody who's stable."

"Are you here because you believe that she might be responsible for what's happened to Ben?"

The question was painful for him — he'd had to put aside his pride to come here and tell me this stuff — and as he struggled to formulate an answer, I watched him try to put aside his love for his wife too, but he didn't quite manage it.

"I wouldn't go that far, I just thought you ought to be aware of our situation. She hasn't even told her sister."

"Thank you, Mr. Forbes. I can't tell you how grateful I am."

I walked him to the main entrance; it felt like the least I could do.

Outside, on the top of the steps, waxed coat done up and leather driving gloves pulled onto thick, strong-looking fingers, he spoke again.

"I don't know what my wife has or hasn't done, Inspector. I can't guess at that. I'm just telling you what I think you should know. And in return I ask that you respect our family's dignity as much as you possibly can. I want to avoid inflicting any further pain on our daughters. Ben's disappearance has been extremely difficult for them as it is."

"Have you told your sister-in-law about this?"

"To be honest, I assumed Nicky would have told Rachel, but when I realized that wasn't the case, I thought I would spare her this, which is why I'm here, telling you. Rachel must be going through a living hell already."

As soon as he'd turned his back on me, I bolted back into the building and took the stairs up to the incident room three at a time.

Rachel

On Sunday night, after dark, I still thought of nothing apart from the fact that Ben had been gone for one week. Seven days, one hundred and sixty-eight hours, thousands of minutes, hundreds of thousands of seconds. And counting.

My thoughts were suddenly full of the woods as if, now that seven days had passed, the memories had swollen, and germinated into a vivid sensory overload.

The bright blue sky and the kaleidoscopic intensity of the backdrop of beautiful, colorful, crisp autumn leaves replayed in my head like a movie reel. I saw Ben's flushed cheeks, the gauzy mistiness of his breath, floating momentarily, a piece of him, of his warmth, in the air, then evaporating into nothing.

I would have seen more, lost myself in those memories, but my phone rang. It was the police, letting me know that a DC Woodley, my interim FLO, was on his way to call on me. They apologized for the lateness of the call. It was already half past eight at night.

DC Woodley arrived at nine. He was very tall and very skinny with an elongated neck and a large nose. He looked as if he was about seventeen years old.

He introduced himself awkwardly, and then he said that we should probably sit down, and he licked his top lip nervously when he said it.

At my kitchen table we sat under the stark central light. Unlike my sister, I didn't think to make the room cozy by switching on other lights, or boiling a kettle. I'd lost my social niceties a week ago. I only wanted to hear what he'd come to tell me.

"We've arrested somebody," he said. "We haven't charged them yet, but they are at Kenneth Steele House and they are under arrest."

"Who?"

"Lucas Grantham. Ben's teaching assistant."

My mind curled around this information and then recoiled at the ghastliness of it. Lucas Grantham spent all day of every weekday with my son. He spent more hours with Ben than I did. And I didn't know him at all; he was a stranger to me.

For DC Woodley, and his patient, insistent questioning, I tried to remember anything I could, any mention of Grantham that Ben had made, but there was nothing beyond the entirely bland. Ben had hardly ever mentioned him, favoring Miss May, whom he had known for longer.

I scraped my mind for my impressions of him. They'd been fleeting. We were only a few weeks into term, after all, and Lucas Grantham was new to the school, like the headmaster. I forced my mind to work back through any memories of him when I'd collected Ben's schoolbooks from school just a few days before, but I had none really, just the vaguest sense of him being there at all. And then those thoughts were interrupted by a question that I had to ask:

"If Lucas Grantham took Ben, then where is he?"

"We're undertaking extensive searches at his property, and at properties he's associated with. We're doing everything we can to locate Ben. In the next twenty-four hours we're going to be questioning everybody around him. I'm afraid I can't give you any more information than that at present, but we wanted you to hear this from us, and not from anybody else. Please know that we are doing what we think is best in order to return Ben to you safe and well. That's our priority."

"Do you believe that?"

"That we're doing our best? Yes. Absolutely. I'd swear on my mother's life."

He actually put his hand over his heart when he said that. Then, just as he was readying himself to leave, he said, "One more thing, Ms. Jenner?"

"Yes?"

"Have you heard from your sister?"

"No," and I realized that she'd never phoned me back. "Why?"

"It's the role of the FLO to make sure that all family members are doing fine, so it's really just a follow-up after the difficult interview she had with DI Clemo."

"She's fine so far as I know."

When he'd gone I tried to phone Nicky, to tell her, but it went to voicemail. I didn't leave a message. I'd heard about voicemail hacking. I knew we would be targets. I wasn't going to give the journalists that advantage.

I tried Nicky's house in Salisbury but her youngest daughter answered and said that her mummy wasn't there and her daddy wasn't either and her sister who was looking after her was on her mobile phone. I gave up, I didn't even say who it was because

Olivia was only nine and leaving a message with a nine-year-old is complicated and unreliable. I knew Nicky would phone me back when she saw my missed call.

I thought again about the TA and thought about what he might have done.

In one sense it allowed me to feel a surge of relief. It allowed me to let go of the germ of suspicion I'd been guiltily harboring about my sister. That was a release of pressure I was grateful for, definitely. I gave silent thanks for the fact that I hadn't accosted her with my suspicions about her, or accused her outright. That might help us repair.

On the other hand, the news threw up a scenario that made my guts clench, because the question that lurched around my head was: What would a man like Lucas Grantham want with a boy like Ben?

There was no answer I could come up with that wasn't somehow horrific. And so I didn't feel a complete sense of relief, as I might have at the news of the arrest, of course I didn't, because that would be impossible until Ben was back in my arms again.

I went online again later, curious to see if the arrest had been made public. Not yet.

Instead, some members of the online community were marking the week's anniversary of Ben's disappearance by saying that he was probably dead. That he had to be.

As if to underscore this theory, one or two of them had posted photographs of lit candles to mark the anniversary. Online shrines, the flickering flame a public display of emotion, which I found sanctimonious, ugly, and cruel.

Others took a more cerebral tack, including one who caught my eye because he was quoting the same websites that Nicky had been looking at before she left, to prove his hypothesis. I clicked on the link he provided, and instantly I wished I hadn't, because right in front of my eyes was one of the research documents that Nicky had tried to stop me from reading in the first few days after Ben disappeared:

> Abduction Homicide . . . victims were more likely to be killed immediately or kept alive for less than 24 hours, with a few victims being kept alive for 24 to 48 hours or more than three days (Boudreaux et al., 1999). Hanfland, 1997, reported even more shocking findings. He stated that 44% were dead in less than an hour, 74% of the victims were dead within the first 3

hours, and 91% within the first 24 hours.

It sickened me. I closed the window on the computer, stabbing the mouse with sweaty, shaking fingers. I was ready to shut the machine down, unplug it, retreat from it, but behind the window I was looking at was another, left there by Ben.

It was the login page for Furry Football, the online game that Ben and his friends loved to play. It was like Club Penguin, or Moshi Monsters, a child-friendly online forum where you could play games and interact with other people's avatars. The difference was that it was football themed and if you won points you could buy players for a Furry Football team. Ben loved it. All his friends did.

I clicked on it. The page refreshed and invited me to log in. Ben was the manager of two separate virtual teams and I had a choice of which one to log in as: "Owl Goal" or "Turtle Rangers." I chose "Owl Goal" and I typed in Ben's password. A message appeared: "YOU ARE ALREADY LOGGED IN."

I tried again. Same message.

I leaned back in my chair, confused. Somebody was logged in as Ben. I remembered him saying that he couldn't log in if he'd already done so on another machine, but his iPad was at his dad's house, and I had no other computer.

I clicked on "Turtle Rangers" instead, entered his password again, and this time it worked. I was in. I was Turtle0751, the captain of the Turtle Rangers, and my avatar appeared on screen: a plump turtle in football boots holding a clipboard.

"WHICH SERVER WOULD YOU LIKE TO JOIN?" the computer asked me, and then my stomach roiled as an idea took hold. What if Ben was logged in somewhere else, playing the game as his owl avatar?

I selected the server that I knew Ben always chose to play on: "Savannah League."

A cartoonlike scene popped up — the African savannah. A meerkat invited me to choose a game I'd like to play. I selected "Baobab Bonus," Ben's favorite game.

On screen a glade of cartoon baobab trees appeared. About twenty avatars cruised among them, little speech bubbles coming from their heads now and then. It didn't take me long to see Ben's other team captain: Owlie689.

"It's you," I said. "It's you."

My fingers gripped the mouse so hard that its edges dug into them and I stared at the screen as Owlie689 moved around it.

I navigated my avatar so that it stood by Ben's. I was clumsy with the mouse. I wanted to talk to him. It was hard to work out how to make a speech bubble. I wasn't practiced at this like Ben; I'd never paid attention to the detail of the game.

After numerous failed attempts, I finally clicked on the right tab. A list of possible phrases appeared, but it was safe chat. Of course it was. I hadn't allowed Ben to do anything other than communicate with phrases that were provided by the game. For his safety.

I scrolled down the list of phrases available, desperate to say something meaningful, but they were entirely bland, designed to stop children from upsetting or offending each other.

I clicked on "Hello." After a few seconds Ben's avatar said, "Hello."

"How was your day?" my avatar asked.

Owlie689 displayed an emoticon. It was a frowning face. I scrolled down the list of phrases I could use.

"Sorry," my avatar said.

Owlie689 began to move. I followed. It stopped underneath a baobab tree.

"Want to visit my team?" it said to me.

"Yes," my avatar replied and the screen

dissolved and reformed and we were in a training area. The positions of players were laid out around the edges of the screen and above four of them were animals that Ben had earned enough points to buy.

"Cool," my avatar said.

"New player," said Ben's avatar. He moved toward his center forward. It was a giraffe. He hadn't had it last Sunday because he'd talked about it, about wanting to get a giraffe because they were good at doing headers. In fact he'd gone on and on about it in the car on the way to the woods until I made him change the subject.

"It's you," I said. "It's definitely you."

I searched the list of phrases for something else to say, something that would tell Ben who I was, that it was me communicating with him. He must suspect it, I thought, because who else would use his other avatar? He had to know it was me.

But I was too slow. Before I selected a phrase Owlie689 had gone, just disappeared. My avatar was alone on screen.

I reached for my phone.

Jim

Fraser and I were huddled in the meeting room we used for briefings. Lists and interview notes littered the table between us. We were planning.

Woodley put his head around the door. "Rachel Jenner's just phoned, she says she's seen Ben playing an online game."

"What game?" Fraser asked.

"Furry Football. She says he's logged on as one of his avatars."

"What in God's name does that mean?"

"You have characters that you become when you play the game. Ben has two. She logged on as one of them and met the other in the game. She thinks that means that Ben was logged on."

"And does it? You're the IT expert."

"It could, obviously, if he has access to the Internet, which would seem unlikely. Equally, anybody who had access to his login details could have done it."

"How likely do you think that is?"

"It's impossible to say, but people often know their friends' passwords etc., it could be one of his mates or anybody who knew him."

"Does Rachel Jenner have a view on that?"

"She doesn't know. It's hard to get sense out of her, to be honest, boss. She's pretty hysterical."

"We need to find out who might have known. Can you contact that man who was in the woods, the father of Ben's best friend? Ask him if he knows about this stuff, and ask him if we can interview his boy in the morning. He might know."

"Will do."

Once he'd gone, Fraser turned back to me. "What's your feeling, Jim?"

"Could be something, could be nothing. Just like the schoolbook."

"I'll get the IT folks onto it. Now, Lucas Grantham versus Nicola Forbes. I want a plan of action tonight, so that we don't waste a minute tomorrow morning. Not one second. What's your feeling about resource allocation?"

I took my time before answering. We had a very strong suspect in custody, and I knew he looked good for it, but there was something about Nicky Forbes that I just couldn't let go.

"In my view, Nicky Forbes is very intelligent and potentially very manipulative," I said to Fraser. "Chris was certainly very clear that the sort of trauma Nicky's suffered could cause all kinds of psychosis or delusions. If her own husband is coming in to warn us about her, I think we need to take it very seriously."

"You favor her for it?"

"If I have to stick my neck out, I do."

And, as I said it out loud, I felt my conviction build. I said, "I think there's a danger that Lucas Grantham might be another Edward Fount. Looks good for it because he's a lying little idiot who lives with his mother, but he could be telling the truth about why he went to the woods."

"Telling the truth about his lie?"

"Yes."

"If that's the case I'm going to have him on wasting police time."

"Agreed."

Fraser sighed, massaged her forehead. She looked old suddenly. "But I'm not sure it is, and part of me wants you here to run the investigation into Grantham. Clock's ticking."

I knew that. I kept quiet, let her think, and watched her massage her forehead as she did so. I knew there was no point pushing her. She came to a decision quickly.

"Right. I'm going to let you go and interview her, Jim, tomorrow morning, not tonight. It's far too late."

I felt a surge of adrenaline, as if I'd had a shot of it into my arm.

"Thank you, boss." I stood up. "I'm going to get familiar with everything in her file."

I wanted to know every detail by heart; I wanted to pull off the interview of my life. Nicky Forbes had got to me right from the start.

"Now listen to me, Jim. You do no such thing. You go home and you sleep. You look like shit." She paused, let me absorb the insult, and then she asked, "How are you feeling about Emma?"

That blindsided me. Totally. It took me a moment to pull together a reply.

"Disappointed, of course. But I'm focused on moving forward, boss."

"Don't fuck about with me; you know what I'm asking. I'm not blind."

"Honest truth, boss, I am focused on moving forward, but I'm gutted too. Of course I am."

"I'm only going to ask you this once: do you think it's affecting your judgment?"

"Not at all. Not one bit."

She leaned back in her chair, her mind working it through, before she replied. "OK. So you go first thing to interview Nicky Forbes, because I don't want to leave any stone unturned. Get back here as quickly as you can afterward. We couldn't be more stretched for resources so I shouldn't really be letting my deputy go."

"Boss —"

"I'm indulging you here, Jim, so don't push it. I've got a list of interviews as long as my arm that relate to Lucas Grantham."

"I just wanted to know if I would go alone or not."

"I can't send anybody else. I need every body I can get."

She took off her glasses, which made her look suddenly vulnerable, and she rubbed her eyes, which were reddened around the rims. As it was late, and her guard seemed to be down just a little, I asked her something: "Boss, do you think he's still alive?"

"You know the statistics as well as I do. We just have to do what we can."

Back at my flat, I looked through the case files, poring over every detail, memorizing the events that took place when Nicky Forbes was a girl, rereading all the notes I took after Simon Forbes came in.

It was a jubilant phone call to Fraser that I made at midnight.

"I found a hole in Nicola Forbes's alibi. Last Sunday she said she was attending a food festival. She was definitely there in the morning, but nobody can confirm that they saw her between 13:30 and 22:00 when her husband maintains that she Skyped him from the cottage."

"I thought we'd confirmed her alibi?"

"People said they thought they'd seen her, but it's a really big event. Tons of stalls selling produce, cookery demonstrations, that kind of thing, hundreds of folks attending and although she's quite well known, nobody can actually guarantee that they saw her during the afternoon. They all say she was definitely there that day, and a friend says that they had lunch together, but after 13:30 none of it's reliable."

"Good work, Jim," she said. "Take Woodley with you in the morning."

"I thought you couldn't spare anybody."

"I've changed my mind."

I didn't have the energy to go to my bed. I lay on my sofa, the window cracked open even though it was freezing outside, and I smoked and tried to fight away the memories of Emma that could upset the perfect balance I felt: the poised moment when a case is about to come together one way or another, and when you're right in it.

I checked my phone. Woodley and I had been texting and emailing, finalizing directions and details for the morning.

What I didn't expect to find in my inbox was an email from Emma. Its title: "Sorry."

Email
To: Jim Clemo
<jimclemo1@gmail.com>
From: Emma Zhang
<emzhang21@hotmail.co.uk>
October 28, 2012 at 23:39

SORRY
Dear Jim
I hope you read this because I owe you an explanation. If you are reading it: thank you.

I should never have done what I did. It was unforgivable. I should never have contributed to the blog and I should never have expected you to help me. It was a terrible position to put you in.

When I walked past you in the incident room this morning it was the hardest moment of my life because all I wanted to do was rewind the clock, and not do what I did, so we could still be together. When I was with you I felt happy, and protected, and I threw all that away for the worst and most stupid of reasons.

I owe you an explanation for why I did it, and here it is. It's not an excuse:

When I was six years old my dad went outside to mow the lawn and asked me to look after my little sister. She was two. Her name was Celia. We were playing in my bedroom. I left her for just a few minutes to go to the loo. When I came back I couldn't find her. I called my dad. He found her wedged down the side of my bed. She'd got stuck, and suffocated. She died before we got her out.

My dad blamed me for her death, but I was just a child too. What he did wasn't responsible because he was the adult in charge, he shouldn't have left her in my care. I didn't know you could die like that.

But he was tough like that, always, you've no idea how tough he was. He never let me be a child. I miss Celia every day.

When I heard what Rachel Jenner did to Ben, how she let him run ahead, I wanted to punish her, because you shouldn't leave kids unsupervised. They can come to harm. I thought it meant that she was a person who didn't deserve to have a child, that she didn't love him properly. I thought she was like my dad. I realized I was wrong when I saw the photographs she'd taken of him. They were so beautiful, I felt as though they would break my heart there and then.

I didn't mean to do what I did. The blog sucked me in. It was a kind of compulsion, so hard to resist.

I don't know if that's because the FLO role was too much for me. Perhaps I'm not good at bearing other people's problems. It freaks me out. I should have been stronger, more professional, and I should have pulled out of the investigation, but I didn't, and then it got so hard to fight the urge to contribute to the blog because I felt so angry. I try hard to quell it, but I carry a lot of rage with me about what happened to Celia and to me, and I confused my history, and my anger at my dad, with Rachel's present, and I wanted to punish her for his sins.

I try not to let it show, because I'm usually very good at pleasing people, and making everything right, but I'm not always a well person, and even when I work hard to keep it under control, my past messes with my mind sometimes.

I behaved in an arrogant and disgusting way, and that's something I'll have to live with, just like I'll have to live with losing my career, and I deserve that.

I know we can't be together anymore, but I hope you can find it in your heart to forgive me just a little, or try to understand.

I've told all of this to Internal Affairs. I'm in the process now. They've suspended me and I'm under investigation. I'm not allowed to communicate with you so please delete this after you've read it.

Know this though, Jim. I love you. Our

times together were amazing and I'll miss you always. So thank you.

Emma x

When I finished reading I hit "delete." But then I went into my trash folder and moved the email back into my inbox.

In one of my kitchen cupboards I found a bottle of whiskey, a gift from my parents when I moved in, so far untouched. Normally, I'm not much of a drinker, but that night I opened it. I didn't bother with mixers. I drank a large quantity of it, much more quickly than I should have. It was enough to make the room tilt before I passed out.

▪ ▪ ▪ ▪

DAY 9
MONDAY,
OCTOBER 29, 2012

▪ ▪ ▪ ▪

. . . children have difficulty determining who will harm them and who will not. For this reason, the onus is on parents to screen those persons supervising and caring for their child, and to educate their children on how to stay and play safe.
— Marlene L. Dalley, and Jenna Ruscoe,
"The Abduction of Children by Strangers in Canada: Nature and Scope,"
National Missing Children Services,

National Police Services, Royal Canadian
Mounted Police, December 2003

Hope is essential to your survival.
— "When Your Child Is Missing:
A Family Survival Guide,"
Missing Kids USA Parental Guide,
US Department of Justice, OJJDP Report

Rachel

I logged on to Furry Football countless times that night. I was hoping to encounter Ben again, of course I was. You would have done the same thing.

But he wasn't there. Not anywhere. I trawled the online game until I knew every inch of it, every server, every area you could play in. Overnight, avatars with foreign-sounding names came and went, and I could see the ebb and flow of the time zones as they logged on and off: hundreds, thousands, tens of thousands of children online from all over the world. But not Ben. I never encountered him again. Not once.

The hours searching didn't breed any doubt in my mind, though, because my conviction that it had been Ben just grew and grew, that feeling so powerfully strong it was as if he'd actually flitted past me in his red anorak, met my eye for a second, and then gone again, just out of reach of my outstretched hand.

I wanted to tell John. I thought he of all people would understand, would feel the enormity of this fleeting contact with our child.

I called the hospital in the hope that he might have improved, that he might even be conscious. A voice that was compassionate and tired-sounding told me that there was no change in his condition. He was stable, that's all she could confirm, she said.

I imagined him as I'd seen him the night before, the absence of him, his mind curled up tight beneath the bleeding and the swelling and the trauma. Did a very small part of me, just for a moment, envy him that oblivion? Maybe. Was it because I was finding it harder than ever to exist? Probably.

But two things kept my mind engaged that night, kept me alert, jittering. Two things nagged at me with the persistence of a noose slowly tightening around your neck.

If Lucas Grantham had taken Ben, then why would Ben have disappeared so abruptly from Furry Football? If Lucas Grantham had taken Ben, then who was looking after him while Lucas Grantham was in custody?

I passed my phone from hand to hand, my fingerprints oily on its screen. Silent, it felt to me a useless object, its very existence mocking both my reliance on it and the isolation that bred that reliance.

I wanted a phone call from the police to let me know that they were searching properties, that they were knocking down doors and smashing windows as they looked for Ben.

I didn't want process. I didn't want twenty-four hours of questioning. Them and Lucas Grantham in a room, with the tea, and the biscuits, and then after that no charges brought and all that time Ben could be somewhere with nobody to care for him, nobody to bring him food, or water, or he could be somewhere with somebody else, somebody who made him log off Furry Football late at night, in a hurry.

But my phone remained mute.

Silently, in its depths, I knew that emails would be pinging in: media requests, contact from friends and families we knew, those who were too scared to speak to me, people who were most content monitoring me from afar.

But the phone itself didn't ring. The police didn't call me. Nobody did.

And in that silence those two thoughts went around, and around, and I didn't know what to do with them. I felt as if I was no longer the wild-eyed fighter, the scrapper, who stood up at the press conference and dared Ben's abductor, who looked down a lens and into every corner, trying to find an assailant to challenge.

Instead, my nerves were scraped so raw that they lent me the perfect purity of feeling of the addict, ecstatic in the midst of a high, so those two questions loomed large and unanswered in my psyche, like a high-pitched note that will not stop, and, when morning came, I acted as if in a trance.

There were no voices in my head telling me not to do it when I called a taxi, advising me that it wouldn't be a good idea to turn up unannounced at the police station again. There was just an impulse to make my voice heard, to tell them what I knew, and what I feared. I wanted to communicate.

The morning was bitterly cold and every outside surface was shiny with rain that had fallen in the night and was close to freezing. It still fell, in fat, intermittent droplets that chilled my hands as I opened the taxi door. "Kenneth Steele House," I said to the driver, "Feeder Road."

The driver must have just come on shift; he was too preoccupied with trying to clear condensation from his window to talk to me. I watched the moisture disappear from the windshield incrementally as the fans worked: two spreading ovals of clarity, revealing the city in sharp, unflattering lines. It was 7:45 a.m. Darkness was beginning to lift from the city and the Monday morning traffic was already starting to build, so we traveled in fits and starts, dirty spray showering the pavement whenever the driver accelerated. Red lights blocked our progress at every junction, and he braked late and hard as we approached them. The city felt grimy and hopeless.

At Kenneth Steele House the receptionist recognized me instantly, launching herself out from behind her desk and intercepting me with the purpose of a sheepdog, who can see that one of his ratty, stupid sheep is about to go astray.

"Are they expecting you, Ms. Jenner?" she asked, hand on my elbow, guiding me to the sofa in the waiting area, away from the stream of Monday morning arrivals.

"I need to speak to somebody on the investigation," I said. I tried to hold my head up straight, make my voice as steady as possible. A hank of my hair fell across my face and I brushed it away, noticing only then that it was unbrushed and unwashed.

They didn't take any chances this time. A scene in reception was obviously not going to be in the cards. It took only ten minutes for me to get an audience with DCI Fraser.

I don't even remember which particular characterless room we met in, but I do remember DCI Fraser. I hadn't seen her for a week in the flesh, though I'd watched her updating the press on TV. She looked like she'd aged, but I supposed that I did too. Her skin was grayer than before, the crow's-feet by her eyes more pronounced. She'd brought a black coffee in with her and she drank it in three gulps.

"Ms. Jenner, I know you're aware that we currently have somebody in custody," she said.

"Yes."

"And this morning I've already begun a string of interviews that I hope will bring us closer to being sure that we have the right man in custody and therefore to locating Ben."

She was spelling it out to me. It was Policework 101.

"OK, so that is my priority this morning, but I wanted to see you personally because I know how difficult it is for you to wait at home for news."

"Thank you." I did appreciate it. I could

tell that she was being kinder to me than she need have been.

"But I would request that you try to be patient, and do just that. We did get your message last night, and we are acting on it. We've done some research this morning, we've already talked to one of Ben's friends, and it seems that the boys who play Furry Football often share identities and passwords."

"I know it was him," I said. The knowledge was an itch that wouldn't go away, and her words, however kind, were failing to act as a salve.

"I realize that the idea is terribly attractive, Ms. Jenner. Believe me, it's a tantalizing thought that we might be able to communicate with Ben, but you must realize that there's no way we can confirm that it's him, and I don't want you to raise your hopes too much."

"Did any of his friends admit that it was them?"

"Nobody has so far, but you must remember that children aren't always truthful. Not because they want to lie, but sometimes they're scared. And it could have been another friend; we've only been able to talk to one boy so far this morning."

"I'm his mother. I know it was him. He

had a new player on his team, a player that he was talking about wanting on Sunday morning. It was a giraffe."

She ran her index finger up and down a deep line between her eyebrows.

"Could another child have got the new player?"

"It was Ben. He's alive, DCI Fraser. I know he is."

"God knows, Ms. Jenner, I hope he is too, and I am taking this seriously. It is very useful information, of course it is, and I will not forget it, I am listening to you. But, it is important that we view it in the context of what else is happening in the investigation at this moment."

She shifted toward me, her eyes penetrating and sincere.

"Believe me, I shall do everything in my power to return Ben to you safe and sound. I understand that waiting for news must be desperately difficult for you, but we are working around the clock here to make progress, and the bottom line is, every moment we spend with you is time taken away from the focus of the investigation."

Her words, finally, got through to me, for what worse sin could I commit than to divert their energies from the investigation?

I began to cry again and I wondered if

that would ever stop happening, that public leaking of emotions. I didn't apologize for it anymore, it was just something that happened to me that other people had to get used to, like your stomach rumbling, or a sweat breaking out.

"I didn't mean to waste your time," I said.

She took my hand in hers and the warmth of her hand surprised and disarmed me. "You're absolutely not wasting my time. You're informing me, and the more information I have, the better. But I can't just go out there and search every house in Bristol where somebody logs on to Furry Football. It's impossible. At this stage in the investigation my quickest route to finding Ben is via whoever took him, using all the information I have at my disposal, and this information is logged in my noggin now. I won't forget it, nor will my team. We'll have it in mind whenever we interview somebody or whenever we make a decision. Do you understand that?"

I nodded.

"Your information is valuable."

"OK."

"I'll arrange for somebody to drive you home."

"Ben's alive," I said.

"I'll be in touch," she said, "as soon as

there's any news. Wait at home."

Heading down to the foyer, vision blurred still, unsteady down flights of identical stairs, feet slapping on the linoleum treads, feeling things slipping away. In the foyer downstairs I was surprised to see Ben's teacher.

A picture of composure in contrast to my wrecked self, Miss May was perched on a sofa in the waiting area, handbag on her knee, hands draped on top of it. She wore very little makeup. Her hair was pulled back neatly and fastened at the nape of her neck. When she saw me, she got up.

"They asked me in for an interview," she said. "About Lucas." She whispered the name, eyes wide with disbelief, red-rimmed and bloodshot. I wondered whether that name would be whispered more now, only spoken of in hushed terms, because Lucas Grantham might be a child abductor, a predator, a monster.

"What did they ask you?"

"I'm not allowed to say."

That didn't stop me. "Anything? Did you think of anything? Do you think they're right?"

"I told them absolutely everything I could think of," she said.

"Do you think he did it?"

There was a heightened quality about her, flushed cheeks and quick movements.

"Honestly, I don't know. Maybe, definitely maybe. I'm trying to think back over everything, in case there were signs, I'm really trying. There was nothing obvious or I'd have said before, but there are some things, little things that —"

She opened her mouth again as if to say more, and I felt as if she was going to confide something in me, give me a drop of hope, but our conversation was brought to a halt because the officer who had retrieved the book from me and John a few days earlier appeared suddenly beside us, car keys jangling in his hand. "DI Bennett," he said. "OK if I drive you both home together? Apparently you live reasonably close to each other."

It was nine a.m. and the rush hour was abating. Bennett drove us through the city center, where the roads were hemmed in by smog-drenched modern buildings throwing endless reflections of tinted glass back at each other, OFFICE TO LET signs, boarded shopfronts, student accommodations with jauntily colored plastic windows, and concrete sixties edifices rotting in the pollution, graffiti-covered and stained. At street level, office workers were arriving for work, trainers on, coffees and briefcases in hand.

I broke the silence in the car. There was something I wanted to say to Miss May. "I'm not sure I've ever thanked you properly for all the effort you made with Ben last year, when we were going through our divorce. I really appreciated it. He did too."

"He did have a hard time." She gave me a wan smile.

"Well, you helped him a lot."

"It was the least I could do," she said. "They're such little souls. It's a privilege to be a part of their lives. You must feel so very empty without him."

Bennett cursed at a cyclist who was climbing laboriously up the steep slope of Park Street, wobbling into our path with the effort. I fixed my gaze on the tall Victorian Gothic tower at the top, dominating the skyline, Bristol University's most recognizable building. Beside it was Bristol Museum. I thought of Ben's favorite things there: the ichthyosaur skeleton, a case of glowing blue crystals, a stuffed dodo, and the painting by Odilon Redon.

"I don't feel empty," I said to Miss May, "because I know he's alive. I know he is. But I do feel very afraid."

My words petered away, the last few dregs of sand falling through an hourglass.

She looked out of the window, and I worried I'd spoken too freely, exposed the depths of my misery without enough filtering. It's a line I've crossed many times since. If you talk too openly about terrible things people shrink from you.

Her handbag was on the seat between us. It sagged open and in the silence my gaze fell on its contents. A set of keys, phone, plastic-wrapped tissues, A4 papers folded in half, charger cable, hairbrush, a leather document wallet, and yet more stuff underneath: the assorted paraphernalia of a life.

When Miss May turned back toward me, her expression was unreadable.

"I'm so sorry," I said. "It's just hard."

"No, it's fine. I just can't imagine how awful it must be for you. I mean I can't sleep at night, and that's just me. I think all the time about how difficult he must be finding it to settle without his nunny."

My hand went to my mouth, knuckles pressing on it, trying not to let myself break down again.

"Sorry." This time the word caught in my throat.

"Please don't be sorry. I totally understand. I'm the one who should be sorry. I didn't mean to upset you any more than you are already."

I took deep breaths that shuddered and ached, got control of myself eventually.

"I'm fine," I said. "And you're right. I don't think he's ever slept without his nunny before."

She nodded. The light was murky in the back of the car and her face looked drab and shadowed. Behind her, through the window, prettier streets flashed past now, houses painted in pastels or mellow in Bath stone, attractive even under the flat gray sky.

When I think of it now, that moment has a filmic quality, as if time was stilling.

"Poor little soul," she said.

The parting and closing of her lips was mesmerizing. An unsettled feeling prickled at the back of my neck.

I glanced at DI Bennett. He was oblivious to us, concentrating on a turn he was waiting to make, indicator light thudding, his lips slightly parted in concentration.

"Are you all right?" said Miss May. "Really?" She was peering at me.

"I . . ." I started to say something, but lost my train of thought. I was trying to deal with the unease I suddenly felt, the sense that something didn't fit.

"Ms. Jenner?"

Her neck looked long and white as she leaned toward me. I turned away from her and toward the window as I tried to concentrate, to pinpoint the source of my edginess. I replayed our conversation in my head, and the unease crystallized into a thought, a moment of perfect certainty, a bright white light that was terrifying for its clarity.

My throat went dry.

"Is this it?" said DI Bennett.

The road was narrow, with cars parked on either side, and we were blocking it. We'd pulled up outside a four-story Georgian townhouse, fronted by a broad sidewalk constructed from huge slabs of stone, uneven and worn. The house was part of a long, elegant crescent, which had leafy gardens opposite enclosed by wrought-iron railings. The crescent had far-ranging views across the city and the floating harbor, toward the countryside beyond: trees and rooftops in the foreground, then more buildings falling away below, the glint of the river, and beyond, distant fields and hills under rolling gray skies, and on that morning sheets of rain approaching relentlessly, one after another.

And I knew then that I had only seconds to act.

What I did next, I did on sheer impulse.

Jim

I woke up with my head in a vise, mouth dried out, and the urge to vomit, which turned out to be unproductive. I was still in my clothes.

Woodley picked me up at quarter past seven. It was still dark, and freezing cold. Woodley had the heaters in the car turned up full, pumping warm air around. I'd just finished fumbling with the seat belt when he tapped the dashboard with the flat of his hand. "Ready, boss?" he said.

"Are you going to put the address in the GPS then?" I asked. "Or will we guess how to get there?"

He got going. Tucked into the footwell by my feet was a newspaper. I picked it up. The first-page headline had moved on from Ben Finch:

SUPER STORM SANDY
Hurricane heads toward New York

Sixty million Americans could be affected by high winds, rain, and flooding as super storm expected to make landfall on the East Coast on Tuesday.

I flicked through, found him on page four:

HIT A WALL?
Police investigating missing Benedict Finch still "pursuing multiple lines of inquiry."

I didn't bother to read on. It wasn't good, but at least it wasn't nothing, and they didn't have news of the arrest yet. The blog was bad, negative publicity was bad, but no publicity was worse.

I dropped the paper back into the footwell.

It was dark and shiny wet on the road, taillights ahead of us blurring when the wipers swiped intermittently. We left the motorway and were immediately on country roads that twisted and turned so that oncoming headlights loomed out of nowhere, blindingly, and forced us into the side, where our wheels hit deep puddles, sending spray clattering up onto the windows.

As dawn broke, the landscape around us began to emerge: low rounded hills in washes of black ink against a blue-black sky. The sky finally lightened as we made a steep descent into Pewsey Vale, showing us that it lay flat and wide below us, a dense white mist lingering at its lowest points so that it resembled an inland lake. It was a freezing mist and once we were down into the valley it settled firmly around us so that our headlights were muted and reflected back at us in the whiteness.

As we got closer to the cottage, the lanes got narrower, and the mist thicker still until we could see only yards ahead, and the car decelerated until we were crawling. Tall, dense hedges reared up oppressively on either side of us, and Woodley had to drive carefully to avoid the potholed verges.

We pulled onto the shoulder about half a mile from the cottage according to the GPS. We were too early to call on Nicky Forbes. It was only 8:30 and we needed to kill a bit of time. Fraser didn't want her complaining that we were harassing her.

I got out of the car, and lit a cigarette. I went to stand beside Woodley's window. He wound it down a touch.

"Did you notice if we passed any houses on the way here?" I asked.

"Closest one I saw was about half a mile down the road."

"Same here."

I felt uneasy. The mist was impenetrable, limitless, and disorientating, and inhabited by a deep cold so that my toes were already numb. The cigarette was doing me no favors, so I stubbed it out when it was half smoked, carried the butt back into the car with me, and saw Woodley's nose wrinkle when I stuffed it into the ashtray. I felt a curl of nausea in my gut and I rubbed my eyes hard and Woodley said, "Are you all right, boss?"

"Yeah. Why do you ask?"

He went silent, small shake of his head. He looked nervous. He had his phone in his hand and he started to polish the screen with his sleeve. I felt like I should give him some sort of advice, but it was difficult to think what to say.

"It's not a normal life this, having this job. You're outside society."

I wasn't saying it well. I wanted him to understand what I meant, but he wasn't looking at me, and the motion of his hand polishing the phone continued, around and around.

"Some cases make you grow up fast." As soon as I said it, I thought it sounded patronizing, but he didn't seem to care.

"Have you ever worked on something

that's remained unsolved?" he asked me.

"This case will be solved," I said. "We're close now. I swear it."

"I know," he said. "I just wondered."

I thought about it. There were always things that you never got to the bottom of in cases. A dog walker who was never identified, a random white car supposed to have been at a scene, which nobody ever confessed to driving past. That was normal, though sometimes it drove police officers mad, seeking answers that they never got. They couldn't let it go. I'd seen that happen once or twice, but I'd never worked on anything where we hadn't got our perpetrator, and I didn't want this to be the one. Not with a young boy's life in the balance. Not with the worst of crimes a possibility.

"Not yet," I said.

"Do you think she'll cough?" Woodley asked.

"A woman like Nicola Forbes won't hand us a confession on a plate. We've got our work cut out."

We moved on cautiously through the mist and found the cottage half a mile farther along the lane. Above us you could sense the weight of huge trees looming, although only their lower branches were visible as suggestions of their might.

We parked beside a red Volkswagen Golf in front of a wooden fence that was warped and green-gray with lichen. I knew from the car's registration that it belonged to Nicky Forbes.

We approached the cottage through a white wooden gate, and up a short garden path paved in uneven stone. Wet leaves were banked against the threshold and the path was lined with rosebushes, pruned back to their bare bones. The cottage was pretty, cream painted with a silvery thatched roof and small windows set into thick walls. It wasn't a large place. I guessed it had maybe three bedrooms, one bathroom. Some of the curtains were drawn upstairs, but through a window beside the door I could see into a compact sitting room. The furnishings were plain and tidy. There were books lining the walls and an open fireplace. Yesterday's papers were spread on the coffee table.

As far as I could see, there were no outbuildings at all, but with the mist reducing visibility severely, it was hard to tell.

I pulled hard on the doorbell and we heard it clanging inside.

Rachel

Miss May peered out of the car window at a house with a glossy black door.

"This is it. Perfect. Thank you," she said.

"Thank you for helping us with our inquiries," Bennett said.

"It was the least I could do."

She got out, taking a moment to straighten her coat. Her bag was still on the seat beside me. I could see her keys, but before I could move she leaned down and peered into the back of the car.

"If there's anything I can do for you. Truly. Please let me know."

"Thank you," I said.

A car had pulled up behind ours, and the driver sounded the horn sharply, wanting us to move on.

"They'd better mind their manners," said DI Bennett. I could see his narrowed eyes in the rearview mirror, watching the car behind.

I had one chance. Miss May reached for her bag but before she could get to it I picked it up.

"Here you go," I said. I held it out to her, but as I did so I let it tilt and then fall, so that its contents tipped out onto my lap, and down into the footwells.

"Oh, I'm so sorry!" I said.

I leaned down and scooped up her belongings from the dark recesses, blocking her view. I stuffed most of them back into her bag. Half-eaten granola bar, purse, phone, charger, tissues, packet of painkillers, document wallet.

The keys I kept for myself. I slid them between the seat and my thigh.

Behind us, the car horn sounded again.

"Come on, ladies," said DI Bennett.

I handed the bag back to her, careful to hold it by the top so that it didn't gape.

"It's all there," I said.

"Are you sure?" she asked.

The car behind flashed its headlights.

"All there," I said. "Bye."

"Take care," she said, and shut the car door.

DI Bennett accelerated away. In the side mirror, I could see her standing on the side of the road.

Her keys were digging into the underside

of my thigh and I moved them into my coat pocket, careful not to let them make a sound.

It was a ten-minute drive from Clifton Village to my house. We drove along the edge of the Downs, flat, muddy, and green, dog walkers and joggers plowing around its perimeters, trees dotted across the parkland like abandoned livestock, water tower looming.

I listened closely to the police radio. I was terrified that Miss May would contact the police as soon as she tried to get into her house and realized the keys weren't in her bag. She'd ask for DI Bennett to drive straight back there. I wished I'd taken her phone too.

We skirted around the edge of suburbia, 1930s row houses mostly, John and Katrina's house just around the corner. A few minutes to my place. The radio was spitting out little bits of noise. Nothing about the keys so far, but panic was making me swallow, my mouth awash with warm saliva, which had a bitter, tannic edge from the police station tea.

"DI Bennett," I said.

"What's up, love?"

"It's what Miss May said, about Ben's nunny."

"What did she say?" His eyes met mine in the rearview mirror.

"Well, it's just that she wouldn't know about his nunny."

"I'm not sure I'm following you."

"He's embarrassed about his nunny, that's the thing. It's an old crib blanket, a ragged thing. He's had it since he was a baby. He uses it to get to sleep. He would never have told her about it."

Silence, as he negotiated a roundabout. "Couldn't he have told her about it?" he asked. Victorian terraces now, narrow streets climbing up and down hillsides.

I leaned forward, between the front seats. "He would never tell her, that's what I'm telling you."

The radio sputtered again and I raised my voice to drown it out. DI Bennett parked on my street, a few doors away from my house, and turned to face me.

"Right," he said, stringing out the word, skepticism the subtext. "Are you sure about that?"

"I've never been so sure of anything in my life."

"I'll tell you what I'll do then." His careful tone of voice made me think he wasn't taking me seriously, that he was just humoring me. "I'll pass that information on to the boss. Would you like me to do that?"

"Could we call it in now? I think it's important."

"I'm heading straight back now and I'll let them know and that's a promise."

"DI Bennett, I don't think you understand . . ."

"I've promised, haven't I? Can't do more than that. They'll ring you if they think there's something in it. You'd better get out, love. Don't worry about that lot. Come on. I mean it."

A few journalists were in front of the house, watching us. He wound down the window. "Clear off out of her way," he shouted. "Go on. Get away."

Another blast from the radio and I knew I had to go, or the news about the keys would surely come through.

I climbed out of the car, my head down and my hood up, and ran for it.

Inside the house I stood there with the keys in my hand, and tried to think what to do. Skittle, still in his cast, wove clumsily between my legs, his tail wagging, wanting affection.

I called Kenneth Steele House and yet again I asked to be put through to Fraser, but I was told she was busy and would call me back. They assured me that they understood how urgent my request to speak to Fraser was, and that they'd pass my message on and somebody would get back to me.

Nicky answered her phone, listened in silence as I blurted the whole story out: Lucas Grantham's arrest, Miss May in the car on the way back home, everything. "Tell the police again," she said when I'd finished. "Call them back. Make them listen."

In the background I heard the distinctive sound of the doorbell at the cottage.

"Where are you, Nicky? I thought you were at home."

"I've got to get the door. Sorry. I'll call you back."

"Don't go."

"OK, hold on, let me just see who it is. I'll get rid of them."

I heard the sound of her footsteps, the click of a door opening, a male voice, then Nicky was back on the line, saying: "I'm so sorry, I really have to go," and it went dead.

Jim

Nicky Forbes was on the phone when she opened the door. Her expression told me that we were the last people she expected to see.

She was dressed already but her face was void of makeup and she wore her paleness like a mask. She looked like she was sucking a lemon as she led us into the small kitchen and gestured to us to join her at a small table that was set against the wall.

A smoking cigarette lay in a circular ceramic ashtray that had fag ends crushed into its base. The table and chairs were a shiny orange pine, dented in places. The floor was tiled with small white squares grouted in black and the cabinets were white with a wood trim around the edge.

The room was a throwback to the 1980s, nothing had been updated for years. It wasn't what I expected from Nicky Forbes, because I'd seen her blog, the pictures of her cooking on her AGA in a perfectly equipped and decorated modern kitchen.

The kettle had just boiled, but she didn't offer us a drink.

"Are you a smoker, DI Clemo?" she asked, and she held out the cigarette packet that was on the table.

"No, thank you," I said. Woodley shook his head too when she aimed the packet at him.

She dropped it back onto the table, where it landed with a slap, and retrieved her half-smoked cigarette from the ashtray.

"I gave this up years ago," she said. "When I got pregnant with my first daughter."

She sucked smoke in deeply, her eyes on mine, her gaze direct and challenging.

"I'm wondering why you're here," she said, exhaling the smoke slowly so that it billowed between us, "when my sister is in Bristol frantically trying to get hold of somebody who'll listen to her when she tells them that she has evidence that Ben's alive? I'm also wondering why you're here when you have a suspect in custody? Ben's teaching assistant? Is that right? Shouldn't you be trying to gather some evidence against him? Maybe?"

She looked from one of us to the other, and when neither of us replied, she slammed the side of her hand on the table, a show of temper that made Woodley jump, but not me.

"What is the matter with you people?"

Her face was angry red and her manner was that of a teacher demanding an answer. It was all about control with her, I thought. This was an attempt at a display of control from somebody who had lost it. But I wasn't worried about cracking her; I knew I was a good interviewer, very good.

When I was in my first couple of years of training I spent hours with my dad, honing my interrogation skills, role-playing until he'd caught me out with every dirty trick in the book, and then taught me how to recognize those tricks and work with them.

"You'll hear excuses," Dad said to me one night. I was visiting the family home and it was after dinner. Mum was washing up and Dad and I were talking in his study. The window was wide open and outside the late summer heat had just folded itself away, so we were sitting in the early gloom of a cool, velvety night. "Blokes will say that you aren't a magician," Dad went on, "that you can only do what you do. That's bullshit. It's whining. It's for people who aren't good enough. If you're worth anything, you can get the truth out of anyone. But you've got to be good."

Two cut-glass tumblers sat squat on the table between us, two whiskeys. My dad shut the window and switched on his desk lamp. The shade glowed dark emerald and dropped a rectangle of light onto the surface of his desk.

He sat back down. "Again," he said.

In the kitchen of Nicky Forbes's cottage I took a chair and pulled it close to her, so we were practically knee to knee.

Rachel

So here's the thing.

What do you do when it's just you? When you know something and nobody will listen? When you want to do something, but you don't know how dangerous it is, or how much you will be risking? When you have only minutes to decide?

I was used to making decisions about my life that were based on my complicated relationships with others.

Do I need to name them? Most of us have them. They're generic. They could include your resentment of parents, or a sibling, or your desire to please your family, or a husband, or your fear of losing him. They could include your ambition, or your perception of what parenthood should be. I could go on.

But, at nine a.m. on Monday, October 29, all those things fell away. There was just me, and I had a choice. I could believe what was written about me, that I was worse than useless, incapable of a sensible or moral decision, and I could obey DCI Fraser's request, and wait quietly at home for news.

Or I could act. I could take the certainty I felt and do something. On my own. Again. Because I was sure.

Don't think that self-doubt didn't course through my veins and threaten to weaken me. Don't think that I didn't consider the possible risks of acting alone. The risk for Ben, and for myself.

I fought both those things. I fought them because I knew I had to rely, purely and simply, on my instinct as a mother.

"Be strong," Ruth had said. "You're a mother. You must be strong."

And that was enough for me. I understood in that moment, on that morning, that being a mother had given Ruth a single silken strand, strong as a spider's web, which had tethered her to her life. It was the string that had led her, time and time again, out of the enveloping and dangerous depths of the labyrinth that was her depression. It had prevented her from slipping fatally and completely away into the dark seductive folds of melancholia, and stopped her sinking into the drowsy escape of a terminal pill overdose, or seeking a tumbling, chaotic fall from a height and its inevitable brutal, shattering end below.

It hadn't stopped my own mother. She'd been overwhelmed by the love she felt, by the fear it made her feel. Her emotions had drowned her sanity; such was their power.

But I was different.

I knew my son was alive, and I knew where he was.

So you might wonder what I did.

I opened a drawer in my kitchen and looked over the contents. I chose a vegetable knife. Short and sharp, easy to conceal. I put it into one of the deep pockets of my coat, blade down, beside my phone. I put the keys I'd taken into the other. Then I left my home through the studio at the back, unseen by anybody, and I began to run.

JIM

Nicky Forbes was disturbed by my proximity. She shifted, tucking her legs under the table, away from me. Her body language was pure avoidance, but I was OK with that. I'd learned to be patient.

Woodley sat on the other side of her, keeping more distance, his posture relaxed. Good lad, I thought, he'd been listening.

We'd planned to use the Reid technique in the interview. It's not very nice, but it's very effective. It's a well-known technique that makes use of a good-cop, bad-cop routine, so Woodley had a role to play. As well as being my foil, he would be my eyes. He would watch her for body language that would betray her.

Nicky Forbes folded her arms over her chest.

"Are you finished?" I said.

She flinched slightly, a small jerk of her head away from her hand, which held her cigarette just in front of her mouth, the smoke curling between us.

"The thing is," I said, "here's how I see it." I kept my voice gentle, but persistent, I wanted her to listen to every word I said.

"I think what you went through as a child was a terrible thing. I think that when you lost your brother, when you lost Charlie, you never really recovered. Did you? Then you had to bring up Rachel and she was ungrateful, wasn't she? She never knew how much you had to suffer, or thought about how hard it was for you to keep the secret about your parents and about Charlie."

She took a deep pull on her cigarette, her eyes on mine. I went on.

"So when Rachel had Ben, that was difficult for you, wasn't it? You had four daughters, but that's not the same as having a son, is it? She didn't know how lucky she was, because for you, having a son would be like having Charlie back.

"So I think you didn't have a choice. I think you thought that Rachel was bad for Ben. You reckoned that she couldn't look after him as well as you. She's divorced, after all, bearing a grudge against her husband and his new wife. That's not a happy home. And Ben's been unhappy in the past year; we know that from his teacher.

That must have pained you. In fact I think it was really hard for you to bear."

She gave a small, brusque shake of her head, then she ground the cigarette out in the ashtray, crossed her arms.

"Four children is a lot, and all girls too. Were you hoping for a son, Nicky? Is that why you wanted to try for another baby this year? Your husband told me. Has it been all about replacing Charlie?"

Her eyes began to glisten with tears, but she didn't move a muscle. I didn't draw breath. You mustn't, because if you do it gives them a chance to deny things, and that can make them stronger, just the act of saying it. You have to carry them on your narrative until they finish it for you, and hand you the ending you're waiting for.

I inched my chair just a little closer to hers. Her head bowed. I leaned forward, put my elbows on my knees, and looked up at her.

"You see, I think it was just too much for you in the end. That Rachel had Ben. You knew you could do a better job than her and you wanted a son of your own."

She shuddered.

"I know what it's like to want to protect," I said. "I can understand why you did it. You'd left your own family; you didn't want them. You wanted him. And you wanted him for the right reasons. It was a mother's instinct, a proper mother's instinct, wasn't it? You knew you could do a better job than your sister."

She covered her face with her hands, let out a moan.

I wondered if she was going to break quicker than I thought.

I could almost smell it.

Rachel

It took me twenty-five minutes to get back there.

I stood in front of Miss May's house, panting and soaked to the skin. The only dry parts of me were the depths of my pockets where my fingers nestled around the handle of the knife and the hard edges of the keys.

The street was empty and in front of me the slate sky was reflected in polished windowpanes that were speckled with rain, and the black wrought-iron railings separating the house from the sidewalk looked sharp and forbidding.

I approached the house and looked at the names and buzzers beside the front door. None of them read "May." I peered over the wrought-iron railings, which enclosed a dank courtyard at least twelve feet below ground level.

It was worth a try.

I took the steps down one at a time,

slowly, stone treads slick and treacherous. The doorbell wasn't named. I rang it. No answer.

I got out her keys and tried the Chubb key in the deadlock. It turned smoothly. In went the Yale key too, soft click, and I had to give the door a bit of a shove but it opened and I saw a dark hallway ahead, daring me to step into it.

"Hello?" I called. It wasn't too late to pretend I was just returning the keys, but there was no answer.

"Ben?" I called. Nothing. I felt almost disabled by fear, but I forced myself to walk down the dark, narrow corridor. Filtered daylight beckoned me from the other end.

I glanced through an open door on my left. It was a bathroom, and it was immaculate: fixtures gleaming, expensive-looking toiletries in a neat row. The door opposite showed me her bedroom. On the bed was a suitcase, lid open, neatly packed.

At the end of the corridor I found her living space. It was large and rectangular, the full width of the back of the house. There was a compact, neat kitchen area and small dining table at one end of it, a sitting area at the other. The room had stripped wooden floorboards and three wide, pretty windows with wooden shutters folded back, sills low and wide enough to sit on. The outside space it overlooked was little more than a light well, but there were pretty furnishings and the whole effect was of artful good taste. It was a flat I might have been envious of under different circumstances.

Standing in the center of the room, I saw myself reflected in a mirror over the mantelpiece. I looked white as a ghost. My hair, blackened by rain, hung in damp hanks around my face, and patches under my eyes were as dark as storm clouds. My skin looked slack and undernourished, and the injury on my forehead was healed, but prominent. My eyes were darting with fear and something else as well: there was desperation in them, and a glint of wildness.

I looked completely mad.

Doubt coursed through me.

This is what a total breakdown must be, I thought. You find yourself standing somewhere you shouldn't be, doing something so out of character that you wonder if you've become somebody else entirely. You've lost the plot, taken a wrong turn, jumped onto a train whose destination is total lunacy.

I must leave, I thought. I must go home.

I would have done that, too, but as I turned to leave I noticed the door. It was in a corner, partially obscured by the kitchen units. An apron, oven gloves, and tea towels hung from it on a neat row of hooks. Layers of paint had dulled the paneled detail on it. It was probably a larder, I told myself, or a broom cupboard, and I should just go.

But I found that I couldn't. I felt compelled to walk toward it, and, as I did so, I heard someone whimper and I realized it was me.

I stopped in front of the door. My left palm was molded around the handle of the knife, and I rested the tip of my index finger on the bottom of the blade, and pressed down a little, feeling it bite into me, making me flinch. There was nothing to be heard apart from the slow drip of rain from somewhere outside. Even the hands on the kitchen clock moved soundlessly.

With a feeling of horror uncurling within, I reached my hand out toward the door and clasped the handle. It turned, but something stopped the door from opening. It was jamming at the top.

I reached up to a bolt that was drawn at the top of the door. Tremulous, unreliable fingers fumbled but managed to draw it back.

I opened the door, stepped behind it, and there was a soft click as I pulled it shut.

I could see nothing. All around me it was pitch black, and I had to use the light from my phone to see that I was at the top of a short staircase, and that there was another door, also bolted, at the bottom of it.

I started to make my way down. The darkness was so dense that I needed my hands to steady me on the narrow walls.

Two more steps and I reached the door at the bottom of the staircase. Once again, trembling fingers pulled the bolt, pushed the door open.

My fingers felt for a light switch, and found one. The hesitant bulb blinked and then glowed the dull orange of a polluted sunset before it brightened, revealing the room to me, making me gasp.

It took me long moments to absorb what I could see.

It was a boy's bedroom: freshly painted walls, bright yellow, thick blue carpet on the floor. A rugby poster, and rugby club scarf, both pinned up, some reading books, a teddy bear on the bed, wearing a scarf. There was some clothing, a pair of small slippers, a dressing gown in the softest white toweling. A wooden-framed bed made up with a cartoon-patterned duvet set on it, a pile of DVDs and a television set on a table in the corner, a chest of drawers with pirate stickers decorating it.

No Ben. No natural light.

I picked up one of the garments: it was a pajama top, for a boy, bright red cotton, a dinosaur printed on the front of it, grubby marks around the collar. "Age 8" read the label. I held the top to my face, I inhaled the smell of the fabric, and I knew that Ben had worn it.

He had been here.

My fingers dug into the soft cotton and I held on to it as if it were a living, breathing part of my son. "Ben," I whispered into it, "Ben."

My eyes roved again, looking for more signs of him.

And what struck me was that there was nothing in that room, nothing at all, not one thing, that was right.

If Miss May had made this space for my son, and I was convinced that she had, then she'd got it wrong. Ben didn't like rugby. He'd never have chosen bright yellow walls, or a babyish duvet set, or the type of reading books she'd left out for him, and he wouldn't have liked the pirate stickers on the chest of drawers because he preferred dinosaurs. The bear on the bed was a version of Baggy Bear, but wasn't him. His ear wasn't sucked.

This was a room made for an imagined boy, not for my boy, who would never have felt at home here.

And then I saw something else.

Scattered all over the bed, beneath a fresh scar on the wall where it looked as though it had made impact, were the components of a smashed laptop: shards of plastic, electrical bits, and keyboard keys, all separated from one another by significant force.

Ben would have liked the laptop. He might have played on it.

But he might not have been allowed to go online, to play his favorite game. The laptop might have been snatched from him, and hurled against a wall in anger.

And would that anger have then been directed toward him?

I fumbled for my phone. The reception was poor, but it was enough. I called 999.

And when I'd finished the call I stood in the middle of that space, with the painful wrongness of it in every corner of my vision, and the shattered computer components a glowering hint of violence, and I began to moan, and it was a dreadful, primitive sound, and the moans turned into a shout for him, a final desperate plea, an ululation, like the one I'd made in the woods one week before.

And I fell to my knees, hope shattered.

TRANSCRIPT
EMERGENCY CALL — 10.29.13 at 10 hours, 17 minutes, 6 seconds

Operator: Ambulance emergency. Hello, caller, what's the emergency?
Caller: I've found a boy.
Operator: OK, where have you found him?
Caller: I'm in the woods, Leigh Woods, just over the suspension bridge. My dog found him. He's lying on the ground. He's covered in a bin bag.
Operator: Can he talk to you?
Caller: He's all curled up. He won't wake up.
Operator: So he's not conscious then.
Caller: No, he's not conscious.
Operator: Is he breathing?
Caller: I don't know.
Operator: OK, do you think you can check for me? If he's breathing?
Caller: He's curled in on himself, I can't see his face properly. Hang on.
Operator: How old is the boy?
Caller: I don't know, maybe seven or eight. He's quite little. He's so white, he's really white. Oh God, you've got to send somebody quick.
Operator: They're already on their way. It doesn't delay them for me to ask you some

questions, so don't worry about that. I need you to have a look and see if he's breathing or not, OK?

Caller: He's freezing cold to touch. And he's in a state. Oh God. Oh my God. He's not even wearing anything except underwear. Jesus, oh my God . . .

Operator: All right, you're doing really well and help is on its way, they won't be long now. Can you tell me whereabouts in the woods you are?

Caller: I'm off the main path. By a swing. Help, quickly, help.

Operator: The whole time we're talking, they're on their way to you, so don't worry about that. Have you managed to check if he's breathing?

Caller: Oh God, it's him, isn't it? I think it's Ben Finch, it's the missing . . . [the phone goes dead]

Operator: [Calls back but gets voicemail.]

Jim

Nicky Forbes's expression was complicated: proud and defiant, but with a touch of something else too that I read as surrender. We were close to getting a breakthrough, I knew we were, but then Woodley's phone rang.

It was the world's most stupid, immature ringtone. Of all things, it was the *Star Wars* theme tune, and just like that it destroyed the moment.

Woodley was mortified. I was furious.

Nicky Forbes laughed. "You are so fucking incompetent," she said.

I felt an ache in my temples as Woodley, instead of turning the phone off, took it out of his pocket and looked at it.

She wasn't as close to giving up as I'd thought. She was combative. But that was OK. That I knew I could work with, but Woodley's phone wouldn't shut up, he said, "It's Fraser. I'd better take it."

Nicky Forbes was watching, not missing a trick. I desperately didn't want her to get the upper hand. The Reid technique depends on the interviewer keeping control of the process, moving from one stage of the interview to the next. It can be a long process and we'd only just got started. As Woodley slipped out of the room, I tried to regain control. "Let's discuss what you were doing on Sunday, October twenty-first."

"No," she said. "Let's discuss why you are here wasting my time and harassing me when you should be looking for Ben. Where's Ben, DI Clemo? Where is he? You actually have somebody in custody, and you are here, targeting me. You know nothing about me! Nothing! Do they charge police for wasting their own time? Do they? Because that is what you are doing. My family is everything to me, it's everything. At this moment in time, I can't cope with it very well, but that is nobody's business apart from mine and my husband's. It's not a criminal offense to take some time out, so stop treating me as if I am some kind of monster. My life has been difficult, and I cope with that the best I can. Do I want a son? YES! Do I want Charlie back? YES! Do I find my family too much to cope with sometimes? YES! Did I take Ben? NO, I

DID NOT! Am I a monster? NO, I AM NOT! Do I love my husband, my daughters, my sister, and my nephew? YES, I DO! Is that it? Is that all your questions answered?"

It was the way she said it, hand slamming down on the table as she made each point, as if her very existence depended on my understanding those things.

Faced with those words and her certainty, I simply felt everything start to slip through my fingers: the interview, and the case I wanted to build against her.

I pulled my chair back, loosened my collar.

Outside the kitchen door the mist was still thick, and it was impossible to see more than a few meters into the garden.

Get a grip, I told myself. Get back into it, hold your nerve, you can do this, but then Woodley reappeared and when I saw the look on his face I knew that I'd be lucky if I came out of this with even a shred of dignity.

He held his phone up as if it had something written on it that I should read. "We have to go," he said. Something about the way he said it made me understand that it wasn't negotiable.

"Thank you for your time," I managed to say to her, and the chair scraped on the floor as I stood. There was a static noise in my head. It had a size and a shape, and it was swelling as if it was being pumped in.

"Get out," she said, quietly, as if she'd never seen a creature more disgusting than me.

Outside, by the car, Woodley said, "They've found a boy. In the woods. And they've found the site where he was held."

"Woodley," I said, but then I didn't know what else to say.

I puked onto the thorny stems of one of Nicky Forbes's neatly pruned rosebushes. Bile and bits of unidentifiable spew spattered around its base, leaving a pattern that can't be mistaken for anything other than the hot disgorging of somebody's guts.

I wiped my mouth, straightened up, and felt pain ripple across my abdomen.

"I'll drive," I said, and Woodley handed me the keys.

Rachel

They pried me up off the carpet, which had been so freshly laid that bits of blue fluff stuck to the knees of my trousers and my forehead and my arms.

They escorted me up from the flat with a blanket wrapped around me and they put me in an ambulance that was parked on the street.

The press was there too, of course they were. Only a few of them arrived quickly enough to photograph me being wheeled into the ambulance, but one person with a camera is all it takes. "Rachel! Rachel!" they shouted, as the shutters fired. "Are you all right? Can you tell us what happened?"

Inside the ambulance a paramedic did checks and asked me questions. They said they were treating me for shock.

I refused to lie down. I sat up, blanket wrapped around me. It was all I had the strength to do. Shaking racked my body, like convulsions.

Then it was the turn of the police. They told me they were in pursuit of Joanna May. They said nothing about Ben. Their faces were grim, and I found I had no voice to ask questions.

I had imaginings. I felt as if chunks of me were separating themselves from my body, falling off. I imagined blood creeping in at the edges of my vision, a red tide. It was because I knew I was too late. He had been there, and now he was gone, and what were the odds that she'd keep him alive?

I felt myself let go. I let go of hope.

And then, cutting through the murmured voices, I heard the ambulance radio. The dispatcher was calling for somebody to respond to a call in Leigh Woods. Precise location unknown. A young boy found. Status unknown.

They had to sedate me. Blackness fell as swiftly as the blade of a guillotine.

TRANSCRIPT
EMERGENCY CALL — 10.29.13 at 10 hours, 38 minutes, 28 seconds

Operator: Hello, ambulance and emergency, how . . .
Caller: Oh my God, thank God. I've been disconnected. Can you hear me? I've been trying to call, trying to call you back. I was talking to somebody, but my phone went dead and I couldn't get a signal again. I've found that boy. I've found him. But he's in a really bad way.
Operator: Where are you, caller?
Caller: Please, hurry up.
Operator: Can you tell me where you are?
Caller: I'm in Leigh Woods, by a rope swing. Off the path. Are they looking for us? Should I go to the path?
Operator: Hold on just a second, OK . . . [consults somebody briefly]. . . . All right, help is already on its way, they're nearly with you, but it's best if you stay with the boy and I really need you to tell me if he's breathing if you can.
Caller: He is breathing, but it's really bad breathing. I can't feel a pulse in his arm. He's freezing cold. I've put my coat on him.
Operator: Right. Is he conscious at all?

Caller: No, he's not.
Operator: All right. You're doing well. Can you see if he's got any injuries on him? Is there any blood?
Caller: I can't see any blood. He's got bruises up his arm. He's making weird noises.
Operator: Right, can you carefully move him onto his back, as quickly as you can, and have a look in his mouth if you can, check there's nothing obstructing it. Keep him lying as flat as you can.
Caller: I'm doing it. God, he's cold, he's soaking wet. Oh God. Where are they?
Operator: They're nearly with you. Can you tell me, how's his breathing now?
Caller: Bad.
Operator: But he's still breathing, right?
Caller: I've got him on his back.
Operator: Look in his mouth. Is there anything in there? Food or vomit?
Caller: No. His lips are blue.
Operator: Is he still breathing?
Caller: Yes, he is. I'm going to lie with him. I'm going to give him my body heat.
Operator: OK. They're a few minutes away from you now; they're making their way along the main path in the woods. Can you give me some more detail about where you are, can you tell me where they

need to turn off the main path?

Caller: There's a pile of logs opposite the entrance. Cut-up logs in a pile. About halfway around the path.

Operator: I'll let them know.

Caller: I'm lying with him. He's breathing really bad.

Operator: Can you shout? I want you to stay with him, and tell me straightaway if he stops breathing, but can you shout, to help them find you? They're very close, but they can't see you.

Caller: HELP! OVER HERE! HELP!

Operator: Well done. They can hear you. Keep shouting.

Caller: HELP US! HELP! OVER HERE! Where are they?

Operator: Don't worry, they can hear you and they can see you now.

Caller: I can see them. HERE! QUICK! HE'S HERE!

Operator: Are they with you now?

Caller: Yes, they're here.

Operator: OK, I'll leave you with them, OK?

Caller: Yes, thanks, all right.

Operator: Thank you, bye.

Jim

We made it to the woods in one hour. I used blue lights.

On the way in the car we got more details. About Ben Finch's condition. About Joanna May, and the room in the basement of her flat.

"We interviewed her," I said to Woodley. "We should have fucking seen it."

He didn't respond.

The paramedics were still working with Ben Finch in the woods. They couldn't get the ambulance to the site so they'd had to stabilize him and move him in stages.

We parked and I ran. I wanted to be with Ben. I wanted to see his clear blue eyes for myself, see if there was life in them. I wanted to tell him that he would be OK, that his mother was waiting for him. I wanted to do that for him at least.

Rain was falling in a downpour, crashing through the canopy above. The trees lining the path were bowed and streaked from it. They arched over me, a skeletal tunnel of bare branches, urging me onward, making me feel as if it was impossible to make progress.

My breathing was ragged and fast, my heart thumping, my clumsy feet tripping over sticks, stones, each other, never moving fast enough. With every step I was soaked some more, but with every step I cared less.

I rounded a bend in the path, and ahead I saw the ambulance, and a stretcher being loaded on board.

I pushed myself, tried to reach them in time, tried to shout out, but it was futile, because they slammed the door shut long before I reached them, and by the time I got there the ambulance had begun the tricky process of turning around.

Mark Bennett was guiding it. I stayed back, stood to the side of the path as the ambulance maneuvered past me, watched him pat the back of it as a farewell.

And Bennett, all dressed up in waterproofs, jaw clenched, and wet from rain, said, "That lad's not in a good way, Jim. Not at all." It had got to him. I could see that.

And I said, "I wanted to see him." I wiped

the rain from my face, felt my sodden clothing cling coldly to me.

"Nothing we can do for him now. It's too late for that. It's in the hands of the medics."

And I hated him for saying that, and I hated him for being there when it should have been me, and I hated myself for letting harm come to that boy, any harm at all.

RECORD OF EVIDENCE: AVON AND SOMERSET POLICE, CID

OPERATION HUCKLEBERRY — EVIDENCE BAG 2

AUTHORIZED COPY OF HOSPITAL ADMISSIONS NOTE FOR BENEDICT FINCH, BRISTOL CHILDREN'S HOSPITAL, MONDAY, OCTOBER 29 AT 12:07 P.M.

Description of text:

Name: Benedict Jonathan Finch Age: 8 years Sex: Male

Date of birth: to be confirmed

Benedict Finch, male, 8 years, identity confirmed by police officer attending scene in the woods. Awaiting confirmation by family member.

On arrival presented with severe hypothermia caused by overnight exposure in Leigh Woods with no shelter and no clothing. Hypothermia-induced coma. Hypotension (BP 78/54); core body temperature 28°C; HR 30 reg. General condition extremely poor. Underweight, dirty, and dehydrated. Significant bruising to left upper arm.

Original stored Item 3, Evidence box 345.112

WEB PAGE — BREAKING NEWS — www.up2theminute.co.uk/asithappens

October 29, 2012, 14:13

UP TO THE MINUTE brings you a timeline of today's dramatic developments in the case of missing eight-year-old Benedict Finch.

The significant developments were confirmed by AVON and SOMERSET CONSTABULARY in a hastily arranged press conference this afternoon led by DS Giles Martyn.

10:15 a.m. The body of a young boy is discovered in Leigh Woods near the site where Benedict Finch went missing just over one week ago. The discovery is made by a member of the public who contacted the emergency services. The boy is alive, but barely.

12 noon The search for Benedict Finch is called off, after the boy's identity is confirmed on arrival at Bristol Children's Hospital.

12:45 p.m. A small number of people begin

to gather outside the Children's Hospital. They light candles and pray for Benedict Finch and there's an outpouring of concern on Twitter for his safe recovery.

1:17 p.m. An arrest is made at Bristol Airport and police confirm that they've detained a person in connection with the investigation.

2:10 p.m. Police confirm that the person detained in connection with Benedict's disappearance is a teacher at his school, Joanna May, 27 years old.

In other developments there are unconfirmed reports that Benedict Finch's mother was treated in an ambulance outside an address in Clifton this morning. It's thought that the address may be the home of Joanna May.

Keeping You Up to the Minute, Every Minute

Spread the word: Facebook; Twitter

RACHEL

Bristol Children's Hospital smelled of cleanliness and sickness in equal measure. The only times I'd been there before had been to meet John after work.

We traveled up from the ground floor in a tiny elevator where Wallace and Gromit's recorded voices told us to "Mind the doors," over and over again. Shock-eyed and sleep-deprived parents got on and off, checking the sign in the lift for their destinations, fingers running down a list, stopping at "Oncology" or "Nephrology."

Among them were a mother and baby boy, she wearing a burqa, even her eyes veiled from the world with mesh. Her baby was in her arms, a tube running up his nose, taped in place, his wide brown eyes staring at the ceiling lights. I wondered how she was able to comfort him when she was confined to that garment, when their eyes couldn't even meet. Did she rest her uncovered fingers on his cheek? Was that skin-to-skin contact enough for them both here, in this hospital?

My heart, hurting for my own son, ached for her too.

The elevator disgorged DI Bennett and me onto the fourth floor.

The decor was wincingly bright, themed in blue and yellow, and featuring aquatic motifs, but somehow all of that felt hopeful; it made my sense of anticipation swell.

In the vestibule outside the elevator doors, where the floor-to-ceiling windows offered us a tumbling, chaotic cityscape view of Bristol, DI Bennett told me that he'd been in the woods with Ben. He couldn't quite meet my eye, but he held open a door for me and then guided me along the corridor with a light hand on my elbow that was touching if not welcome.

I was met in the corridor outside Ben's ward by two doctors, who politely ushered me into a room. A nurse was there. She offered me a cup of tea. The chink of china was the only sound in the room as everybody waited for her to pour it.

Ben had been close to death when they found him, they explained to me, his core body temperature dangerously cold, but they'd warmed him up, and he was stable. Battered and bruised, very weak, but stable.

Relief and happiness that he was alive overwhelmed any trepidation I might have felt. They could scarcely hold me back.

"He's still in a dangerous condition," they wanted to tell me before they let me see him. "Do you understand that?"

I said I did. I left the tea to go cold on the table.

Do you want me to describe our reunion?

I can tell you that a nurse was outside the door of Ben's room and that her hand reached out to touch mine when I arrived, just brushed it lightly, even though we were strangers. We exchanged no words but she held the door open for me.

Jim

By the time we got back to Kenneth Steele House, Woodley and I mud-stained and soaking wet from the woods, Fraser had just gone in to interview Joanna May. They'd picked her up at Bristol Airport waiting for a flight out.

We heard everything secondhand. The incident room was fairly buzzing with the news. Relief had broken out across everybody's faces, though there was an undercurrent of muttering that Benedict Finch was seriously unwell, that it was a wait-and-see job. Nobody was celebrating properly because of that; nobody wanted to.

Fraser had left instructions for Bennett to get down to the hospital and for Woodley and me to go and visit Joanna May's parents at their house. She wanted us to get to the bottom of the alibi they'd given their daughter and find out what else they knew.

It was three p.m. by the time we pulled

into their driveway on a quiet street of semi-detached Victorian villas far enough out in suburbia that streetlights were few and far between.

When we arrived, two uniforms made a discreet exit, leaving Woodley and me with a couple, in their seventies, who looked as though they wished the ground would open up and swallow them.

We sat in their living room. There was no tea or coffee. Vast windows inset with a band of decorative stained glass gave us a view of a pair of raised vegetable beds, where bamboo canes protruded from the dark puddle-pocked earth and were tethered into triangular shapes.

On an ornate marble mantelpiece a vase of flowers was crowded by family photographs, which spilled over onto adjacent bookshelves that reached from floor to ceiling. Among the faces in the pictures was Joanna May.

Hanging above the fireplace was a large mirror in a gilt frame, which threw back a reflection of our sorry gathering: Woodley and I standing in the middle of the room, tall and dark like crows; Mrs. May sunk into an armchair, a walking stick propped up beside her, dressings visible on her legs underneath thick brown tights; Mr. May beside her in a matching chair, wisps of white hair over his forehead, cat hair on his trousers; both of them looking stricken.

"She was our fourth child," said Mrs. May, once Woodley and I had taken a seat on a rug-draped sofa. Her voice was tremulous and careful. "We had five children altogether. Rory died, our eldest son, when he was a toddler, but we were a happy family, weren't we, Geoff?"

Mr. May reached over and took her hand, squeezed it.

"But she wasn't right," he said to Woodley and me, "from the start. As soon as she started interacting with other children, we knew she wasn't."

"In what way?" I asked.

Mrs. May lowered her eyes.

"She was so manipulative," said her husband. "She competed constantly for our attention, she bullied her siblings to get what she wanted, and she was always lying. The lying was constant, it was infuriating."

It was painful to watch Mr. May talk. Everything he shared with us stripped another piece of his pride away, and undermined more completely the life this couple had built.

"If somebody lies to you habitually, Inspector, you can't ever trust them," he said.

"It erodes relationships, even between a parent and child." He ran a trembling hand across the paper-thin skin on his forehead. "We knew the way she behaved was wrong, and that she wasn't what you might call completely normal, but we never dreamed it would lead to something like this."

"Is the child all right?" Mrs. May asked. "The boy?" She didn't seem able to say his name. "We've been watching the news."

"It's a little early to tell," I said, "but as far as I know his condition's stable for now."

She nodded, swallowed, and made a small sign of the cross.

"I believe," I said, "that you provided your daughter with an alibi for last Sunday. Is that right?"

"We did, yes," said Mrs. May. "Your colleague rang us to talk about it, a very nice young lady called, what was she called, dear?"

"DC Zhang," said Mr. May.

"Can I ask you about that?"

"Well," said Mr. May. "Yes, well, Joanna came to have lunch with us on that day, and we weren't really sure exactly what time she went home, but she reminded us it was about four thirty so that's what we told your colleague."

"Joanna reminded you?"

"Yes. We asked her because we weren't sure. We didn't think to question it, because it could have been four thirty, couldn't it, Mary?"

Mrs. May nodded. "We never really checked," she said. "And we started lunch quite late. But I suppose it could have been earlier too. Now that I think about it. We never actually checked the time ourselves."

"So you weren't absolutely sure?"

"Not certain, no, but your colleague said that was normal."

"Would you mind making a statement to that effect?"

"We never thought our daughter would be capable of such a thing," said Mr. May. "If we'd ever dreamed . . . oh dear God . . . would they have been able to find the boy earlier?"

"It's not your fault," I said, but he lowered his eyes and I could see that it was a question that they would be asking themselves for a very long time.

"Can I ask, do you have any idea why Joanna might have done this?" I said.

They exchanged a glance then, and Mrs. May gave a small shrug of her shoulders.

Mr. May said, "Joanna's infertile. That's the only sense I can make of it. She just discovered her infertility last spring after she tried to get pregnant using artificial insemination. We didn't approve. We thought she should be in a stable relationship before she had a baby, but she was insistent, as usual, and so we gave her the money anyway, for the inseminations, and then for the fertility tests, because you try to help your children. You feel responsible for their happiness. I don't think she would have told us if she hadn't needed us to pay for it. She doesn't confide in us. In fact she only contacts us if she wants something. Anyway, it upset her a great deal, the infertility. She wasn't used to not getting what she wanted. My guess is that she took this boy because she wanted a child. But let me tell you this: don't expect her to explain why she did it. She never admitted to anything as a child, and I doubt she will now."

He stood up again, painfully, and made his way to the mantelpiece. He took down a photograph of Joanna May and gazed at it for a moment before showing it to his wife. In the photograph Joanna May was on a beach. She couldn't have been more than ten or eleven years old. In her swimsuit she sat beside a body-shaped mound of sand from which the head of a smaller child protruded. She wielded a spade triumphantly and the child was smiling too.

"I'll move this I think, Mary," said Mr. May.

"Yes, dear." Her eyes slid to her lap as he left the room, fingers picking at the fabric of her skirt.

Together, we waited silently for him to return, but before he did, the sound of breaking glass made Mrs. May flinch.

Rachel

I approached my son's bedside with a lifetime of love to give him, and with the humility of somebody who's been brought to her knees in every way imaginable.

I came to him with a surfeit of relief and emotion that should have made for a perfect Hollywood moment, with full orchestral accompaniment and box of Kleenex required. The works.

But it wasn't like that.

When I entered the room, I saw that he had his back to me, and he lay curled up under layers of blankets, motionless and small, the outline of his body making an angular shape.

I saw the back of his head, his sandy hair unkempt, without luster. One of his arms lay on top of the blanket. A garish hospital gown covered some of it, but his forearm protruded, bare until the wrist, where a thick bandage was wrapped around it, securing a cannula, which was attached to a tube, down which a transparent liquid crawled, dripping into his vein.

Closer. An oxygen mask was on the pillow beside his head, hissing. I could see the side of his face now, his profile. His lips were chapped and paper-thin eyelids covered eyes that were twitching beneath. His eyelashes were long and beautiful as ever, though they did little to mask the deep dark patches under his eyes and the gray pallor of his skin.

"Ben," I whispered. I touched the skin on his temples with the side of my hand; it was the softest skin you could ever touch. I pushed a strand or two of his hair back from his forehead.

He didn't respond. He was sleeping the sleep of the dead.

Behind me, the doctor said, "He may take a few minutes to wake up properly." He was standing awkwardly by the door, keeping his distance. I knew he was there because they were frightened of what my reunion with Ben could do to him.

"Ben," I said. "It's me, Mummy."

I sat down on the side of his bed. I wanted him to wake up, I wanted him to come to me, to pitch into my arms as if he'd been falling from a great height and had finally landed in a place of safety.

His eyelids flickered open, then shut again.

"Love," I said. "It's Mummy. I'm here. Ben."

Another flicker and then I had them: bright blue eyes. They didn't move in the usual way though. They looked past me at first, and it was only when I said his name again that they slid toward me, locked on to mine.

He blinked.

My head sank down onto his, my breath on his face, his head motionless beneath me. I kissed him, and my tears slid from my cheeks onto his. I felt his lips move, and I pulled back so I could see him better, hear him. "What did you say, Ben? What did you say?"

Eyes slid shut again, a twitch of movement in his arm. And I thought, where is my child, the one who could never stay still, whose every movement was brimming with life?

His breathing faltered audibly and I heard the doctor step forward, but it settled again and the doctor contented himself with moving the oxygen mask closer to Ben's mouth.

I felt terrible, terrible sadness building in me, a feeling so powerful that it hurt, and it made my hands shake. I looked at the doctor, his eyes powerfully kind and his words steady: "Give him some time."

And he was right, because Ben stirred, and his eyes met mine again, and even though they seemed to slip out of focus, his lips moved and this time a word was audible on his outtake of air. "Mummy." And tears began to roll slowly, silently down his cheeks.

I took him in my arms, even though the doctor stepped forward as if to stop me, then thought better of it. I scooped Ben up, onto my lap, and I held his limp, small body close to mine and in return I thought I felt some strength in his arms, and then it was a firmer squeeze and he clung to me. He did that weakly, and wordlessly, but we stayed like that for so long that eventually the doctor had to pry him gently away.

After the medical staff had laid him back down, they tidied him up, adjusted his cannula, and checked that he was properly connected to his machines. When they stepped away, Ben's eyes met mine with more consciousness in them than they'd had before.

And I smiled, because that was what I wanted from him most of all, a smile. It was the last thing I'd seen on his face before he left me in the woods, and I wanted to see it again. But my smile wasn't answered, because his eyes moved away again, and the lids slid down over the tears that still fell, and he turned his head away from me.

And here's the thing: I wasn't sure whether that was because he was exhausted and dangerously unwell, or because there were things deep inside his eyes that he didn't want me to see.

It was a beautiful reunion for me. It was. The feel of Ben's arms around me was everything I'd dreamed of, every second he'd been away. But the other bits, his desperate physical condition, the sorrow that was deeply, soundlessly buried within him, and the way he dodged my gaze, I won't deny it — this is supposed to be a truthful account after all — they were profoundly frightening.

Did you want catharsis? So did I. But there was none. I'm sorry.

Epilogue: Christmas 2013 — One Year, Five Weeks After

WEB PAGE — www.twentyfour7news.co.uk/bristol — 3:15 PM GMT Dec 11, 2013

JOANNA MAY GUILTY OF BENEDICT FINCH ABDUCTION

by Danny Deal

Joanna May pleaded guilty to the abduction of 8-year-old Benedict Finch in front of Mr. Justice Evans at Bristol Crown Court today.

The 27-year-old abducted Benedict Finch after becoming obsessed with having him for herself, it can now be revealed, after she discovered she was infertile.

May was arrested and charged with the abduction after Benedict was discovered abandoned in Leigh Woods. She had been keeping him in the basement of her flat in

Mortimer Crescent, Clifton, for nine days during October 2012.

May had displayed symptoms of fantasist behavior in the past and shown an "unhealthy" interest in a friend's baby.

This information can now be reported after the judge, Mr. Justice Evans, lifted an order banning publication.

May stared ahead and showed no sign of emotion during her time in court.

The judge told May she had committed "a heinous and dreadful act that harmed in extreme ways the emotional and physical welfare of a vulnerable young child" and that the abduction had left Benedict's family suffering "eight days of torturous uncertainty" and "unforgivable harassment and vilification by the media."

Julian Paget, QC prosecuting, described May as "calculating, manipulative, arrogant, and extremely dangerous."

Members of Benedict Finch's family were in court to hear the verdict but showed little emotion and declined to comment.

Sentencing will take place next week.

286 comments and 7 people are discussing this article

Simon Flynn
This is a truly chilling case. Let's hope she gets the sentence she deserves. My thoughts are with Benedict Finch's family.

Jean Moller
She is a vile piece of scum. Hahahahahaha Joanna May, everyone inside prison will know what you did and there will be degradation heaped on you. I hope you're never released. Pain to you.

Anthony Smith
Exodus 22:18: "Thou shalt not suffer a witch to live."

Samantha Singh
Hopefully this will be able to bring some closure for her family. Thinking of them and poor little Benedict.

Patricia Gumm
For the sake of the family and for Ben we should be thankful that justice has been done. And we should spare a thought too

for the other poor children who suffered her as a teacher without knowing the evil in her heart.

Jasleen Harper
Are we going to pay for her to wallow in prison with satellite tv and psychotherapy now? People like her should be put to work cleaning up after shit like them.

Cliff Downs
Jasleen, we shouldn't use language like that out of respect for Ben and his family.

Simon Flynn
The news is a 24/7 monster. It devours all information and we feed it with our opinions, so we can't be shy of expressing ourselves even if we don't like the language other people use. It's called free speech.

Comments are now closed

RACHEL

A few weeks ago, somebody asked me if I thought Ben and I could have some closure once the trial was over. I was lost for words, truly; because the fact of it is that we might never have "closure." If only life were that simple. There are some events and uncertainties that you take to the grave, and they threaten to tumble you every single step of the way.

If closure is a search for answers, and an attempt to clear away ambiguity, then let me tell you how far we've got.

Here's what I know for sure:

I know that in the woods that Sunday afternoon, my child willingly walked away with Joanna May, his hand in hers. He looked up into her eyes, he trusted her, and he believed what she told him.

She took him to her car, after making him change into clothes that she provided him with. Skittle followed them. Joanna May hadn't been prepared for that so she kicked the dog, to make him go away, and, in doing so, she broke his leg. Then she drove Ben away. She avoided routes where CCTV cameras lay in wait for her.

Out of everything that happened to him in that week, Ben talks about her treatment of the dog most of all. His mind circles around it, trying to make sense of her cruelty. What bothers him most is that she made him leave Skittle there, in pain, whimpering on the ground. It was the first sign he had that she wasn't a stable person.

After that, I know very little for sure, except that it was Ben I met on Furry Football one week later. There is a void, a seven-day hole in his life between the two events.

The evidence tells us a little more. The smashed laptop and bruising consistent with finger marks on Ben's upper arm indicate that her anger at finding him playing the computer game pitched her into a state of mind dangerous enough that she drove him back to the woods and dragged him through the darkness back to the place where she first took him.

She left him there, dressed only in his underwear and with a black bin bag to shield him from the rain. In doing so, she humiliated and frightened him and the exposure almost killed him.

We know that once she'd returned home after that she booked a flight for late the following morning, and packed a suitcase, and placed her passport in a travel wallet, which she put in her bag.

We also know that Lucas Grantham was her downfall, because the police phoned very early that morning to ask her in for an interview about him. She took a gamble, and went to Kenneth Steele House, not wanting to arouse suspicion, knowing she could still make her plane.

Though she wasn't to know that we would end up in a car together, and that she would make a little verbal slip, which would lead me to steal her keys.

I imagine her standing on that broad sidewalk outside her home as DI Bennett and I drove away, rifling through her handbag for the keys to the flat, not finding them, and then replaying the moment in the car when her belongings fell to the floor, and most likely putting two and two together, or at least deciding that she couldn't afford the time to retrieve them or to track down a spare set. As far as the police could tell, she made absolutely no attempt to enter the flat and gather her stuff before I got there, probably because she had her passport in her bag already. We know that she was in a cab to the airport only twenty minutes after DI Bennett and I dropped her off, so she didn't dither. I like to think it was the moment when the hunter became the hunted, when her breath quickened, and she began to look over her shoulder.

And that is the sum of all I know for sure.

Here's what I don't know:

Why she took him, or how she treated him.

Why don't I know that?

Because Ben won't speak of it.

Why not?

We don't know. I guess that aside from the things he's willing to say, there must be other things he can't remember, things he's confused about, or things he might be frightened of talking about.

I think he doesn't like the way the eyes and attention of everybody around him sharpen when he so much as mentions that room or Miss May. I think that makes him feel uncomfortable, and ashamed. He doesn't want to be the center of attention; he would rather it all went away.

So we have to be careful, because we don't want to make things worse, damage him further, or send him into a shell where he doesn't communicate at all. That can happen to children in his situation. I've read about it.

And though I hate to say it, I do sometimes wonder if he's trying to protect her with his silence. They did, after all, have a close bond before this happened.

And why can't we get the rest of what we need to know from Joanna May?

Because she and Ben have something in common, beyond the eight days he spent in her home. What they have in common is that she refuses to speak about it as well. She has ever since her arrest. Her guilty plea has been her only word on the matter.

Just when we need her to talk, she has decided to remain silent. As is her right.

And so we speculate. We have built a story that seems to fit the scant evidence. And the story goes like this:

In return for Ben's trust, for the way he slipped his hand in hers so easily, Joanna May led him to a place where she incarcerated him against his will.

I think she did it because she either loved Ben or she wanted to very much. It was a distorted, selfish love that was the product of a damaged mind, but I think it existed.

I think that she formed a bond with him during the first year she taught him, and she began to want him for herself. Her diagnosis of infertility, which has emerged in the public domain now, was simultaneous with my divorce, with me asking her to help us support Ben, and I think that at this very vulnerable time in her life, when her urge to be a mother was strongest, she might have mistaken him for a child who wasn't loved enough, or cared for enough, and thought that taking him could solve both her longing for a child and Ben's sadness.

That thought must have grown stronger for months until it was fully fledged, and formed into a careful plan, which she executed flawlessly one year ago on Sunday, October 21.

Once she'd incarcerated him, I think she began a process of trying to make him believe that his family was bad for him and she was the right person to care for him.

We don't know what her long-term plans were, but Ben has hinted to us that she might have been planning a trip for them and I suspect she was going to take him away. I don't know where, or how.

The bedroom she made for him is testament to her desire to make his environment nice, to look after him well, and I actually think she meant to, even though it was in reality no more than a carefully decorated cell.

But I think it went wrong, the reality of having him. I don't think she anticipated how much he would miss home, or miss me, and his father and his stepmother, or his dog. I don't think she expected him to be so desperately unhappy without us. She didn't realize that he was already deeply loved, and that he loved so much in return.

Those are the motives we attribute to her, the timeline we fabricate to explain things. And we continue to try to fill in more gaps.

We speculate that Joanna May underestimated the tech savvy of a young boy. Why else would she have let him have access to a laptop? Was she tired of trying to entertain him down there, had she exhausted all other ideas? Did she think it was safe because it would be impossible for him to log on? How enraged was she when Ben found a WiFi signal down in that basement that didn't need a password?

Enraged enough to put his life in danger, and I think that was because it made her feel that she'd lost control, that she'd bitten off more than she could chew. Her solution? To take him back to the woods and abandon him there, then to come home and organize her exit.

Is it because she really did love him that she didn't take that final step and murder him at that point, to silence him forever? I think so, although the thought makes me recoil.

To confirm our various hypotheses, we've all tried to coax more information out of Ben: therapists, doctors, psychiatrists, us. But for the most part he's chosen silence, perhaps as a way of feeling in control. And we must accept his silence. We must content ourselves with our guesswork.

I wish now that I'd valued more the words that tumbled freely out of him before he was taken. I wish I'd collected them and kept them safely in packages that I wrapped up carefully, secured with a ribbon, and stored in a safe place for the future. I wish I hadn't been too distracted to listen to every word he said. I wish I hadn't let him run ahead of me. There is so much that I wish, and all of it is pointless now. Beyond pointless.

Ben is not the child he used to be. Trust is difficult for him, because he doesn't understand why John and I didn't find him earlier, or why the teacher he adored turned out to be somebody bad.

He has pretty good attendance at school, considering, though it's not uncommon for

John or me to get a phone call to say that he's unable to cope, again, that he's gripped by a migraine so severe that he can't open his eyes, again, and then we go to get him.

Emotionally, his daily existence is volatile and unpredictable. He can be fine for days at a time, and then something sets him off balance. Then he can be desperately clingy, or angry, depending on the form his sadness takes. His emotions are powerful and visceral. Very, very occasionally he fights us, kicking and hitting. More often, he cannot last the night without waking and screaming in terror.

When that happens, I run to him and lift him from his bed, and I bring him into bed with me, where we lie, eyes wide, bodies together, and I hold him to me and wait for his teeth to stop chattering, and watch carefully for the sheen of sweat on his brow that signals the fever that sometimes rises after these nightmares.

I bring Skittle to sleep on the bed with us too, because the dog is the object of Ben's most uncomplicated affections. I get pleasure from watching them play together, Ben's gentleness with Skittle, and the dog's adoration of him. When Ben goes to John's house now, the dog goes with him. Her claws have made scratches all over the parquet floor, but nobody minds.

And even when Ben and I lie together during those long nights, even though our hearts pump fast and in unison, I wonder if sometimes we remain a hundred miles apart, because his mind still crouches in the woods on his own, cold to the core, or perhaps in that basement, flinching as a laptop shatters against a wall, pieces falling around him, sensing the advance of a person who wants to drag him away, even though he's covered his face with his hands, even though he cowers.

These are my imaginings, for, as I said, Ben won't speak of it.

His silence torments me, because I want to make him better, but it's her silence that I truly loathe, for Ben can't help it, but she is an adult and she knowingly withholds information that could help us to understand better what happened, and therefore to heal him more quickly, and that I cannot forgive her for.

Jim

Addendum to DI James Clemo's report for Dr. Francesca Manelli

Transcript recorded by Dr. Francesca Manelli
DI James Clemo and Dr. Francesca Manelli in attendance

Notes to indicate observations on DI Clemo's state of mind or behavior, where his remarks alone do not convey this, are in italics.

FM: I've read your account of what happened on the last day of the Benedict Finch investigation.
He nods curtly.
FM: I'm sorry that things went wrong for you that day.
JC: That's putting it mildly.
FM: How have you been feeling lately?

He's moving a lot, he can't settle. His gaze is shifting around the room. He's expressing avoidance with every movement he makes. He doesn't answer.

FM: Can I be frank with you?

JC: Please.

FM: We have almost used up your allocation of sessions that CID is prepared to fund. You arrived late to the second to last session we had, and you didn't turn up at all last week. I am concerned about your commitment to this process.

JC: There's nothing wrong with me. I feel much better, in my head, I mean.

FM: That's not good enough, DI Clemo. That judgment has to come from me.

JC: I just said: I feel better.

FM: Do you want to know what I think?

I catch him off guard with this, and his reply is a little petulant.

JC: Isn't this supposed to be about what I think?

FM: My professional assessment of the situation is that you avoided our last session because it's getting painful for you to talk. Which means that this is exactly the point where you need to attend.

He worries at his hairline with his fingertips. The signs of profound fatigue are written all over his face, and obvious to see in his body language too. You would not have to be a professional to spot these.

FM: When did you last get a night's sleep?

JC: I can't remember.

FM: Is there any improvement in your insomnia since we began these sessions?

Clemo shakes his head slowly, resignedly.

FM: Do you know why that is?

I don't wait for a response.

FM: It's because you aren't engaging with this process. And if you don't engage then we cannot work toward treating you, and improving your quality of life, and that includes the insomnia, and the panic attacks, all of it. To date, across all of our sessions, I would say that your responses to my questions are mostly about avoidance. That must be exhausting for you. Isn't it? It must exhaust you dodging my questions, working out ways to preserve that facade of toughness. My question to you is why you are so willing to expend so much energy avoiding this process when it would be so much easier if you would open yourself up to it? I'm not a quack, DI Clemo, I've worked with many people in similar situations to yours, and helped them.

JC: And what would you say my situation is, Dr. Manelli?

FM: You suffer from severe, debilitating depression leading to insomnia and panic attacks, all of which have affected your ability to do your job. Based on our discussions, I would say that they have their roots in a combination of factors, which arose at the time of the Benedict Finch case.

JC: And what were those factors?

FM: You tell me. What do you think they were?

He is stony-faced.

JC: I thought that was your job.

FM: My job is to help you. Let me. Talk to me.

Clemo sits absolutely still for a moment, then puts his head in his hands. He sobs, and the sound is awful and strangulated, but it's what I've been waiting for. I take my chance.

FM: Play a game with me.

JC: What?

FM: I'm going to say a word, and I want you to tell me how you feel about it. No! Don't argue about it, just do it. Will you?

He holds his fingers over his eyes now, trying to stem the tears.

FM: Emma.

He gets control of himself, and then the silence in the room seems endless, capa-

cious, but just when I think I've lost him, he speaks.

JC: I loved her.

FM: I know you did.

JC: So much.

FM: Do you still love her?

JC: Yes.

FM: Have you seen her since the case?

JC: No.

FM: Do you miss her?

He looks at me, and his eyes are burning with something.

JC: I miss her every day. I miss the months we haven't had together and I miss the future I thought we were going to have, because without her it feels pointless, it feels, just, totally flat. Fuck!

This is the kind of candid answer I've been waiting for. I hold my breath and I wait because he needs to pull himself together again before we continue. Then I proceed very carefully.

FM: OK. I'm going to give you another name.

He just looks at me, bruised and weary eyes have a note of defeat in them now. He is playing my game. He feels as if he's being beaten, but he's not.

FM: Joanna May.

JC: I should have seen it when I interviewed

her. I'll never forgive myself for that. Never.

FM: You're not responsible for what Joanna May did to that child.

JC: If I could have ended it earlier that would have made a difference, at least spared Ben Finch that night in the woods.

FM: You're not responsible.

JC: But I'm responsible for making the wrong decision, for going after Nicky Forbes. That was my call.

FM: As I understand it, that was a joint decision with DCI Fraser.

JC: It was me who had the hunger for it. I thought it was her, so I went after her. It was the wrong call. I humiliated myself.

FM: I'm going to give you one more name. You're doing well.

He flinches as if he knows what I'm going to say.

FM: Benedict Finch.

JC: I should have been there for him. In the woods. At the end. It should have been me.

FM: Why does that matter so much to you?

JC: Because all along it was all about him. It was about his suffering, because we all knew he was. And I missed my chance to prevent that and I missed my chance to be there for him at the end.

FM: Do you think it might have helped, if you were there?

JC: I wanted to be with him, to comfort him.

I am very touched by his words. They are humble, and moving. I have to make an effort not to let this show.

FM: Is that what most keeps you awake at night, DI Clemo?

JC: All of it keeps me awake at night. It obsesses me. It replays over and over again. It won't let me rest. I made mistakes. I broke that family apart and I let the light go out in that boy's eyes.

FM: Are you in contact with the family?

JC: I saw them once.

FM: What happened?

He cries again now, but this time it's just a few tears that slip down his cheeks and dampen the fabric of his shirt when they fall. He doesn't speak.

FM: Will you believe me if I tell you it is possible to move forward from this? Not to forget, but to move onward, and make it a manageable part of your life.

JC: I don't deserve it.

FM: You do deserve it. This doesn't have to be the end of your career, DI Clemo. This case, and everything that happened around it, represents a very significant time in your life, of course it does, but it doesn't have to define you, or break you. Don't do that to yourself. Instead, you can think of it as something you can learn to live with, to get past, and even to build on. Benedict and his family will be doing that too. Think for a moment of your life as a path that you're moving forward on, not a place you're stuck in. You can deal with this appropriately, and respectfully, and if you do that it will be possible to put it behind you. If you'll trust me, I can guide you through that process.

Quite honestly, at that moment, I'm not sure if DI Jim Clemo wants to be fixed at all.

FM: Will you, Jim? Trust me?

Time hovers then, waiting, with me, for his response. This is a good man. I want him to heal. Eventually, he exhales slowly and deliberately, but even when he opens his mouth to speak I'm still not sure if this is going to be the beginning or the end of his attempt at recovery.

JC: I'll try.

Rachel

We might never have closure, but we do have a future to consider. We must consider it.

As a family, we now spend a lot of time together, trying to provide a network of security around Ben. We want to comfort him, to sustain him. Katrina is a rock, and so is Nicola. She went back to her family after Ben was found and they welcomed her with open arms, as do I. We have slowly begun to relearn each other, to reconfigure our relationship now that there are no lies, now that we both know who we are. It's made us more forgiving of each other, and that's a relief.

John is not doing so well. His shock and sadness at what happened live on in his haggard features, and a listlessness that's characterized him since he recovered from his head injury. They never caught the person who attacked him. John feels guilt, because he still thinks that if he hadn't left us, none of this would have happened. He's probably right, but he's not to blame.

He's a father again now, and this does make him smile. Katrina had a baby girl, whom they named Chloe, a glorious chubby baby, who at six months old showers smiles on everyone, and pumps the air with playful fists and feet.

Chloe is a delight for us all, and especially Ben. When he's with her he'll stretch out a hand and let her clutch his finger in her fist. He'll bring her toys and fool around to make her smile, he'll plant kisses on her chubby tummy, which makes her shriek with abandoned laughter. It brings us all joy.

Laura, I don't see. Our friendship didn't survive. Some things are too big for other people to bear. I mourn the loss of her, but not much, because I give my time to Ben, and to my family.

Ruth and Ben have resumed their closeness. She learned of what happened to him after he was back. We couldn't avoid telling her and she was mostly lucid enough that we felt she deserved to know. And if when we visit her Ben snuggles closer to her than he used to, then she either doesn't notice or simply knows better than to comment on it.

Her family's history has been suffused with the necessity to bear sadness.

We brought her out of the home recently, to watch Ben play his violin in a concert, a little school recital.

Alone at the front of the room, facing the audience, Ben straightened his back, and put his violin to his shoulder. He looked remarkably free of nerves, but I was so petrified on his behalf I felt as though I could hardly breathe. Ruth pulled her head up straight — so often it sags down nowadays — and she looked at Ben attentively, as if she were adjudicating his playing at a high-level competition.

He played a little patchily at first, rushed the piece here and there, and I panicked, because it wasn't very long and I knew he could do it better, but somewhere in the middle of it he hit his stride, and, by the time he reached the complicated final passage, the playing was exceptional and he achieved a tone that was just simply lovely.

The small audience was silent while he played, completely so, because there was an honesty about his performance that captivated. The round of applause he got at the end was more than warm.

But what meant the most to me was Ruth's reaction. Her cloudy eyes brimmed and her stiff hands wrapped around my own as best as she was able and she said, "He has such musicality, darling. There were mistakes, he must find discipline, but the musicality, this is a gift."

And my heart lurched because when I'm able to see through the blackness this is what I hope for. It's that, in spite of his problems, Ben might be learning to live again, and that he might still have that capacity to find things that can drive him onward: that the beauty of music, or of a painting in the Bristol Museum, or of his connection with his baby sister, or of any damn thing he likes, can occasionally eradicate the blackness, and make it a life worth living.

So what is our plan for the future?

We want to eradicate Joanna May from our lives, to eradicate the legacy she tried to leave us when she put Ben through such a terrible ordeal and ripped our family apart.

We have a plan to tackle this.

The plan is that we wait.

We wait to show Ben that we're there for him, to prove to him that he's worth it, no matter what's happened to him, no matter what she's told him. We wait for him to understand that we love him, all of us, and that he can trust us, each one of us. We wait for him to understand that we did everything we could to find him.

We hope that time will heal him. Time has become a very precious commodity for us.

We've waited a year, and in that time I've come to think a lot about what happened before Ben was abducted, and I've observed the way our family has closed in around him since he's been back, with vibrant butterfly wings that fold softly over him, while he heals.

I understand now that my priorities were wrong before he was abducted, that I worried too much about the divorce, that I let life happen around me, and I didn't take responsibility for it.

When John left I missed him and our companionship, of course I did. I don't know if I missed being loved by him, though, because I'm not sure now whether we ever loved each other very deeply, or if it wasn't more that we were two lost souls when we met, huddling together for comfort.

What interests me now is that it might have been the betrayal of convention I felt most keenly, because in some way I felt I was owed the life we had together, and that I didn't deserve the public humiliation of him leaving me for another woman.

But here's the thing: none of us deserve anything. That's an illusion we all exist under.

What I know now is that even after the divorce I should simply have been grateful for what I had. I should have celebrated my life as it was, imperfections, sadness, and all, and not forensically examined its faults. Those faults were largely in the eyes of a critical and sharp-edged society anyhow, and I had learned to recognize them by osmosis, by following the herd.

I had not yet learned to use my intelligence, or to trust in my instincts.

I see more clearly now, and I shall never make that mistake again.

This attitude is how I deal with my sorrowful family history, which Nicky hid from me and DI Clemo forced her to reveal. I try not to cast blame for that.

Instead, I count my blessings every day for my blemished, damaged family, which is full of love, and that is fine, and that is all we need and all Ben needs to know.

But among these moments of rationality, I fear too, we all do. We are living through the short-term effects of Ben's abduction, but we also fear for its long-term effects. Perhaps the greatest of these is that Joanna May will break her silence one day, and that will damage Ben all over again.

That is why I'm telling you this now, because I want to get this out there first. I want to try to claw back some of the power she's taken from us, I want to try to loosen her grasp on our family, on my son. I want us to be grains of sand that slip through her fingers and fall, so that they're undetectable from all the others on the beach, impossible for her to find again. I don't want her, or you, to own us anymore. I want anonymity for my family. I want dignity.

There's one more thing I should tell you, because you might want to know this. The detective came to see us: DI Clemo. We thought it might help Ben if somebody from the police could come and tell him how hard we all looked for him; how we did everything we could to find him. I felt Clemo owed us that.

He came to our house and we sat in the kitchen together and Ben stared at the table while Clemo talked, and when he'd finished, Ben left the room without a word and went upstairs to his room and began to build with his Legos. It's what he does when he doesn't want to talk about things. He makes amazing contraptions. I don't know if Ben took in the detective's words or not. Clemo and

I were left alone at the table. Ben had not made eye contact with either of us.

Afterward, I watched Clemo get back in his car, and his head fell onto his hands and his shoulders shook, but I couldn't feel sympathy, because all of me must be dedicated to Ben, to his recovery. So I turned away and went upstairs. I sat beside my boy while he built. I didn't speak, I just hoped to reassure him with my presence. I waited for him to finish so that he could explain to me what he'd made, and how it worked, so that he could show me how creative he'd been.

Clemo emailed me shortly afterward, from a home email address. He sent me an extract from a poem by W. B. Yeats:

Verse from "To a Child Dancing in the Wind" by W. B. Yeats

Has no one said those daring
Kind eyes should be more learn'd?
Or warned you how despairing
The moths are when they are burned,
I could have warned you, but you are
young,
So we speak a different tongue.

"You couldn't have saved him from her,"

Clemo wrote. "There was nothing you could have done. If you'd tried to warn him of dangers this extreme, you'd have ruined his childhood. Nobody could have predicted this situation. I know how much you love him. I saw that. I hope he believed me when I told him that."

I thought the email was sad, and painful, and kind too.

I also suspected that Clemo was seeking reassurance for himself as much as he was offering it to me, and I wondered if he was having some kind of breakdown.

I wanted to reply, but I didn't know how to help him. I wanted to offer him solace, but I couldn't find the words.

Because I have only one job to do, and it requires all my focus. I must be patient as I hope for my son to come back to me, to come home in mind as well as in body and to do so completely. And so I struggle my way through the blackness, and I wait.

And I hope to do that in private.

And that is all anybody needs to know.

ACKNOWLEDGMENTS

I am hugely grateful to the following people:

Emma Beswetherick, my brilliant editor, whose enthusiasm, support, guidance, and suggestions have improved this book beyond measure. Thank you.

Caroline Kirkpatrick, Grace Menary-Winefield, Dominic Wakefield, Kate Doran, Victoria Gilder, and Jo Wickham. Thank you so much to you all, and also to everybody else who has worked wonders on the book at Little, Brown, especially Sean Garrehy.

Amanda Bergeron, my wonderful editor in the United States, and the rest of the team at HarperCollins, with special mentions to Elle Keck, Mumtaz Mustafa, Molly Waxman, and Kaitlyn Kennedy. Thank you all, you've been such a pleasure to work with, and I'm extremely proud of this edition.

Nelle Andrew, my fabulous agent, who has a very big heart. A massive thank-you for taking a punt on a bit of a dodgy first draft and for contributing so much to help me turn it into something better. Big thanks too to Rachel Mills, Alexandra Cliff, and Marilia Savvides at PFD.

Abbie Ross, my writing partner. Thank you so much for reading and rereading, for tirelessly offering your comments and for the friendship along the way.

Philippa Lowthorpe. Thank you for the lengthy dog walks, for all the encouragement, and for the advice on storytelling and much more that I couldn't have done without.

My two retired detectives. Thank you for so kindly giving up your time for coffees and a very long chat about all things police and procedure related. It was invaluable. Any errors in the book are all mine!

My parents, Jonathan and Cilla Paget. Thank you for filling my childhood home with books and encouraging me to read them.

Jules Macmillan. Thank you for all the spaghetti carbonara, and plot suggestions, for being Jim Clemo's biggest fan, and for backing the book all the way.

Rose, Max, and Louis Macmillan. You've been brilliant, because I couldn't have done it without your support. Thank you for that, but most of all for making me smile every day.

BIBLIOGRAPHY

The following websites and papers were used as a valuable resource in this novel:

www.rcmp.gc.ca, the website for the Royal Canadian Mounted Police, and specifically a paper available to download on that site: Marlene L. Dalley and Jenna Ruscoe, "The Abduction of Children by Strangers in Canada: Nature and Scope," National Missing Children Services, National Police Services, Royal Canadian Mounted Police, December 2003.

The NISMART Bulletin Series (National Incidence Studies of Missing, Abducted, Runaway and Thrownaway Children), and especially NISMART-2, which is available to download from www.ojjdp.gov/publications, the website of the Office of Juvenile Justice and Delinquency Prevention (OJJDP) in the United States.

www.missingkids.com, the website for the National Center for Missing & Exploited Children in the U.S., and in particular the download "When Your Child Is Missing: A Family Survival Guide," *Missing Kids USA Parental Guide,* US Department of Justice, OJJDP Report. The download is also available at www.ojjdp.gov/childabduction/publications.html.

Preston Findlay and Robert G. Lowery, Jr., eds., "Missing and Abducted Children: A Law-Enforcement Guide to Case Investigation and Program Management," Fourth Edition, National Center for Missing & Exploited Children, OJJDP Report, 2011. This is available to download from www.missingkids.com/en_US/publications/NC74.pdf.

www.missingkids.co.uk, the CEOP (UK National Crime Agency's Child Exploitation and Online Protection Centre) website for missing children and young people.

www.ceop.police.uk and specifically a study called "Taken: A Study of Child Abduction in the UK," by Geoff Newiss with Mary-Ann Traynor.

M. C. Boudreaux, W. D. Lord, and R. L. Dutra, "Child Abduction: Aged-Based

Analyses of Offender, Victim, and Offense Characteristics in 550 Cases of Alleged Child Disappearance," *Journal of Forensic Sciences* 44(3), 1999.

P.S.
INSIGHTS, INTERVIEWS & MORE . . .

About the Book

READING GROUP DISCUSSION QUESTIONS

1. At the very beginning of *What She Knew,* Rachel states that "in the eyes of others we're often not who we imagine ourselves to be." How much do you agree with this statement and do you think it's a liberating idea or an unsettling one?

2. The narrative in *What She Knew* is presented in some unusual ways, including through social media excerpts, transcripts, and the alternating viewpoints of Rachel and Jim. What did you make of this?

3. Do you think Rachel and Jim change as the story evolves and, if so, how?

4. Does Rachel deserve the criticism that she gets via social media?

5. Do you think that the influence of social media has a negative impact on how the

case develops for both the police and Rachel?

6. Rachel feels that the media would have treated her differently if she hadn't been a single mother. Do you agree with this?

7. Do you think it was understandable for Rachel to follow her instincts at the press conference?

8. Does the ending of the book work for you? Would you have liked to see it resolved differently?

9. Were you surprised when you discovered who was responsible for Ben's abduction? Do you think having a position of trust or authority means that people can get away with more than they would otherwise?

10. Did you sympathize with Jim by the end? Should he have let his instincts or personal feelings interfere with his rational judgments about the case?

11. What is the importance of secrets in this novel?

AUTHOR Q & A

Have you always wanted to be a writer?

I've always wanted to write and have loved writing. Ever since my early twenties I've written bits and pieces whenever life hasn't got in the way. Most of it was fairly unstructured, but as I got older I began to wonder whether I had it in me to write an entire book. However, I'm not sure I ever thought I could actually be a writer. That always felt like an impossible goal.

***Can you tell us a little about what inspired you to write* What She Knew?**

By the time I started *What She Knew* I had already tried to write two different books, and had abandoned them for various reasons. I was at a point where my children had all begun school and I realized I probably had one more shot at actually trying to produce an entire book before it would be essential for me to go out and get a "proper job." With that in mind I decided the best idea might be to try writing in a genre that I absolutely love and to get on with it. I'm a massive fan of crime novels, and psychological thrillers in particular, so I thought I would see if I could write a page-turner.

At the time I had just read Linwood Barclay's book *No Time for Goodbye,* and that book inspired me because of its domestic setting and simple, strong premise, which I found deeply unsettling. An everyday life suddenly and shockingly turned upside down is something we can all imagine and which we all fear. I tried to think of what would be my worst nightmare as a mother, and it didn't take me long to decide that it would be for one of my children to disappear without a trace. So the book started with that one idea: a mother, walking in the woods on a beautiful Sunday afternoon, feeling hopeful, and then minutes later her son is gone and her life will never be the same again. The idea made me shudder then and it still does now.

Once I'd thought of that, I set myself a goal of writing a thousand words a day for five days a week, which was just manageable between school runs. That was how the first draft of *What She Knew* was produced.

What does it feel like to see your debut novel in print?

Absolutely amazing. And terrifying.

Were there many stumbling blocks along the way?

The biggest stumbling blocks were the rewrites I had to do in order to take the book from its first incarnation as a pretty dodgy first draft to the finished product that it is now. I was lucky enough to find my agent, Nelle Andrew, fairly quickly, and with Nelle's help I had to work on getting the book into shape for submission to publishers. Among other things, this involved sorting out the pacing of the plot and adding the character of Jim Clemo (as Rachel was the only narrator in the first draft), so it was a lot of work.

Just over a year later Emma Beswetherick, my editor at Little, Brown, acquired the novel, and we embarked on another round of rewrites to improve the story further. Emma worked very closely with me on those so that they weren't as painful as they might have been. All in all, the rewriting process has been an extraordinarily good discipline for me and I've learned huge amounts about pacing and putting together a strong plot, as well as many other things along the way.

Did your characters appear fully formed or did they evolve along with the story?

Rachel's character appeared fully formed. The parts of the book that haven't significantly changed during its evolution are her prologue and the scenes that take place in the woods, as well as her attitude toward Ben and her strong love for him. The other characters definitely evolved as the story did. For example, I had to work very hard to get Jim right: his personality, his motivations, and his feelings about the case. That was a particular challenge, as I was also concerned about writing effectively and believably in a man's voice.

You've written about a very sensitive subject. How difficult was that for you?

At all stages of writing this book I have been very, sometimes painfully, aware that I was tackling an extremely sensitive subject. That thinking informed the way I approached the story. I feel boundless amounts of respect and sympathy for any family who has not only suffered the disappearance of a child, but has had the additional burden of doing so in the public eye.

Most of all, I wanted Rachel's voice to be as strong and as truthful as I could possibly achieve, and I spent a long time trying to imagine what it must be like to be her, and the experience she has to go through. To help with this, and to try to find an authentic voice for her, I did a great deal of research on missing children. I also read a lot of accounts written by parents, and others, in order to try to get it as right as possible.

Of course, *What She Knew* is a figment of my imagination, and I haven't experienced what families who've gone through this in real life have — no doubt there are places in the book where I might have got it wrong — but I have tried my hardest to imagine it truthfully and respectfully. I was determined that the book would not trivialize or sensationalize any part of their experience, or that of their children.

What made you want to include so much social media in the novel?

A response on social media to big news stories is inevitable these days, and I felt that to tell a story like this without it would be to omit a large part of many people's everyday experience. I've always been staggered by the vast gulf between the actual experience of families who find themselves in desperate situations and the public's often swift and judgmental response via social media. Because people are able to remain anonymous, or comment from the safety of their own homes, it gives them courage to make judgments that they might not be brave enough to articulate otherwise.

If you watch stories evolve in the press and online, as I did as part of my research, it quickly becomes clear that the nasty opinions expressed in social media can become absorbed into the narrative of that particular story, usually for the worse. The danger of that is that swiftly it becomes, at best, a rather shocking invasion of privacy, and, at worst, downright cruel. In the book, invasive social commentary and press attention turn into an act of vandalism and then violence against Rachel — the scary thing is that I don't feel that is taking it too far.

If I were in Rachel's situation, I feel strongly that the trial by online and media commentary would be one of the most difficult things to bear.

Did you have to research a lot of the police procedural? How important was it that you got this right?

It was incredibly important to me, because I wanted the book and the action within it to feel as realistic as possible. I am most terrified by thrillers when everything that happens feels as if it could happen to me. Having said that, you inevitably take some liberties when you're writing fiction, so I'm sure there are mistakes in the book that the better informed or eagle-eyed might spot. To try to get things right, I met two retired detectives who very patiently talked me through processes that were relevant to the story, and gave me all sorts of other bits of information that were invaluable to the book.

There are many ways this novel could have ended. How did you decide on the ending?

The ending! It has tormented me! I rewrote the end of the book at least three times in the quest for the perfect resolution. I needed it to strike the correct balance between something that wouldn't be too neat and easy (Draft 1) or be unpalatable to readers (Draft 2). Above all it had to be realistic and believable for all the characters involved, as well as resolving the story in a way that would satisfy readers, and it also needed to maintain the pulse of the story as a whole. I think (I really hope!) that I've achieved that now. The finished ending is as truthful as I could make it.

What advice would you give to aspiring novelists?

Read as much as you can, especially within the genre you're writing in; write as much as you can so that you are always developing; be willing to listen to and collaborate with agents and editors because they almost certainly know the market far better than you do; be prepared to work very, very hard to get a finished book out there; and sometimes, most difficult of all, hold your nerve while you do all of that!

What are you working on now?

I've just put the finishing touches on my second book, which is another psychological thriller called *Butterfly in the Dark* (in the UK). I'm really excited about it because it has a complex plot and a cast of characters who both thrilled and unnerved me as I was writing. The action takes place over a short time scale and is intense and claustrophobic.

The main character is Zoe Maisey — child genius, musical sensation — who, several years earlier, caused the death of three teenagers. She served her time and now she's free. Zoe's story begins with her giving the musical performance of her life, but by midnight her mother is dead. The book is an exploration into the mind of a teenager burdened by brilliance. It's a story about the wrongs of our past not letting go in the present and how hard we must fight for second chances.

Read On

GILLY'S TEN FAVORITE PAGE-TURNERS

***Miss Smilla's Feeling for Snow* — Peter Høeg**

This book is so good that I almost wish I hadn't read it, because I can't ever again experience the utter thrill of discovering it. It has everything: it's thoughtful and intelligent; the prose is rich and evocative from the very first sentence to the last; and both the plot and the characters (especially outsider-turned-detective Miss Smilla) are complex and intriguing, and embedded in a setting that feels vivid and chilling, in both senses of the word. This was the first contemporary psychological thriller I ever read, and I was instantly hooked on the genre.

***No Country for Old Men* — Cormac McCarthy**

This book grips me by the throat every time I open it. Extraordinarily well written in prose that is lyrical and sparing yet tremendously powerful, this is an absolute masterpiece of a book. Not a word is wasted, yet the picture of shattered lives that's painted is as realistic and gripping as you can get, and the plot is a vortex you desperately want the characters to be able to extricate themselves from.

***The Secret History* — Donna Tartt**

A perfect mystery story. Ingredients: an East Coast American college setting, a group of privileged, refined students, an outsider desperate to get in with them, and a murder. Throw in large doses of intrigue, beautiful prose, and characters you end up knowing so well they feel like your roommates. What more could you want?

***Black and Blue* — Ian Rankin**

In my view, this is one of the best Rebus books, but they're all fantastic. It has the usual Rankin cocktail of great characters; superb Edinburgh setting; some of the most realistic dialogue in the business; deadpan, perfectly placed prose; and a high-stakes, twisty-turny plot to keep you devouring the story right until the end. Rankin's Rebus books have a kind of rhythm and fatalism to them that I find irresistible.

***The Tin Roof Blowdown* — James Lee Burke**
This book is hard-hitting and unflinching yet poetic at times, and a powerful humanity hangs from every word of it. All of James Lee Burke's powers are at their mightiest in this incredible Dave Robicheaux thriller set in a vivid and terrifying New Orleans in the aftermath of Hurricane Katrina.

***Gone Girl* — Gillian Flynn**
Clever, stylish writing, sensationally well structured, and with a shocking twist that I didn't see coming. The disappearance of a wife from her picture-perfect marriage reveals more than you could possibly have imagined. Unputdownable.

***The Ice Princess* — Camilla Läckberg**
Camilla Läckberg's brilliantly drawn lead character sucked me right into this book. She's a feisty, curious, clever girl determined to get to the bottom of a mystery in a small Swedish coastal town. It's another one of those books where location, characters, plot,

and good writing all combine to make you race through the book to find out "whodunit."

The Lovely Bones **— Alice Sebold**
I was completely gripped by this compulsive story from the start. The narrative, in the voice of a murdered fourteen-year-old girl, is carefully and compulsively rendered. Her tale is horrific yet hauntingly ordinary too in its depiction of both her family's grief and her murderer's sinister suburban existence. This is one to make you shudder.

Faithful Place **— Tana French**
This is my favorite title in Tana French's Dublin series. She has a talent for superb plotting, funny, über-realistic dialogue, and keen social observation. I loved Detective Frank Mackey, who is the lead character in this one, and his crazy family, who leap right off the page.

No Time for Goodbye **— Linwood Barclay**
This book's disarmingly simple premise sucked me right in and kept me going: it's a domestic nightmare of a situation, which

you would never want to find yourself in, but can imagine all too easily.

ABOUT THE AUTHOR

Gilly Macmillan grew up in Swindon, Wiltshire, in the UK and spent a few years living in Northern California in her late teens after her family relocated to Menlo Park. She returned to the UK to study History of Art at Bristol University and then did an MA in Modern British Art at the Courtauld Institute of Art in London. After a short time working in commercial galleries in London, Gilly got her dream starter-job in the editorial department of *The Burlington Magazine* and then worked in the Exhibitions Department of the Hayward Gallery before starting a family.

Since then, Gilly has been a full-time mom and a part-time photographer and photography lecturer. Nowadays she sometimes accompanies her son to the set of the BBC TV show *Call the Midwife,* where he's a member of the regular cast, but she mostly writes whenever she can.

Gilly lives in Bristol with her husband, three children, and two dogs. This is her first novel.

The employees of Thorndike Press hope you have enjoyed this Large Print book. All our Thorndike, Wheeler, and Kennebec Large Print titles are designed for easy reading, and all our books are made to last. Other Thorndike Press Large Print books are available at your library, through selected bookstores, or directly from us.

For information about titles, please call:
(800) 223-1244

or visit our Web site at:
http://gale.cengage.com/thorndike

To share your comments, please write:
Publisher
Thorndike Press
10 Water St., Suite 310
Waterville, ME 04901